A STRANGE DECEPTION

Richard Coward was born in 1955. He studied Politics, Philosophy and Economics at Wadham College, Oxford before taking a further degree at the London School of Economics and joining the Foreign Office. The success of his first novel, "A Strange Deception", enabled him to become a full-time novelist. He has since written two further mystery thrillers, "A Dream Too Far" and "Castles in the Air". He is married with two sons and lives in North London.

A STRANGE DECEPTION

by

RICHARD COWARD

LONDON
Richard and Erika Coward
WRITING AND PUBLISHING PARTNERSHIP
1990

First published in 1990 by
Richard and Erika Coward
Writing and Publishing Partnership
16 Sturgess Avenue
London
NW4 3TS

Reprinted 1991
Reprinted 1992
This edition 1994

Photoset by B P Intergraphics
Printed in Great Britain by
The Guernsey Press Co. Ltd, Guernsey, Channel Islands

ISBN 0-9515019-5-X

To my parents

LONDON, JUNE 1975

Kate had nagged him into going yet now he simply had to admit he was rather enjoying it. Instead of being buried away in the basement canteen at the Foreign Office, it was refreshing to find himself basking in the summer warmth of a brightly sunlit Trafalgar Square and sharing a picnic lunch with his eldest son Justin.

It was not that Robert Creighton Stanton was a man to neglect his family responsibilities. But the manner in which he viewed those responsibilities was perhaps somewhat remote. He had always conceived of himself as the breadwinner, not the babysitter, and the times in his life when he had inevitably found himself in the latter role he had usually found distinctly unsettling. Yet now, watching the ten-year-old dividing his banana sandwich roughly equally between his own mouth and those of the attendant flock of overfed and undergroomed pigeons, the thought crossed his mind that he might after all have been missing out on something important.

A tourist walked by and the pigeons vanished. Freed from the need to satisfy so many appetites simultaneously, Justin turned to his father with an enquiring look.

"Dad, didn't you ever make a family tree?"

After lunch they were going to make their way down the Strand to St Catherine's House, where they were planning to undertake some systematic research into the identity of Justin's forebears. When his schoolteacher had set her young charges the project to complete by the end of the summer holidays, she had probably envisaged a series of animated conversations with ageing relatives over afternoon tea, but Justin had become so involved with the venture that Kate had felt they should give the child some positive encouragement by showing him how to compile the detailed information he needed from public records.

"No," Robert answered, helping himself to a particularly juicy-looking red apple, "and anyway, I went to school in Hong Kong so I couldn't have come up here to look them up properly, could I?"

"But weren't you ever curious?" Justin persisted, seemingly unaware that his father's answer constituted an entirely self-contained and satisfactory explanation.

"Well, I suppose I was. I just never came up here to look."

1

Justin helped himself to another banana sandwich and looked thoughtfully across the Square.

"Weren't you named after one of your grandparents, Dad?"

"Yes, that's right, grandpa's father. But I never knew him or my grandmother. They were killed in a car crash in 1945, just after the end of the war."

Although he had only been two years old at the time, Robert knew of the events that surrounded his grandparents' sudden death well. During the early years of his life, while his father was away on active service with the army, he had lived with his mother and her parents-in-law in a large rambling country house high on the Yorkshire moors. He had been conceived during a brief wartime reunion and had never seen his father. Then, after long months of anxious waiting, news had finally arrived from the regiment that the family was to be re-united. Robert's father's tour of duty was over.

It was early autumn and the heather on the moors was in full bloom on the day he came home. Although the sun was shining brightly, a biting autumnal wind was sweeping low across the open hillside and bringing with it the distant menace of approaching winter. Yet inside the Stanton home the log fires crackled cheerfully as the family prepared for the long-awaited reunion lunch. The table was laid, the champagne cooled, and all that remained was to fetch the star guest from the railway station, a good ten miles away across open moorland.

Robert's grandparents had taken the car and gone to the station, leaving his mother alone with her child to complete the last minute preparations for lunch. They never arrived. Half-way to the station, where the narrow moorland road twisted sharply round a rocky out-crop, the remains of the car and its lifeless occupants were later found smashed against some rocks about fifty feet below the edge of the road.

"Can you remember them, Dad?"

"My grandparents? No. I must have been too young. I was only two when it happened."

Robert paused for a moment, wondering whether to say anything or not. But he had to tell the boy, otherwise he might really put his foot in it one day.

"Justin."

"Yeah."

"Listen, Justin. When you go round to granny's, do me a favour and don't talk about it."

Justin looked puzzled. "Why not?" he asked.

2

"Well, because it upsets her, that's all. Just don't mention it."

* * * * * *

As they walked along the Strand towards St Catherine's House, Robert wondered why he had never found time to explore his own family background more fully. He had, after all, always regarded himself as a fully-fledged representative of the British establishment and as such firmly rooted in the traditions of his country. It had never seemed necessary to go through the tedious process of actually drawing up a family tree to confirm an identity which was to him completely self-evident. He had always regarded an obsession with family trees as being a sure sign of a man's insecurity about himself – the kind of thing that afflicted second-generation Canadians or Australians trying to overcome their hidden fear that they did not actually belong anywhere.

His family, certainly on his father's side, had loyally served their country as army officers for a number of generations and, as a child, Robert had naturally assumed that he would follow in the family tradition. But in 1956, at the tender age of 13, events far distant from the drab and dreary boarding school existence of his everyday life had occasioned a sudden change of heart. When the news of the Anglo-French invasion of Egypt first broke, Robert and his classmates – many of whom came from military homes – had been filled with an overpowering sense of nervous enthusiasm as they crowded round the old radio in the common room listening to the latest bulletins. Brought up in the shadow of the Second World War, surrounded by the lingering mystique of the British Empire, they yearned for further proof of British greatness. The humiliating end of the crisis, and the disillusionment it brought in its wake, led most of his school-fellows to turn their minds and energies to other more parochial concerns, but Robert had refused to turn away. He realised, as he lay in bed night after night wrestling with the ignominy of defeat and its implications for his own future, that the key to Britain's future role in the world no longer lay with the sheer size of her navy or the efficiency of her standing army, but rather with the political skill with which she conducted her reduced role in the world. He resolved to join the Diplomatic Service.

It was symptomatic of Robert's personality that from that day on he had worked single-mindedly towards achieving his chosen goal. And it was symptomatic of his ability that it was beginning to look as if he was going to succeed. At thirty-two, and after only eleven years at the Foreign Office, he was working in a job concerned with the political aspects of Anglo-American relations which was widely regarded as a staging post for those going on to very senior posts within the Service. Although Robert could not pinpoint exactly why or when he had been chosen, it was becoming increasingly clear that he had been singled out for accelerated promotion.

Glancing down at his son by his side that sunny June afternoon in 1975, he could not help but wonder why he should have been so fortunate. Others were also successful in their jobs, but he had managed to combine a promising career with two delightful children. Justin and his younger brother Tim were shaping up fine; they were thoughtful and bright, attentive to their schoolwork and at all times polite and respectful to those around them. No father could ask for better children.

Their arrival at the public research room of St Catherine's House interrupted Robert's thoughts. He had always imagined it to be a dark, rather dusty place, rather like the Bodleian Library in Oxford or the reading room at the British Museum. He had expected to find learned family tree researchers, their backs bowed low as they patiently studied ancient volumes of certificates. But this place bore a greater resemblance to the international ticket office at Victoria Station, with crowds of people of every description milling noisily around between shelves full of dark red and black books. Every now and then someone would eagerly grab a volume off a shelf and heave it to a nearby table where they could hunt through the tens of thousands of names for details of the tiny little specks of humanity about which they cared.

It soon became apparent that the red books contained births and the black ones deaths: a large notice pointed to another room where marriages could be found. The volumes were arranged in chronological order, each bookcase labelled with a large white sign listing the years covered on the shelves. Since the red books were attracting far more interest than the black ones, and the age of the thick red volumes seemed closely correlated to the age of the people busying themselves about the shelves, it seemed clear that most of these people were not in the least little bit interested in investigating their family trees; they had simply lost their birth certificates and had to get hold of another one urgently for some official purpose. The black volumes attracted less activity for the simple reason that the people listed within them no longer required full documentation to conduct their affairs.

"What do we do now, Dad?"

Justin was pulling at his arm, eager to get started. Why was it

4

little children had this annoying habit of thinking that grown-ups know everything?

"Well, Justin, I suppose we might as well work backwards. Does that sound sensible?"

His son nodded his head wisely, clearly trying to make sense of his father's incomprehensible plan without appearing stupid. He failed miserably.

"What d'you mean, Dad?" he asked with obvious embarrassment.

Robert looked fondly at his boy and smiled. Justin reminded him so much of himself as a child: he so desperately wanted to be an adult but couldn't quite pull it off.

"What I mean, Justin," he said reassuringly, "is that we'll start with you, because it's your family tree that we're going to investigate. We'll start by looking you up."

The penny dropped instantly and a look of profound relief came over Justin's face.

"You mean we want to look up my birth certificate."

"Yes, look yourself up. Go and find yourself in the red volumes over there marked 1965."

Justin quickly located the correct volume and dragged it over to one of the high benches set aside for examining the records. He took only a few minutes to find the correct page.

"Hey, Dad, come and look at this," he declared with a growing sense of excitement. "I think I've found myself but they've put me down twice."

For a moment Robert was startled, puzzled at why his son's name should have been entered more than once. But as he looked over Justin's shoulder at the ageing volume all became clear.

"No, Justin, those two entries aren't both you. That's you, registered at Epsom. The other boy called Justin Stanton came from somewhere else. It's just that you were both registered on the same day."

He watched while his son wrestled with this information. Another boy with exactly the same name, registered on the same day! Robert shuddered. On the one hand this was a perfectly straightforward government building, full of the perfectly straightforward population records required by any advanced society. But it was also a powerful symbol of the devastating insignificance of each and every one of us: rich or poor, famous or unknown, kind or brutal, we were all just simple one-line entries in a vast building full of books. And even our names we had to share with others.

Justin's shocked reaction to this realisation did not last long. Those

5

people who cannot build defences against the triviality of their own existence quickly end up in a mental institution, and this little boy had no intention of wasting his life in that particular fashion.

"What do I do now, Dad?"

"Well, let's see . . ." Robert paused, wondering how best to proceed. "This entry isn't actually the full birth certificate, so I suppose we've got to fill out a form to order a copy. Then we'll be able to work backwards."

"Dad?"

"Yes."

"Don't you know when you and Mum were born?"

Robert paused, unsure for a moment what Justin was driving at. Then he started to laugh.

"Of course, Justin, you're absolutely right. Let's go and look us up now. I'm 1943, and your Mum's 1945. You know the birthdays don't you?"

He followed his son to the 1943 shelves, intending to watch him carry on with his work. But then his eye fell on an ancient clock prominently displayed on the wall: it was nearly half past three. Only one-and-a-half hours to closing time and they still hadn't found out anything they didn't know already.

"Justin!" His son looked up from 1943. "The time's getting on. While you're looking up your mother and I, I'll go and get started on your grandparents and great-grandparents. Write down everything you find out and then come and get me when you've finished."

His parents didn't take long to find. His father, John Wilberforce Stanton, was in the 1919 volume, his birth registered at the small town in Sussex in which he had grown up. His mother, Peggy Stanton, was registered at the Devon market town of Bideford under her maiden name of Turner in the 1920 volume. His mother's parents were also straightforward. They had been dead for over ten years, but he could remember both their birthdays and the approximate year of their birth.

Up until now, the researches had been straightforward since he had known the date of birth of everyone concerned. But when he came to think about his father's parents things became more complicated. He had no idea of their birthdays and only the most approximate idea of the years in which they had been born. Yet his father's one-line entry in the red volumes did not include sufficient information to work backwards in time. He thought again of filling in a form to order a copy of his father's full birth certificate only to realise that the copies could not be obtained straightaway.

6

Robert dithered for a minute, wondering whether to sacrifice his lunch break the following day in order to return and pick up the document. But then a thought occurred to him and he strode back to 1945, where Justin was by now copiously reproducing the information from Kate's entry.

He tapped his son on the shoulder. "Justin. You wait here. I'm just going out to a call-box to ring grandpa."

He didn't know his grandparents' dates of birth, but his father would be sure to remember when his own parents had been born.

Outside, the rush hour was just beginning to get under way. People were walking along, their tired and strained faces set on getting back to their homes at the end of another long hard day. It was a feeling Robert knew all too well, but it was curious and strangely pleasant to find himself the observer of the phenomenon rather than an integral part of it.

Several street corners later a telephone box appeared. He dialled his parents' number, hoping that he would get a reply. His mother answered.

"Hallo. This is Upper Trumpton 5793."

Robert always found the stilted upper class voice with which his mother answered the telephone rather amusing. She gave the impression that she was expecting a telephone call from the Queen.

"Hallo Upper Trumpton 5793. It's me."

"Oh, hallo dear, how nice."

That was better, now she was speaking properly again, her broad Devon vowels honestly articulated.

"Mother. I'm up in London with Justin. At St Catherine's House. He's doing a family tree."

There was a short silence.

"Oh yes, dear." Robert couldn't help thinking that his mother's voice seemed rather strained.

"Are you all right, mother?"

"Yes, dear, perfectly all right. How can I help you?"

"I've tracked down your parents but I've got stuck with Dad's. Do you happen to know exactly when they were born?"

Another silence.

"Mother, are you there?"

"Yes, dear, I'm just thinking. I know his father's birthday was in the autumn and his mother's sometime in the spring, but more than that I can't really remember. And I really don't have a clue in which year they were born. But I should think your father will know."

7

"Is he there?"

"No, I'm afraid not, dear. He's just popped out for a game of golf. He won't be back until about six. Can you ring again then?"

Robert swore inwardly. Why did his father have to play golf all the time?

"That's no good, mother, the place closes at five. Never mind, thanks for trying. I'll be in touch. Bye."

As Robert put the phone down and started walking back along High Holborn towards St Catherine's House, he found himself wishing he had prepared himself better for the afternoon's outing. He really could have collected this kind of basic information from his living relatives in advance. It was just that he hadn't given it sufficiently high priority. With a sharp twinge of guilt, he realised that he would never have allowed himself to be so sloppy at work.

A screech of brakes shattered his thoughts.

"You bloody git, why don't you look where you're going!"

Crossing a side road, Robert had completely failed to see a taxi swinging round from the main road. It had swerved and avoided him, but the driver was not amused. He started to apologise, but the taxi was already accelerating away.

Still shaken from the experience, Robert wondered just how Justin would have felt if his father had managed to get himself turned into an entry in the black volumes during their trip.

That was it! Why hadn't he thought of it sooner? The black volumes.

He turned and walked briskly back to the telephone box. A stout middle-aged woman was inside, so he had to wait, impatiently pacing up and down and looking at his watch. Come on, come on, why couldn't she finish gossiping? But the more impatient he got, the more involved the woman appeared to become in her conversation. He couldn't wait all day, not with Justin all alone.

Eventually the woman finished. Grabbing the phone, he dialled his mother's number again.

"Hallo. Upper . . ."

"Mother, it's me again. Listen, I've had an idea. Tell me when they died."

"Who, dear?"

"Dad's parents. I know it was in the autumn of 1945, but when exactly did they die?"

For a few moments there was silence. And then his mother's voice again, except this time her voice was really strained, as if she were making a tremendous effort to control herself. "It was October 5th."

With a shock, Robert suddenly realised that he had ignored the advice he had given his son only hours before. Embarrassed by his own stupidity and uncertain how to react, he muttered his thanks and put the phone down. Over twenty years of studied silence had changed nothing, and his mother's reaction to the mention of her parents-in-law's sudden death was as odd as it had been on the first occasion he had witnessed it.

It must have been when he was about eight, while he was living in Hong Kong with his parents. Although he had already known that his father's parents were dead he had somehow never got around to asking exactly what had happened. Then one day he did ask, quite in passing, as they were about to sit down to lunch. To this day he could see in his mind's eye the extraordinary look that had transformed his mother's face, a kind of strangled grimace as she struggled unsuccessfully to prevent her little boy from witnessing emotions that were too powerful to control. His father had risen quietly from his chair and taken Robert by the hand into the garden, leaving his mother alone in the house. They had sat down together on the little wooden bench at the bottom of the garden and his father had recounted to him the sad story of that fateful day in 1945. And as he had listened to his father's words, he could hear the haunting sound of his mother's inconsolable sobs drifting towards them from the room they had left behind.

* * * * * *

In later years, Robert often found his thoughts turning to the driver of that black taxi-cab in High Holborn who had so nearly run him down. What was his name? Where did he live? What kind of man was he? Robert felt that he wanted to establish some kind of contact with the man who had changed his life for ever. Sometimes he felt grateful to him. But more often he cursed his very existence. And there were even times of bitter despair when he wished with all his soul that the driver of the taxi-cab had killed him instantly that day.

For as the taxi-cab had made him realise, it was the death records that held the key.

Entering the crowded records office once again, he quickly located Justin. Robert was expecting him to have become anxious as a result of the long wait, but the boy was eagerly searching through a volume from 1922.

"Hallo, Justin, what are you doing?"

Justin looked up and smiled. "Mum gave me some information about her parents and grandparents. I'm just looking them up."

That was typical of Kate. She was nothing if not thorough. Again he felt the twinge of guilt at his own lack of preparation.

"Listen, Justin, grandpa's playing golf so I couldn't find his parents' birthdays but grandma did tell me the date they died. I'm going to look them up in those black books over there. Come and get me when you've finished what you're doing."

There were only a few people looking at the death records. In the aisle with the 1945 records there was just one other person, a thin elderly man with glasses closely examining a volume propped onto a high bench. He looked lost in thought. Robert picked up the volume containing October 1945 and placed it quietly on the bench opposite the old man so as not to disturb him.

He opened the book and quickly found the right page. As his eye ran down the entries he saw that there were only three Stantons registered as deceased on October 5th. Two of the entries were definitely his grandparents – Robert K. Stanton, aged 51, and Isabel W. Stanton, aged 47.

At first he assumed it was a coincidence. There, neatly printed on the line below his grandfather, was the third Stanton entry for that day: 'Robert C. Stanton, aged 2.' How extraordinary that another child of the same age and with the same name as him had died that day.

But when his eye moved to the column in the book which indicated the place at which the death was officially registered the sensation of curiosity began rapidly to turn to panic. For the three deaths were all registered at exactly the same place, and that place was the small Yorkshire market town of Uffley near where his grandparents had lived and died.

He was tempted to walk away. It was absurd, ridiculous. Surely it was just a coincidence. He should shut the book and put it back. But he didn't. He just stood there, rigid, peering down at that simple little line of writing in the book and trying to work out an explanation.

There were of course lots of perfectly innocent explanations for what appeared to be an entry recording his own death. Perhaps it really was a coincidence, and another boy of that name and age had died in the same place on the same day. It might even have been a cousin from another branch of the family, although he was not aware of the existence of any such branches. And there again perhaps it was simply a mistake, a typing error, some information about the next of kin of his grandparents incorrectly transferred into the death records. After all, it couldn't be what it appeared to be since he, Robert C. Stanton, was clearly not dead.

He looked around the room, seeking the solidity of the familiar world. The bookshelves with their ageing black volumes, the ancient clock on the wall, the elderly man with the glasses, all looked exactly as they had done a few moments earlier. This was ridiculous, a dream from which he would soon awake.

"Dad!"

Robert slammed the book shut and turned to face his son.

"You all right, Dad?" Justin looked surprised at his father's reaction.

"Yes, you made me jump, that's all."

"Did you find them?"

What should he do? Justin was so damned observant, he'd be sure to spot the third entry if he looked.

"Oh, grandpa's parents. Yes, they're in there."

"Oh good. Have you written the entries down?" The boy was already opening up his notebook ready to start writing.

Robert had to think fast. "Justin," he said, trying to sound as relaxed as possible, "I'll write down the entries in here, you go and look up Aunty Susan; she was born two years after Mum."

Justin looked sour. "I'm not interested in all Mum's boring old brothers and sisters. I want to find out about my ancestors."

"Listen, young man, if you want to do a family tree properly you've got to do it, so get cracking."

The ten-year-old must have sensed the tension in his father's voice because he went quietly away, clearly wondering to himself what exactly he had done to annoy his father so much.

Pulling a pen out of his pocket Robert grabbed a form and filled out a request for a full copy of the infant's death certificate. He took it over to the counter.

The clerk looked up. "Can I help you?"

"Yes, I'd like to order a copy of this, please. I'll pick it up tomorrow lunchtime."

The clerk looked at the form for a minute, checking that all the details had been properly filled out. Robert turned to walk away.

"Excuse me, sir," the clerk called after him.

Robert turned. "Yes."

"I don't think you've filled the form out properly, sir. You've put your own name down twice."

With a shock Robert realised what the clerk was saying. But he hesitated for only a moment before replying.

"No, it's all right. It's a relative of mine. Happened to have the same name, that's all."

11

The following morning at the office was hard to endure. As Robert tried to concentrate on his work, he found his mind returning again and again to that simple line of writing at St Catherine's House. Eventually he gave up trying to do any useful work and settled back in his chair with a copy of the 'New York Times' open in front of him. It gave him time to think.

The night before, after Kate had finished putting the children to bed, they had sat together in the garden enjoying the long warm summer evening. All the way home on the Underground, throughout dinner with the kids, Robert had intended to tell his wife about his discovery as soon as they were alone together, but when the opportunity had finally arrived he had failed to do so. Normally he was quite happy to share any problem with Kate, and now he was troubled about why he hadn't.

He tried to console himself with the thought that the deceit was only a very temporary one. By lunchtime he would know for sure the identity of the tiny child who had shared his name and died in the same district and at the same time as his own grandparents, and then he would tell her.

Over the road, Big Ben started slowly telling the world that the morning was over. Unable to wait any longer, Robert rose from his desk. He remembered how he had felt at Oxford on the day the final examination results had been posted. It was a strange combination of eager anticipation and dread, a desire to know the truth mixed inextricably with a fear of what the truth might hold.

Twenty minutes later he was standing once again amidst the crowds at St Catherine's House. Robert was about to go and ask at the counter for the certificate he had ordered when he suddenly turned away. This was all too absurd. Perhaps he had simply misread the entry. He walked over to the aisle with the black volume containing October 1945 and heaved it off the shelf and onto the bench. But the entry was still there, still taunting him to go and identify the dead child.

This time there was no escape. He approached the counter.

"Good morning, sir, you're the chap with the namesake, aren't you?" the clerk said brightly.

Inwardly, Robert squirmed. "Yes, is it ready?"

"Of course, sir, just a moment."

He started to look through a pile of certificates in front of him.

"Ah, here we are," he said, handing the certificate over.

Robert was ready for this. Without looking at the writing on the paper, he folded it in two, thanked the clerk and walked away. He wanted to be on his own. In the far corner of the room was an empty table and chair, and Robert went over and sat down, placing the folded death certificate on the desk in front of him. Then, bracing himself, he opened it up and started to read.

The certificate was quite straightforward. It stated the name of the deceased, the age of the deceased, the date of death, the occupation of the deceased, the cause of death, the place at which the death was registered and the name of the person reporting the death. But as Robert read and re-read the simple entries there could no longer be any mistake, any confusion. The document lying in front of him was a certificate recording his own death.

Eventually Robert looked up from the desk. He felt tired, as if the discovery had suddenly drained all his energy from him. Now that he had the information, he didn't have the faintest idea what to do with it. He looked down again at the certificate.

The cause of death was recorded as 'Motor Accident'. Robert stared at the entry, realising that therein lay something important.

And then it all suddenly fitted together. Only the day before he had encountered once again that strange reaction from his mother when he had broached on the telephone the subject of his grandparents' death. He had always felt that her reaction to the subject was too extreme for such a normally sane person. Why should a woman become so distressed at the simple mention of the deaths of her parents-in-law so many years before? But now it was all absolutely clear. There must have been three people in the car that crashed on the moors that windy October day in 1945, not two. And his mother was not distressed because of the deaths of her parents-in-law, she was still consumed with a burning hidden grief for her own child, a small defenceless two-year-old boy who had been allowed by his mother to go to a railway station to meet a father he had never seen.

For a moment he felt an overwhelming sense of compassion for his mother, a desire to rush and hold her, to give her the consolation she had denied herself for so many long years. But the emotion did not last long. For as he reconstructed that terrible scene on the moors in his mind he realised with a shock that he was no longer a passive observer. He was actually in the car that was smashed to bits on the rocks that day. At the moment of impact he – Robert Creighton Stanton – had been written out of the script. And if his mother's previously incomprehensible reactions were now beginning to make

13

sense, the disturbing question remained of who he – the man sitting at the little desk in St Catherine's House on 10th June 1975 – actually was.

He looked again at the certificate. There was an entry giving the name of the informant, the person who had reported the death to the authorities. And in the case of the infant Robert Creighton Stanton, the name of the informant was John Wilberforce Stanton. It was Robert's own father.

With a grim look on his face, Robert stood up and looked round the room one last time. Then, tucking the copy of the death certificate neatly into his breast pocket, he turned and left the building, heading for the telephone box he had found the previous day.

First he rang the office. He told his secretary that something had cropped up at home and he wouldn't be in that afternoon. Then he dialled his parents' number. A few moments later, the call was answered.

"Hallo, this is Upper Trumpton 5793."

This time the fake upper class accent was more disturbing than ever before. He didn't yet know what it was, but he had himself been the lifelong victim of some kind of sophisticated deceit. But this was not the right moment to find out what it was.

"Hallo, mother, I'm just phoning to find out if you're in this afternoon. I was thinking of popping down to visit you."

"Oh, how lovely, dear. We're both in. But aren't you at work?"

"No, I've got the afternoon off. I'll see you in a couple of hours."

"Lovely. I'll make some scones. Bye for now."

* * * * * *

There was no denying that the summer of 1975 was turning out to be a particularly fine one. As Robert walked through the quiet streets of the little Sussex village which had been his childhood home during all the years his family had spent in England he could not fail to be aware of the beauty of his surroundings. Upper Trumpton was like every American's dream of what England should be: the village green where the men would gather dressed in white on a warm Sunday afternoon to play cricket to the accompaniment of an occasional gentle ripple of applause from the bystanders; the lanes lined with tiny half-timbered thatched cottages and small carefully-manicured gardens; the old stone church with its low twelfth-century tower; and, of course, the local pub – the 'Hare and Hounds' – sitting proudly at the heart of the village, advertising its importance to communal life with a large painted sign in front of the door.

The only surprising thing about Upper Trumpton was that it was still in possession of its own railway station. When most of the other small villages in Britain had lost their stations during the Beeching cuts of the early 1960s, Upper Trumpton had been spared the axe. The most likely explanation of this particular piece of good fortune was that the station lay on one of the more profitable branch lines in Sussex, but the explanation most popular in the 'Hare and Hounds' was rather different. In the minds of the villagers responsibility lay with a rather elderly gentleman by the name of Sir George Burberry, who had represented without a break the Parliamentary constituency in which Upper Trumpton lay since just after the war. Sir George was not only known to be a well-respected and influential member of the backbench transport committee, but also a lifelong resident of Upper Trumpton and frequenter of the 'Hare and Hounds'.

It was two-thirty by the time Robert came into view of the pub, and the old regulars were beginning to emerge from their lunchtime sojourn. Unusually, though, they were accompanied on this occasion by the upright figure of Sir George himself. Spotting Robert, he quickly made his apologies to his companions and strode purposefully towards him, his crisp military manner still apparent even after nearly thirty years in civilian life.

"Well if it isn't young Robert Stanton," he called as he approached, holding his hand out in greeting while he was still at least fifty yards away.

Waiting for the hand to approach sufficiently closely to make contact, Robert wished he had chosen a different route from the station. In point of fact, he very much liked the old fellow, even though he considered him to be hopelessly out of his depth in the world of late twentieth century legislative affairs. It was just that he had other more pressing matters on his mind.

The hand arrived, closely followed by Sir George.

Robert tried to sound relaxed. "Good afternoon, George, how nice to see you."

Sir George smiled broadly. "Come down to visit your old parents, have you?"

Robert nodded, trying for some reason to think of an innocent explanation of why he should be coming down to Upper Trumpton. It was unnecessary.

"Don't seem to have seen you for ages, young man, even though we work right next door to one another, so to speak. You ought to come over to the Commons one day for lunch and we can have a good old chin-wag, just like in the old days."

Robert knew Sir George well, since he had been a good friend of his father for many years. The M.P. had never married, preferring the life of the London gentlemen's club, and it often seemed as if he had adopted Robert as a kind of honorary nephew.

'Uncle George' had been a larger than life figure to Robert during his childhood. Whenever he came to visit, he would generally greet the young boy before his parents, swinging him high into the air and then enquiring at great length about his studies before putting him back down on the ground. Later, when Robert was at boarding school and his own parents were away on a tour of duty overseas, Sir George would drive down to the school and take Robert out on a Sunday. Together they would eat a hefty meal at a local hotel before going on a lengthy route march through the nearby country-side, where Robert would recount all the latest gossip from his school and Sir George would recount all the equally trivial gossip from the House of Commons.

They had never spoken of it, but Robert knew that Sir George was secretly hoping that his adopted nephew would one day join the Conservative Party and enter public life. The M.P. was aware that he was getting on, and whereas most people want to pass on their material wealth to their nearest and dearest, Sir George wanted above all else to be able to pass on his Parliamentary seat to the boy he knew and liked so well. And such was his enormous influence in the local branch of the Party, he could almost certainly have achieved his goal if only the young Robert Stanton would dismount from the political fence on which all British civil servants inevitably find themselves sitting.

"I'd love to lunch with you, George, I really would. Perhaps next week, but I must dash now, mother's getting some scones ready."

"Scones! Your mother's making some of her wonderful scones this afternoon and I've promised those stupid whips I'd be back for a vote later on."

And with another shake of the hand Sir George was off, striding away briskly towards the station.

Robert stood and looked after him for a long time. Did he know what had happened all those years ago in Yorkshire? Did he realise that the real Robert Creighton Stanton was really dead? Or was he simply another victim of the gigantic lie to which Robert was now certain he had been subjected?

Sir George turned a corner and vanished from sight as Robert continued along the lane towards his family home. Looking at the tidy cottages, he began to wonder just how many people were aware of the truth. He had known many of these people all his life: old Mrs Simkins at Rose Cottage, the Browns at the little house on the corner, Reverend Potter and his family in the old vicarage. Did they all know? Were they all part of some obscene conspiracy of silence?

The thoughts were absurd and he pushed them hard to the back of his mind. He should get a grip on himself or he would not be able to handle what was clearly going to be a difficult encounter with his parents. With a shock, he realised that he had not really planned what he would say when he arrived.

But it was too late to think about it now. He had arrived at the old wooden gate set into the hedge surrounding his parents' garden. He pushed against the gate and, as it always did, it made a kind of tortured squeaking noise. Robert had often asked them why they didn't oil it. He had even offered to do it himself. But his mother had always refused, saying that she liked some advance warning when people were coming up the garden path so that she could tidy her hair before they arrived.

Before he reached the house the short, plump figure of his mother appeared at the front door.

"Bobby, here you are. How lovely to see you." She was clearly delighted by the unexpected visit.

Robert embraced her, uncertain how to behave. "Hallo, mother, how are you keeping?"

"Oh, not so bad, dear," she said with a welcoming smile. "But come along inside, won't you, and tell us all the news."

Robert stepped into the house. In contrast to the summer heat outside, it was pleasantly cool in the quiet wood-panelled hall. The old grandfather clock which had been in the Stanton family for generations ticked patiently away to itself in the corner and, as always, freshly cut flowers from the garden were carefully arranged on the hall table.

"We're in the sitting room, dear," his mother said, leading him through to a large, airy room into which the sun was streaming through a wide picture window overlooking the garden.

His father rose as Robert entered the room. John Wilberforce Stanton was a tall, rather distinguished-looking man who managed to exude an air of quiet authority, even when he was at home. He greeted his son warmly.

"Hallo Robert, how good that you could come down to see us."

Robert shook his father's hand in the rather formal way to which he was accustomed.

"How long can you stay, dear?" his mother asked.

17

Robert looked up, trying to hide from her the tension he felt.

"Oh, not very long. Until about five, I suppose. Kate's expecting me."

"Oh well, in that case I'd better get the tea things on." She turned to her husband. "John, dear, why don't you go and show Bobby the garden?"

"Very well, my love. Come on Robert, you might as well see all the work your mother's been making me do out here. And while we're at it you can give me some advice on what to do about that old apple tree down at the bottom of the garden."

Together they walked out across the meticulously well-groomed lawn towards the rougher area at the back of the garden where several large and ageing fruit trees were located. As they walked in silence across the lawn, Robert knew that this was as good a time as any to confront his father with the small piece of paper in his breast pocket. In view of his mother's obvious sensitivity on the subject, it was better to speak to his father alone.

He lifted his arm to draw out the certificate from his jacket pocket but before he could say anything his father had started to speak. His tone was serious.

"Robert, there's something I'd like to have a chat with you about while your mother's out the way. Just between you and me."

It was clear that he was not thinking of the apple tree. Robert's arm dropped away from his pocket, leaving the certificate hidden within.

"Yes, Dad."

"I was playing golf yesterday." He paused, as if uncertain how to proceed. The silence started to become awkward.

"Yes, Dad, I know you were."

"Yes, golf. But that's not really the point. The point is, I was playing golf with your Uncle George."

Another silence. His father had never been very good at getting to the point.

"I met George down at the pub as I was coming here," Robert observed.

"You did?" His father looked rather shocked. "Did he say anything?"

"Well, of course he said something. Asked me to come and have lunch with him one day at the Commons, in point of fact."

John Stanton's face relaxed. "He didn't say anything else?"

"Nope. Nothing important. Should he have?"

The older man shook his head, still wondering what to say. Robert decided to force the issue.

"You were going to tell me what George said to you while you were playing golf yesterday."

"Oh yes." Now his father was slowly beginning to relax, as if he had been given permission to proceed by a superior officer.

"It's like this, Robert," his father continued, "George is getting on a bit, as you know, and is rather hoping he might be offered a peerage in the not too distant future. Anyway, he's been thinking about what to do with the constituency." He paused.

"Well, it's not really for him to decide, is it?" Robert muttered.

"Oh, you know George. He thinks the constituency belongs to him and in truth he does carry a lot of personal weight in Tory Party circles round here."

Robert remained silent until his father was forced to continue.

"The point is, he's trying to find out if you want it?"

Robert looked at his father in amazement.

"You mean, he asked you if I want his seat?"

"In so many words, yes."

"But I'm not even a member of the Conservative Party."

"Mm. That's what I said to him. But he seemed pretty sure that wouldn't be a problem, what with you being a diplomat and all that."

The sun was beating down overhead. Robert was beginning to get a headache and this wasn't helping. But the proposition Sir George had floated was certainly an intriguing one.

"But just how does he imagine I could stand for Parliament doing my job. He must know I'm not allowed to indulge in party political activity."

"That's the point. That's why he's bringing it up now. If you do want him to help you get the seat, you'll have to give up your job well before the next election. He knows that's a big risk for you, so he's proposing to square the local party management committee privately for you in advance of your resignation."

Robert looked at his father incredulously.

"What! Just like that."

"That's what he said. Once the management committee's on your side, the election itself is just a formality. George reckons the Tory Party could put up his old dog Rufus and he'd get elected around here. Couple of speeches, couple of leaflets and you're in. Anyway, it's your business so that's all I'll say, son. But when you've had a chance to think about it, let me know, will you, and I'll have another game of golf with the old chap. In all fairness, you ought to let him know how you react to the idea."

Although Robert had known for years that Sir George secretly wanted to push him forward in politics, this was far more than idle dreams. For a minute, it almost made him forget the purpose of his trip.

But not for long. His own death certificate was still in his pocket, urgently demanding an explanation, but as he raised his arm to pull it out his mother called down from the house, summoning them to tea. His arm dropped to his side and he meekly followed his father back into the sitting room.

Over tea the conversation was concerned, as it generally was, with inconsequential matters. Robert's mother had something of an aversion to serious topics of conversation, particularly when food was being consumed. So Robert talked about Tim's swimming lessons, Justin's planned trip to Devon with the cubs and the family's latest plans for the summer holidays, while his parents briefed Robert on all the latest comings and goings in the busy social life of Upper Trumpton.

The clock on the mantelpiece began its slow melodious chime. It was already five o'clock, soon time to go, and he could put it off no longer. As soon as there was a lull in the conversation, Robert withdrew the piece of folded paper slowly from his breast pocket and held it on his lap.

"Dad." he said calmly, looking his father square in the face. "I was at St Catherine's House yesterday with Justin – helping him draw up a copy of his family tree. While I was there, I found this." Without a further word, he handed over the crisp new copy of the death certificate.

As he spoke, he could see his mother out of the corner of his eye. She seemed paralysed, her hands tightly clenched on her lap.

His father remained still for a long time, looking down at the piece of paper. The only sound in the room came from the clock on the mantelpiece, its slow methodical tick seeming to mock the agitated pace of Robert's heartbeat.

Eventually John Stanton rose slowly from his chair. Without so much as glancing at Robert, he went quietly over to his wife and touched her arm.

"Peggy, darling," he said gently, "I think you should go upstairs and have a little rest. I'll come up later on."

Like a person sleep-walking, Robert's mother rose and walked stiffly from the room. Through the open hallway door, the two men watched her silently as she slowly climbed the stairs. When she was gone the older man closed the door and turned angrily on his son.

Although he didn't raise his voice, the deep hurt within him was plain to see.

"Why did you have to ask me in front of her? Why?"

Robert looked up at the tall figure of his father and knew he had every right to be angry. Whatever the truth, whatever the twisted reality of that distant October day nearly thirty years before, Robert could not have asked for a better mother or a better childhood. And this was how he had now repaid her.

He searched unsuccessfully for the words to express himself, to apologise for an act of crass insensitivity that could so easily have been avoided. But his frantic search for a satisfactory explanation was unnecessary, since his father's anger seemed to subside as quickly as it had arisen. He sat down heavily in his armchair and as he did so Robert could see that his father was turning into an old man.

And now it was his father who was apologising.

"I'm sorry, Robert. That wasn't fair of me. You must have had a terrible shock when you found it."

"I've just got to know the truth, Dad. I've got to. I didn't search it out; I found it quite by accident. But now that I have found it, I've got to know the truth." He leant over and took the little piece of paper from his father's limp hand. "It's me, isn't it? That's my own death certificate."

John Stanton looked up at his son and gazed into his eyes. But Robert could tell that his father was not looking at him, but at some other image far away. When he spoke, his voice was barely audible.

"I should have told you. I've always known deep down that you've got a right to know."

He fell silent again, as if trying to find the inner strength to continue.

"During my life in the army I often had to face situations that required courage, sometimes tremendous courage. And I think I can honestly say that I've never run away. But I've never been able to find sufficient courage to tell the boy I brought up and loved as my only son the truth about himself."

Robert rose from his chair and walked over to his father. He could see that the old man was fighting hard to retain the dignity and self-control of which he had always been so proud. Squatting down on the floor in front of him, he gently took hold of his father's arm.

"Dad, I know something terrible happened. And you know you've got to tell me about it. But I want you to understand that whatever it is, whatever the truth, I'll still love you and mother after I know it. You can't wipe away thirty years of love and caring just like that."

By now tears were flowing freely down his father's face. It was the first time that Robert had ever seen him cry. But eventually he stopped, pulling a large white handkerchief from his trouser pocket to wipe his eyes. Robert stood up and went over to the drinks cabinet.

"I think we could both do with a large Scotch, Dad."

He poured a couple of drinks and handed one to his father.

His father took a gulp and smiled weakly at Robert. "Before I tell you, why don't you ring Kate and tell her you'll be late back tonight. It might take a while."

Robert nodded. There was a phone in the living room and he went over and dialled his home number. It was Kate who answered.

"Hallo, darling, it's me. Listen, I've got held up at a meeting. I'll be back a bit late tonight."

Kate didn't sound at all annoyed. Unlike the wives of the other men at work, she always seemed so understanding when he was held up at the office. Reminding her to give his love to the children, he put the phone down and returned to his chair.

His father was looking at him with a penetrating look.

"Why didn't you tell her you were here?" he asked quietly.

Robert looked surprised. "I didn't want to worry her, that's all. She knows I'm often delayed at work. She understands that. But if I say I've come down here without any apparent reason, she'll think that something dreadful's happened."

His father smiled. "Lies always start like that, don't they? We've always got a good reason for them. To understand a lie, you've got to understand the circumstances in which it was born. If you can understand why we lied to you, it's just possible you might not feel so bitter about it.

"It all started at the end of April 1945. As you know I was posted as a military liaison officer with the Russian troops attacking Berlin. The war was drawing to a close in Europe; the Russians had drawn a tight ring around Berlin and everyone knew that it was only Hitler's insane obstinacy that was prolonging the fighting. To tell you the truth I was wasting my time; the Western Allies had decided to leave the capture of Berlin to the Russians and the Russians weren't in the least bit interested in liaising with anyone about their local operations, least of all me. So I ended up driving about pretty aimlessly in a rusty old jeep between Russian field command posts looking for something useful to do.

"Sitting here in England today it's hard to imagine what it was like in Germany at that time. The old Nazi administration had collapsed but the Russians were far too busy with their military operations to put anything coherent in its place. Yet the German civilian population was terrified of what the Russians would do to them after the war. They knew how Hitler had treated the Slavs and were convinced that the Russians would now pay them back in kind. In the chaos of those closing weeks of the war, whole families were trying to escape westwards, away from the advancing Russian troops and towards the British and the American lines. As I drove around the countryside I could see them walking along by the roadside, their faces completely dead of emotion, dragging their few pathetic possessions with them as best they could. That's where I found you, Robert."

Robert stared at his father incredulously.

"I was driving down a small side-road to the south of Berlin. It was early in the morning, with the sun just beginning to rise over the surrounding fields, and there were no people to be seen for miles around: if it hadn't been for the distant pounding of the Russian artillery bombardment of Berlin, you could have been forgiven for forgetting there was a war on. But I wasn't alone. I turned a bend and there, just ahead of me at the side of the road, I saw a heavily pregnant woman and a small child. At first I thought there must have been a car accident or perhaps even some fighting, because the woman was lying on the ground, her body writhing in pain. Clinging to her head was a terrified little infant of no more than two, sobbing uncontrollably as he watched what he must have believed was his mother's death agony.

"I pulled up and jumped out of the jeep. The woman's pain seemed to subside and she became aware of my presence for the first time. Clutching her sobbing child tightly to herself, she started dragging away from me, making a futile attempt to reach the undergrowth by the side of the road.

"It occurred to me that in her pain she must have mistaken me for a Russian soldier. I held back, pointing to the Union Jack fluttering at the front of my jeep. In German I told her not to be afraid, that I was a British officer and that I wanted to help her. I think she must have understood, for the fear in her face started to subside. But soon it returned, if anything more strongly than before.

"By now I was becoming convinced that the woman was suffering from some kind of internal abdominal bleeding. If that were true, I knew from bitter experience that there was little I could do for her other than try to relieve her suffering. So I ran back to the jeep, planning to fetch some morphine I carried in my medical kit, but before I could find it she let out another terrified scream. I turned to look, and as I did so I suddenly realised that far from being injured she was in the process of giving birth. I had no idea what to do, no idea how to help. She had ripped her undergarments away and I could see that the baby's head was already half-way out, the smooth crown of its head thrusting out between her naked legs. Then she screamed again, and as I knelt down by her side the head and then the tiny body came out from within her and into my arms. The woman was sobbing, the little boy was sobbing, but now there was also the plaintive crying of a third human being, as the little baby I was holding in my hands tried to grab its first desperate breaths."

Robert looked at him in astonishment. "Are you saying that that was me? Are you saying that I was that baby?" he said faintly.

The man opposite him, the man whose face was so familiar and whom he had always known as his father, looked up with surprise.

"The baby. No, you weren't the baby. The baby was a girl. Don't you see, you were the boy, the terrified little boy who had convinced himself that his mother was dying.

Unanswered questions were swirling around inside Robert's head. But he remained still and said nothing. John Stanton looked at him and saw his inner struggle. "Why don't you let me finish the story, Robert," he said quietly, "and then you can ask me as many questions as you like."

Robert nodded.

"I handed the baby to its mother. It was still attached to the afterbirth, but I remembered somehow that it didn't matter. The woman's agonised screams melted away into a kind of gentle whimpering, a strange mixture between infinite sorrow and infinite happiness. Your mother took hold of your little hand and held it on the baby's body. As she did so, you stopped crying and sat gazing at your new sister with a look of complete wonderment.

"I stood back and watched the little family lying there by the roadside. Nearby I could hear the sounds of birds singing and in the distance the sounds of my fellow men killing and maiming each other on the streets of Berlin. For several minutes they seemed to take no notice of me: their world was just the three of them, and whatever else was happening on that crazy planet where they lived was as nothing compared to the human bonds that tied them together.

"But it couldn't last. The world had to come along and shatter their peace sooner or later. I couldn't wait with them for ever, and the woman obviously couldn't be left there in her condition. I went over and sat down next to her on the ground, waiting quietly as she recovered her composure. I felt intensely sorry for her: before she had had one child to care for in an utterly hostile world and now she had two. The woman must have been completely exhausted by the birth, but she was able to speak with me quite coherently.

"I told her that she couldn't stay there by the roadside. She was unwell; she needed to rest. I said I would take her to a Russian field hospital that I knew to be nearby where she could stay until she was better. She remonstrated with me, insisting that she had to go on, that she must at all costs get to the Western sector. She seemed terrified of what the Russians would do to them all if they found her. I remember she made a pathetic attempt to get up, to carry on walking, but she was far too weak to get more than a couple of paces. As she fell back to the ground I could see that she accepted I was right. With a brave attempt at a smile, she apologised for being so stupid and agreed to come with me. I tried to reassure her, to tell her that the stories circulating about the Russians were untrue, and that she would be doubly safe if brought in by a British officer.

"By this time you had got fed up with looking at your little sister and were beginning to fidget, so I sent you off to pick a bunch of spring flowers from a nearby field. Your mother watched as you tottered off and from her face I could see that an idea had suddenly occurred to her. She turned to me and asked if I had any reason to go to the south-eastern outskirts of Berlin, to a place called Köpenick. She had heard that the Russians had already taken the suburb. In fact she was right. It was a long way from the city centre and had been captured a few days before. As it happened, I was due there later that day to prepare a provisional report on the developing position in that sector for my superiors in London.

"When I told her this she looked tremendously relieved. Apparently she had an older sister there, a sister with whom she had once been very close. She begged me to take her to the house with her children. I looked at her in amazement, trying to think of a good reason to refuse. But I couldn't. She was weak, but if it was true that she had relatives so close at hand then she would certainly be better off with them than in a dirty and overcrowded Russian military hospital. There was actually no reason why I shouldn't do it: I was not under Russian military command and was pretty well a free agent. Nobody would stop me taking her.

"Finally I agreed. She was tiring, so I pulled the jeep over and lifted her gently onto the back seat. I could tell the movement was painful for her despite her attempts to conceal it. I let you ride in the front beside me, and I remember the way you gurgled with pleasure at the thought of a ride in an army car.

"We hadn't gone far when I realised something was going badly wrong. I could hear your mother moaning quietly behind me on the back seat and pulled the jeep to a halt. When I looked round I could see that blood was seeping out increasingly rapidly from under her dress. This time I didn't stop to discuss the matter. I swung round again and drove as fast as I could to the place where I knew the nearest field hospital to be.

"I don't mind telling you, Robert, that when I drove into that awful place I nearly turned round and drove straight out again. It comprised a dilapidated farmhouse and its equally dilapidated out-buildings together with a ramshackle collection of army tents. The stench was the first thing I noticed as I approached, a strange combination of rotting human flesh and antiseptic. As I came closer I became aware of the sounds of many human voices. But these were no ordinary voices, they were the voices of war. For when the guns have finished their work there are always people left behind; shattered, crushed wrecks of human beings who have been smashed to pieces in a tiny instant and are then left to suffer for the rest of their mortal lives. And it was the pitiful moaning of these men that I could hear as I drove into the yard. They were lying all around me, inside the buildings and tents and outside on the bare earth. They still had their uniforms on and I could see that some of them were Russian, more of them German. It didn't seem to matter any more. They were just lying there, many with injuries so severe that they would clearly not survive the day. And their moans were those of men wishing that they had never been born.

"But it was no good. The woman behind me was clearly in dire need of medical help. I had no choice but to leave her there.

"The arrival of a British officer had caused quite a stir and I could see a harassed-looking Russian who I took to be the officer in charge hurrying towards me. I showed him the woman with her baby in the back and briefly explained to him in Russian what had happened. He turned and barked an order, and two orderlies came briskly over carrying a stretcher.

"Up to this point you had been sitting quietly beside me, more interested in the car than in your mother's moans, but at the sight of the orderlies you really started to panic. As the orderlies began loading your mother and sister onto the stretcher you began scream-ing, trying desperately to climb out of the car. The Russian looked at you with tense frustration and told me curtly that he could take the baby but not you. He gestured around him as if to drive home his obvious inability to spare any staff to deal with a troublesome toddler. At that moment, as if to reinforce his point, another lorry rolled into the yard to deposit its grisly cargo of human debris.

"You must have followed his meaning because your screams became even louder and more intense with every word he spoke. Your mother was on the stretcher by now, her blood dripping through the rough material onto the ground beneath, but she was shouting at the orderlies not to take her away until she had spoken to me. I could see that they didn't understand her German and I told them in Russian to wait. Breathlessly, urgently, she told me to give her paper and a pen. When I did so she wrote for a few moments on the paper and handed it to me. It was the address of her sister, she said, the sister in Köpenick. She told me I should take you to her sister and that she would follow as soon as she could. And with that she lay back on the stretcher and allowed herself to be carried away, her baby still held tight to her breast.

"I will never in my life forget the scream you gave that day as you watched them take your mother away. I don't know how, but somehow in that young and immature mind of yours you must have known it was to be the last time you would ever see her."

John Stanton stopped talking. He looked weary, and an echo of the tension of those distant hours was stamped upon his face. Then he rose from his chair and, without saying anything, walked slowly over to the old bureau in the corner of the room. Reaching down, he opened the bottom drawer and pulled out a small metal box which he placed on top of the bureau. Then he quietly left the room.

A few moments later he was back, a key in his hand. With it he opened the box, removing a small yellowish piece of paper which he laid carefully on the bureau. Then, equally carefully, he locked the box and returned it to its place in the drawer.

He walked back across the room and gave the piece of paper to Robert.

"There you are, you can have it now, Robert. I've carried the burden long enough."

Robert looked down at the piece of paper in his hand. It was written in the distinctive italic script used by Germans of the older generation. But the words were still clear, if fading with age. 'Katherina Hagenau, Krämerstrasse 15, Köpenick, Berlin.' His natural mother, the woman he must have last seen carried off into a filthy barn on a blood-soaked stretcher at the age of two, had written those words. They were her only testament.

As Robert sat and stared at the writing on the paper, John Stanton stood silently by the window and looked out. For several minutes the only sound that could be heard in the room was the patient ticking of the clock on the mantelpiece.

This time it was Robert who broke the silence.

"You're not my father, are you?"

The man by the window didn't look round. "No," he said, "I'm not your father. I don't know who your father was."

There was another pause, but this time not for long.

"Did I have a name?"

The man by the window turned.

"I suppose so, but I don't know what it was. Your mother never used it, at least I can't remember her using it. She just referred to you as 'the child', and when she spoke to you she called you 'little mouse'."

Robert suddenly remembered the death certificate.

"But you did have a child, didn't you? A child named Robert Creighton Stanton. A child that was killed with your parents in that car accident on the moors. That's right, isn't it?"

"I'm sorry, Robert, I haven't finished the story yet." He fetched the whisky bottle from the side and brought it over, filling Robert's glass and his own again. Leaving the bottle by the side of his chair, he sat down and continued.

"As soon as your mother had disappeared from sight I turned the jeep round and drove out of the hospital yard as quickly as I could. It was difficult to drive, because I had to hold you down to prevent you climbing out of the vehicle and running back to her. As soon as we could no longer see, smell or hear the dreadful place I pulled over to the side of the road and tried to tell you what was happening. You didn't really understand, but you calmed down a bit and I started driving towards the eastern suburbs of Berlin. I had missed an appointment in the morning, but I knew that in the chaos of those last days of the war nobody would notice my absence. I felt a complete idiot driving around with a two-year-old German refugee in my jeep and decided it was best to get you to your aunt as soon as possible.

"Before long I found myself entering the eastern suburbs of what had once been the proud city of Berlin. Red Army soldiers stood guard over the smashed and twisted remains of people's homes and Russian military vehicles were still flowing freely backwards and forwards along the main arteries of the city that led to the battlefield in the centre. But alongside and parallel with all this military activity I could see other people moving about. Old men, women and children who must have been hiding for days in underground cellars as the fighting passed overhead, were beginning to emerge again into the late April sunlight. They could be seen wandering in the shadows by the roadside and clambering amongst the ruins, hunting for scraps of food and firewood or perhaps for loved ones they had lost.

"As I looked at the total devastation around me, I could feel a growing sense of unease. It was the first time I had entered the built-up area of the city and I realised how ill-prepared I was for what I found. I had expected to find some ruins, but not the complete destruction of every human habitation. I realised with a shock that the address to which I was driving was almost certainly a pile of rubble and that there was no guarantee that anyone would still be left alive there.

"I was only stopped once as I drove towards your aunt's address. A Russian officer flagged me down at a junction and asked me where I was going. I explained to him, truthfully as it happened, that I was preparing a report on the situation in the south-eastern sector of the city. He looked at you sitting next to me with a puzzled look and then waved me on, warning me not to approach the city centre because heavy street fighting was still taking place.

"I didn't find your aunt. The road was like all the others, just a heap of rubble. There were a few people around, and I asked them all where she was, but although some had known her, nobody knew where she had gone. One man I spoke to said that he had actually lived in the same building as she had, but that she had disappeared several months before without saying goodbye. I tried to get some more information out of him, something that would help me find your aunt, but he didn't have anything more to say. He just stood there silently, clutching a stupid little rag doll in his hands.

"So there I was, and I had to do something with you. I had to find you somewhere to sleep, somewhere to be safe. If I could, I would have taken you with me there and then, but I was staying in a Russian army barracks and I knew it was impossible.

"There was nothing more to be done in the street where your aunt had once lived so I drove away, uncertain of what to do. I couldn't find your aunt and I couldn't take you back to the field hospital. But then I had a stroke of good fortune. As I turned a bend I could see in front of me a large group of young children, some of them little more than toddlers like you. Some women were herding them along next to the road rather like a flock of ducks. I pulled up the jeep and called to an elderly woman who appeared to be in charge. She stopped the ducks with a crisp, business-like command and strode over to speak to me.

"She was a tall, rather gaunt-looking woman, whose haggard appearance suggested she had found little food and even less rest for many weeks. But although the state of her clothing and outward appearance were much the same as all the other German civilians at that time, there was an indefinable quality about her that was very different. For whereas most people I saw had been completely crushed by those final bitter days of defeat, she seemed to have remained completely unbowed by adversity.

"I asked her what she was doing. She looked at me with rather disdainful surprise and gestured at the waiting group of tiny humans by the side of the road. Her piercing eyes glared aggressively at my military uniform. 'Can't you see what I'm doing?' she said. 'I'm collecting up the little ones who are left behind when you men have finished your games of toy soldiers.'

"They were dangerous words for a German civilian to speak to an enemy officer. If I had reported her to the Russians she would in all probability have been shot. But as I looked around me at the smashed city and at the pathetic band of children she had gathered from the ruins, I could not help but see her point.

"She noticed the silent child beside me and the anger in her eyes melted away. She must have suddenly realised why I had stopped and asked me quietly, so that you could not hear, if the child was an orphan. I explained to her what I knew, told her that I had nowhere to take you, and she agreed to take you with her. As she lifted you into her arms with gently soothing words, I was struck by the look of tranquility that came over your face for the first time that day.

"I asked her where the orphanage was, intending to return to the field hospital and tell your mother. She smiled at the stupidity of my question and gestured with her arms to the ruins. But then she explained that she was planning to set up a kind of temporary shelter in the cellar of an old warehouse not far away. Asking for a map, she produced a remarkably grand fountain pen from the recesses of her clothing and made a neat little cross showing the exact spot.

"I thanked her for her help and started up the jeep. But I'd only gone a few yards when a thought occurred to me and I slammed on the brakes, reversing the jeep back to where the children were still waiting. I called to the woman again and she came over to me. Reaching over into the back I dragged up my ration box, pulled out the food and medicines in it and thrust them into her hand. For a moment she hesitated, but then she thanked me for my kindness and explained that they were indeed very short of food.

"As she turned away and went to rejoin her growing flock, I suddenly felt a sense of almost unbearable guilt. Every day I sat down to several substantial meals and yet here were these innocent little children, these children who could in no conceivable way be held responsible for the rise of Adolf Hitler, going without enough food to fill their tiny stomachs."

John Stanton's voice trailed away and he took another gulp of his whisky.

"I couldn't get back to the field hospital that day. I was way behind with my work and I had a report to file so it wasn't until the following day that I drove into that foul smelling yard to tell your mother where I had left you. This time no one came to greet me, and so I left the jeep and started to look around for her. She wasn't anywhere to be found, so eventually I stopped one of the orderlies and asked him where she was. He looked at me with an expression of amazement, wondering why a British officer should be concerned about a German civilian. He didn't know anything about it, but he took me to the same officer I had met the day before.

"I could hardly have arrived at a worse time. The officer was bending over a Russian soldier lying on a table, and as we came closer I could see that he was operating. One of his patient's legs was already lying on the floor and the officer, who was clearly a surgeon, was half way through removing the other one. He looked up as we approached and nodded a greeting before continuing with his grisly work.

"Eventually he finished, and as the orderlies removed the inert body from the table to replace it with another, he came over to speak to me. He told me that your mother was no longer there. She had gone into a coma during the night and they had decided to send her and the baby on a night transport going to a proper hospital further east.

"I asked him where exactly she had been sent. Throwing a glance at the blood-stained wreck of a man lying impassively on the operating table, he looked at me with scarcely disguised impatience and told me he didn't have the faintest idea. He thought that the lorries carrying the injured went to a central rendezvous some twenty kilometres to the east of Berlin and were sent on from there. She could have ended up anywhere. He told me where the rendezvous point was and then, with a hurried apology, turned his back on me and continued with his work.

"As soon as I had the chance, I contacted the rendezvous point by radio and when they failed to give me a satisfactory reply I drove over to see them in person, but they simply had no idea where they had sent your mother and sister. It could have been any one of a dozen places, and even they might not have been the final destinations.

It was hardly surprising that they didn't know: with so many people moving around, so many lorries passing through, no one could remember what had happened to two inconspicuous German civilians.

"Over the next few weeks I tried phoning nearly all the places where they thought your mother could have been sent. Where I couldn't phone I wrote, explaining what had happened to you and where you could be found. But none of it did any good because she never returned. For all I know, she died that night along with her baby in the back of a Russian army transport.

"The war in Europe was soon over. But although the guns fell silent the shadow of war still hung over the shattered remains of Berlin. By day people would work clearing the piles of rubble with their bare hands, and by night they would hide away in their cellars and makeshift shelters, trying to find the strength to face another day. I was surrounded by human suffering, I should by rights have become completely immune to it, but I just couldn't get you out of my head."

Robert looked up sharply.

"Why did you care so much?"

John Stanton smiled.

"I suppose that's a good question, although I never stopped to think about it at the time. It might have been because I was sick of the killing after six years of war, or maybe it was because I had watched your mother giving birth. But I suppose the most likely explanation is that I associated you with my own little two-year-old son in England whom I'd never seen.

"I found myself dreaming about you at nights. Sometimes you were crawling along in the sewers and the tangled ruins of Berlin. You never cried out, you never turned round, you just kept on crawling in search of the mother you had lost. On other occasions I dreamt you were my own son and that we were playing on the lawn of my parents' house in Yorkshire. Everything was so settled, so peaceful, and you were always laughing and happy.

"Although the war had ended I was still attached to the Russian forces as a British liaison officer. The Allies had agreed to govern the city jointly, with each government responsible for the day-to-day administration of a particular sector. But British and American soldiers didn't really start arriving in large numbers until early July and so I remained one of the few Western officers in Berlin for quite some time.

"The Russian troops who were responsible for the administration of the city in the immediate aftermath of the capitulation had not the slightest interest in the welfare of the civilian population. Their primary task appeared to be the removal to the Soviet Union of the few objects of value that still remained in Berlin.

"By now I was staying in a barracks set aside exclusively for British officers. I befriended a soldier working in the kitchens and told him about the plight of the children in the cellar. The man, who was himself a father of four, put aside a little food each day from the army rations with which we were supplied and I would quietly load them into the back of the jeep when nobody was looking and drive across to visit you and the other children in the makeshift orphanage.

"Helga – that was the elderly woman's name – was not short of customers. The cellar she had found was teaming with children who had lost their parents. During the day it seemed to be exploding with the sound of children playing, children fighting and children crying. At night it was quiet, but in the glimmer of the candlelight you could see that many of the children remained awake long into the night, alone with their memories and their secret hopes and fears.

"Helga was an extraordinary woman. Only once in the six months that I knew her did I see her spirit begin to sag. It was when she had managed to arrange an appointment with the Russian officer in charge of that district of Berlin in order to try and arrange proper supplies of food and medicine for the children. I arrived one night with my food parcel just as she had returned from her visit and she told me that in response to her plea for more food he had told her that he was glad that the little German children were close to starvation because it would teach them never to start a war when they grew up. As I sat and talked to her, it turned out that the reason she was so upset was not because the Russian had been so heartless but rather because she secretly feared he might be right.

"Whenever I came to the orphanage I would come to see you. I would sit and hold you on my lap in a corner somewhere and try to tell you what I was doing to try to find your mother. It seemed unlikely that you would grasp the full meaning of what I was saying but I told you anyway. At first you missed your mother terribly. When I spoke of her you would immediately start to sob, the tension held within you suddenly released by her mention. But after a few months you started to detach yourself from her: instead of crying when I spoke of her, you would start to fidget as if you found the whole subject increasingly boring.

"Two people came to dominate your life at that time. Helga was one of them. She had a knack of making every child under her wing feel that he or she was the most important person in all the world.

Despite the tremendous administrative burden involved in keeping that place functioning, she always found the time to cuddle and reassure a frightened child. And in the evening, when you were all lying down, she would sit in the middle of that damp and overcrowded cellar and make up stories to tell you.

"If I could, I would try to come at story-time. Helga would tell of faraway places and faraway times where life was good and people were eternally kind and happy. For young and old alike during those terrible months, the stories she told held out a tempting hope for the future and were a soothing relief from the grim realities of the present.

"I soon became aware that the other important person in your life was me. I don't really know why, because you didn't see nearly as much of me as you did of Helga. Perhaps it was because I was the living link with your mother. Perhaps it was because I reminded you of your own father, of whom you only seemed to have the haziest of recollections. Or perhaps it was simply because you could tell that I actually cared about you in a world which was still trying to rediscover the meaning of the word after so many years of senseless hatred.

"For six months or so I kept on visiting you in the cellar. But then, at the end of September, my tour of duty in Berlin came to an end and I was given extended leave in England. Many other soldiers had to wait longer than I did to go home, but I was given preferential treatment because I had a child at home whom I had never met.

"My last day in Berlin arrived and I knew I could put it off no longer. I took the jeep and some food and drove over to the orphanage to tell you I was leaving Berlin, probably for ever. Although I was pleased to be going home to see my own child at last, I was terrified by the effect my departure might have on you. You had been torn away in front of my own eyes from your mother. Helga and I had tried to replace her for you, to give you something to hold on to, and from your reaction to us it was clear that we had at least partially succeeded. Yet now I was going to tear up that trust by walking out. As I drove towards the cellar that day I found myself praying that your obvious affection for Helga would help pull you through the pain of separation.

"But when I arrived at the orphanage I immediately knew something was badly wrong. There was a Russian army bus parked outside, and the children were gathered in a group on the pavement, each holding a little cloth bundle. Two burly Russian women in military uniform were busy counting the children, who were evidently about to be loaded onto the bus.

"I could see several of the German women who helped out in the orphanage, but I noticed they were standing a little way apart from the children, on the other side of the bus. From their faces I could see that they were frightened. Helga herself was nowhere to be seen, so I went over to ask one of the German women what had happened. She whispered that Helga had become angry that morning because promised supplies of food had failed to turn up for three days in a row. She had gone to demand action from the Russian authorities but had not returned. The next thing they knew was that the bus had turned up and they had been told that the orphanage had been closed on the orders of the Russian authorities. The children were to be transferred to a town outside Berlin but the women had been told that they were not permitted to accompany them.

"It didn't make any sense. There should have been advance warning if the orphanage was to be moved. And what had happened to Helga? I approached one of the Russian women and asked her what was going on. She looked at me in surprise, puzzled at the concern being shown by a British officer, and then explained that the children were being moved to better accommodation elsewhere. I expressed astonishment, pointing out that no advance warning of the move had been given, and asked what had happened to the elderly lady in charge of the children.

"At this the woman took fright. She turned on her heel and walked off to speak to her colleague, who was still sorting out the children by the bus. They conferred anxiously for several minutes, unsure of how to deal with a British officer. Then the second woman, who was of a more senior rank, came over to me. She asked me what my connection was with the orphanage and why I was enquiring. It was a dangerous question, because I had no business to be interfering in the eastern, Russian-administered sector of the city. Hoping that she would know no better, I told her that I was preparing an Allied report on the condition of German children in Berlin and, to my immense relief, she accepted my lie at face value. Taking my arm, she led me out of earshot of the children and the group of German women and whispered to me that the lady who had previously been in charge of the orphanage had been arrested that morning for violating the Russian occupation statutes. Then, after glancing around again to check that nobody was listening, she explained that the real reason for the arrest was that the woman had insulted a particularly touchy Russian officer.

"It was all too easy to imagine. Helga's trouble had always been that she didn't know when to keep her mouth shut. But I was still puzzled as to why the orphanage was to be moved and why all the other women who worked there were to be left behind. I asked the Russian woman to explain. She pointed at the ruin and told me it was no place to keep young children. Then she turned to the group of women and explained that the Russian commander did not feel that the staff appointed by a known law-breaker should be left in charge of impressionable children. New, more reliable staff were therefore to be appointed when the children arrived at their destination.

"I tried to reason with her, to tell her that Helga and the other women were in no way unreliable and to explain that the children had formed a desperately needed relationship with them. But I could tell that the Russian was becoming increasingly suspicious at my concern so I stopped, thanked her for her help and walked away.

"When I had got back to the jeep I stood and watched the children. You were all standing quite calmly in a group by the door of the bus waiting for the order to get on board. But although none of you were crying, I could tell that you were all perplexed and confused by what was happening. I wanted to come and say goodbye to you, to hold you one more time in my arms and wish you well, but I couldn't see how I could approach you without arousing the Russians' suspicion. So I held back, wondering what effect it would have on you when you realised that you had again been deserted by the people you had learned to love and trust.

"But then it happened, and when it happened, it happened fast. One of the Russian women started loading the children onto the bus, lifting the little ones up over the big steps, and as she did so you suddenly spotted me standing by the jeep. Your eyes, which had previously appeared dull and lifeless, were suddenly filled with a kind of desperate hope. Without any hesitation, you started to totter straight towards me, your eyes fixed on my face. You stumbled into the mud on the road, but managed to pick yourself up and stagger on towards me. I bent down as you approached and you fell into my waiting arms, tears of fear and relief flowing freely down your little face as you clung onto my neck.

"It took several seconds for the Russian women to react to these events. But then the more senior one came running towards me and with a muttered apology tried to pull you from my arms.

"But you wouldn't let go. You gripped your arms around my neck with all your strength and screamed at the top of your voice. The harder she pulled, the harder you gripped and the louder you screamed. I had no time to think, only time to react. I pulled away from the Russian and told her in the most authoritative voice I could muster that I would deal with this particular child myself and that she could get on with her duties. Her mouth fell open but before she could recover her senses I had climbed into the jeep and started the engine.

"By now the woman had started to remonstrate, shouting at me that it was abduction and that she would report me to her superiors, but I didn't wait to listen. I just drove off down the road at full speed with you still clinging with all your strength to my neck.

"I didn't stop driving until I was safely in the British sector. Then I pulled up and turned off the engine. You looked up at me, looked around to check that nobody was waiting to take you away, and then you started to grin all over your face. You were exceedingly pleased with yourself.

"But I suppose you had every right to grin. As I looked at you that moment I knew already what I was going to do. I had tried dumping you once before, six months previously, yet now you were back with me in my jeep all over again. And this time I knew that you were with me for good. I had decided to take you back to England with me.

"It wasn't easy getting you out of Germany. I was frightened that the Russian women would make a fuss and that I would be forced to hand you back. At the barracks that night I told them that you were a young Jewish child who had been in hiding with a German family since your mother had been picked up by the Nazis. I explained that the family had found out that I was going to London and had asked me to take you with me to your grandparents who had escaped to England before the war.

"The story worked incredibly well. You had no papers, and I had no papers relating to you, but ever since the revelations about the camps everyone was feeling so shocked about the way the Jews had been treated that nobody tried to check out my story or create any difficulties on the journey home.

"And so I arrived back in England after over three years away. All the way back on the train I had been wondering just how I was going to explain you to my wife. I had never seen my own child, yet here I was bringing another child of almost exactly the same age back with me from Germany. It was bizarre and I knew it was. I decided that the best thing to do was say nothing in advance and simply turn up with you at my parents' home in Yorkshire. I reckoned that if only Peggy could see you with her own eyes she would understand why I couldn't just hand you back to the Russians. So I rang Peggy from the station in London and told her which train I would catch without saying a word about you. She told me that my parents would come to the station by car to fetch me."

John Stanton paused, and then turned to Robert with a grim look.

"I think you've already worked out what happened next, haven't you?"

Robert nodded.

"I think so. But I'd like you to tell me anyway."

"My first reaction on getting off the train was one of annoyance. Despite my phone call, there was nobody there to meet me. But then I remembered that my dad had written to me shortly before saying that the car was playing up so I assumed that he had had trouble starting it that morning. There was a taxi outside the station so I took it. As we drove off across the moors I could feel a growing sense of excitement at the prospect of meeting my son for the very first time.

"We turned the bend where the road climbed up the hillside and drew to a halt. The road was blocked by several police cars and an ambulance. I looked to see what had happened and realised that a car must have gone over the edge, but from where I was sitting the wreckage was hidden from view. At first I didn't react. But then I suddenly remembered my parents' failure to meet me at the station. Leaving you sitting on the rear seat of the taxi I got out of the car to go and see what had happened.

"I knew as soon as I looked over the edge that it was my parents' car. It was the same old black Ford in which I had learnt to drive before the war. And as I stood by the road looking down, I could see some policemen dragging the lifeless bodies of my parents from the vehicle and loading them onto stretchers.

"But worse was to follow. Instead of carrying the stretchers back up the hillside, one of the policemen returned to the smashed car. A few moments later, I could see him dragging another body from the vehicle. But this time it wasn't the body of an adult, it was the lifeless corpse of a tiny child. And I knew it was my only son."

John Stanton stopped talking. From his face, it was clear that he was reliving the dreadful desolation of that terrible moment. The clock ticked patiently on the mantelpiece. It was an old clock, and Robert found himself trying to estimate how many times it had ticked since October 1945. It was ticking about once a second. Sixty seconds in a minute, sixty minutes in an hour. That was three thousand six hundred ticks an hour. Twenty four hours in a day. Roughly ninety thousand ticks a day, or thirty million ticks a year. Thirty years, nine hundred million ticks, but the pain written on his father's face at this moment was as if it had all happened only yesterday.

Unlike the rest of the story he had heard that day, the scene by the Yorkshire roadside was familiar to him. Only the previous day he had told his own son the circumstances of his grandparents' death. But now there was a twist in the story, a twist he had suspected from the moment he had examined the death certificate, and it was clear that the child whose name he bore had also died in that terrible road accident.

Robert's mind raced on. The couple who had brought him up, his 'mother' and 'father', had obviously done a complete switch. They had simply replaced the little German child for their own. For some reason the thought made Robert angry. He interrupted his father's reverie.

"You switched me, didn't you? I just stepped into his shoes, as if he had never been killed."

His father looked up at him with a confused look, as if uncertain how to respond.

"Not at first," he replied quietly.

"Well, when then? And why?"

"I'll try and tell you if you'll only listen, Robert. And then you must judge for yourself whether what we did was right or wrong."

The anger subsided and Robert settled back again in his chair.

"I waited by the roadside as they carried the three bodies up the hill to the waiting ambulance. They were covered by sheets, but when they lifted the sheet for me to see my child I took an involuntary step backwards. The child looked almost exactly like you. The same hair, the same eyes, the same build. I found myself looking back at the taxi to check that you were still there, to check that you had not somehow vanished.

"But there was another strange emotion at the same time. I found myself almost relieved that it was my own son and not you that had been killed. The smashed body of the little boy lying on the stretcher was a stranger to me, but you were already a part of my life.

"The days that followed were hard to endure. Although it was my parents who had been killed it was actually harder for Peggy than for me. The dead child was hers much more than mine for she had brought him up and knew him well. Her reaction to you was predictably cool at first. It must have redoubled her grief to share a house with a little child who looked so remarkably similar to the one she had lost. But a part of her must have understood that you too had lost someone close and I think in the end that fact drew you both together.

"We didn't plan the switch straight away. But after the funeral had taken place we had to start thinking again. We had to decide what to do with you. One possibility would have been to apply for adoption, but there were several problems attached to that course of action. We didn't have any idea as to your true identity; we didn't even know your name. And I was well aware that the circumstances of my removing you from Germany were hardly correct; there was a good chance that the authorities would have regarded it as abduction and returned you to East Berlin.

"I remember that the idea of a switch occurred to us about two weeks after the funeral. You had gone to bed and Peggy and I were sitting up by the fire talking. Earlier in the day we had been out walking on the moors and had met some distant acquaintances who had not heard about our bereavement. You were wearing the dead child's clothes and the people had completely mistaken you for Robert. It was only when you spoke that you gave yourself away, because although you had picked up a few phrases in English you still spoke in those early months with a most atrocious German accent.

"At first we discussed it almost as an intellectual exercise. It was indeed remarkable how similar you looked to our dead child and we wondered whether it would be possible to arrange a switch. Peggy was sceptical, but the more I thought about it the more I realised that we stood a pretty good chance. Nobody knew about the accident other than people who lived in the village and they were primarily friends of my parents rather than me. We could simply move away from the area and lose contact with everyone who knew. Peggy's parents had emigrated to Canada before the war and for some reason we hadn't found the time or the energy to write and tell them yet about the accident. The same went for all our other friends.

"A more tricky problem in the short run was your accent, which had given you away that day up on the moors. But we knew that it would not take many months before you would sound like any other English child of your age; it was simply a matter of keeping you out of public circulation until you were ready. If people came to the house to visit us, it would be straightforward to tell them that you had a contagious illness and that they should stay away from your room.

"Your memory was another potential problem. When you arrived in England you were roughly two-and-a-half years old and had clear memories of what had happened to you in Germany - particularly of the orphanage. But it was clear that your conscious memory of your real mother had already faded away to just about nothing and it seemed likely that the same process would eventually occur with your memories of Helga and everything else in Berlin, particularly if we avoided all reference to them. Again, it was just a matter of time.

"Peggy and I talked all through that night, trying to think of every possible objection to the plan. But instead of thinking of more problems we only came up with more advantages. In your true identity, for example, you were a German. But in Britain in 1945 the Germans were the scum of the earth. Other children, adults even, may well have reacted badly to you.

"We eventually decided that we would give it a try. At first we didn't do anything dramatic, we just carried on in the village as we had done before. But we didn't tell any new people, such as Peggy's parents, about what had happened. We put my parents' house on the market and I told the army that I was very keen on an overseas posting after my spell of leave was over.

"With you it was more difficult. I had always called you 'little mouse' – in German – but now I told you that I was going to call you Robert because that was an English name and you were now an English boy. You rapidly became used to the name and forgot that you had ever been called anything else. Ever since my arrival in England I had spoken English to you as much as possible, only using German when you clearly failed to understand. But now I started to avoid German altogether, telling you carefully the English word or phrase every time you came out with the German.

"The most difficult part of the transition for me was the way I had to react when you spoke of Helga and the other people and things you had known in Berlin. Peggy and I knew we were walking a tight-rope. Within months, certainly by the time you were three years old, you would become capable of remembering things in later life. I was afraid that if we spoke of your mother, or of Helga, or of anything else that reminded you of your early life in Germany, then you would somehow remember talking about the past even if you didn't remember the past itself. So every time you brought up the subject I would be evasive and refuse to join in the conversation.

"It was only much later, when we had left Britain and were living in the Far East, that we started to implant within you stories about an early life that was in fact not your own. For example, you would ask us what your first word had been and we would tell you what the dead child's first word had been. Or we would show you photographs of our own son as a baby and tell you the stories that accompanied them."

Robert's father rose from his chair and returned to the bureau. This time he took out a large photograph album and laid it down on the table beside Robert. It was an album Robert knew well, full of pictures of himself as a little boy. His own children, Justin and Timothy, had only recently taken great delight in looking through the pages and laughing at the pictures of their dad as a youngster.

"Have a look, Robert," his father said. "See if you can tell where the switch occurs."

The familiar volume suddenly took on a sinister form. The baby photos which he had always assumed to be his own were nothing to do with him, they belonged to someone else.

He flicked back through the photos of his early teens. They were definitely of him, and he could actually remember when many of them had been taken. He turned the pages backwards still further and the little pre-adolescent boy portrayed in the images became younger and younger but was still recognisably himself. But now the photos were those of a pre-school child and he realised with a shock that the memories of the events they portrayed were actually second-hand memories. They were the stories of childhood events that are passed on from parents to their children as they grow up and become a kind of substitute for a real memory that does not exist.

Robert turned to the first page. He was looking at a copy of a baby photo he knew well. Another copy was upstairs by the side of his mother's bed. The tiny baby was holding in its hand the little silver-coloured rattle which his own children had held when they were babies and which was now carefully put away in a drawer at home for his grandchildren. But the baby in the picture was not him, it was somebody else, a little human being who had not had any life other than a babyhood with a rattle.

He turned the page and looked at more photographs of the baby. Holding the page close to his face, he tried to find a clue that it was not him, but he could see nothing. He did the same with the pictures of the toddler but without success. Finally he gave up.

"Which is the earliest picture of me?"

Without saying anything his father pointed at a photograph of a smartly dressed little boy of about two wearing short grey trousers and a stripy open-necked shirt. On the same page there was another picture of what looked like the same boy wearing the same trousers and the same shirt.

His father noticed him comparing the two.

"You're right. One of them's you, the other isn't. The one on the left was taken by my father on the day before the car accident. My son was looking so pleased with himself because he knew he was to meet his dad for the first time. I took the one on the right with the same camera the day after we decided to try the switch so that we could see how similar you appeared in a photograph."

Robert peered at the two children. It was true that they both looked virtually identical. At a casual glance no one would think that they were different boys. But as he studied the photographs he could see that they really were different people. The real Robert Creighton Stanton was proud, upright and happy, a boy surrounded throughout his life by love and security. But the other boy, the boy who had lived, was standing with a stooped and depressed appearance. In his face could be seen the anxiety of one who has learnt from bitter personal experience that life is nothing but a precarious joke. And that boy was him.

Robert silently closed the book. Rising from his chair, he went over to the window and looked out over the garden. The flowers, the lawn, the apple trees, it all looked so real. Yet he had supposed himself to be real, to be a person with a particular identity and a particular past. He had taken it utterly for granted, just as he took the existence of the flowers for granted. And if he had been deceiving himself about his own identity, what else was there on which he could rely?

He pushed the thoughts to the back of his mind. It was ridiculous. He was no different because of the discoveries of the previous two days. He was essentially still Robert Creighton Stanton, successful British diplomat, and the fact that he had borrowed a name from a child who quite evidently no longer needed it was not going to change that fact.

He turned to the man who was still his father.

"I've got to go, Dad. Kate'll be expecting me back."

The older man nodded silently.

"Shall I go up and see Mum?"

His father shook his head. "No, I'll talk to her when you've gone. She'll be all right."

As his father spoke, Robert could hear the emptiness in his voice. It was as if he felt that he had lost his only child. Robert went over to him and laid a hand gently on his arm.

"There's something you've got to know, Dad," he said. "You'll always be my father and Mother will always be my mother. Nothing you've said today changes that."

His father attempted a smile and quietly showed him out through the front door. But he had only taken several paces down the garden path when he stopped and turned.

"One more thing, Dad."

His father looked at him.

"Thanks for what you did. Thanks for bringing me up."

And with that he turned and walked briskly away without looking back.

LONDON, NOVEMBER 1978

The phone on Robert's desk started ringing and he picked it up.

"Robert, it's your old Uncle George. I was wondering if you could pop over for lunch today. There's something I'd like to have a chat about."

Robert smiled to himself.

"Hallo, George. I guess so. What time?"

"Oh, whenever you like. Shall we say 12.30. Come and meet me in my office."

"O.K. I'll be there."

He put the phone down and returned to the papers on which he was working. But to no avail; however hard he tried, he couldn't get his mind back onto his work. There was only one reason why George wanted to see him in such a hurry and his mind went back to the last time they had lunched in the House of Commons. It had been over three years before, in the summer of 1975, only a few days after his father had told him the extraordinary story of his early life in Germany.

Robert had arranged the meeting to tell Sir George in person his thoughts about standing for Parliament. The meeting had come at rather a bad time. He had found it difficult to settle back into his normal routine after the discoveries he had made about his past and had felt a pressing need for the relative security of his career in the Foreign Office. Kate must have sensed his unease, for when he had asked her for her reaction to the idea she had argued strongly against taking any precipitate action.

And so it was with some considerable regret that Robert had told Sir George that he was not yet prepared to resign his job in order to start a new career in politics. He had expected that to be the end of it, but Sir George had not looked in the least bit taken aback.

He had simply asked Robert whether he would like to be Foreign Secretary one day.

It was an unfair question. What other answer could there be for an ambitious young diplomat? And then he was hooked. Sir George had explained that a resignation was not required so long before the election, just a private expression of interest to a small and select group of people in inner echelons of the constituency party.

Robert had been shocked by Sir George's obvious contempt for his electorate. They were his faithful flock, and would follow the guidance of the Conservative Party elders in the constituency in these matters. All the important people were on the management committee, and George had arranged for him to meet privately with each and every one of them. Nothing further had been required at that stage and the M.P. had promised to speak to him again nearer the next election. Shortly afterwards, Robert had been posted to South America from whence he had only recently returned.

Outside the office, Robert heard the deep tones of Big Ben striking the hour: it was twelve o'clock. Putting on his overcoat to protect him from the bitter November wind, he left the office and emerged into the teaming bustle of Whitehall. When he arrived at the door of the Commons he found Sir George waiting for him, his large brown overcoat wrapped tightly around his large form.

"Thought I'd come down and meet you, Robert."

Robert looked surprised. He had been expecting to lunch at the Commons, but George clearly had other plans.

"I thought we'd go and eat at the Club. The food's better."

As they set off together along Whitehall, George did not waste any time in coming to the point.

"I wanted to talk about my inheritance, Robert."

Robert looked up. The man's arrogance in these matters seemed to know no bounds.

"Sorry?"

"You know, the constituency. There's election fever in the air and I'm coming under a bit of pressure to tell the committee what my plans are."

Robert had discovered from long experience that it was best to remain silent in these situations. He did so.

"The thing's yours if you want it. I'll stand down and the committee will see to your selection as soon as you resign your job and join the Party."

Robert was uncertain what to say. He was being offered a safe seat in the House of Commons as if it were a rotten borough.

"You mean you've decided you want to stand down."

Sir George pulled his coat more tightly around his shoulders. It was several seconds before he replied.

"I didn't say that, Robert. I said it's yours if you want it."

Something fishy was up, that was plain. Sir George continued.

"Listen, Robert, you know I think you'd be an excellent person to take over from me. You're bright, you've got better judgement than most of the young upstarts in the Party and you're a damn sight more up-to-date than I am. I said all that to you three years ago and I still think it. And I more-or-less said to you three years ago that you could take over the seat at the next election. That's why its yours for the asking. Your old Uncle George is not someone to go back on his word."

"But something's wrong, isn't it? There's something troubling you George."

"Mm, yes, I suppose there is."

Robert decided to force the issue.

"Well, I'm not going to tell you my answer until you've told me what it is that's troubling you."

George looked utterly miserable.

"Well, it's to do with this peerage business."

So that was it. George had not been offered the expected peerage. All along he had been reckoning on an honourable retirement to the red benches of the Upper House, but now he was facing the bleak prospect of total exclusion from the Parliamentary world that was his only life.

"I'm not going to be on the list this time. Don't know why the buggers have left me off after all I've done for the Party. But I'm not on it."

There was a long silence. George really was a pathetic creature in his own way. He had had a long and successful career, he should be proud of himself for what he had achieved. But here he was, a crumpled heap who felt he was not being given a much deserved pat on the head on the occasion of his retirement.

It was obvious what was going through his mind. He was hoping that Robert would let him off the hook and allow him to stand again for another five-year term. He was caught between his promise to Robert to allow him to take over the seat and his own burning desire to stay in Parliament. Robert swallowed hard. Ever since his return from Latin America he had been expecting George to make the offer. And this time Kate and he had decided he would accept. However dim a view Robert took of the manner in which he had been offered the seat, the fact remained that it was too good an opportunity to let pass.

"You want to carry on, don't you?"

George looked at his feet. "I'd relied on that bloody peerage."

"But you can't carry on for ever, you know that."

George's face brightened.

"I don't want to carry on for ever. I'm sixty-nine years old. If I carry on for another full term I'll be nearly seventy-five." He chortled to himself. "They'll have to offer me a peerage then, the old buggers, because they'll be scared witless that I'll stand yet again and start going ga-ga on television."

Robert glanced sideways at Sir George. The thought of him going ga-ga on television was certainly amusing and perhaps not totally beyond the realms of possibility.

Sir George was evidently still uncertain about Robert's response.

"Robert, I shouldn't really be telling you this, but there's another reason why it might be no bad thing to hold your Parliamentary career over for a few more years. I've been keeping my ear to the ground and I've heard some pretty encouraging things about where your diplomatic career's heading."

Robert looked up. One of the best kept secrets in the Service was the career plans that were laid down years in advance for individual diplomats. He had sensed from his recent jobs that he was a high-flyer, but Sir George was obviously privy to some more concrete information. George looked around, as if to check that nobody was listening.

"The word's out that you could get quite a decent Ambassadorship next time round."

Robert looked genuinely surprised. He was only thirty-five years old.

"I thought you had to have a good supply of grey hairs to be shortlisted."

Sir George's face cracked into a smile.

"You should look in a mirror some time, young man."

Robert was shocked that the older man had noticed. He had been carefully pulling them out for several years now.

"I don't know for sure, of course, but I gather one of the Latin American countries is on the cards. That's why you were sent out that way last time."

"How do you know all this?"

Robert regretted his words as soon as he had uttered them. Sir George frowned.

"You should know better then that," he grunted.

"Sorry. I shouldn't have asked."

"The point is this. If it happens that my information is correct, you'll come into the House from a position of considerable strength. A Prime Minister with an erstwhile Ambassador sitting on the back benches would be very unlikely not to offer him some sort of junior ministerial post in the Foreign Office. And that's exactly what you want, isn't it? I've been happy to stay a back-bencher, but I know damn well you want to get on, to get a bit of real power."

They walked on in silence. On their left the Foreign Office building rose imperiously from the Whitehall pavement, its grand façade a relic of past imperial power. Robert had always been aware of the limitations of his job as a professional diplomat. However high he rose, even if he rose to the very top, he would still be the servant of others, of political masters whose chronic ineptitude was all too often apparent.

George was a clever old manipulator, for all his apparent idiocy. He wanted Robert to leave him the seat for another five years so he had found a good reason to persuade him that such a course of action was actually in his own best interests. For a moment Robert couldn't help wondering whether the old schemer had actually fixed up an Ambassadorship with one of his old cronies at the Club, but he swiftly rejected the idea as being too far fetched even for George.

There was nothing to be done except capitulate gracefully.

"Listen, George, if you want to carry on, you carry on. Like you said, it's your seat."

Now Sir George looked really happy.

"Thanks. I'll keep it warm for you, Robert. You're still young, it'll wait."

* * * * * *

It was gone three by the time Robert returned to his office. The meal had been an excellent one, washed down with plenty of very fine claret, and he was hardly in the mood for work. He had no meetings planned for the afternoon and was looking forward to spending a quiet few hours reading some background papers before slipping off home on the early train.

He was shocked therefore to find a message on his desk from no less a person than Sir Percival Sotherby summoning him to a 'chat' as soon as he returned from his lunch. As he read the note, Robert dearly wished that he had drunk orange juice instead of claret with his meal. Sir Percival was the senior Under- Secretary concerned with Foreign Office staffing matters and a man of stern temper. He combined a razor sharp brain with a keen perception of human nature, which probably accounted for his current job.

Robert left his office and, after calling in at the cloakroom on the way to wash his face, comb his hair and collect his wits, walked the several hundred yards of corridor to the office of Sir Percival's secretary, a friendly woman who had been a good friend of Kate's since the days before their marriage when she had also worked there as a secretary. She greeted him warmly as he entered.

"Hallo Robert, you got the message then. The old man's been expecting you for some time."

Robert grimaced. If only he'd known about this, he'd have come back from lunch more promptly.

"Hallo, Shirl, I got held up at lunch." He went up to her and whispered into her ear. "Does it look as if I've drunk too much?"

She found it hard to prevent herself from laughing.

"Not as much as it did the last time I had dinner at your place. And just as well, you know what he's like about diplomatic drinking."

She pressed a button by her telephone and a rather metallic version of Sir Percival's voice could be heard through the intercom.

"Yes."

"Robert Stanton to see you, Sir Percival," she announced, her voice crisp and business-like.

"Send him in, will you," he grunted. "I've been expecting him for nearly an hour."

Robert went through the large door into the imposing wood-panelled inner sanctum. You could sense the power this man held from the physical surroundings, as he shuffled diplomats backwards and forwards across the globe and planned the careers of younger staff well into the twenty-first century.

Robert closed the door and approached the huge mahogany desk behind which Sir Percival could be seen scrutinising a single piece of paper. It was the only thing on the desk. He looked up as Robert approached.

"Afternoon, Stanton, I've been expecting you."

The comment did not seem to require an apology, so Robert waited for him to continue.

"Sit down, won't you, sit down."

Robert sat, being careful to choose the least comfortable of the available chairs arranged around the giant desk. It would help him keep alert.

"Something's cropped up where I think you can be of some help, Stanton. How do you like the idea of going abroad for a while?"

Robert wondered what it could be. He'd only recently returned from overseas and had not been expecting a new posting for several years. But then he remembered his recent conversation with Sir George, and for a moment the thought of an Ambassadorship crossed his mind.

"You know Jeremy Brookman, I'm sure."

Robert's heart sank. Jeremy Brookman was a nice enough chap, but most definitely in the slow lane of the Service.

"Of course, we were in Tokyo together."

Sir Percival's lips moved in what may possibly have been an attempt at a smile.

"I know you were. I sent you both there."

Robert felt his face turning red. He should have seen that one coming.

"Anyway, I'm afraid he's gone and fallen ill on us."

Robert was genuinely surprised. Although a good ten years older than he was, Jeremy was one of those men who never seemed to catch anything.

"Nothing serious, I hope."

"No, we don't think so. Some sort of mild attack of hepatitis. The point is, he's had to come back home again to rest up. Doctor's orders."

Robert waited, confident that Sir Percival would continue.

"Anyway, he's been involved in some pretty important negotiations and we'd like you to go out and pick up the threads while he's off sick."

Robert tried to remember where Jeremy's last posting had been but without success.

"Where am I going?"

"Somewhere completely new for you, Stanton. This one's behind the Iron Curtain. East Berlin."

* * * * * *

The pen in his hand wouldn't keep still. It turned around over and over again, his fingers reluctant to release it. Robert tried to concentrate on its movements; first the nib was uppermost, then the remains of the chewed stubby end. He had never been able to break the lifelong habit of chewing his pens. But however hard he tried to distract himself, his thoughts kept coming back to exactly the same place.

There was a whole world out there. Why on earth did it have to be East Berlin?

It was beginning to get dark outside, but Robert didn't turn the office light on. He sat in the gathering gloom, trying to make sense of the conflicting emotions swirling round inside his head.

His mind drifted back to that fine June day over three years before when he had learnt the truth about his origins. He had walked away from his parents' home uncertain how to react to the story he had heard. At first he had supposed that he would go home and tell Kate, but somewhere on the train journey home he had changed his mind. He had not told her. He had not told anyone. He had carried the burden alone.

That first day it had seemed too much trouble, unnecessary. He had had a bad headache, and he didn't want to have to recount the whole story to Kate on his arrival home. In any case, he had lied to her about working late that evening, and an admission that he had done so would undoubtedly have upset her.

He had gone to bed that night supposing that he would find a convenient moment to tell her the following day, but no suitable moments had presented themselves and he had again failed to tell her. The same went for the following week and the following month. It had just never happened.

And since he hadn't told Kate, he certainly wasn't going to start telling anyone else.

His father asked him once, when they were alone, whether he had told anyone. He remembered the look of pity that came over his father's face when he said he hadn't, as if the older man understood only too well the burden that Robert was now carrying and which he had himself carried for so long. For three years he had told no one, but he had never really sat down and tried to justify in any systematic fashion the reason for the deceit. As he watched the pen turning over and over in his hand, Robert decided that that was the first thing he had to resolve.

There were obvious reasons for not shouting the truth from the rooftops, the most devastating of which was his job as a diplomat. He didn't know for sure how they would react if he told them since there were hardly a large number of precedents, but he was pretty sure that the likes of Sir Percival Sotherby would take a pretty dim view of it. Robert was, after all, a human being without an official identity, operating on stolen papers and a stolen name. And even if a genuine birth certificate could somehow be traced, it would record the birth of a little German child far away in central Europe. Hardly the correct background for a high-flying British diplomat.

They might not sack him, that would potentially cause a most embarrassing and unseemly row. But as Robert thought back to his recent interview with Sir Percival he could easily imagine the way it would be handled. Sir Percival would quietly ring up Shirley in the outer office and ask her to bring him the confidential file on Robert Creighton Stanton. For a few moments, that file would be the only thing sitting on that large mahogany desk. He would examine the file, casting a clinical eye over the forward plans for Robert's career, and then a few discreet strokes of the pen would be sufficient to sort out the little problem. Shirley would be summoned once again, the file would be returned to its correct place in the registry, and Sir Percival would summon the next piece of paper requiring his attention.

It would only take two minutes, three at the most. But it would effectively be the end of Robert's diplomatic career. The Ambassadorships and the top ministerial advisory jobs in London would have been quietly removed with one stroke of Sir Percival's pen, and an alternative career in some obscure backwater of the consular service would have been substituted with another. And that would be that.

There were other considerations. The possibility of a political career opened up by Sir George's patronage was one of them. But how would Sir George react if he knew the truth? Would it make a difference to his view of Robert if he knew that he was really a German by birth. On the one hand it seemed likely that George knew Robert sufficiently well to disregard his early origins, but on the other hand Robert knew full well that Sir George couldn't abide what he still persisted in calling the 'filthy kraut'. In short, it seemed better if he didn't know.

The pen stopped turning and Robert started chewing it instead. He really should have told Kate. She never blabbered. He used to tell her everything, and now he felt guilty that he had said nothing all these years. Could it be that he was worried that it would change the way she thought about him? That seemed more than unlikely. But there must have been a reason; it didn't really happen just by accident.

Perhaps it was because it was simply irrelevant. It introduced a complication into life where none need exist. If he told Kate they would either have had to tell the children or he would have had to involve Kate in his deceit. Yet it was one thing for him to lie, quite another for him to expect his wife to lie on his behalf. And if the children became aware of it, there was no telling where the information would end up. As he sat and chewed his pen, Robert began to understand better why his father had chosen to hide the truth.

In the months after the discovery, Robert had wondered whether he would try to investigate his own past quietly, on his own, without telling anyone. But there was no point: the whole of Eastern Europe was strictly out of bounds to diplomatic personnel unless they were on official business and without going there, there was little he could do. So for three years he had done nothing. He had convinced himself that it didn't matter, that it was utterly irrelevant to his present life.

And now they had to send him to East Berlin.

Robert got up from his chair and went over to the window. It was nearly dark, and as he looked out over St James's Park he could see people beginning to hurry for home through the gloom. As he watched them, he became aware of a growing sense of envy welling up inside him. All those people knew who they were. They knew where they came from. They knew who their parents were even if they had never actually known them. Yet he didn't have the faintest idea of any of these things.

Robert turned away from the window. Without hesitating, he walked out of the door, along the corridor, up the stairs and into the imposing Foreign Office library. Walking straight over to the section containing street maps of foreign cities, he pulled down the volume containing Berlin from the shelf and turned to the index. Krämerstrasse. He turned to the correct page and searched the map.

There it was, the little black letters standing out clearly on the map. How different his life would have been if his aunt had still been there at the end of the war? What would have become of him? And what kind of person would he be today?

BERLIN, DECEMBER 1978

They pulled up at the traffic lights. Angus MacPhearson gestured at a ruined façade to their right.

"The Anhalter Station. Used to be one of the busiest railway terminals in Europe before the war."

Robert looked at the ruin. All that was left was a part of the main entrance, but you could see that in its day it had been a magnificent building.

"Why have they just left it like that?"

"Berlin's a city of shadows, Robert. For some reason best known to themselves, the West Berliners have left it there as a reminder of the folly of war."

The lights changed to green and they drove on. Although Kate and he had flown into West Berlin two days earlier, this was his first visit to East Berlin and the Embassy. Kate had wanted to use the car for some shopping, so Angus MacPhearson, the British Ambassador to East Germany, had offered to give him a lift to the office.

"You haven't been over this border before, have you?"

"No. I've never been posted to Eastern Europe at all, as a matter of fact."

"So you haven't seen the Wall?"

Robert shook his head. He had meant to come with Kate and have a look at it over the weekend but they hadn't found the time.

The Scotsman pulled up the car with a jolt by the side of the road.

"Come on, then, get out. Checkpoint Charlie in a diplomatic car is no place to meet the Wall for the first time. You've got to see it on foot to really appreciate it."

Climbing out of the car, he hurried after the Ambassador, who was already striding off down the road.

They turned a corner into a small side street and were confronted by a solid barrier of smooth concrete stretching right across the road some thirty feet in front of them. It was approximately twelve feet high and surmounted by a rounded concrete pipe running along the top. Every available inch of the Wall appeared to have been covered in graffiti, much of it very colourful, but it still presented a grim aspect. Robert shuddered. Although he was perfectly well aware of the history of the Wall it was still a shock to come face to face with it.

Angus must have seen him react.

"I've been here nearly two years and it still gives me the creeps," he muttered.

Robert could see why. It was so incongruous. From the moment of his arrival at the airport, West Berlin had seemed in every respect just like any other modern European city. But whereas most cities peter out into suburban hinterland and rural fringe, this one just stopped dead at a twelve foot high pile of solid concrete.

"The funny thing is," Angus continued, "that the West Berliners seem to take it totally for granted."

"What's on the other side?"

"Another world, laddie. You'll soon see."

"I mean it's not just this wall, is it?"

Angus laughed. "Oh no. If they get this far then they're virtually home and dry. The Wall itself is just the final obstacle. Coming from the East the first thing is a high barrier designed to stop the East Germans from even looking at the border defences. Then there's a wire fence, followed by a trip wire which sounds an alarm and releases flares. And if you get past all that lot there's the watchtowers, the bunkers, the dog runs, the patrols, a five metre deep vehicle ditch and a wide strip of raked sand before you get to the Wall. And the whole lot's floodlit at night."

Robert looked at the solid barrier of concrete in front of him. "Not much chance, then."

"Not any more. Used to be easier of course, but it's getting more difficult all the time. There's even a rumour circulating that the East Germans are going to install automatic devices on the Wall which shower you with little bits of razor sharp metal when activated."

Robert grimaced.

"The crossing points are getting tighter, too," Angus continued, "In the sixties they were the weak link in the chain, and there were quite a lot of successful crossings by people smashing their way through or smuggling past the guards. But the border police are getting wise to all the methods. They can stop most attempts pretty easily these days."

Robert looked enquiringly at the Ambassador.

"What do they say about it?"

"Who?"

"The East Germans you meet. The East Germans in the government."

Angus had taken out his pipe and was lighting it up. He didn't reply until he had finished.

"If you want to take a tip from me, young man, you won't mention it with them. Just assume it doesn't exist."

"But you work just next to it, and so do they. How can you pretend it doesn't exist?"

"Oh, don't get me wrong. You won't flounder them in the least little bit if you bring it up. They'll give you a quite boringly predictable little blurb about it being an anti-fascist protective wall set up to prevent C.I.A. agents luring honest East German workers away from the fatherland in an attempt to undermine the economy and frustrate the inevitable triumph of socialism."

"But surely they don't believe all that rubbish."

"No doubt. But they're not going to tell you that, are they? So it just causes upset for no very great benefit to anyone. Therefore the best thing to do is to bite your lip and pretend it doesn't exist."

And with a puff of his pipe Angus turned away from the Wall and led the way back to the car.

They had not driven far before they turned into the Friedrichstrasse and came to a halt at the Western side of Checkpoint Charlie. Angus pointed at the British, American and French flags flying in a row by the side of the road and the American G.I.s hanging about with bored expressions by the roadside.

"You wouldn't think this was Germany, would you, looking at that lot? This crossing point is only used by non-Germans and it's where most of the diplomatic traffic passes through. Get your papers out."

They drew to a halt at a barrier and a bored-looking American serviceman waved them on with hardly a glance. The car moved forward and through a high gate set into the Wall.

"That's the border, as you probably realised. Now notice the way the road twists around."

It was true. The road on the East German side twisted and turned past a collection of obstacles clearly designed to prevent a vehicle from smashing its way through to the West. Angus indicated a barrier being raised in front of them as they approached.

"Have a look at the way the barriers are designed. When they're lowered, they have those little metal spikes hanging down below the poles. Someone once got through here using a funny little flat car that could squeeze underneath the poles. After that they fitted the spikes."

They pulled up underneath a kind of covered shed that served as the East German customs post. A smartly dressed border guard inspected their papers and saluted before waving them on.

"There you are, Robert, it's as easy as that. Just show them your diplomatic papers and you're through. You'll get quite used to it."

Angus pulled the car up a few yards from the border.

"Look at that and just try to imagine you're an East German going for a Sunday afternoon stroll with the kids."

He was looking at the road on the East German side that ran parallel to the border. On one side was a drab and dirty tenement building in which could still be seen bullet marks left over from the last war. On the other side of the road, running along the pavement adjoining the border just next to the road entrance to Checkpoint Charlie, was a high metal grill about fifty yards long that bore a striking resemblance to a lion enclosure in a zoo. Set into the bars of the cage was a small metal door, also made of bars, and there, attached to one of the bars, was a doorbell.

"That's the way out if you're on foot," he commented drily. "You press the bell and they let you into that cage where they look at your papers. If you're a visitor they process you on from there through a series of other cages towards the West. But if you're unfortunate enough to be an East German and try ringing the little bell, you'll simply get arrested for making a nuisance of yourself."

Robert looked with disgust at the metal bars running along by the pavement. It seemed that the authorities did not even have the sensitivity to disguise the fact that this so-called sovereign state was a giant prison camp with sixteen million inmates. He turned to Angus.

"Do you get much chance to talk to ordinary East Germans?"

"None worth speaking of. It's not as bad as some other parts of the Soviet block, where contact would be virtually a crime, but I spend nearly all of my time with the apparatchiks."

He chuckled as he started driving again.

"The Embassy cleaners are the best bit. They're simply too well spoken for cleaners and are obviously employees of the State Security Service."

They soon arrived at the British Embassy in Unter den Linden, a rather grand building only a stone's throw from the Brandenburg Gate and the border. As they passed through the rigorous security check at the door and up to the Ambassador's office on the top floor, Robert felt a growing sense of tension. The morning's encounter with the Wall had been sufficient to make him realise that he was in hostile territory, a representative of what was to the East Germans an enemy power. And he was very far from a free agent in this place.

Why was Kate always so slow getting herself dressed for these occasions? It was the last Friday evening before Christmas, nearly a month after their arrival in Berlin, and they were due at the Embassy party at eight. Yet it was already gone seven.

"Hurry up, Kate," Robert called from the sitting room. "What are you doing to yourself?"

"You'll just have to be patient, darling," came a muffled reply from the bathroom, and with a feeling of despair Robert could hear the rush of water as the shower unit was turned on.

Robert knew full well that these occasions were very important to Kate and he knew better than to argue with her about the time she spent dressing. He got up from the sofa and helped himself to a drink before settling down for what was obviously going to be a long wait.

Robert was determined to have a good evening with his wife since it was going to be their last together for quite some time. The following morning she was flying back to England to spend Christmas with her parents and the children. He had been hoping to be able to accompany her, particularly since he hadn't seen the children since early in the autumn, but the difficult trade negotiations in which he was involved did not allow him to get away.

The Berlin job was proving to be a dead bore from a professional point of view, nothing like the political work he was used to, and he had found himself wishing on several occasions that Jeremy would hurry up and get better so that he could take over again. Robert wondered why they had picked him for the job: after all, trade was not really his field. Then it occurred to him that it was probably because he was the only fluent German speaker they could get their hands on at such short notice.

The thought was a disturbing one. Even as a schoolboy he had wondered why he had found German so easy to learn and everyone had always commented on his excellent accent. In the past he had attributed his fluency to a natural talent for languages, but now of course he knew better. It was, after all, his own mother tongue.

In the four weeks that had gone by since his arrival in the East German capital, he had made no attempt to visit the address in the south-eastern suburb of Köpenick where his aunt had once lived. It was strange, because on the day when he had heard about the posting from Sir Percival and had looked up the address in the Foreign Office library he had resolved that he would go and look at the street as soon as he arrived. As he sat and listened to Kate finishing her shower, he found himself wondering why he had not yet got around to it.

But he didn't have long to speculate. The water stopped running and Kate appeared at the door, her lithe body completely naked and still dripping.

"I've had a thought, Robert," she said excitedly.

"Yes, love."

"Do you suppose that I'll be able to host a party like this when you become an Ambassador?"

Robert had regretted telling Kate what Sir George had said within minutes of so doing. He looked at her scathingly.

"I suppose so. Does it matter to you so much?"

Kate's face showed a mixture between hurt and anger.

"You don't need to be so insufferably stuffy about it, Robert," she complained. "It's all right for you, you've got your job. But all I get for my trouble is the chance to go to a few half-way decent social events."

And with that she turned and walked out of the room, leaving a small wet patch behind her in the middle of the carpet.

Robert looked disconsolately into his drink. What was the matter with him these days? He had found Kate increasingly irritating in the last few weeks yet he couldn't put his finger on why. There was nothing wrong with her looking forward to being an Ambassador's wife, just as there was nothing wrong with him looking forward to being an Ambassador. And she was a damn good wife to him, following him about the globe in pursuit of his career without so much as a hint of a grumble.

Robert got up and went into the bedroom. Kate was now in her underwear, sitting combing her hair at the dressing table.

"I'm sorry, love, that was a silly thing for me to say. Of course you'll be the hostess at Embassy do's. If I get the job, that is."

Kate looked round and smiled at him. She always seemed to bounce back so quickly when she was upset. Robert sat on the bed with a rather uncomfortable look on his face.

"What's the matter with you, Robert. You've been so miserable recently."

Robert tried to cheer up. She was only trying to help, but he wasn't really in the mood for being helped just at the moment.

"I'm sorry, love," he muttered, "I don't know why I've been so low. Maybe it's going across that damn border every day. It still gives Angus the creeps after two years."

"I know, darling, its pretty grim, isn't it? But cheer up, at least you're allowed to go across it. It's the poor East Germans I feel sorry for, not you."

Robert felt obliged to provide an alternative explanation. "It's the job too, I suppose. I was doing interesting political work in London, but now I'm grappling with the exciting intricacies of the stupid textile trade. It might be very important to somebody but frankly I find it a giant bore."

Kate put down the comb and came over to him, kneeling down beside him on the floor.

"Just so long as it's not me you're finding a giant bore," she murmured, gently unbuttoning his shirt with one hand and pulling her underwear off with the other.

Robert threw a glance at the clock on the bedside table. It was already twenty to eight. But Kate's warm hand was already beginning to explore him, arousing a desire that was hard to control. As he lay back on the bed he knew there was no point in resisting.

And perhaps she was right. Perhaps she understood better than he did why he was feeling so incredibly tense.

* * * * * *

They were already an hour late for the reception by the time they arrived at the East German side of Checkpoint Charlie. Robert smiled at the border guard, a friendly enough chap with whom he was already getting on quite good terms, and fumbled in his jacket pocket for their papers.

The guard was shivering in the cold December night.

"It's a cold night," remarked Robert, handing him the passports.

"Yes, Herr Stanton, a very cold night. But tomorrow I start my winter holidays so I can put up with it."

The guard was about to hand the documents back when suddenly he pulled back and looked up in alarm. A little way to their left, somewhere in the border strip next to the crossing point, some dogs had started snarling and barking.

Then, almost immediately, all hell let loose. A siren started wailing, searchlights began sweeping the protective zone just to the left of the control point and some soldiers started running frantically out of one of the huts in the direction of the commotion. In front of his car, Robert could see an additional metal barrier swinging into place, and when he turned round he saw that the concrete tank barriers set into the road behind them had already slid neatly into position.

Kate was clutching his arm.

"What's happening, Robert?" she whispered anxiously.

"I don't know. Just stay in the car."

The commotion lasted for no longer than a minute. Then the siren and the searchlights were switched off and the additional barriers blocking the border quickly retracted. Only the continued barking of the dogs served as a reminder that anything untoward had happened.

Some of the soldiers who had earlier run out of the hut in such haste could be seen returning at a relaxed pace. Two of them were laughing and joking together, but the rest were looking very glum.

It did not take long before the explanation of what had happened became clear. Two young civilians, a boy and a girl, walked slowly through a small gate from the death strip into the covered customs area, closely followed by two heavily armed border guards.

Robert stared at the approaching couple.

"They must have tried to jump the Wall, the stupid fools," he whispered.

Kate's face showed a mixture of amazement and horror.

"But look at them. They can't be more than sixteen or seventeen years old," she said.

The couple approached closer and closer, obviously heading for the building to their right where the guard had disappeared with Robert's papers when the alarm had first sounded. The girl was sobbing as she walked along, making no attempt to hide her tears. But the boy's face was still tense and alert, like a hunted animal searching in desperation for a way of escape.

He was only a few yards away from the car when he saw his opportunity. Suddenly, without any warning, he ran forward towards the open window on Robert's side, bending down so that his frenzied face was only inches away from Robert's own.

"Help us, please. Our names are Ingeborg Schmidt and Rudolf Lichtenstein." He paused and then repeated the names more slowly and deliberately. "Ingeborg Schmidt. Rudolf Lichtenstein. Try to remember. Please try to get help for us? Please."

He did not have time to say anything else. The armed guards were quick to react, pulling him roughly away from the car and frogmarching him swiftly into the guardhouse.

It was nearly a minute before someone appeared from the guardhouse with Robert's papers. But it was not the guard they had spoken to before. From the insignia on his uniform, it was clear that this was a much more senior officer. He saluted as he approached.

"I am sorry about the incident," he said politely, passing Robert back his papers. "And I am particularly sorry that the guards failed in their duty by allowing that hooligan to molest your car in that fashion. I can only assure you that the lout will be severely punished for his insolence."

Robert looked at the man incredulously. He felt desperately sorry for the young couple, stupid though they had been, and wished there was some way he could help them. But there was absolutely nothing he could do.

"It's all right, I don't want them punished on my account," he muttered, starting up the engine as he spoke. The officer saluted again, the final barrier was raised, and they drove out into the dark and deserted East Berlin street.

Robert was still shaking as they entered the crowded room in the Embassy where the Christmas party was being held. There were several hundred people milling around, clutching their drinks and little plates of titbits. As usual on these occasions, they were all talking too much. As Robert glanced around, it was apparent that the Embassy staff were heavily outnumbered by guests from other diplomatic missions in East Berlin and from the East German establishment.

As they entered the room, a corpulent East German from the Ministry of Trade with whom Robert had spent several hours in difficult negotiating sessions spotted him and elbowed his way over, bringing a small rather sallow middle-aged lady in tow. Normally a rather dour individual, he seemed full of Christmas cheer.

"Ah, Herr Stanton, a real pleasure to see you here. And this is your lovely wife about whom I have heard so much?"

Had he? Robert was only aware of having spoken with the man about textiles. Oh well, such was the nature of diplomacy.

"Good evening, Herr Lechner. Yes, this is indeed my wife, Kate. Kate, this gentleman is Herr Lechner, with whom I've spent a fair amount of time recently."

Kate smiled graciously, pleased that her reputation had preceded her. Herr Lechner pulled the small lady forward.

"And this is my dear wife Lotte."

She nodded nervously. Unlike Kate, she clearly did not enjoy diplomatic receptions.

Herr Lechner smiled.

"I hope you had a good journey here," he enquired politely.

For a fraction of a second Robert forgot the advice the Ambassador had given him on his first day at the office.

"Well, actually we ran into a little trouble on the border."

A look of concern spread across Herr Lechner's face.

"You did," he said with amazement. "Surely our customs officials did not interfere with your passage. Tell me what happened and I will ensure it is investigated immediately."

Robert wished he could extricate himself but knew he couldn't.

"No, no, it wasn't anything like that. Some people tried to escape while we were coming across."

If Herr Lechner knew what Robert was talking about, he certainly showed no signs of it. But his wife flinched visibly and seemed to shrink back even further from the conversation.

Robert felt obliged to spell it out.

"Two young people tried to go over the Wall into West Berlin just as we were coming across the border."

Herr Lechner sighed.

"Oh, I see. And what happened?"

"They got caught, of course. They were just kids. Couldn't have been more than sixteen or seventeen years old."

Herr Lechner looked solemn.

"How sad," he murmured. "And how unnecessary. If they wanted to leave the country they should have filed an application through the usual channels."

Robert nearly choked on his drink. He looked at the East German with disbelief.

"I beg your pardon," he said.

"They should have filed a request for an exit permit."

Robert was speechless. If it was so easy to leave, why on earth did the East German government have fifty thousand armed guards preventing people from doing just that?

Herr Lechner smiled.

"You have not been with us in East Germany for very long yet, Herr Stanton. Did you not know it was possible to file a request for an exit permit?"

Robert could feel himself being sucked into the kind of conversation that a diplomat should not have, particularly a diplomat at a Christmas party. He should have politely acknowledged the East German's point of view and started talking about the Berlin weather.

"Well. Actually I didn't. But there must be a catch to it. Otherwise they'd be no point in going to the expense of the Wall, would there?"

Herr Lechner smiled, not in the least bit taken aback by his remarks.

"Herr Stanton, there are a lot of very strange ideas floating about in the West in connection with our border, on which as you rightly observe we spend a considerable sum of money which we would rather spend on other things. The intention of the border defences is not to prevent people who have a genuine desire to emigrate from doing so." He hesitated before continuing. "I'm sure I don't need to remind you that East Germany is a signatory to the Helsinki Declaration on Human Rights."

"But why do you have it, if not for that reason?"

"I do not know how much you know about our history, Herr Stanton, but you will certainly know that we have been in the front line of socialism for over three decades. Foreign powers, and I do not mean yours in particular, have long been interested in undermining the economic foundations of our socialist society. They have been prepared to sink to any depths, even trading in human beings themselves."

Robert remembered the Ambassador's warning. If only they could talk about the weather. But there was no escape.

"By the end of the 1950's the situation was becoming intolerable. The secret service of the United States, aided by the capitalists in Bonn, was luring our best workers away with false promises of a wonderful new life in the West. It was ruining our economy, and the leadership therefore decided they had to strengthen the border to protect the German working class from this evil menace."

Robert remembered the boy and girl he had seen dragged away to an uncertain future in an East German prison earlier that night and wondered what right this intelligent man had to talk such rubbish.

"Herr Lechner, I do not know a great deal about your country's history but I do know that two million people left East Germany – one eighth of the entire population – prior to the building of the Wall in 1961. Surely you cannot believe that they were all carried away by C.I.A. agents and the West German government?"

Herr Lechner smiled broadly. He seemed to be enjoying the conversation tremendously.

"I did not say they were physically carried away. I said they were seduced by false promises. And the figure you cite, far from being a refutation of my argument, is surely proof of it, since it indicates the seriousness of the attack to which we were being subjected by the capitalist states."

For several moments Robert could not find the words to express himself. It gave the East German time to press home his advantage.

"And so you see, Herr Stanton, the border defences are only there to ensure that our people are not ensnared by false propaganda. If the young people you saw tonight had a desire to leave and had applied for an exit visa through the proper channels, and if they had been sincere in their desire to go and had fully understood the dangers that would have awaited them in the West, they would certainly have been allowed to leave."

Kate looked at the East German, whose rotund face looked so calm and kind.

"Excuse me, but does that mean they will be allowed to go. They were so very young."

Herr Lechner smiled politely.

"I am sorry, Frau Stanton, but I know nothing about these particular young people. You must remember that they have committed a crime by trying to leave without an exit permit. They may well have damaged state property during their illegal attempt. So I imagine they will be punished first for what they have done. I am sure that you would agree that people should be punished if they break the laws of their country."

Kate was about to say something but before she could do so Angus MacPhearson, who had overheard Herr Lechner's last words, interrupted her.

"Of course the laws of a country should be respected, Herr Lechner," he said with a reassuring smile.

He turned to Robert.

"Did something happen tonight?"

Robert nodded, and briefly explained what they had seen. But the Ambassador, the same man who had told Robert about his own continuing horror of the Wall, reacted hardly at all. Instead, he looked downcast for a suitable length of time and then turned to Herr Lechner with an enormous grin.

"Reminds me of the story of this crazy West Berliner in the sixties who spent his entire time trying to break into East Berlin. The trouble was, every time he succeeded your government used to put him in a bus and dump him straight back out over the border again."

At the thought of this Herr Lechner collapsed with laughter. Even his wife could not resist a wry smile. Taking his opportunity, Angus's face turned serious.

"But you must excuse us, Herr and Frau Lechner, I have something important that I must discuss with Herr and Frau Stanton."

And without a further word he shepherded Robert and Kate quickly out of the room, up the stairs and into his office. They sat down on the sofa.

"Sounds like you've had an exciting time tonight," he muttered, "but quite frankly I wouldn't spend the entire evening going round discussing it with our guests. We've got some pretty important people from the Party here tonight and we're trying to build a few bridges."

Robert felt like a naughty schoolboy being told off by his housemaster.

"I'm sorry," he said quietly, "but I didn't just find it exciting. I found it disturbing."

Angus's face softened.

"Do you think I enjoy talking to these bastards?" he asked. "This whole country stinks and the sooner its government sinks into a big hole in the ground the better as far as I'm concerned. But you and I can't do anything to change things. And in fact change could be dangerous. It's my view that it could destabilise the entire situation here. And that doesn't necessarily do the poor East Germans any good."

Robert looked glum. Intellectually he knew the Ambassador was right.

"The boy spoke to me, you know."

"You what!"

"While they were leading him away, he broke away to where the car was parked and told me their names. He begged me to do something to help. It's hard to keep your distance."

"I know it is," Angus repeated. "But as far as tonight's concerned, you've got to."

The Ambassador paused for a moment before continuing.

"There was something else I wanted to tell you both, something that I think will cheer you up. Jeremy's nearly better. He should be able to come back to work shortly after Christmas."

"Does that mean we'll be going back to London?" Kate asked.

"Yes, for the time being. And then, who knows?"

The look on his face suggested that he had at least an inkling.

"Look," he said, rising from his chair. "I've got to go back down again but why don't you two sit here for a while and help yourselves to something to drink. It'll give you both a chance to collect your wits before you have to face all those tedious East Germans again."

He opened the door to go. But then a thought occurred to him and he paused.

"I tell you what," he said, going over to his desk and handing Robert a piece of paper, "jot down the names of the people you saw arrested at the border. I'll pass them on to one of the West Germans I know who's in the business of buying them out for hard currency. He just might be able to arrange some kind of deal."

Robert wrote the names down on the slip of paper and handed

it to the Ambassador, who promptly turned on his heel and left the room, leaving Kate and Robert alone.

Kate was bubbling with excitement.

"Isn't that wonderful, Robert," she exclaimed as soon as the Ambassador had closed the door, "we're going to get out of this dreadful dump."

Without saying anything Robert rose wearily from the sofa and opened the drinks cabinet, pouring himself a large Scotch. He turned to Kate with a downcast expression.

"Do you want something too?" he muttered.

Kate looked at him coldly.

"What's the matter with you?" she said, trying to control the anger rising within her. "Earlier this evening you were going on and on about how awful it is here yet now you're told you can go back to London soon it doesn't seem to cheer you up in the least little bit."

Robert said nothing. He walked over to the closed window and looked down at the bustle in the crowded thoroughfare of Unter den Linden several storeys below. He so wanted to be alone for a few moments, to have some time to work out what exactly he was going to do. But Kate was sitting there getting increasingly angry with him, so it obviously couldn't be now.

Trying to control his feelings, he downed his Scotch in one gulp and went over and sat beside Kate. Her anger was temporarily subsiding, only to be replaced by a growing feeling of self-pity. He put his arms around her but it only seemed to make things worse and she started to cry.

"Ever since we came here I've felt you're drifting away from me, Robert. If only you'd tell me what's happened to you. But you won't. You've become so secretive, keeping all your thoughts locked away from me."

Robert held her to him, trying to find the energy to comfort her. But then, quite abruptly, Kate stopped crying and pulled violently away.

"You've got someone else, haven't you?" she hissed, rising from the sofa and backing off as if he were contaminated. "You've found someone else, someone younger than me."

Robert jumped from the chair and moved towards her, shocked by her ridiculous accusation. But she backed away even further, as if she had suddenly convinced herself that she had found the only plausible explanation for his peculiar behaviour since leaving London.

"No, love, no. I promise."

Kate was becoming increasingly angry. "Don't give me that 'I promise' rubbish. Now it all makes sense. I'm thirty-three years old, I've had two children for you and I'm losing my looks. And now you've decided to jack me in and take up with some young tart in the office."

Her anger was rapidly turning into hysteria. "I used to work here. I know exactly the kind of thing that you high and mighty diplomats get up to. On the bloody carpet, I wouldn't be surprised, with the door locked so that no one comes in to catch you at it."

The motive force of her accusations became ever more powerful as she gradually filled in all the missing details of her new-found theory. Robert watched the onslaught with horror. He knew perfectly well he had only himself to blame for the accusations, however ill-founded they might be. How was she to know what was really bothering him? How was she to know that every time he went out in the streets of East Berlin he found himself staring at all the women over fifty who went by, wondering whether one of them might be his own mother? And how was she to know that the gigantic lie he had lived for the last three years, or was it thirty-three years, was rapidly crumbling to pieces within him despite his increasingly desperate attempts to hold it together?

* * * * * *

It was three o'clock in the afternoon by the time the British Airways plane rose gracefully into the air from the runway of Tempelhof airport in West Berlin. As Robert watched the crisp winter sun glinting off its streamlined form, he breathed a sigh of relief that Kate was gone at last. As soon as the plane had disappeared from sight he hurried towards his car and headed straight for the border. There was no time to lose.

Unlike the night before there were no difficulties at Checkpoint Charlie and he quickly found himself in a relatively empty street on the East German side of the frontier. Pulling up at the side of the road, he pulled out his Berlin street map from the glove compartment and carefully checked the route to Köpenick.

As he set off, he realised with something of a shock that this was the first time he had ventured away from the government buildings in the centre of the city. The contrast between the West Berlin streets he had recently left behind and the East Berlin streets in which he now found himself could hardly have been greater, especially bearing in mind that the West lay only a few miles away to his right on the other side of the Wall. The cars, the shops, the trams, the buildings, even the clothes in which people were dressed, all looked grey and drab compared to the modern, throbbing, colourful thoroughfares of the West. In West Berlin it was only artificially preserved relics such as the bombed-out ruins of the Anhalter Station that served as reminders that this city had been completely annihilated by foreign troops less than thirty-five years earlier. But in the Eastern sector, although a great deal of rebuilding had admittedly been done, the scars of war were still to be seen on buildings still pockmarked by Russian bullets and artillery shells.

He slowed down. About a hundred yards in front of him a policeman was indicating with a little round sign that he should pull over. Apprehensively he brought the car to a standstill and the policeman approached, saluting politely as he did so.

"Are you aware that you have been speeding?" the officer explained with a stern expression on his face as Robert wound down the window.

Robert turned round in alarm and looked at the road behind him. He had only been driving at fifty kilometres per hour, fully aware from conversations with his colleagues in the Embassy both of the East German obsession with speed limits and of the extremely dim view the Ambassador took of his staff pleading diplomatic immunity in order to evade traffic penalties.

"I'm sorry, officer, but I was being most careful only to drive at fifty kilometres per hour. That is the speed limit in built-up areas, isn't it?"

"But you were driving at fifty-two kilometres per hour, sir," the officer explained reproachfully.

Robert looked at him in astonishment.

"What! Exactly fifty-two?"

"Yes, sir, we measured it. May I see your papers please?"

Robert fumbled for his diplomatic passport and handed it to the officer. He took the papers and returned to his patrol car. Robert watched as he spoke with someone over the car radio: he seemed to be reading out the details on the passport and obtaining instructions from higher authority. After a few moments he strolled back and returned the passport to Robert.

"In view of your diplomatic status no charges will be brought, but the matter will be reported to your Embassy. Please can you ensure that you respect our traffic laws in future. Good day."

The policeman saluted crisply and returned to his roadside vigil.

Robert drove on, careful now to keep his speed well below forty-five.

"Damn!" he muttered to himself. He had got on the wrong side of the Ambassador at the reception only the previous evening for shooting his mouth off. And now the Ambassador would come in on Monday morning and discover a note on his desk to the effect that his Special Assistant on Trade had broken East German law and was pleading diplomatic immunity to evade the consequences. It was hardly appropriate behaviour for a future Ambassador and Robert just hoped that Angus would be decent enough not to include it in any reports on his work that he sent back to Sir Percival Sotherby in London.

After he had been driving for about three quarters of an hour a roadsign indicated that he was entering the suburb of Köpenick. He parked the car, and, after checking his map, realised that Krämerstrasse was now only a few blocks away. He thought for a moment and then decided to leave the car and go the rest of the way on foot. Although there was nothing illegal about him walking down any street in East Berlin, he felt nervous about advertising his movements too openly.

He soon arrived at Krämerstrasse. Since his father had told him the story of his early life he had often imagined coming to this street, but in his mind he had always supposed that it would be as his father had described it, scarred with shell-holes and lined with the remains of bombed-out buildings.

It was of course a ridiculous notion, and Krämerstrasse looked much like any other suburban street in East Berlin, perhaps rather better than some he had seen. The rows of terraced apartment blocks were of the rather drab design so typical of the immediate post-war re-construction phase. Some six storeys high, the buildings were provided with large doors along the pavement which served as communal entrances. At ground level, adjoining the pavement, were several shops selling the usual dreary assortment of standardised Eastern European household artifacts.

Robert walked slowly down the street looking for his aunt's address. It was strange to think that the last time he had been in this road had been when he was only two years old, carried by a young British army officer who was then a complete stranger but was later to become his father. But try as he might, he could not summon up any memories of that distant day.

He arrived at number 15 and studied the names written by the bells of the fourteen or so separate apartments in the building, looking to see if a Katherina Hagenau still lived there. With a feeling of disappointment he realised that there was no one of that name. Robert stared at the doorway for quite some time. He had always supposed that if he could only pluck up the courage to search out his past he would find it, but now that he had found the courage to look he had drawn a complete blank. He smiled wryly to himself at his own stupidity; had he really supposed that his aunt would be still living there, over thirty-three years after the end of the war?

He pushed open the tatty communal door to the building and went inside, climbing over the old prams, pushchairs, children's bikes and other assorted junk which was lying about at the base of the stairwell. It was dark in the hall, with a single low-powered electric bulb hanging disconsolately from the ceiling. From behind the doors of the flats leading off the stairwell came the sounds of children playing, televisions blaring and, to his right, a man and a woman having what sounded like a monumental marital row.

After only a moment's hesitation, he pushed one of the doorbells to his left. The door opened and a harassed-looking woman in her early twenties appeared. Several young children could be seen playing in the tiny hall behind her and she was holding a young baby in her arms.

"Excuse me," Robert began uncertainly, "I wonder if you can help me. I'm looking for a lady by the name of Katherina Hagenau."

"Katherina Hagenau?" she muttered, "No, I don't know anyone by that name." She turned away as if to close the door.

"Do you know, is there anyone in the building who lived here before the war?"

The woman turned.

"Well, there's old Max. Lives by himself up on the top floor – number thirteen. He's pretty old, and I know he's lived here a long time. But whether he was here before the war I really couldn't tell you."

She closed the door and left Robert alone in the hallway. Nearly tripping over a small children's tricycle lying at his feet, he started climbing the dark stairway. It was a high building and the stairs seemed to go on for ever. The dark green paint on the walls was crumbling with age, and Robert wondered why the people living in the block didn't go out and get themselves a pot of paint to brighten the place up a bit. After six flights he reached the top of the stairs and rang the bell at number thirteen. There was no reply. He rang it again before realising that it was not working. There was an old knocker on the door which he banged loudly.

The door creaked open and an old man appeared wearing an ancient double-breasted suit.

"Good day," the old man said politely.

"Good day. I was wondering if you could help me. Your neighbour on the ground floor thought that you may have lived at this address before the last war."

"I did," he muttered, "although it wasn't the same building then, of course. The old building was bombed in the war."

Robert felt awkward standing in the stairwell.

"I wonder, would you mind very much if I talk to you?"

"Yes, if you like. Pleased for the company. Don't get a lot of visitors these days."

He stood back from the door and beckoned Robert through to his living room. In sharp contrast to the communal hall, the interior of the old man's apartment was immaculately clean and filled with some fine old pieces of furniture. Every wall seemed lined with books, most of which looked at least as old as their owner.

"My name is Maximilian Schmidt," the old man said politely, holding out his hand, "and may I know yours?"

Robert shook the proffered hand. "Of course, my name is Stanton. Robert Creighton Stanton."

The old man appeared taken aback.

"Then you are foreign? British?" he exclaimed. "I would never have guessed from your accent that you were not from these parts. Anyway, please sit down."

Robert lowered himself into an old leather armchair and looked the old man straight in the face.

"When you lived here before the war, did you ever know someone by the name of Katherina Hagenau?"

The old man thought for a while before replying.

"Katherina Hagenau. Yes, I did. She lived on the ground floor, if I remember. Yes, that's right, on the ground floor. Why do you want to know?"

Robert hesitated. He didn't want to tell the old man the truth, but he had to have a reason.

"She was a friend of my father," he said. "He knew her well a long time ago and asked me to look her up."

The old man nodded. "Well, I can't help you then. I haven't seen Katherina Hagenau or her children since I left for the army in thirty-nine. For all I know she isn't alive any more."

Robert could feel a sinking sensation. He had come all this way, he had even found someone who knew his aunt, and yet he had found out nothing that he didn't know already. He had found no clues that might help him in his quest.

"Can you remember anything, anything at all that might help me trace her?" he asked, realising as soon as he had spoken that he sounded too anxious.

But the man didn't seem to notice. "Let me think," he said, "she had some children, three I think. They used to play in the hallway with my own little girls."

He paused for a while, as if searching through his memory for something of importance.

"And I think she had a sister, a younger sister with long blond hair who lived with her for a while. At least I think it was a sister, because they seemed very close and the children used to call her 'Aunty'."

Robert looked sharply at the old man.

"Can you remember her name?"

The old man thought hard before replying.

"Yes, I think it was Frieda, but I don't know her surname."

Robert could feel a growing sense of excitement. "Can you remember anything about her, about Frieda?"

The old man thought again.

"I can't remember much, to tell you the truth. She was always very friendly when I saw her in the hall. But she left quite a long time before war broke out. I think she went to East Prussia, but I can't be sure. Maybe she got married or something, she was always a pretty little thing."

"And you've not seen her since," Robert asked.

"No, not since 1937, or was it 1938? But I wouldn't even recognise her now, even if I did see her."

There was nothing further to be drawn from the old man and Robert rose from the armchair. His earlier elation had passed only to leave a heavy depression in its wake and he felt a strong desire to return to the fresh winter air outside. The old man rose too and Robert held out his hand.

"Thanks for being so helpful."

"That's nothing. Like I say, I'm always pleased for a bit of company."

The old man moved to show him to the door. But then he stopped.

"I've just remembered something," he said. "Once before an Englishman came to ask me about Katherina Hagenau. It was just at the end of the war, shortly after the Russians arrived. I'd dumped my army uniform and come back home to hunt for my wife and my two little girls. I remember a British army officer came clambering over the rubble clutching a little child in his arms and asked me if I knew where she was."

The old man's face was fast clouding over but in his excitement Robert didn't notice.

"A British officer? And what did you tell him?" he asked.

The old man didn't reply immediately. Instead, he moved slowly over to a ancient dresser and, opening a drawer, pulled out an old rag doll.

"I can't really remember," he said, struggling to retain his self-control. "You see, I'd just found this in the rubble. It was my little Sophie's favourite toy. I dug out her body along with her mother and sister a few hours later."

It was clear that the old man needed to be alone. With a twinge of guilt that he had been responsible for stirring up such painful memories, Robert touched his arm and thanked him again before turning and quickly leaving the flat.

Outside the weather had changed. Heavy black clouds had pushed aside the winter sun and large puffy snowflakes were beginning to drift down into the deserted street. But instead of walking back to the car as he had intended, Robert pulled his coat up around his neck to protect himself from the bitter cold and started to walk in precisely the opposite direction.

So now he knew his mother's name. Frieda. He was her first-born, and she had called him 'little mouse'. And he had screamed and screamed when he had been torn apart from her after two years in her arms. He thought of her, trying as he had tried so often before to summon up a picture of her face in his mind. But there was nothing there, an empty space which should have been full. Was she still alive, or had she really died during that dreadful night in 1945? And if she was alive, did she still sometimes lie awake at night and think of her 'little mouse'? Or had she forgotton him as he had forgotten her, and turned her thoughts to other things.

The snow was falling more heavily now, covering up the drabness of the street with a soft coating of brilliant white. He reached the far end of the road and, turning a corner, found himself walking along the bank of a wide river lined with trees.

One thing was now painfully obvious. He wanted to find his mother, or at least his aunt or some other relative, before he left East Berlin. The previous night at the Embassy he had come to understand that simple unavoidable fact. He had tried to hide away from the truth for years, to pretend within himself that he really was Robert Creighton Stanton, but the strain was finally beginning to tell. Like his father before him, he had supposed it would be a kindness to himself and those he loved to keep the truth hidden. But Kate's frantic accusations had made him see the falseness of that approach. The heart of the problem was that he was not being honest with himself by trying to pretend that it didn't matter. And if he could only start being honest with himself then everything else just might begin to fit into place.

He had almost walked past the telephone box when the thought occurred to him. Looking through the glass, he could see a grubby copy of the East Berlin telephone directory sitting in a little rack. Pushing the door open he went inside, brushing the snow from his coat. Then, searching through his pockets, he dug out a good supply of East German coins.

He looked at the directory. 'Frieda' wasn't much help and he didn't know her surname. It would have to be his aunt, 'Katherina Hagenau'. 'Hagenau' would almost certainly have been his aunt's married name.

When he found the right page, he noticed to his horror that there were a good two columns of Hagenaus. And that was just East Berlin, never mind the rest of East Germany. There were only eight Katherina Hagenaus, although looking at the entries it seemed probable that quite a lot of them were listed under the husband's name.

Stacking his coins neatly on a ledge next to the telephone, Robert started dialling the first Katherina Hagenau. A woman's voice answered.

"Hallo, is that Katherina Hagenau?"

"Yes," came the reply.

Robert took a deep breath.

"Excuse me. Did you live in Krämerstrasse before the war and have three children and a sister called Frieda who lost a little boy in 1945?"

There was a brief silence.

"Sorry?"

Robert repeated his words more slowly.

"No. I wasn't even alive in the war," the woman said, obviously puzzled by the call.

Robert muttered an apology and put the phone down.

The snow outside got deeper while Robert's pile of coins got smaller until eventually he had exhausted all eight Katherinas as well as his supply of appropriate coins.

There was no one near the phone box and Robert sat down on the floor, reluctant to leave until the worst of the storm had passed. If this were West Berlin, a systematic telephone search, even though time consuming, would probably have produced results. He could ring all the Hagenaus, every single one of them, and would probably come across either Katherina or someone related to her who would recognise the description. But this was not West Berlin, it was East Berlin, and in East Berlin only a very small percentage of households actually possessed a telephone. He would probably draw a blank.

And anyway, perhaps she wasn't in East Berlin. Even if she was still alive, perhaps she had gone to the West. For that matter, perhaps his mother had too. Two million East Germans had fled to the West before the Wall was built in 1961, so why not his mother and aunt? After all, that was precisely where his mother had been trying to reach when John Stanton had discovered her by the roadside.

It was beginning to get dark and yet the snowstorm showed no signs of abating. Robert pulled his coat around him in an attempt to keep out the cold. He felt stupid sitting in the telephone box, but he didn't want to return to the car just yet. The car symbolised a borrowed life, a life that wasn't his. He knew he would have to return to that life eventually, but he couldn't face it just yet.

He was trying to make some sort of sense of the situation he found himself in when the door of the telephone box swung wide open. Robert looked up in alarm and saw the pretty face of a girl of about nineteen or twenty staring down at him. He scrambled to his feet as quickly as the confined space would allow.

"Sorry," he mumbled.

"That's all right," she grinned, standing to one side of the open door to let him pass.

Robert edged past her into the snow outside and started walking back in the general direction of the car. But he had only gone a few paces when the girl pushed open the door of the telephone box and called after him.

"Excuse me!"

Robert turned.

"Yes."

"You haven't got any change, have you?"

Robert retraced his steps and started fumbling in his pockets for his coins. It was dark outside and he couldn't see what he was doing.

The girl watched him for a moment.

"Why don't you come inside out of the snow," she said with a smile. "You'll be able to see better."

Robert looked at her and half entered the telephone box. He had pulled out all the coins in his pocket before he remembered that he had already used up all the ones which fitted a telephone box with his own calls. Most of the coins in his hand were West German.

"I'm sorry," he said, "I should have realised before. I used up all my coins myself just now."

The girl looked at them.

"Oh well," she said, "never mind. It's not important. Thanks anyway."

Robert left the telephone box and retraced his steps by the river-bank. The girl followed him out and walked by his side.

"Are you from West Berlin?" she asked.

Robert looked at her with surprise.

"No. What made you think so?"

"East Berliners don't generally walk around with West German small change in their pockets."

They walked along in silence for while.

"But you're from the West, aren't you?" she persisted.

"Yes. I'm from the West."

"So why were you sitting in one of our telephone boxes?" she asked with a grin on her face. "Aren't your telephone boxes comfortable enough?"

Robert looked at her, wondering whether to be annoyed by her impertinence. But then, despite himself, he burst out laughing. It was the first time he had laughed for a long, long time.

"I don't make a habit of sitting in telephone boxes," he said with a smile.

"So why were you?"

"Well . . . it was snowing outside."

"That's not an answer."

"No, I don't suppose it is."

"So why were you?"

Robert stood still and looked at her. "First, let me ask you a question."

The girl stopped too and returned his gaze. Robert was struck by the intensity with which she looked at him.

"O.K. Fair enough."

"Are you so direct with everyone you meet in the street?"

"I didn't meet you in the street. I met you in a telephone box. I've never met anyone in a telephone box before."

Try as he might, Robert couldn't keep a straight face.

"Neither of us seem to be very good at answering straightforward questions with straightforward answers, do we?" he said with a smile, starting to walk again.

The girl shrugged her shoulders.

"Maybe that's because the answers aren't as straightforward as the questions," she murmured, but Robert couldn't quite make out whether the remark was intended for his consumption.

He turned into Krämerstrasse but the girl stayed by him.

"Do you live near here?" he asked.

"Not far," she said. "I don't live far. And you?"

"I live in West Berlin."

"I thought you said you didn't?"

"I said I wasn't a West Berliner."

"So where are you from?"

They were walking past the door of number 15. Robert thought for a moment before replying. He had lied so much recently, and he just didn't feel like lying again.

"I suppose you could say I'm from here."

"Here? How old were you when you went?"

"I was only two."

She looked at him in amazement.

"Only two?"

"That's right, only two. You see that house, the one just there. Number 15. My aunt used to live in that house, or at least in the house that was on that site before the war. I came to try and find her."

They were approaching the end of the street and Robert looked at the girl thoughtfully. He had already told her more than he had told his wife, more than he had told his employers, more than he had told anyone else he knew. But he had only just met her.

They turned out of Krämerstrasse and into the road where his car was parked. Robert wished it wasn't. It made him feel better talking to this pretty young girl with the penetrating eyes who could make him see the funny side of life. He didn't want to drive back to his empty flat on the other side of the Wall. But there didn't seem to be much alternative.

They arrived at his car and he stopped, feeling in his pocket for his car keys.

The girl looked at him and looked at the car.

"Your car?"

"Yes."

A cloud passed over her face, a look of sadness, almost of loss.

"Did you find her?" she said.

"Who?"

"Your aunt."

"No."

The girl was staring at him intensely.

"Do you have to go right now?" she said quietly.

In his pocket, Robert could feel the car keys already in his hand. Yet the directness of her question caught him completely off guard. He dropped the keys and took his hand out of his pocket.

"No," he said, returning her gaze. "I don't have to."

The cloud passed from her face and her eyes brightened.

"Let's go and have a drink. I know a place not far from here," she suggested.

"Shall we go in the car? It's cold."

Her eyes flashed at him for an instant, like an animal sensing danger.

"No," she said quickly, recovering her composure, "I'd rather we walked. It's really not far."

She led the way down another side street.

"What's your name?" she asked.

Robert looked at her and smiled.

"Well," he replied, "that's another difficult one,"

"Come on," she said, "surely you've got a name. Or is it that you don't want to tell me?"

Robert laughed.

"Sorry. My name's Robert. Robert Stanton."

Her reaction was exactly the same as the old man's.

"Robert Stanton. What kind of a name is that? It's not German."

"No, it's English."

"You come from East Berlin. You live in West Berlin. You've got an English name. You a drive a car with diplomatic number plates and you sit in telephone boxes," she said with a grin. "Maybe you're right. Maybe I'd better stop asking so many questions."

Robert burst out laughing. How did this girl manage to make him feel so happy?

"Well," he said, "and what's your name?"

"Ah, at last a question with an entirely straightforward answer. My name's Sonja."

They turned another corner and arrived outside a small pub. Sonja pushed open the door and led Robert into a brightly-lit room filled with square plastic-topped tables. Singularly uncomfortable-looking upright chairs had been positioned in neat fours around the tables, on each of which some kind soul had lovingly arranged a selection of dull plastic flowers in an unsuccessful attempt to soften the atmosphere.

There were quite a few people in the room and Sonja nodded a greeting to most of them. But she didn't attempt to join any of the groups already there. Instead, she led Robert across to a small empty table next to the far wall. Above the table was a large photograph of the East German Party leader.

Before they had time to sit down a waiter came over.

"Hallo, Sonja," he said with a smile.

"Hallo, Fritz," she replied, and then turned to Robert.

"What do you want?" she asked.

"Something warming, a Scotch perhaps."

The waiter looked at Robert and then threw a glance at Sonja.

"Try again, Robert! You're in East Berlin, remember. And this isn't an Interhotel."

Robert realised what he had done and felt incredibly stupid.

"Sorry. I'll have a beer."

"Two beers, Fritz. Big ones. And some schnaps. It's freezing out there."

The waiter vanished. Robert took off his heavy winter coat and went behind Sonja to help her off with hers. As he lifted it from her shoulders, he was struck by the sensuous outline of her young body, firmly clad in a tightly fitting pullover and jeans. For a fraction of a second he let his gaze descend, thinking that she could not see, before turning away to hang up the coats.

When he had returned to the table and sat down Sonja leant across to him.

"Did you like it?" she whispered.

"I beg your pardon," he said.

"My body. You were looking at my bum when you were helping me off with my coat. Did you like it?"

Robert had met a lot of people in his life but never anyone who spoke like Sonja. He just didn't know how to handle her.

"I'm sorry," he said, "I didn't mean to."

She laughed her infectious laugh and looked him straight in the eyes.

"Do you really think I mind?"

Robert looked down, aware how flushed his cheeks must look.

"I don't know. Some people would, I suppose."

The smile disappeared and was replaced by a look of savage contempt.

"I hate people like that. People who aren't honest. Why shouldn't you look at my bum if you want to?"

Robert couldn't think of any good reasons, but he was relieved when Fritz arrived with the drinks and interrupted the conversation.

Sonja smiled and said nothing while the drinks were served. But as soon as Fritz had gone she leant across to him and spoke again.

"That's what I can't abide about this bloody country. The fact that nobody says what they think. Not at school, not at work, not anywhere. They all pretend to think one way but in reality it's all fake."

She picked up the small glass of vodka and downed it in one, following it up with some beer.

"Sorry," she muttered. "It's not your problem, is it?"

Robert smiled at her. "I don't mind listening to somebody else's problems for a change. I've got rather fed up with my own problems over the last few days."

She returned his smile.

"I'll do a deal with you," she said. "If I tell you my problem then you can tell me yours. That way we'll both feel better."

"Let me try and guess yours," Robert offered. "You're this side of the Wall, and you want to be the other side. Right."

She looked at him glumly.

"Right in one. You make it sound very straightforward."

"Hmm. Very. Trouble is, your problem doesn't have a solution."

"You could always take me back in the boot of your car."

Robert nearly choked on his beer before he noticed that she was laughing at him.

"It's all right, don't panic. It was just one of my little jokes."

If it was a joke, Robert didn't find it very funny. He looked at her seriously.

"Is that why you started talking to me tonight? Because I'm from the West and you think I might be able to help you."

The laughter vanished from her face.

"I don't know," she said sadly, looking into her beer, "I talk to nearly everyone I meet from the West."

She looked up at him, her large eyes pleading with him to believe her.

"It's not because I want to use them. I never want to use anyone. It's just because I find people from the West so refreshing to be with. I find you refreshing to be with."

"I can't see why anyone would find me refreshing at the moment," said Robert. "My wife certainly doesn't."

"You're married?"

Robert looked at her. "Yes, happily married with two children." He didn't mean it to sound cynical but somehow it came out that way. "It's funny. Last night she accused me of having an affair with a younger girl. It wasn't true, I've not been unfaithful to her in thirteen years of married life."

"I'm not getting married to anyone until I get out of this dump.

81

Once you're married they've got you in a trap," she said bitterly, jerking her face up at the photograph of the Party boss above the table.

Robert looked at her, and as he did so a feeling of pity for the girl began to overcome his own sense of misery. She was so young, so pretty and yet she was convulsed with such a hatred for the society in which she lived that she would reject even love itself.

"Why do you hate it so much? It can't be that bad. I've been to quite a lot of countries with my job. All over the world. Lived in quite a lot of them. East Germany's better off than most places."

"But there you have it. You've been to those different countries. You've travelled. If I want to know about faraway places and faraway people, I have to watch television or read about them. There isn't a chance for me to see them for myself. I can't even visit the other half of my own city."

"But other people seem to manage here. They survive."

"I survive. But I want to do more than survive like a caged lion. I want to roam free, to be free. You've travelled the world. Don't you understand that? Living by this Wall, it just burns me up inside until I want to scream."

Robert thought of the two people he had seen arrested at Checkpoint Charlie the night before. They must have been roughly the same age as Sonja. Perhaps they had felt the same.

"Sonja," he said, "I saw something horrible last night. On the border."

She looked at him.

"I was coming across to a diplomatic reception in East Berlin with my wife. Over Checkpoint Charlie. While we were waiting to get through some people tried to bust the Wall."

"What! Right there."

Robert nodded.

"They didn't stand a chance. Not a bloody chance. You can't get across so don't even think about it."

She looked at him coldly, like a child who has been told they cannot have an ice cream but refuses to accept the fact.

Robert remembered his conversation with Herr Lechner.

"I met someone later at the Embassy. A senior official from the Ministry of Trade. I told him about what had happened and he said you can now apply for permission to leave."

Sonja stared at him and then started to laugh. But this time her laugh was not a laugh of happiness, but a laugh of bitterness.

"That's funny. That's really funny."

"I didn't think it was true," he said.

"But that's what's so funny. It's perfectly true."

"Sorry, Sonja, I'm not with you."

"You are looking at one bona fide exit visa applicant of two years standing."

He looked at her in astonishment.

"You mean you actually applied?"

"Yup. I was only nineteen at the time. I'd always got good marks at school, and I'd landed myself a job in a local library. It was pleasant enough work compared to what a lot of people have to do, even if it wasn't very stretching. I tried to kid myself that I could stomach it here. I was even thinking of getting married to someone, a boy I'd known from school for years. Lots of people do that here, you know, get married really young and have children. Unless you're in the Party it's all you've got to look forward to.

"But the library was having a terrible effect on me. When no one was there I would sit flicking through the books on other parts of the world. London. Paris. New York. It was all there in the pages of the books but I knew I could never see any of it. I suppose it became a bit of an obsession. One day I couldn't stand it any longer. I took a day's leave from the library and without telling anyone I walked down to the police station and asked for the forms to apply for an exit visa.

"At first they tried to humour me. They asked if I was unhappy at work, told me that they could try and get me a different job. They offered to help find me a better place to live. But I said no, I didn't want a new job, I didn't want a better place to live, I just wanted a new life in the West.

"Then they got nasty. A policewoman took me into an office on my own and gave me the forms to fill out. She ordered me to fill them out there and then. I was frightened. I didn't know what they were going to do. Then she started shouting at me, accusing me of being a traitor to my parents, to my schoolfriends, to my country, to everybody she could think of. I told her I didn't want to hurt anyone, I just wanted to live somewhere else. Suddenly, she stopped shouting and put the forms I had filled out in the drawer of her desk. She said they would be processed and that I would hear from the authorities in due course. Then she told me to leave."

"I heard sooner than I had been expecting. Three days later I got a letter saying that I had been reallocated to a different job. The library no longer required my services. I was to report the following Monday morning to the offices of the S-Bahn. That's when I got my present job."

Robert looked up at her expectantly, but she didn't say anything.

"What is it?" he asked.

"I clean toilets," she said eventually. "From six in the morning until six in the evening I clean the toilets on the S-Bahn. Actually I think it's their idea of a little joke - they know perfectly well I can see the smart blocks of flats in the residential districts of West Berlin from some of the platforms."

She looked down into her empty glass.

"Shall we have another drink?" she asked.

Robert nodded silently. He didn't know what to say.

She went over to Fritz and collected some more drinks from the bar. When she came back she was smiling again.

"There you are," she said with a grin, "I told you that you feel better if you get your problems off your chest."

She sat down and gave Robert another beer and another schnaps.

"Cheers," she said in appalling English, holding up her schnaps glass. "That's what you say in English, isn't it?"

Robert held his glass up and touched hers.

She smiled at him for a long time. Then she leant back in her chair.

"O.K. I've had my turn. Now it's yours. What is it that makes Robert Stanton sit looking so glum in telephone boxes?"

Robert looked at her for a moment, and imagined her bending over filthy toilets in East German railway stations for twelve hours a day within sight of a world to which she could never go. And suddenly he felt bitterly ashamed of himself.

"They've gone, Sonja. You've made them all vanish."

She smiled at him and then her face became serious.

"We seem to be good for each other," she said, her eyes meeting his. For a long time they said nothing.

"I want you," Robert said at last.

She didn't reply straight away. But then she slowly reached her hand across the table and touched his.

"I know you do," she said quietly, "and I want you too."

* * * * * *

The first thing Robert could hear when he awoke was the sound of a distant train. It must have been going round a sharp curve because it was making a most excruciating kind of rasping noise which seemed to grind on without ceasing. He wished it would stop so that he could drift back to sleep but no sooner had it done so than another train started making exactly the same noise. He opened his eyes.

Sonja was still asleep, her face only inches away from his in the cramped single bed. He watched her for a long time, reconstructing the events of the previous day and trying to work out exactly how it was that he had ended up in the bed of a girl some fourteen years younger than himself with whom he had only just struck up an acquaintance. It was still dark outside, but he couldn't help wondering whether the arrival of the cold light of day would make him regret what he had done. He knew he should feel guilty, but he felt no guilt. He felt only a deep sense of tranquility, a peace of mind that had evaded him for many months, or was it even longer? He wished he could lie there for ever watching the peaceful face of the girl by his side.

Her long hair was dishevelled, strewn across the shared pillow, and he touched it gently with his hand. Why was Sonja so different to Kate in bed? Why was she so much better? Perhaps it was that his wife tried too hard to please: lying there beside Sonja, he began to realise that Kate had always used sex as a kind of tool, a way of hanging on to him. From the first, she had responded flexibly to his every whim: when he had been tired she had soothed him, when he wished to be dominant she had been passive, when he wanted her to climax she had climaxed. But in thirteen years of married life, had she ever really done anything at all to please herself?

Sonja's eyes opened but she made no sudden movement. She seemed to be in a dream, reluctant to disturb a precious moment of peace in a world where peace was hard to find. And so they lay together, face to face, gazing into each other's eyes and hoping against hope that time would stand still.

There was loud gurgling noise from behind the wall rather like a dinosaur suffering from indigestion. It went on and on until it could no longer be ignored.

"What on earth is that?" Robert whispered.

She smiled at him.

"It's six o'clock. The man in the flat next door is having a bath. He always has a bath before he goes to work."

"Doesn't it bother you?"

"No. I'm usually gone by five-thirty."

Robert fell silent. Sonja looked at him sweetly.

"I think you'd bother me, though, if I slept with you every night," she said, a gentle smile spreading across her face.

Robert looked at her with a puzzled expression, unable to grasp her meaning.

"What does your wife do about it?" she continued.

"Do about what?"

"When you start snoring like that?"

"I snore!" he said. "Kate never told me I snore."

"Well in that case I'm having a bad effect on you, because I had to tell you at least five times in the night to shut up."

Not for the first time with this girl, Robert couldn't think of what to say.

"Sorry," was the best he could manage.

"Never mind," she said, "I expect it happens to us all when we start getting old."

Robert rolled over onto his back and examined the ornate plaster-work on the ceiling. Bearing in mind it was such a crummy flat it had remarkably fine plasterwork.

Sonja's arm reached across his chest and she buried her head into his shoulder.

"You're not cross, are you? It's not your fault if you snore."

Robert smiled to himself and put his arm around her. If Kate had started saying these things to him he'd have gone off in a huff for the rest of the day. But with Sonja it didn't seem to matter. He pulled her closer, relishing the warm pressure of her firm young breast against his chest.

"You're a very direct young woman, Sonja, it could get you into trouble."

"It already has," she said with a laugh, "but I still take it as a compliment."

Robert ran his hand down the smooth skin of her back and could feel her body shudder with pleasure at his touch. He knew she liked it not just from her reaction, but because she had told him so in no uncertain terms the night before.

She let him stroke her back for a long time without speaking.

"Sonja," he said at last.

"Yes," she whispered.

"How many men have you slept with?"

She didn't react at all.

"You're the second," she replied quietly.

Robert stopped stroking her. He had assumed from the speed with which she had agreed to go to bed with him the previous night that she had slept with many men.

"Are you surprised? You didn't think I was a virgin, did you?"

"No," Robert exclaimed, rather too quickly.

"I told you last night. There was a boy. The boy I nearly married when I was working at the library." She laughed. "I was a law-abiding girl in those days. I'd known him for years at school, but I didn't let him get me until the night of my sixteenth birthday!"

"What happened?" he asked.

"He left me after I got the sack from the library. I don't know why. He probably took offence to the fact that I hadn't discussed my application for an exit visa with him. Or maybe he didn't want the same thing to happen to him as happened to me. Anyway, he's married to someone else now and they've got a little baby. I think he's happy enough."

"And you've had nobody since. Not for two years."

"No," she said quietly, "not until last night."

Robert lay still for a long time.

"So why me?" he said finally.

She shrugged her shoulders.

"I don't really know. Why did you choose me after thirteen years with your wife?"

Robert thought for a while, searching for a satisfactory answer, but before he could find one she had pulled away from him and got out of bed.

"It's always so bloody freezing in here," she said, pulling a dressing-gown around her naked body. "Will you give me a hand with the oven?"

Robert quickly got up and went over to an old iron stove in the corner. She was right: away from the warmth of the bedcovers his body was shivering in the bitter cold of the December night. He started raking out the ashes from the previous evening. Sonja threw him his coat.

"Put this on, you silly man," she laughed, "or you'll freeze to death before you're done."

It did not take long to light the fire and by the time he had finished Sonja had returned from the tiny communal kitchen she shared with the other occupants of the flat with two mugs of coffee and some rolls.

Besides the bed, the tiny room contained little furniture other than an old wooden chest of drawers and a single upright chair. Sonja sat on the floor by the oven, warming her hands on the cup of coffee, and Robert sat down beside her, pulling his coat around them both. Sitting there sipping the coffee reminded him in a strange sort of way of distant student days at Oxford.

"I'll bet you've got a nice house," she remarked, but there was no hint of jealousy in her voice.

Robert nodded. He didn't particularly want to pursue the topic.

"I'm lucky to have got this place," she said. "You probably think it's pretty tatty, but I'm lucky not to be living with my parents still."

The coals in the oven were now beginning to pump out an impressive amount of heat into the tiny room and Robert could feel himself slowly relaxing.

"How on earth do you manage to remain so cheerful, Sonja?" he asked, watching her smiling face as she sipped her coffee. "If I were in your shoes I'd never smile."

"Sunday's a good day," she said, "but you should see me on Monday mornings."

"I'd like to see you every morning," he said quietly.

"Your wife would like that, wouldn't she?"

"She's in England. She went back for the Christmas holidays to be with our children. She's not coming back for several weeks."

Sonja peered into her mug of coffee and thought for a while.

"I don't mind," she said, "you're welcome to come as long as you want. I'm not going anywhere. But you're taking a risk, aren't you?"

Robert looked at her, wondering what she was talking about.

"If I understand it correctly," she said, "you work for the British Embassy in East Berlin. Right?"

He nodded.

"They'd be thrilled to know you were having an affair with me, wouldn't they?"

Robert looked miserable. He had been expressly warned before departing for East Berlin, as all diplomats posted to Eastern Europe were warned, against forming any kind of romantic attachments behind the Iron Curtain. He knew full well that it was a ploy frequently used by Eastern Bloc intelligence services.

"How do you know I'm not an agent of the State Security Service?" she asked, looking him directly in the face.

Robert sat still for a while, thinking.

"I don't," he said with a glum expression. "I just choose to believe you aren't."

"Well, I'm not," she said, "and just to prove it I promise I won't ask you any questions about your work."

Robert nodded.

"But your employers won't believe that I'm not, will they? They'll think I'm bad news."

Robert nodded again.

"So don't risk it, Robert. I don't want to hurt you, I really don't.

I'm not in the business of hurting people. Last night was fun, more than fun. In fact it made me happier than I've been for years. But I don't want it to be at the expense of your marriage or your job. I don't want to have to be responsible for that."

She looked down at her cup and Robert could see that she was fighting to prevent tears from forming in her eyes. He knew that everything she had said was right. He was risking a lot if he carried on seeing her. In point of fact he was probably risking everything of value he had ever possessed.

The room was warmer now. Leaving the coat with Sonja, he got up and walked over to the small window. The flat was near the top of a high building and outside the still dark city of Berlin was spread out before him. The snow from the previous evening lay thickly on the ground and in the distance there was a passenger train, its lights moving like a glistening snake through the darkened buildings. And as it went round a bend and approached a bridge over a wide river it started making the dreadful scraping noise to which he had first awoken that morning.

He looked at the dark shape of the bridge and the train crossing over it and thought about his own life. It seemed as if he were crossing a bridge as well, although he was not very sure when he had started crossing it and had even less idea of what he would find on the other side. But Sonja was refusing to let him cross with his eyes closed. She was forcing him to think about where he was going. He watched the train to see if it would stop and return to the side from which it had come, but it carried on moving relentlessly forward. Up until this morning, up until this very moment perhaps, Robert had assumed that he would just go back to his previous life after he had returned to London from Berlin. Looking for his mother, sleeping with Sonja, he had perceived both these events as interludes in his life, the half-time intermission at the cinema before continuing with the main film.

He turned to look at her. She was still sitting on the floor, his overcoat pulled around her shoulders, her eyes staring down at her cup. And as he looked it became clear that there could be no turning back. He walked over and knelt down in front of her, pulling her face up so that he could look into her lonely eyes.

"It was kind of you to say those things, Sonja. Kinder than I had a right to expect. But I know what I'm doing. I take the responsibility for what I'm doing. And I still want to see you again."

Sonja gazed at him for a moment, trying to take in what he had said. And then, letting the coat and the dressing-gown drop to the floor, she drew him to her and lowered him to the floor. And as he felt her warm lips move ever lower down his naked body, he was sure he could hear the sound of her crying.

* * * * * *

"It's in here. On the fifth floor. I hope she's in."

Sonja pushed the door of the building open and went inside, holding the door open so that Robert could follow. There was no bell by the front door and as they started to climb the stairs they had no idea whether Sonja's friend was at home.

"Remember, Robert, I'm not promising anything. She might not want to help. And don't forget to let me do all the talking."

It was nearly midday and the bright winter sun was shining in through the grubby hallway windows. Climbing flight after flight of steps, Robert was beginning to regret that the dreadful racket of the squeaky trains had awoken him so early that morning.

"At least you get fit in this country, climbing all these bloody stairs," he panted.

Sonja laughed.

"Didn't you know? Lifts are a symbol of a decadent capitalist life-style."

Robert grunted. Sonja really didn't seem to mind all this running up and down. Perhaps it was just another sign that he was getting older, rather like the snoring.

They got to the fifth floor and Sonja knocked loudly on one of the doors.

"Don't forget," she whispered, "let me do the talking. You just smile sweetly and nod occasionally."

The door swung open and a rather overweight girl of about the same age as Sonja appeared at the door. She had a large towel wrapped around her generous form and had obviously just emerged from the shower.

"Sonja! What a surprise."

"Hallo, Heidi, I hope you're not too busy."

"Not busy. Bored. Come on in, won't you."

Heidi smiled at Robert and welcomed him in.

"This is Robert. He's a friend of mine."

She offered a hand and Robert shook it. Earlier, Sonja had explained to him the special meaning that was attached in East Germany to the expression 'friend'. It meant a person who could be trusted, a person with whom you did not have to keep your mouth shut.

Heidi's flat was strikingly different to Sonja's. For whereas Sonja's was a run down and dreary establishment, as if nobody cared, Heidi had clearly taken a great deal of trouble, for although most of the furniture was cheap and simple, the impression created in the flat was warm and cosy.

Heidi directed them to an old settee.

"Sit down," she said. "Would you like some coffee?"

"Please," said Sonja, "we'd love some."

Heidi vanished from the room and could be heard clattering around in the kitchen.

The walls of the flat appeared to be covered in bookshelves and it was apparent that Heidi was an exceedingly well-read young woman with a wide range of intellectual interests. Sonja watched him eyeing the books.

"She's a bright girl. Don't underestimate her just because she's got such a shitty job."

Just then a little child of about two years old tottered into the room. Sonja jumped to her feet and picked him up with a grin.

"Well if it isn't little Hansel," she said, throwing the young boy high into the air. Hansel gurgled with pleasure.

"Hansel's her kid," she explained to Robert, sitting down again with the boy on her lap.

The boy looked at Robert suspiciously and then picked up a little car and started showing it to Sonja. She put him down on the settee beside her with his car and he seemed quite content.

"It's a struggle for her on her own," she said quietly so that her friend would not hear from the other room. "I've got a lot of respect for her."

Sonja had already explained that Heidi was a single parent. It seemed she had had a stupid affair with a useless apology of a man and had ended up carrying his child. The man had promptly vanished.

Eventually Heidi returned carrying a tray with the coffee things and some home-made cake. She was no longer wrapped in the towel but had changed into casual slacks and a tea-shirt with 'Ohio State University' printed on the front.

Sonja looked at Hansel. "He gets bigger and cuddlier every time I see him," she said.

Heidi looked at him fondly.

"Yeah. He's great. He really is."

Sonja didn't waste time getting down to business. As Robert had already observed, getting to the point was not something she seemed to find overly difficult.

"Heidi, I've got a favour to ask. Quite a big favour."

91

Heidi looked at her with interest.

"It's not like you to ask a favour, Sonja. It's usually me asking you the favours. I'll do what I can."

"It's not really a favour for me, it's a favour for Robert. He's trying to trace someone – a relative – who he thinks might live in our wonderful fatherland. But he doesn't know much about her other than her name."

A strained expression came over Heidi's face.

"I see," she said.

Sonja continued. "Robert's English. But some of his family came from here around the time of the war. He has an aunt who used to live right here in Köpenick."

Heidi gave Robert a searching stare.

"And you want me to try and find out about her at work?" she asked.

Robert nodded. Heidi worked in the department of the Ministry of the Interior dealing with the issue of identity cards to East German nationals.

"Yes, that's right," he explained, "I'd love to trace her. I've been to the house where she used to live but drawn a blank. And I've even tried telephoning all the people listed under her name in the telephone directory but without success. Sonja thought you might be able to help."

Heidi picked up her coffee and sipped it slowly, playing for time while she thought.

"It's not easy," she said finally. "I'll have to think."

Robert felt acutely embarrassed.

"If it's too difficult, don't worry, I'll understand."

Heidi looked at him and smiled.

"I didn't say I wouldn't do it," she said, "I said I'll have to think how to do it."

"The problem is," Heidi continued, thinking aloud, "that they're so security conscious these days. Paranoid, I call it. I'll have to think of a good reason for doing a search and then find a way of smuggling the information out of the office." She paused. "But never mind, I'll find a way. What's her name, this aunt of yours? I'll do a run on her and see what I can come up with. And then I'll get in touch with Sonja and give the information to her."

Sonja leant over to where she was sitting and gave her a kiss.

"Thanks, Heidi, I knew you'd do it."

Heidi grinned.

"I tell you what. If I get caught and lose my job, I'll apply to come and help you clean the toilets on the S-Bahn."

They laughed and Sonja turned to Robert.

"Heidi's one of those survivors you talked about yesterday, Robert. She'll always stick it." She turned to Heidi and continued.

"Robert's widely travelled. He thinks East Germany is pretty good compared to most places in the world and that I'm making too much fuss."

Robert sat forward in his chair with an embarrassed look.

"I didn't quite say that, Sonja." he exclaimed.

But before Sonja could say anything Heidi interrupted.

"I think you're right, Robert," she said decisively. "It's not so bad as all that compared to a lot of places. And since there's nothing we can do about it anyway, what's the point of spending your entire life feeling bitter about things." She turned to Sonja. "After all, look what's happened to you for all your trouble-making."

Sonja said nothing but helped herself to another piece of cake.

"I'll get out of here one day," she said, her mouth full of cake. "I don't plan on cleaning those disgusting toilets for ever. And then I'll write and tell you if it was all worth while."

* * * * * *

It was nearly four o'clock by the time they left Heidi's. During the day the temperature had risen slightly, but now that the sun was sinking it was getting colder fast. Sonja was holding his hand and leading him back towards her flat through a large park in which a few hardy souls were still out gathering some fresh air before scurrying back to their warm burrows to celebrate Christmas Eve.

Suddenly Sonja stopped walking and let go of his hand.

"I've got a surprise for you," she said, "but you've got to shut your eyes."

Robert stopped walking and closed his eyes. He could hear the sound of Sonja moving quietly behind him in the snow. Then, with lightning speed, her hand pulled open his coat and thrust a large pack of compressed snow down his back.

He jumped back at the shock, wincing as the icy snow slithered slowly down his back.

"What the hell d'you do that for?"

Sonja laughed.

"It was an experiment. I wanted to see how trusting you are?"

With a malicious grin, Robert bent down and slowly picked up a large snowball. Sonja started to run away, leaving a series of small footprints behind her in the snow. Robert dropped the snowball and ran after her. She was quick, and the horrible thought crossed his mind that she might be able to outrun him. But eventually he started gaining on her. Grabbing her from behind, he held her struggling body in a vice-like grip.

"Sorry!" she pleaded. "I'm sorry."

"Do you deserve to be punished?"

"Yes."

"If I let you go and tell you to hold open the collar of your coat ready for me to drop a nice big snowball down your back will you try and run away?"

"No."

He let go of her and watched while she pulled her scarf up and exposed the bare skin at the back of her neck.

"Are you ready?"

"Yes."

He picked up some more snow and packed it into a huge snowball.

"Pull your coat down a little bit more, please."

She obeyed without a word.

"When it drops in it slithers down your back and runs all the way down to your bottom."

"Get on with it, Robert," she begged.

"Now shut your eyes."

As she did so Robert looked at her standing there in the freezing cold park, her head bent low and the collar of her coat open, passively awaiting a punishment she knew she deserved. Throwing the snowball away, he bent down and kissed her gently on the neck.

She opened her eyes and turned to face him.

"Why didn't you do it?" she asked, a sense of relief spreading across her face.

He shrugged his shoulders.

"I'm not telling you," he said, "you'll simply have to work it out for yourself."

As she reached up and kissed him on the face, he noticed how serious her expression had become.

"Robert. I've got to go soon. I don't want to, but I've got to. My parents are expecting me for Christmas Eve."

Robert looked at her sadly.

"That's all right. I understand."

"What are you going to do?" she asked.

"What, tonight?"

"Yes."

"Oh, not much, go back to the flat and watch a film on television,

I expect."

"That's sad," she said, "you've got nowhere to go on Christmas Eve."

Robert could still feel the dampness caused by the snowball on his back. Suddenly the idea of being back in his smart, comfortable diplomat's flat seemed quite appealing. He would be able to have a long hot shower followed by a stiff Scotch and settle down in front of the television for the late evening film.

"It's O.K.," he said, "don't forget I'm an Englishman. The English don't generally celebrate Christmas Eve. And tomorrow I've been invited by the Ambassador and his wife to have Christmas dinner with them. I think they must be feeling sorry for me."

He looked at her for a moment, wondering how best to say goodbye.

"Where's my car?" he asked.

"Over there," she replied, "along that street to the end and turn right. You can't miss it."

"I'll be back some time next week, Sonja."

Sonja looked at him.

"If you want to," she said quietly. "You know where to find me."

Robert put his arms around her and held her close to him for a moment.

"Happy Christmas, Robert," she said. "Take care."

He squeezed her tight.

"Happy Christmas, Sonja."

And with that he released her from his arms and turned away, walking quickly across the snow towards his car without glancing back.

* * * * * *

Mrs MacPhearson had just finished serving up the bread sauce.

"It's a pity you haven't had a chance to get to know any of the locals while you've been here," she said to Robert in her broad Highland accent.

Robert winced inwardly.

"Yes, Mrs MacPhearson, a great pity."

Angus leaned over the table with a new bottle of wine and filled Robert's glass. The Ambassador had already drunk rather too much before dinner had started.

"Hardly worth the trouble, if you ask me," he said, his words slurring ever so slightly. "They're a boring lot of old time-servers. Can't stand yakking with 'em, bunch of parrots. Robert here knows what I mean."

Mrs MacPhearson looked at her husband with an expression of faint reproach and continued her conversation with Robert.

"But I expect you've at least had a bit of a chance to look around the city."

Robert smiled at her.

"Well, actually I've been pretty busy. Haven't had a lot of time for sightseeing. Kate's probably seen more than I have."

"But you must have had time to see something."

Robert suddenly remembered the speeding ticket. Maybe the traffic police had simply forgotten the whole episode, but he couldn't be sure.

"I did have a drive around East Berlin the day before yesterday," he said, pausing temporarily while he wondered whether to mention his brush with the police.

Angus sipped his wine and looked at Robert with an amused expression.

"That must have been fun," he said. "I'll bet you got stopped on some pretext or other."

Robert looked at the Ambassador and decided to risk it. After all, he was in as good a humour now as he would ever be.

"I'm afraid I did. I didn't realise quite how ferocious the traffic police were."

Angus collapsed with laughter.

"What was it?" he said when he had recovered his self-control. "Speeding? Tyres? Drunken driving?"

"Speeding, but I wasn't going more than fifty."

Angus pretended to put on a serious face and addressed Robert.

"Now you know, young man, that I am supposed to take a very dim view of these matters when they are drawn to my attention."

Angus chortled to himself.

"But in view of the fact that you're soon going to be leaving us, I'll overlook your dreadful crime against the German Democratic Republic."

He thought for a minute and then his face suddenly grew serious.

"No I won't!" he said abruptly.

Mrs MacPhearson and Robert looked at him in consternation. But a broad smile was slowly spreading across the Ambassador's face.

"I'll expel you. That's what I'll do. I'll formally expel you. Here, want some more wine?"

Robert was staring at him, trying to make sense of what he had just heard. Surely it was not possible that his whole diplomatic career could be under threat just because he had been caught driving two kilometres per hour over the speed limit?

"Cheer up, old son. It won't affect you in the slightest little bit," the Ambassador continued. "I'll tell London it's a set up job. You've got to look upon yourself as a martyr in a good cause."

"I'm sorry, Angus, I'm not quite with you."

"They've been needling me and the other Western Ambassadors with this silly nonsense about traffic offences and the like for a long time now. God knows why. It's always utter trivia compared to what their diplomats get up to in London, but they make out that it's an attack on their national sovereignty, almost an act of war. Of course it puts us Ambassadors in an awkward situation so we try to stop our people breaking any of their silly rules. But they always seem to find something they can nag about. Now, if I kick you out it will have a two-fold effect. First of all it'll make my staff doubly vigilant about keeping to the rules since they're much more scared of me than the East German traffic police. And secondly it'll tell the East Germans how seriously we regard these petty infringements of their law by our personnel. Kills two birds with one stone. Not bad, eh?"

Mrs MacPhearson looked at her husband sternly.

"Are you sure this will not rebound on Robert, dear," she said. "That wouldn't be fair."

"Won't even affect him, my dear, that's the beauty of it. In fact . . ."

You could almost see his mind ticking over.

"You want to get out of here, don't you, Robert? Get back to that interesting political job you've been doing in London."

Robert shook his head in denial. How on earth did the Ambassador know that he was fed up with the work?

"It's no good denying it. It's written all over your face every time you talk to me about textile quotas. The point is, I might be able to do you a favour and kill a third bird with that stone of mine at the same time."

Mrs MacPhearson had finished serving the dinner.

"Angus, dear, I think you're likely to give our guest indigestion if you carry on nattering away like this. Should we not talk about something more relaxing over our Christmas dinner than your plans for turning Robert into a kind of international sacrificial goose?"

"All right, dear, all right. But I must just tell you my idea and then I promise I'll stop. The point is this; the East Germans want us to hurry up and conclude the textile deal Robert is working on.

It means lots and lots of lovely hard currency to them. For a variety of reasons, we're not quite so keen. So as soon as they get around to complaining about Robert's driving, I'll pack him off on the next plane to London, with a severe reprimand, before his feet have had a chance to touch the ground. And then I'll ring the Minister of Trade and tell him the negotiations will simply have to wait until Jeremy's got back from his illness." He paused, contemplating the beauty of his scheme. "If Robert's going to be the sacrificial goose, we might as well let the East Germans cook him! The Ministry of Trade will be hopping mad with the Ministry of the Interior for slowing down the negotiations with their stupid traffic nonsense and I'm sure that'll be the last time I get bothered with this kind of thing ever again."

Robert could feel his stomach turning inside out and hoped that it didn't show on his face.

"It sounds like a clever scheme, Angus," he said.

The Ambassador was already tucking into his turkey with considerable gusto.

"Glad you like it," he said with his mouth full. "And if you take my advice, young man, you'll get your bags packed as soon as you get home tonight. When it happens, we'll make damn sure it happens fast."

* * * * * *

Robert kicked off his shoes as soon as he had shut the door of his flat and went to lie down on the bed. He closed his eyes and tried to rest, tried to blank out everything that had happened over the previous few days. Things were simply moving too fast.

It was pleasantly warm in the centrally heated room and he could feel his body slowly relaxing on the comfortable double bed. He had drunk several glasses of wine and a large brandy at the MacPhearsons' and his head was swimming gently from the effects of the alcohol.

He tried to think of something pleasant, and his mind drifted back to some of the Christmas Days he had spent at Upper Trumpton when the boys had been younger. They had always gone to Upper Trumpton for Christmas. In the mornings the whole family would go to the village church for the service and in his mind Robert could still hear the congregation singing the old time-honoured Christmas carols, led as ever by the village choir under the capable direction of Henry Fitzpatrick. After the service they had gone home for the turkey, and as soon as the dinner things had been cleared away there had been presents and family carol singing around the huge Christmas tree in the living room. In the after-glow of his memory, it all seemed so idyllic.

The bureau was sitting in the corner of the room, not far from where the Christmas tree was set up, and Robert found himself watching it apprehensively while the family began to sing 'Silent Night'. Throughout the first verse it just sat there, as it had always done, the brass handles on the old mahogany drawers decorated as usual with little paper Christmas snowmen.

The family started to sing the second verse, with Kate attempting a harmonic as she sometimes tried to do when she was in a particularly good mood. But then he pulled back in his chair and stared at the bottom drawer. It was beginning to move, creeping slowly forward on its runners. He looked at his family, but they were all continuing to sing as if nothing had happened. Robert turned away and looked with determination at the tiny fairy adorning the top of the tree, trying to join in with the singing. But he couldn't help himself; he looked again at the drawer and it was half open now, moving completely by itself as if pushed by a hidden force within.

Robert's chair crashed to the ground as he stood up, staring in horror at the drawer, which was now nearly fully extended. He glanced at his family, at Peggy and John, at Kate, at Timothy and Justin, but they had clearly noticed nothing unusual.

The drawer was now wide open, the front of it resting on the carpet, and Robert could feel himself drawn irresistibly towards the bureau. He walked forward, past his parents, past his wife, past his children, and looked down into the dark hole presented by the open drawer. And then, as if his mind had somehow become disembodied from his body, he entered into the drawer.

It was dark inside, and there was no sound except for the faint echo of his family singing 'Silent Night' in the room he had left behind. He started to crawl forward on his hands and knees. The singing was getting fainter all the time and he noticed, for the first time, that he could hear his own voice singing in the distance along with the rest of his family. It was now completely still and he stopped crawling forward. He was surrounded by emptiness, floating in a dark sea that was strange yet somehow reassuring. He became aware of a faint beating in the distance, a rhythmic pounding that seemed familiar but that he could not quite place.

There was a loud metallic sound which repeated itself over and over again. Robert tried to hang on to the warmth, to force the annoying sound to go away. But it refused to stop and he opened his eyes. The telephone on the bedside table was ringing.

He shook his head to clear his mind and picked up the handset.

"Hallo." he said blearily, still half asleep.

"Hallo, Dad. Happy Christmas!" It was Justin's cheerful voice on the telephone.

Robert stood up from the bed to force himself to wake up more quickly.

"Oh, hallo son. Happy Christmas. How're you doing?"

"Fine, Dad, although we're all missing you here."

Robert winced. He felt guilty enough about sending his children to boarding school, let alone not being with them for Christmas.

"Have you got some good presents?" he asked.

"Yes, Dad, they're great, especially the bike you gave me. Thanks."

Robert thought for a moment. Why didn't he know that he'd given his son a bike?

"Oh, glad you like it."

"Have you opened your presents yet?"

"No. In fact I didn't know I had any presents here."

There was a pause on the other end of the line.

"Mum said there were. I'll go and get her and she can tell you where they are. Bye."

"Goodbye, Justin."

Robert waited while Justin went to fetch his mother and suddenly felt terribly alone. He should have been with his kids on a day like this.

Kate came on the line. And although her voice was calm and controlled, he could hear the edge in it.

"Hallo, Robert, I forgot to tell you where your presents were. I packed them on Friday but completely forgot to tell you about them before I left."

Kate was still seething with anger, or was it hurt?

"Hallo, love," he said, realising that it was pointless to try and clear the air over a long distance telephone line. "Happy Christmas. I've just got back from the MacPhearsons."

"That's nice. Did you have a good time?"

"Fine, just fine, although I'd much rather have been with you and the boys."

Kate let the remark pass without comment.

"The presents are at the bottom of the wardrobe in a large plastic bag," she said. "One of them is from me and there are some from the children. There's also a package from your parents that came by post."

There was a silence, as if Kate was trying unsuccessfully to pluck up the courage to say something.

"How are you, love?" Robert said eventually, trying to break the impasse.

"I'm all right." she said, her voice carefully controlled, "I'll give your love to Timothy and my parents. Goodbye."

"Kate..." Robert began, but it was no good. She had put the phone down and was gone.

Robert put the handset back and sat down heavily on the bed. Kate deserved better than he was giving. He thought of her at her parents, trying bravely to pretend that everything was fine. She did not generally own up to the truth with herself, let alone those around her. It was simply not her style.

He rose and walked wearily over to the wardrobe in the corner of the room. Sure enough, there was the plastic bag full of carefully wrapped Christmas presents. She must have got it all ready for him before he had come home from work on the day of the party and then completely forgotton to tell him about it after they had had that terrible row at the Embassy later in the evening.

He pulled out the bag, carefully removing the contents and placing them on the bedcovers. There were four presents and a number of cards. He opened the cards from his children first. They were home-made and clearly had had a lot of work put into them. He looked at them thoughtfully for a long time before standing them up on the bedside table.

He opened Kate's card. 'To the man of my life,' she had written, 'with love from your ever-adoring wife." He quickly put the card next to the others.

The presents from Kate and the kids were, of course, really all from Kate and comprised the usual dreary assortment of shirts, towels and other 'useful' household objects. Then he turned to the parcel from his parents, which from its general size and feel looked like a paperback book. He tore the wrapping paper away and looked nonplussed at the contents. The present was an ancient dog-eared copy of a Berlin street-map.

Robert picked up the map. In the top right-hand corner of the inside cover were the words 'Captain John W. Stanton.' The words were written in his father's hand and dated from the period when he had used the book at the end of the war. But in the middle of the page, recently written in the same hand, were the words: 'To Robert, to help you find your way.'

He put the book down and quickly opened the envelope from his parents. There was a Christmas card together with a short letter from

101

his father. 'Dear Robert,' it began, 'I hope you are having a good stay in Berlin; I am sure that it has changed a great deal since the last time I was there. You may find the enclosed present a little strange, but I found it recently while going through some old junk in the attic and thought you might be interested. If you look through you'll see some of the places I used to frequent during my time in Berlin. One spot well worth looking at is the place marked on page 57 where I used to spend quite a lot of time in the evenings. I think I might have told you about it once but I couldn't quite remember where it was. Love, dad.'

Robert read the letter several times. His father was writing in code, that much was clear. He knew perfectly well that Robert had not told Kate about his origins in Berlin and was not certain whether she would be there when he opened the letter.

He put down the letter and picked up the book again. The pages were yellowing with age, and the book had that rather musty appearance that comes from being slightly damp for a considerable period of time. Then he remembered his father's letter – the book had been stored away in the attic, and the attic at the house in Upper Trumpton was always damp. He turned the fragile pages carefully until he got to page 57. It showed the same area, around Köpenick, where he had been the previous day with Sonja, and he immediately recognised several of the places marked. He could see the river, the park where he had chased Sonja with the snowball, even the railway bridge with the squeaky bend. The page had been particularly well-thumbed by his father and he could see a fading ink cross on one of the streets not far from the park.

He looked closely. It was not Krämerstrasse, that was quite a way over to the left. It must have been the site of the orphanage, the place that had been his home for six months and where, according to his father's account, he had found some kind of refuge with a brave old woman by the name of Helga. Robert piled the pillows up behind him and lay back on the bed before looking at the book again. Why had his father sent him the old map? Was it just a passing fancy, or did it have some other meaning? He looked again at the inside cover. 'To Robert, to help you find your way.' They were strange words that his father had chosen to write. Berlin in 1978 bore little resemblance to Berlin in 1945 and his father could not really have supposed that he didn't have a street map of the city.

And then he remembered with crystal clarity his father's words three years before when he had given him the piece of paper with the scrawled address written by his real mother, the piece of paper that had for so long lain untouched in the drawer of the bureau about which he had only minutes before had such a peculiar dream. 'You can have it now, Robert. I've carried the burden long enough.' He had not really understood those words at the time, but now they began to make more sense. 'To Robert, to help you find your way.' Did his father, quietly playing golf in the evening of his life, realise what kind of effect being in Berlin was having on his adopted son? And by sending the present was he trying to reassure him that there was at least one person in the world who understood what he was going through?

As he held the book in his hand, Robert felt his eyes beginning to glaze over. John Wilberforce Stanton, even though he might not be his real father, was certainly a most remarkable man. How many other men would have done what he had done in time of war? How many other men would have had such courage?

The words in the book kept going round in his mind. 'To Robert, to help you find your way.' John Stanton was telling him to look, telling him to go and search out the places in Berlin where he had lived for so much of the formative part of his life, telling him to face up to the truth and not to run away. His own father was telling him that he was doing the right thing.

Robert closed the book and lay back. Had his father just stumbled across the map? It seemed unlikely. He had probably turned the house upside down, driving mother crazy by searching every nook and cranny for that ancient little book. And he had done it so that he could reassure his only son that he was not alone.

* * * * * *

Robert stepped briskly out from the Embassy into the early evening gloom and started heading for his car. But he had not walked more than several hundred yards before a well-dressed young man emerged from the shadows of a doorway adjoining the pavement.

"Want to change some money?" the man whispered, furtively glancing round to check that no one was looking.

"No thanks," Robert muttered in reply, and the man returned silently to his roadside vantage point.

This chap was obviously new to the game, or had perhaps been away for the Christmas holidays. Glancing down the street, Robert could recognise several of the regulars, the illegal money-changers who prowled up and down Unter den Linden from early in the morning till late at night in search of day-trippers from the West. But the regulars had either asked him already and been refused, or else had noticed that he worked at an Embassy, for they studiously ignored him as he passed them by.

Being approached by such people was part of everyday life in East Berlin, just as being approached by beggars was part of everyday life in most poor countries, and on previous occasions when he had been asked he had scarcely given it a second thought. But this time he found the man's approach disquieting and his hitherto brisk and purposeful pace slowed to an uncertain crawl.

Counting the night before Christmas, this would be the fourth night he had spent at Sonja's flat.

He decided to play safe. Resisting the temptation to glance over his shoulder, he turned casually around and started walking towards the S-Bahn station on the Friedrichstrasse. It was a tricky problem knowing what to do with the car: if he left it in West Berlin he would have to cross the border on foot or by train, and either way the unusual behaviour would be likely to attract attention. Yet if he left the car in East Berlin overnight it would probably be reported to the authorities. Better in the circumstances to vary his behaviour, not to let anyone notice a clear pattern emerging.

It was the first time he had travelled on the S-Bahn. Built long before the Wall had split the city in two, its snake-like tracks threaded backwards and forwards across the divided city without any regard for the arbitrary course of the border. It had presented the postwar rulers of the city with a practical dilemma which had been resolved by the simple expedient of allowing the whole network to be run from the Eastern Sector. And so it was that the railway continued to operate throughout the city, with trains shunting backwards and forwards across Berlin almost as if the Iron Curtain did not exist.

But not quite. One line of the S-Bahn which lay predominantly in West Berlin ran straight across a chunk of the city centre lying in the Eastern Sector. The stations along that section had been closed down, so that passengers travelling from the northern part of West Berlin through to the southern part had the eery experience of passing through a series of ghost stations which had seen no passengers on their platforms for several decades. As far as the railway network was concerned, the Friedrichstrasse Station was the Border. Citizens from West Berlin passed through it every day on through trains from one part of West Berlin to another without hindrance, but anyone alighting from the train at the station had to pass through the daunting gauntlet of East German customs control. The same of course applied in reverse, and many an East German must have lain in bed at night and dreamt of boarding a train at the Friedrichstrasse and travelling the short distance down the line to a new life on the other side of the Wall.

Reaching the station, he bought his ticket and boarded the train, jostling with the massed ranks of the weary rush hour crowds. Robert shuddered at the sheer familiarity of the scene, for the fact that the rush hour in East Berlin looked much the same as the rush hour in London or Paris or New York served only as a reminder that the inhabitants of East Berlin were much the same as the inhabitants of London or Paris or New York. The only essential difference was that these people were locked in behind a death strip and fifty thousand armed guards.

The train rattled noisily along towards the south-eastern outskirts of the city. In the distance he could just make out the lights twinkling in the tower blocks of some of the smarter residential districts of West Berlin. They must have been the ones Sonja had described to him, the ones she could see from the platforms on the raised sections of the line when she was working. From so far away, they looked like a kind of paradise, a world where all your troubles would somehow melt away. It was a complete illusion, of course: within those homes, just as much as within East Berlin homes, people squabbled and argued, had divorces and suffered bereavements. Yet by the very act of building the Wall, the East German authorities had succeeded in creating a myth about the West which was far more tempting than the reality could ever be.

The train pulled into Köpenick Station and Robert alighted. He was just about to leave the platform when he heard a voice behind him.

"Robert!"

He turned and saw the small figure of Sonja elbowing her way through the crowds towards him. She was wearing the dingy blue overalls she wore to work.

"Robert," she said when she finally reached him, "what are you doing here? What's happened to your car?"

Robert looked at her nervously.

"I didn't bring it."

She nodded.

"If you wait a few minutes I'll come with you. I come off duty at six."

The other passengers who had left the train were rapidly clearing the platform, leaving them alone together. But then a short middle-aged man dressed in the uniform of the railway staff emerged from a little office adjoining the platform and approached them. He did not look very happy.

"Frau Braun," he said to Sonja with scarcely an attempt at courtesy, "What are you doing?"

Sonja turned to him with a surly look.

"I'm talking to someone," she said. "I'm allowed to talk, aren't I?"

The man looked at her angrily.

"You are obviously allowed to talk, Frau Braun, but not when you are working."

"What the hell do you care?" she snapped. "I'll get your bloody toilets clean before I go, even if I do have to do it in my own time. I've been working since six this morning and I've got a right to talk for two minutes, even in this God-forsaken country."

Robert touched Sonja's arm, trying to calm her down. In the platform lights he could see that the man's face was rapidly turning red.

"You may be sure I will report your insolence to your superiors, Frau Braun," he hissed at her, turning and walking away down the platform. But he had only gone a few paces when he stopped and looked back.

"You're nothing but a worthless little slut," he snarled, "and a traitor to your country with it!"

Something suddenly snapped within Robert. Perhaps it was because of the nervous tension that had been building up within him over the last few days or perhaps it was simply because he felt sorry for Sonja's situation. He strode forward and caught hold of the man's arm.

"That's no way no speak to a lady," he said, his voice cold and angry. "I think you'd better apologise."

The man looked blankly at him for a moment, seemingly unable to comprehend what had just happened.

"And what, may I ask, has it got to do with you?"

"I have just heard you insult this lady. That's what it's got to do with me."

Now it was Sonja pulling at his arm.

"Stop it, Robert, there's no point," she said urgently.

"Who are you, anyway?" the man said angrily, pulling his arm free.

Robert fixed him with a penetrating glare. The situation was dangerous, yet having recovered a little from his initial uncontrolled anger, his brain was once again functioning normally.

"A witness to an incident," he said with an air of quiet authority. "And you should know that I have made a careful mental note of the number on that little red badge you are wearing."

The expression on the man's face suddenly changed. He was no longer angry, just plain scared.

"Perhaps I did overstep the mark," he mumbled. He turned to Sonja. "I apologise for those last remarks, Frau Braun."

Sonja looked at the man incredulously.

"That's all right," she said.

He was breathing more easily now.

"Provided that the toilets are in good order before you leave, I will consider the matter closed."

He turned and scurried quickly away down the platform, eventually disappearing from sight into his little office. When he had gone, Sonja started to snigger.

"How on earth did you do that?" she whispered.

"I think he knew he'd gone too far," Robert replied, himself surprised at the speed with which the man had capitulated. "He must have been afraid I'd report him."

"He's the station master here," Sonja explained, "but he's also a member of the District Party Committee. That's probably why he knows about my background. He's terribly proud of his position in the Party."

"You surely don't mean he actually likes it here," Robert exclaimed.

"Actually, I feel sorry for him," Sonja said quietly, and Robert was struck by the genuine look of compassion that came over her face.

"Why?"

"Different people cope with this country in different ways," she said, shrugging her shoulders.

"What do you mean?"

"Well, I'm one extreme: an outright enemy of the system and don't make any bones about it."

"I shouldn't think there are many people quite like you, Sonja."

She laughed.

"Lucky them. Anyway, it's just as well, they'd run out of toilets to clean."

"So are you saying that most East Germans are like that little rat in there?"

"Him. Oh no, he's pretty exceptional too. Most people are like my friend Heidi: amongst their friends they grumble and curse about all the stupidities and injustices of their everyday life and in the evening they watch West German television as a kind of release. But they'd never do anything active to change things or to escape."

She paused, and then gestured towards the little office.

"But there is a definite type like our friend here. He's the other extreme to me, which is probably why we get on so well together. His way of coping with life is to believe absolutely everything his government tells him."

"You're not serious!" Robert muttered, looking at the closed door behind which the man had scurried.

Sonja smiled sweetly. "Go and ask him yourself if you don't believe me. I'll introduce you."

Robert shook his head. He could never tell for sure whether Sonja was joking.

"Another day, perhaps. But you really think that deep down inside he thinks it's great here?"

"Yup. To him, the West is a den of inequity and exploitation in which the fat cats of capitalism live a life of unjustified luxury generated by the endless sweat of the downtrodden workers, while here in the East everything is always getting better and better under the enlightened rule of the working class. He knows it's true because he reads it every morning in his newspaper and he watches it every evening on his television."

"But surely he watches Western television too."

"Someone like him would run a mile to avoid watching a Western television programme. It would raise too many difficult questions. Don't you see, it's simply his way of coping with a lousy situation. It stops him getting hurt."

Robert thought for a moment. He could not help admiring the dispassionate way in which Sonja seemed able to analyse her own society, even though she had been so savagely treated by it.

"I can see that applies to him," Robert said, gesturing in the direction of the station master's office, "but what about someone like Lechner. He's one of the big bosses in the Ministry of Trade. Do you think your description of the station master would fit him too?"

Sonja thought for a minute before replying.

"I don't know your Lechner," she said, "but I can imagine the type you mean. I would guess he's probably in a fourth category, the special category of the ruling class. There's a fundamental difference between old dumbo in there and a member of the ruling class, and the difference is largely a material one. A station master in the West probably earns a packet compared to a station master in the East. So our friend has got to dupe himself into thinking he's better off here, because in reality he's much worse off. But your average senior Party boss, he's got a good lifestyle, he lives in a good house in Babelsberg, he has access to special health care, good schools, good restaurants, Western money which he can spend in the foreign currency shops. In short, he's got an awful lot to lose if the system collapses."

"So are you saying he believes in the system or not?" Robert interjected.

"Don't you see. For the party bosses it no longer matters, because they've got too much to lose. All that matters is that they pretend to believe. It's our station master here who's got to believe, precisely because he has absolutely nothing to lose."

Another train was drawing into the station, preparing to disgorge its quota of homeward-bound humans onto the empty platform.

"I'd better go and finish polishing up the gents," Sonja said with a smile, "or I might yet get the sack! Wait outside for me, will you?"

Robert nodded and walked off in the direction of the exit. As he passed the window of the station master's office, he could just see the frightened little man's face peering nervously at him through the glass.

It was not long before Sonja had finished her work and emerged from the station, her blue overalls replaced by a warm winter coat. As Robert watched her approaching he longed to get back to her flat and make love to her, slowly peeling off the many layers of clothes in which she was clad to reveal the soft and tender human form beneath.

Sonja came up and kissed him on the cheek.

"I'm afraid you can't just yet," she said with a grin, "I've promised we'll go to Heidi's this evening."

Robert smiled. He was gradually getting used to the disconcerting manner in which Sonja would read his most intimate thoughts and then pass comment on them. He took her by the hand.

"Later, then," he said quietly, giving her hand a squeeze.

Sonja looked up at him and smiled.

They started to walk in the direction of Heidi's flat.

"Heidi's pretty efficient," Sonja explained, "unless something's cropped up to stop her she'll have done what she said she'd do."

They walked in silence for a while. Finally it was Sonja who spoke.

"Robert?"

"Yes."

"It's a bit awkward, and it's not necessary, but you couldn't give her a little something, could you?"

Robert looked at her.

"Heidi, you mean?"

"Yes, Heidi. I mean she's doing it for me, really. I've done her a few favours in the past. You know, things like babysitting and so on. But it would still be nice."

Robert put his arm around her.

"It's all right, I'd already thought of that. I've bought her little boy a big mountain of Lego. It's in my briefcase."

A look of relief came over Sonja's face.

"That's lovely, Robert. It's the ultimate children's status symbol in these parts. She'll like that."

He looked at her fondly. Over the past few days he had realised that the girl possessed considerably greater powers of tact than he had at first supposed. She had never asked about his work and, perhaps more strikingly, she had never asked him to explain his family connections with Berlin. She knew he had an aunt from Köpenick, she knew it was important for him to trace that aunt, and that was all she seemed to want to know.

Robert wondered why he didn't tell her the whole truth. He nearly had on the first day they had met and the fact that the complete story of his early origins had not come tumbling out was little more than coincidental. But since then he had become a little more restrained in his dealings with her. Without really knowing why, he felt with Sonja as if they were on a long sea journey together to a distant continent. At the end of the journey they would disembark at different ports in different countries and would in all likelihood never set eyes on one another again. To get too close was likely to be dangerous and could only lead to unnecessary hurt: better simply to live each day as it came and be happy.

In Robert's mind the most perplexing thing was that just at the moment he didn't seem to find the idea of living one day at a time particularly distressing. He was normally such a calculating man, and ever since his schooldays he had planned his life years in advance. Yet although he found the sudden sponteneity in his life rather disconcerting, he also found it strangely exhilarating.

They had arrived at the building where Heidi lived and started climbing the interminable stairs. Robert could not help noticing that he was beginning to find climbing stairs easier: was it possible he was actually getting fitter? Heidi was waiting by the open front door as they trudged up the last flight.

"Hi, I thought I heard you coming," she smiled, shepherding them through to her cosy book-lined living room. Hansel was sitting on the floor fingering a large heap of old wooden bricks with a bored expression on his face, but as soon as he saw Sonja he stood up and ran over to her, jumping up to hang onto her neck as she bent down to greet him.

Heidi looked at Hansel with a long-suffering look.

"He's been grumbling and moaning ever since I picked him up from the nursery," she complained, "so I'm glad you're here. You always seem to cheer him up."

Sonja held him up in the air and pretended to look sternly at him.

"You've not been causing trouble for your poor mummy, have you, Hansel?"

Robert reached into his bag and pulled out the large box of brightly coloured Lego bricks. He gave it to Heidi.

"Perhaps this will help keep him quiet," he said, "it's just a little something to say 'thank you.'"

Heidi looked at the box and smiled kindly at Robert.

"Thanks. That's very kind of you. He'll love it."

She gave Robert back the box.

"Why don't you give it to him yourself?"

The boy had been tracking the Lego excitedly round the room with his eyes ever since Robert had produced it from his briefcase and he clutched eagerly at the proffered toy. Without further ado he scuttled off across the room to unpack his unexpected gift, leaving the old bricks forgotton on the floor.

Heidi fetched three beers from the kitchen and came back.

"Do you drink beer?" she asked Robert.

"Thanks," he said.

"The brewery's just round the corner," she said, pouring out the beers and passing them round. "It's not that bad, all things considered."

"I did it," she said at last when she had finished distributing the drinks.

Sonja looked at her.

"You found his aunt?" she asked.

"Well, I found one hundred and forty-three married ladies by the name of Katherina Hagenau, complete with ages and addresses. I suppose one of them might conceivably be Robert's aunt."

Robert thanked her. But inside he became aware of the same sensation of sinking helplessness that had come over him the night in the telephone box. One hundred and forty-three was too many.

Sonja must have seen the expression on his face.

"You've got to narrow it down, Robert, you can't possibly visit all one hundred and forty-three."

"Heidi," Robert asked, "have you got the list?"

"Yup," she said, leaving the room and returning a few moments later with a small notepad filled with handwritten ages and addresses. "Here you are, it's yours." She held out the book for him to take but as he did so she placed her hand on his arm. "Sonja says I can trust you and I do. But please be careful with it. I'll be in a lot of trouble if they find out I've done this."

Robert looked at the girl for a moment. She had taken an enormous risk for him, and unlike Sonja she could ill afford to lose what little security she had built for herself.

"I will be," he said. "I'm used to keeping secrets."

He turned to the book and eagerly started flicking through the pages.

"Some of them are too young," he murmured.

"I thought I'd let you sort them out. You know who you're looking for."

"How old was your aunt?" Sonja asked.

Robert thought for a moment.

"I don't know," he said, "but I may be able to make a pretty good estimate."

He didn't know exactly how old she was, but he should be able to work it out give or take a few years. He had been born in 1943 and he knew from his father's account that his real mother, Katherina Hagenau's younger sister, had been fairly young at the time when he had met her. That meant, perhaps, that she was between twenty and thirty at the end of the war. But the old man he had visited who had known her in the late 1930's had also spoken of her as a young woman and not as a child. So if she had been over eighteen when she left Krämerstrasse in 1938 then she would certainly have been over twenty-five by the end of the war. So that narrowed down his mother's age to between twenty-five and thirty in 1945 – in other words between fifty-eight and sixty-three in 1978.

But how much should he add to get the sister's age, that was the tricky question. When the old man had known her in the 1930's she had already had three children, at least some of whom had been old enough to play independently with his own children in the communal hall, so she must have been considerably older than Robert's mother. A fair guess would be between five years and ten years older.

Robert reached into his suit pocket and pulled out a pen and a scrap of paper. Adding five years to the lower estimate of his mother's age of fifty-eight and ten years to the higher figure of sixty-three, he jotted the answers down.

"At a guess," he said, pausing to check the arithmetic, "I'd say we're looking for someone between the ages of sixty-three and seventy-three."

Sonja grabbed the little notebook from his lap.

"Give it to me," she said, "I'll see who I can find for you."

It took her only a few minutes to go through the names. Every now and then she tore out a page from the notebook and put it in a small heap on the arm of the sofa. By the time she had finished there were six slips of paper in the heap.

"Six people," she said. "Six people in the right age group."

Robert picked up the little pile of addresses. One of these addresses might conceivably be the home of his mother's sister. He looked carefully through the pile and finally pulled out a single address. Heidi and Sonja looked at him expectantly.

"I wonder if it's this one?" he said quietly.

"Why that one?" Sonja asked.

"Because she's the only one of these six women who lives in Berlin. And what's more, she lives right here in Köpenick."

* * * * * *

Robert looked at the door of the flat and suddenly felt extremely stupid. Sitting in Heidi's living room two hours earlier it had seemed so logical, but now he was actually there, ready to knock on the prim front door with a metal plate neatly inscribed with the words 'Katherina Hagenau', he began to doubt that his search could be so nearly at an end.

He knocked loudly on the door. There was no reply. He knocked again. Perhaps she was out. He cursed inwardly. It was Wednesday evening: Kate was not due back until the following Tuesday but he was well aware that Angus had meant what he said about expelling him from the mission as a diplomatic ruse. It was possible he would be on a plane back to England the following morning.

The flat was on the second floor of the block and he could hear someone slowly making their way up the stairs. His heart skipped a beat. Perhaps this was her. An elderly lady came around the corner of the stairs and into sight, dragging a heavy load of shopping. She looked up when she saw Robert.

"Excuse me," he said politely, "but are you Katherina Hagenau?"

The woman's face showed surprise.

"Not me. I was her neighbour, poor dear."

What did she mean 'was'?

"Has she left?"

The lady carried on dragging her bags up the last few stairs.

"You could say that," she said. "Are you a friend of hers?"

"Not a friend. More a friend of a friend."

"You didn't know, then? She's passed away, she has."

Robert glanced at the door.

"But it says her name here. On the door."

The woman laughed.

"Give 'em a chance," she said, "the poor dear only died yesterday. For all I know, she's still in there."

Robert looked back at the front door. It was not possible. Surely it could not be true.

"But she can't have. Not yesterday."

"Well, she hadn't been well for a long time. Something to do with the arteries. I think it was her heart that finally gave up. But it's a pity you didn't get here a few days ago, that's for sure."

The lady had opened the door of her own flat and was about to disappear inside.

"Can you tell me anything about her?"

The lady turned and shrugged.

"Not a lot," she said, "she used to keep herself to herself of late. She was a pretty lonely old soul. What did you want to know?"

Robert thought hard. His only decent lead was about to slip away and he didn't even know if the dead lady was his aunt or someone else altogether.

"Did she have any children?" he blurted out.

"Children? Well, if she did have some children they weren't a lot of use to her. You know, I had to help her whenever she needed anything heavy done in her flat. She couldn't manage, the poor dear."

"Did she have a sister? A husband? Anyone?"

"Well, there was one woman who used to visit her sometimes, but not very often. It might have been a sister, I suppose."

"What was her name? Do you know the name of the woman who might have been her sister?"

The woman's eyes flashed at him suspiciously.

"You're asking an awful lot of questions for a friend of a friend."

Robert checked himself. There was no point in pushing his luck too far.

"They'll want to know," he muttered unconvincingly.

"If they're a friend of hers they'd know that sort of thing already," she said.

Robert mumbled some thanks to the woman for her help and started down the stairs. He was furiously angry with himself. If only he had got there a few days before, he may have found the answers that he wanted. Yet now he couldn't even be sure it was the right woman. By the sounds of it she may have had a sister, but then on the other hand she didn't seem to have any children. And yet the old man had been sure that his aunt had had three children.

He started walking disconsolately in the direction of Sonja's flat. He had promised her that he would come round as soon as he had visited the address, but he wanted to be alone for a while. He needed time to think, time to work out what, if anything, he could do about the increasingly absurd situation in which he now found himself. Perhaps it was still not too late to call off this ridiculous search for a mother who had probably died over thirty years before in a Russian army transport. Perhaps it was still not too late to carry on with his life as before.

He could see the S-Bahn station on the other side of the road and stopped dead. He was taking the most absurd risk by sleeping at Sonja's. For all he knew she really was a member of the State Security Service; after all, she wouldn't tell him, would she? And even if she wasn't and the British security team at the Embassy found out what he was up to at night, it would most certainly be the end of any hopes of advancement in the Service.

There was no point in dragging it out. It wasn't going anywhere. Kate would be back on Tuesday and in any case he'd soon be recalled to London. Robert could feel his briefcase in his hand: he had all of his office papers with him and he was wearing his suit and coat. There were only a very few unimportant things of his in her room.

He remembered Sonja's words after their first night together. She had told him herself to go, to leave the memory of something good unsullied by a bitter ending. She was a clever girl, maybe she had been right. He crossed the road and entered the station, joining the small queue of people waiting for tickets. It was hard to leave Sonja. At this very moment she was probably having a shower and getting ready for his return.

"Well, mate?"

He was at the front of the queue.

"The Friedrichstrasse, please. A single."

He handed the man the money and waited while he stamped out the ticket. Then he wearily climbed up the steps to the platform.

On the other side of the track he could see the place where he had stood with Sonja only a few hours before, laughing and joking with her about the ridiculous little bureaucrat who ran the station. Tomorrow she would be here again, puzzled and perhaps a little hurt by the manner of Robert's departure, and the man would no doubt take his revenge on her, aware that her powerful protector was no longer within earshot.

It was the first rule of diplomacy to keep a sense of detachment from the foreign countries in which you worked, and Robert knew full well that he had already broken that rule several times since being posted to East Germany. But as he thought about the life to which Sonja was doomed he realised that he hated the country in which he found himself with a deep and profound loathing. Pacing up and down the platform, he could not wait for the train to arrive. With luck, by tomorrow evening he would be on a plane back to England, the kids, his interesting job, and everything he had always valued so dearly.

The train appeared in the distance and Robert waited impatiently while it approached, rattling jerkily along the track. Why did it have to be so incredibly slow? Didn't the driver realise people were in a hurry? The whole idea of searching out a mother he could not even remember had been a completely ridiculous one, starting an affair with a young girl like Sonja had been equally stupid, and the best thing he could do now was sober up as quickly as possible and stop all this silly nonsense once and for all.

The train ground to a halt and the doors opened. Robert waited while two elderly women got off, one supporting the other by the arm.

Robert stared at them.

"My God!" he said out loud in English, and the ladies turned to glance at him in surprise before continuing on their way. It was utterly obvious. How could he have been so incredibly stupid?

The doors of the train slammed shut and it started rattling out of the station. But Robert was not on it. He was standing alone, staring after the two old women walking down the platform together towards the exit.

* * * * * *

"Do you want to stop, Robert?" Sonja said softly. "I don't mind if you do, you know."

For a few moments Robert ignored her words, trying desperately to reach the climax that had for so long evaded him, but then he gave up and pulled himself free of her, lying back on the covers and staring glumly at the ceiling.

"I'm sorry," he said. "It's not your fault, Sonja."

"I know it isn't, Robert. I'm not stupid."

He turned his head and looked at her soft naked body lying next to his on the bed.

"Do you want to talk about it?" she said quietly.

Robert put his arm around her and pulled her to him.

"I don't know," he said.

"Is it because she died?"

Robert shrugged.

"I really don't know why it is?"

Sonja looked at him, her gentle eyes fixed on his.

"You nearly left me today, didn't you?"

"Yes," he said, finding himself unable to lie. "How did you know?"

"A single ticket from Köpenick to the Friedrichstrasse Station fell out of your trouser pocket when you were taking them off. It's got the date and the time stamped on it."

"I thought it might be for the best," he said.

Sonja buried her head in his chest.

"So why did you change your mind?"

"It's not easy to explain, Sonja. I don't really understand what's going on at the moment. My life always seemed so well organised, and now it's all gone crazy. Maybe I was just trying to pull it straight again and simply failed."

There was a long silence. It was finally Sonja who spoke.

"You never loved your wife, did you?"

Robert looked at her. He had always assumed that he had loved Kate, that despite everything he still did love her. They had been through a lot together.

"No," he said. "Now that you say it I don't suppose I did."

"I don't understand how it's possible to marry someone and live with them for year after year without loving them. Why did you do it?"

"She seemed right at the time. She fitted in with what I wanted. And she's never let me down."

Sonja sat up in bed, her face turning red with anger.

"How can you say that?" she fumed. "If she'd never let you down you wouldn't be screwing me, would you? Of course she's let you down."

Robert looked up at her. He really didn't have the energy to get agitated.

"It's not her fault, that's all I'm saying."

"So whose fault is it?"

"Mine, of course. Who else's?"

"So what are you going to do about it?"

"That's just the point, Sonja. I don't know what I'm going to do about anything any more. I just don't have the foggiest idea. When I was standing on that damned platform earlier on I thought I did know, I thought I wanted to get the hell out of this God-forsaken country and get back to my own life and my own future once and for all. But then the train came and I didn't get on it. I seem to be set on a crazy kind of self-destruct course at the moment and I can't shake free."

The anger passed and Sonja started to laugh.

"You really are like me, you know, Robert. Only maybe I'm just a little bit further down that self-destruct road than you are."

He looked at her for a moment. Why was it people did such crazy things? Sonja could have had an easy enough life, working in a little library, married to a good husband and bringing up a family of loving children. She had had it all set up, the whole thing, until she had walked into a police station one day and chucked it all away for a dismal and uncertain future. Perhaps she was right and that was what they had in common, a kind of dogged refusal to take the easy way out.

* * * * * *

Robert sat at his desk nervously fingering his pen. He had to be in Köpenick by two o'clock, but that was exactly when the next negotiating session at the Ministry of Trade was due to begin. In some ways it would have been easier if the Ambassador had sprung his expulsion plan into action during the morning, since at least then the meeting would have been called off, but Angus had sidled conspiratorially into the office about an hour before and told Robert in a whisper that no word had yet been received from the traffic department and that the meeting in the afternoon would therefore go ahead as planned.

It was gone twelve o'clock and the time for indecision was past. He put down his pen and walked the short distance along the corridor to the Ambassador's office. When he entered, Angus was sitting at his desk reading the day's issue of 'Neues Deutschland', the official Party newspaper.

"Ah, thank goodness," he said with relief as Robert knocked and entered the room, "an excuse for me to stop this purgatory. Why oh why can't they write something interesting for a change? All this stuff about bumper harvests on the collective farms and doom and gloom in the capitalist West."

Robert took a deep breath.

"I'm afraid I can't attend the working party this afternoon, Angus. I'm feeling absolutely dreadful."

Angus put the paper down and looked at Robert with concern.

"Oh dear," he said, "you poor man. What's the trouble?"

"I've got the most awful stomach ache and I think I might be developing a fever."

Angus grinned.

"Probably too many Chinese take-aways from those sleazy joints on the Kurfürstendamm while Kate's away. Oh well, never mind, we'll manage. In fact, it'll give me another excuse to stall over those negotiations." A thought occurred to him and he chuckled to himself. "A diplomatic tummy-ache, you might say."

Robert tried to smile but it didn't quite work. Angus looked at him.

"You do look pretty dreadful, come to think of it. You'd better go straight home and get to bed. I'll deal with everything here."

"Thanks, Angus. I'm sorry to have to let you down."

Angus grinned broadly.

"That's all right. Reminds me of the time when I was in Rangoon as a young man. I'd only just arrived and was really trying to impress everyone with my elegant appearance, sizzling intellect and suave sophistication. But almost within hours of getting off the plane my stomach started turning inside out. I was booked to go to a diplomatic reception in the evening with all the Burmese bignobs, and I should have called it off, but I didn't want to look silly so I struggled along. They kept plying me with all this exotic food from one of those sumptuous banquets they lay on out there and I felt I really couldn't refuse without causing offence. But you know it was all the most catastrophic disaster, because half an hour after arriving, just when I was being introduced to the Deputy Foreign Minister, I suddenly threw up all over the carpet!"

Angus stopped abruptly.

"Sorry, Robert, you don't really want to listen to my ramblings when you're feeling so unwell, do you? So off you go, and I'll just settle back to another few pages of over-fulfilled plan targets."

Robert nodded and left the room. That had not been easy. He had never in his life faked an illness to get out of doing something and had always taken a pretty dim view of those who did.

He collected his briefcase and left the building. It had started to snow again, and for a moment he dithered, uncertain of whether to go by car or by train. Stupid. He should definitely take the car, otherwise someone from the Embassy might wonder why he had not taken it back to his flat with him.

By the time he had reached his car the snow was falling more heavily, and as he started driving the windscreen wipers could only just cope with what was rapidly turning into a blizzard. In a few hours he would know; he would either have found the mother from whom he had been dragged away in a dirty Russian field hospital in 1945 or he would have to give up the search for good.

He wondered what she would look like if he found her. For the last three years he had imagined her in his mind's eye as a young woman, as she must have been at the time when he had last seen her. But that was clearly no longer true. If not an old lady, she would certainly be a woman of mature years. But would she be tall, would she be short, what colour hair would she have, what colour eyes would she have? He had no recollection of his father saying anything much about her appearance and he had no idea of what she would look like.

The car was approaching Köpenick and Robert pulled over to the side of the road near a passer-by. Winding down the window, he cursed inwardly as the snow started driving into his face.

"Excuse me!" he called to a tense-looking middle-aged woman walking down the road with a large shopping bag.

The woman came over to him.

"Yes."

"Can you tell me where the crematorium is, please?"

"The crematorium. Yes, it's just round the corner – look, over by that big building."

"Thanks," he muttered, winding up the window again.

As the two old ladies on the train had made him realise, his search for his mother might very nearly be at an end. For if the Katherina Hagenau whose flat he had visited really had been his aunt, then her sister was almost certain to attend the funeral. It had only taken a brief telephone call to the crematorium to establish that the dead woman's final send-off was scheduled for two o'clock.

The crematorium building itself was situated down a side-road on the right of the main road, but Robert turned his car into a road on the left-hand side before parking it. With a sinking feeling, he realised that he was increasingly behaving like a fugitive, always looking over his shoulder, always trying to evade the eyes of the hidden watchers, wherever and whoever they might be.

He shut the thoughts away and got out of the car into the driving snow. The cold air helped him to concentrate. There were only a few other people on the streets, but as he walked briskly along he found himself looking at all of them, particularly if they were walking in the same direction as he was. Perhaps they too were going to the crematorium; if so, perhaps they were among his true relations.

He arrived at the gates of a large building with an ominous-looking chimney from which a thin trail of smoke snaked its way up into the grey winter sky. A sign on the gate confirmed that this was the crematorium, and the smoke seemed to indicate that an earlier party had just finished their business in the place. He walked through the gates and found himself outside an imposing door with a large sign explaining that it was the public entrance. The notice also pointed out that the rear entrance was for use by the deceased and Robert could not help a wry smile at the thought of the dead having to use the tradesmen's entrance when they were, after all, the guests of honour.

He entered the door set aside for the living and was greeted by a short man in uniform sitting behind a little desk.

"Who are you for?" he asked, not meaning to sound as bureaucratic as he did.

"Katherina Hagenau."

The man gestured politely to a door on the left. "Over there, room three. Two o'clock."

Robert pushed open the indicated door and went inside.

The hall was larger than he had supposed, like a modern secular church with seats arranged in neat rows on either side of a broad central aisle. At the front was a raised platform on which lay a coffin and behind the coffin hung a delicately positioned red curtain which presumably concealed the oven.

It was still only a quarter past one and, besides Robert, the occupant of the coffin was the only person in the room. He walked slowly up the aisle and stood beside the plain wooden box.

"Is it really you I was supposed to go to all those years ago?" he murmured gently. "And how different my life would have been if you had been there to take me in your arms."

He stood for a long time gazing down at the coffin and then turned away. Even if it was the body of his real aunt that lay within, she was no longer there. For her he had come too late.

He looked at his watch and saw that it was now nearly a quarter to two. Surely he was not going to be the only person at the cremation. He returned to the back of the room and chose a seat well over to one side, almost as far away from the coffin as it was possible to be. If people did start arriving, he wanted to be the one who would decide when to make the moves.

The door opened and Robert turned to look. An old couple entered and made their way slowly to the front of the room, nodding politely to Robert as they passed. A few minutes later two elderly women entered arm in arm, and then a group of about seven or eight people. Robert stared at them in consternation. They were all fairly old, and most of them were women. Any one of the women could in principle have been his mother. Yet people were continuing to flow into the room, and by now there must have been about twenty people sitting in the chairs near the coffin with yet more entering the door with every passing minute.

The neighbour had spoken of the dead woman as if she had had few friends and Robert had been expecting only a few people at the funeral, not a packed audience.

Another old couple entered and sat in the row immediately in front of Robert.

"There's a good turnout, isn't there, dear?" the man said to his wife.

"Always is when someone at the Club pops off," she replied. "It's only right to come and say goodbye."

So that was it. She must have been a member of a local old folks club. Most of these people must have been from the club.

The door opened again and a man appeared. Although of roughly the same age as the other people present, in other respects he appeared strikingly different. He was wearing a smart Western coat of a similar cut to Robert's own, and his eyes, which were almost hidden behind spectacles, looked alert and keenly intelligent. The rest of his face was cloaked by a full beard and moustache. The newcomer glanced quickly around the room and then started moving silently down the back row of chairs, sitting down a few places away from Robert.

It must have been two o'clock because a small man wearing the sober clothing of a protestant minister entered from a side door and approached what looked like a lectern to one side of the raised platform supporting the coffin. He shuffled some papers around on the lectern and waited for the room to fall silent.

"Dearly beloved," he began, "we are gathered here today to bid farewell to Katherina Hagenau, whom we all knew so well. I know that she was a dear friend to many of you as she was to me and that she will be sorely missed by us all . . ."

Robert listened attentively as the pastor spoke. Perhaps here he would find the proof that he was looking for. But for a long time the man recounted little details about the dead woman's warm personality and her recent activities in the old people's club.

The pastor paused for thought.

"When we remember the little kindnesses that she showed us and the patient forbearance with which she would always find time to listen to our own troubles, it is as well to remember that her own life had been so full of tragedy. Her three children were killed not far from this very spot during a terrible accident at the end of the war and her husband was maimed most horribly at the battle of Stalingrad and did not long survive the end of hostilities . . ."

Robert sat bolt upright in his chair. That surely was the proof he had been looking for. This was indeed the body of his aunt.

The minister was drawing to a close.

". . . and so it is that we consign her body to eternal rest."

As he spoke the last words gentle piped music began to play and the coffin began to role slowly backwards towards the red curtains, which drew slightly apart to let it pass through to the furnace beyond.

The music stopped and the congregation started to rise from their seats. Robert looked around in panic.

The astute-looking man sitting next to him was rising to leave and glanced in his direction.

Robert grabbed his chance.

"Excuse me," he said to the man. "Do you know, did the deceased have a sister, a sister called Frieda?"

The man did not reply straight away. His face looked distant and distraught, as if he had been deeply upset by the funeral.

"I'm sorry," Robert said, "I know it's a bad time to ask, but I must know."

"A sister?" the man replied.

"Yes. A sister called Frieda."

The man's eyes flicked across the room and back again.

"She's there," he said quietly, "just getting up in the front row. You see, the one all by herself."

"Thanks," Robert muttered, but the man was already shuffling off towards the central aisle.

Robert turned and stared. For three years he had wondered what this moment would be like, and now it had finally arrived.

It should have been obvious to him from the moment she had walked through the door that it was his mother. He could recognise so much of himself, and even of his own children, in the outline of her face. She was standing now, next to the place where the coffin had lain, gazing quietly at the curtain behind which her sister had vanished for ever, dabbing her eye from time to time with a small white handkerchief. Robert stood and watched her for a long time, and as he watched her he knew with utter certainty that he had been right to search her out. He had felt in recent days as if his sanity had been falling apart, as if he had been risking everything he possessed in search of a ghost. But the woman standing only a few yards in front of him was no ghost, she was his own mother, the woman who had loved and cared for him under the most difficult of circumstances when he was at his most vulnerable. And it was not his search for her that had been madness, but rather his prolonged attempt to evade that search.

His mother finally turned away from the place where her sister's body had lain and started walking slowly down the aisle towards the entrance. Most of the other people had left, and she glanced at Robert as she passed him. But her face showed no glimmer of recognition.

He waited until she had left and then followed her outside into the snow. She had pulled her coat up high around her shoulders to stop her neck from getting wet and was walking quickly towards the outer gate of the crematorium grounds. He started to run towards her, only stopping when he was several yards away.

"Mutti!" he called out in German, deliberately using the familiar form of the word.

She turned to see who was calling out and saw that it was her he was addressing.

"I think you are my mother," he blurted out, unable to think of anything more appropriate.

His mother continued to stare, and Robert wondered for a moment whether she had heard him properly.

"Heinrich?" she said, her voice uncertain and her face confused.

"I don't know. I mean, I don't know what my real name is. You used to call me 'little mouse'."

She walked slowly towards him, her face transfixed.

"Is it really you?" she said quietly, still trying to absorb the fact that he was there. "I thought that you were dead."

The snow was driving down hard but Robert could see tears of infinite relief beginning to run down her face, as if the accumulated guilt and sorrow of over thirty years was being washed away into the snow. He gently put his arms around her and held her close to him until her sobbing had eased.

It was many minutes before she pulled herself away.

"How strange that you should come on such a day," she said, looking tenderly into his eyes, eyes that she must once have known so intimately.

"On the day of your sister's funeral?"

"Yes. You see, I always assumed that you had been killed by the same bomb that had killed her own children."

Robert remembered the pastor's words during the funeral oration.

"A bomb? But her house was already in ruins when I got there."

"I know. It had been flattened during the final Russian bombardment of Berlin. But that wasn't the bomb I'm talking about. Katherina and her children had moved in with some other homeless families in the cellar of a building a few streets away. On the day when I sent you to Köpenick she was out from early in the day looking for food. When she came home that evening she found that the cellar had collapsed under countless tons of rubble, killing everyone within. Someone must have accidentally triggered an unexploded bomb. Because I could never trace you I always assumed that you must have found that place, that some neighbours in Krämerstrasse had sent you there, and that I had sent you to your death."

Robert stared at her in horror. For thirty-three years she had had to carry that thought with her, the terrible thought that by sending him to her sister's house she had been condemning him to death. He opened his wallet and pulled out the ageing piece of paper on which she had written her sister's address that fine spring day in April 1945.

"It's all I had," he said, "all I had to find you with."

She took the little piece of paper and stared at it for a long time.

"You have no idea how many nights I have lain in bed and been unable to sleep for thinking about this piece of paper and what I came to believe had flowed from it," she said finally.

Robert took the paper back. Little flakes of snow were settling on it and slowly melting, causing the ink to run and the words to fade. For years it had haunted them both, yet now it seemed utterly unimportant. He stuffed it into his pocket.

Taking his mother's arm, he steered her towards the street. They had to find somewhere warm to talk. After all, they both had a lifetime to discover.

* * * * * *

Robert waved farewell as the train jerked into motion. His mother stood by the window, waving back, trying unsuccessfully to hold back the tears in her eyes. It was not long before she was gone from view, but he remained for a long time on the platform as the train pulled away into the distance, until finally that too had disappeared from sight and he was left alone with nothing but his thoughts.

He turned and walked slowly back along the platform to the station concourse. He had found her, he had found his own mother after a separation of over thirty-three years, and he should by rights have been happy beyond measure. But although he had been successful in one search, the meeting with his mother had made him realise that he had to start on another infinitely more difficult one. He had to search for himself.

It was the same problem he had encountered so many times before in the last three years. Every time he found the answer to one question, another more difficult and intractable one seemed to arise. But whereas he had been able to find his mother by applying his intellect, he was far less certain of how to resolve his growing doubts about himself.

He thought of turning to Sonja for help. But deep down he knew that Sonja could not help him now as she had helped him before. She had her own very different problems and, good friend though she was, he sensed that his relationship with her was more a symptom of his condition than a part of the cure. Wearily, he lowered himself onto a bench in the middle of the concourse and closed his eyes. All around him, he could hear the bustle of the surging crowds: it was somehow soothing, a reminder that he was not alone.

His mother had told him so much that it was hard to absorb it all at once. She lived in a small village set in the hill country known as the Thuringian Forest which dominates the southern part of East Germany. Her husband, Robert's natural father, about whom she had said very little, had died before the end of war and she had single-handedly brought up Robert's younger sister Ingrid, who still lived with her. By her account, things had been very hard for many years, but then life had gradually started to improve when Ingrid was coming to the end of her time in secondary school towards the end of the 1950's.

His mother was evidently proud of her daughter's achievements: after leaving school, she had won a place at a prestigious university to study Physics, and after successfully completing a doctorate in the Soviet Union had managed against overwhelming odds to land a job at one of the major scientific research institutes in East Germany where she had been working ever since. And yet, despite her pride, his mother seemed anxious about Ingrid's future: she was now thirty-three years old and still single, and it was clear that her mother was beginning to despair of ever seeing any grandchildren.

It was when they had spoken of grandchildren that Robert had begun to realise the unreal nature of the situation in which he now found himself. He had told her that she had two fine grandsons of whom she could be proud and she had spoken of how dearly she would like to meet them. And then he had been forced to explain that that would never be possible, that even if he himself could continue by some subterfuge to stay in contact with her over the years, he could never risk telling his children that she existed. She had listened in silence and had not brought the subject up again, but however hard she tried to hide her feelings, he could tell that he had hurt her very deeply.

A few minutes before she had left, when they had been saying goodbye only a few yards distant from where he was now sitting, she had taken out a small piece of paper from her handbag and written her address on it.

"Heinrich," she had said, giving him the address, "I know from all you have told me that you may not be able to see me again for a very long time, perhaps never, but you must know that whatever happens, there will always be a welcome for you at my home."

Robert shuddered as he remembered her uttering those words. It was obscene that he should torment a woman who had suffered the pain of separation for so many years in such a way. Yet there was no escaping the brutal fact that the consequences of honesty could be simply catastrophic.

* * * * * *

Robert fumbled for the keys of his flat and opened the door. He had agreed with Sonja that he would not come to her flat that night but would visit her at the weekend. He was, after all, supposed to be lying in bed recovering from a dreadful stomach bug.

He was half-way down the hall when he caught sight of the piece of paper lying near the door. He picked it up and cast his eye quickly over the hurriedly scribbled words.

"Shit!" he cursed loudly, screwing the paper up into a tight ball and slinging it violently across the hall. "Shit and damn!"

Why on earth did they have to be such bloody nice people? Why couldn't they just leave him alone?

Recovering his composure, he picked up the little ball of paper and went through to the desk in the living room, helping himself on the way to a large Scotch to steady his nerves. Unscrewing the note, he carefully read it through again. It was written by Mrs Mac-Phearson and at the top she had put the time - three o'clock. 'Dear Robert,' it began, 'Angus gave me a ring and told me you were poorly so I thought I'd pop round and see if I could do anything to help. I expect you are at the doctor's or something. Give me a ring when you get in.'

Robert looked at his watch. She had come at three o'clock, yet now it was nearly nine; rather a long time to be at the doctor's. Nervously he picked up the telephone and dialled the MacPhearson's home number. To his relief, it was Mrs MacPhearson rather than the Ambassador who answered.

"Hallo, it's me, Robert."

"Robert! Oh that's good," she said with obvious relief. "Are you all right?"

"Yes, I'm fine," he said, trying hard to sound as if he was just recovering from a nasty illness. "I've only just found your note."

"We've been so dreadfully worried. We couldn't think what had happened to you."

"I was at the doctor's earlier and your note slipped under a piece of furniture so I couldn't see it. That's why I've only just found it."

"Well, I just wanted to check that you were all right and see if you wanted me to do anything – you know, some shopping or something."

"It's very sweet of you, Mrs MacPhearson, very sweet indeed. But I'm feeling much better now, thank you. In fact, you can tell Angus that I'll be back at work first thing tomorrow morning."

"Ah, that's fine. That's really fine," she said. "But you'd still better look after yourself, you know, or you'll suffer a relapse - so no more shifting furniture around in your condition."

Robert grimaced.

"I promise, Mrs MacPhearson, I promise. Goodnight."

* * * * * *

Robert picked up the phone in his office and pressed the button to summon his secretary.

"Yes, Mr Stanton," came the crisp voice from the outer office.

"Miss Drummond, would you be so kind as to phone the Interhotel in Oberhof and book me a room for tonight and tomorrow."

"Certainly, Mr Stanton. For tonight and Saturday. Is it just you going?"

"Yes, Miss Drummond, just me."

"Official business?"

"No, I'll be paying for it myself."

"I'll confirm the reservation when I've booked it. Do you want me to make a train reservation too?"

"No thanks. I'm going in my own car."

"Very good, Mr Stanton."

The line clicked dead. Robert rose from his chair and started nervously pacing the room.

There was a knock on the door and the Ambassador strolled in.

"Hallo, Robert, how are you this morning?" he began.

"Oh, much better thanks. It was good of you and your wife to be so concerned about me."

"Oh, that's nothing. What did the doctor think you had?"

"He seemed to agree with your diagnosis about the Chinese take-away."

"Oh well, make sure you have a good rest this weekend, won't you?"

"I will. I've decided to spend a couple of nights down in Thuringia, at the Interhotel in Oberhof."

If Angus was surprised, he didn't show it.

"Oberhof!" he said with a smile, "Not a bad spot by East German standards. I've stayed there myself a couple of times. Quite passable skiing, I believe."

"I know, but I won't be doing any skiing. I just want to get away from the city and breathe in a bit of fresh mountain air, that's all."

"Oh well," Angus remarked, "just as well the old rat-bags at the Ministry of the Interior haven't got around to reporting your traffic offence yet. Maybe the crafty buggers have sensed my little plan and decided to drop the whole thing."

And with that the Ambassador turned on his heel and strode briskly out of the room.

Robert picked up the phone and called the outer office.

"Yes, Mr Stanton."

"Have you confirmed the booking yet?"

"Yes, Mr Stanton. Two nights, room and breakfast, starting tonight. I told them you may be arriving fairly late."

"Miss Drummond, can you give me an outside line, please, I want to phone England."

From his wallet, he pulled out the piece of paper on which he had scribbled Kate's parent's telephone number in Suffolk and nervously dialled the number. Kate could have been trying to get hold of him unsuccessfully at the flat for several days, and in any case he just had to tell her he was going to be away all weekend.

After what seemed like an interminable wait, it was Kate herself who picked up the phone.

"Hallo, Kate Stanton speaking."

"Hallo, Kate, it's me. How are you, love?"

"I'm fine, Robert, fine. How are you, darling?"

Robert was silent for a moment. He had been bracing himself for indifference, anger, even a total refusal to speak to him, but Kate didn't sound angry at all, just a little nervous.

"You really mean it, love, everything's really all right?" As soon as the words came out he could tell that his attempt to hide the surprise he felt had not been entirely successful.

There was a long pause.

"Robert. Can you forgive me?" Her voice was subdued, almost pleading.

"Forgive you! What for, love?"

"I've been frightened to ring you all week, Robert. I've been so frightened you'd still be cross with me."

"Why on earth should I be cross with you, Kate? I thought it was you who was cross with me."

"But that's exactly it. I've had a chance to think these last few days. Calm down a bit, I suppose. I was so stupid to accuse you of sleeping around. I know you'd never ever do anything like that."

Robert swallowed hard.

"I'm not cross with you Kate, really I'm not."

He could hear her sigh with relief at the other end of the telephone, as if he had lifted a crushing weight from her shoulders.

"I love you, Robert."

"I love you too. darling."

There was a pause.

"Kate, I wasn't very well yesterday. Food poisoning, I think. So I'm going down to a hotel in Thuringia this weekend. It's the Interhotel in Oberhof. I'll be back Sunday night."

"Oh my poor love, are you better yet? It's all my fault for not being there to look after you."

Try though he might to push the feelings aside, Robert could feel a growing sense of annoyance. Why did she always have to blame herself for everything that went wrong?

"It's not your fault, Kate, don't be silly. I'll have a good rest this weekend in the countryside and look forward to seeing you early Tuesday evening. And Kate – give my love to the kids and your parents, won't you."

"All right, darling, I will. See you Tuesday. Bye."

There was a click and she was gone.

* * * * * *

Driving down the motorway across the Central European Plain from Berlin to the south of East Germany had been relatively straightforward, but now that he had left the motorway and was climbing steadily into the thickly wooded hills of the Thuringian Massif he was beginning to regret his decision to come by car. The snow by the roadside was getting deeper all the time and, more seriously, he was becoming aware of the treacherous patches of black ice that lay on the surface of the road. There was nothing for it but to slow down. He glanced anxiously at the clock on the dashboard and saw that it was already half past nine.

He rounded a corner and with considerable relief saw a large sign by the side of the road: 'Oberhof greets its visitors!' At last he had arrived, and a few moments later the buildings on the outskirts of the town came into view. Oberhof itself appeared to be a pleasant enough town, the solemnity of its distinctive Thuringian grey slate walls lightened by the brilliant white of the winter snow. It must once have been a sleepy little Central European village much like any other, minding its own business some three thousand feet above sea level, but the East German authorities had in recent years decided to develop its potential as a winter sports centre. And so the streets were crowded with visitors from all over East Germany, drawn to the Thuringian hills as a poor second best to the richer pastures of the great Alpine range away to the south to which they were forever forbidden to travel.

Robert soon arrived at the enormous hulk of the Interhotel, rising like an giant triangular sail into the dark winter sky. This was supposed to be one of the flagships of the East German tourist organisation, a tribute to the triumph of socialism in the pursuit of human comfort. But in truth it had only partially succeeded, for despite a certain pomposity the by now all-too-familiar ragged edges of inadequate maintenance and simple lack of concern were already beginning to show.

Robert checked in at the reception and headed straight for his room, high up near the pinnacle of the triangular concrete tower. The moon was shining brightly now, and looking out over the range of pine-covered hills stretching away into the distance, he realised that somewhere out there lay his mother's home, the home where he himself could well have been brought up if chance had taken a different turn so many years before.

He glanced at his watch. It was just gone ten o'clock and there was no time to lose. He quickly unpacked his things, deliberately leaving them lying about the bedroom in a rather messy fashion. Then he went into the bathroom, brushed his teeth, washed and shaved, pulling together his evening and morning rituals as if there had been no intervening night. Everything was nearly ready. He got into his bed and shuffled around, pretending to toss and turn in his sleep, only rising again when he was satisfied that the bed looked as if it had been slept in for an entire night.

Taking a last anxious look around the room, he pulled open the drawer of the bedside cupboard and removed the 'Do Not Disturb' sign. Then, throwing a few overnight things into his briefcase, he left the room and locked the door, carefully hanging the sign over the handle on his way out.

He looked down at the room key in his hand. It had a large knob attached of the kind used by many hotels to deter absent-minded guests from walking off without handing it in. Glancing around to check that no one was looking, he quickly opened his briefcase and pushed the key inside before heading for the lift.

A few minutes later the bustle of Oberhof was fading into the distance, as the road plunged back into the dense snow-covered forest surrounding the town. Robert estimated it would take only about ten or fifteen minutes to get to his mother's address and, ignoring the cold, he wound the window down as far as it would go so that he could absorb the crisp chill of the fresh pine-scented air all around.

Before long he turned off the main road onto a narrow side-road marked to the village of Rittershausen where his mother and sister lived. In sharp contrast to the gentle gradient of the main road, the road he found himself on began to descend steeply through the thick pine forest, twisting and turning down the hillside as it went. Robert rammed the car into first gear to try and control his speed, cursing inwardly that he had brought a car to these parts in the middle of winter without proper winter tyres.

A bend was approaching and he gently touched the brakes. But there was no response. Beneath him, he could feel the car slipping away uncontrollably over the snow beneath his wheels. Like a film in slow motion, he was sliding inexorably towards the approaching bend and the dark emptiness beyond, completely unable to control his descent. There was no time to think. Pulling his seat-belt free with one hand, he pushed open the door with the other and leapt free of the car.

He slipped as he hit the road surface and landed with a sharp and painful thud, looking up just in time to see his car slide gently over the edge of the road and out of sight. Robert listened, half-expecting to hear the sound of the car crashing down the steep hillside to the valley floor far below, but all he could hear was the faint whistling of the wind through the trees and the occasional rustle of snow falling from the overhanging branches to the ground. It was as if the car had simply vanished.

He picked himself up, rubbing his bottom to relieve the pain, and then limped slowly to the edge of the road. There, only a few yards below, he could see the glimmer of his rear lights; it seemed his car had come to rest in a large snowdrift just below the bend.

Robert clambered down across the snow until he was standing next to the car. It had buried itself so far into the snowdrift that the front doors could not be budged, but he was just able to open the rear doors and climb inside. To his amazement, it appeared to be completely undamaged, its impact cushioned by the snow. Although the car had stalled and the engine was silent, the keys were still sticking into the ignition, and as he climbed over into the front seat and gently turned the key, the motor hummed into life. He turned off the engine and the lights and climbed out of the car.

Brushing the snow off a tree stump near where he was standing, he gingerly sat down on his bruised behind, trying to collect his wits. As he remembered the subterfuge he had gone to at the hotel, he realised that his situation was far from straightforward. According to East German law, he should really report the road accident to the police as well as to a local garage, but with their customary paranoia the East German traffic police might legitimately be curious about exactly what a senior diplomat from the British Embassy in Berlin was doing taking a late night drive down a small side-road towards a village deep in the Thuringian Forest, when according to the law he was supposed to be sleeping in a hotel in precisely the opposite direction. And if they were by any chance to make enquiries at the hotel they would discover that he had not officially left the hotel at all but was staying in his room with a 'Do Not Disturb' sign hanging on the door. Awkward questions were bound to follow.

There was another dimension to the problem, a dimension unconnected with him. His mother had warned him not to write to her at her address in Rittershausen, explaining that it might cause some embarrassment for her daughter if he did so owing to the nature of the work that she did. He had let the remark pass at the time, supposing it to be just another example of East German paranoia, yet now it seemed to be another very good reason for not advertising to the authorities the fact that he was going to their house.

He suddenly stood up. It was certainly worth a try.

Climbing back into the car again, he pulled out his briefcase. Then, reaching over into the front, he took out the map he had brought with him and studied it for a moment before setting off down the road on foot.

It was certainly easier to walk on the road than to drive on it, and about half an hour later he found himself striding through the narrow cobbled streets of the village of Rittershausen. The buildings were of identical construction to those in Oberhof, the overlapping slates on the walls reaching right down to the ground, but whereas the streets of the larger town had been crowded with East Germans in anxious pursuit of après-ski, the narrow road along which he was now walking was utterly deserted.

With the help of a large street map attached to the wall of a dilapidated building at the centre of the village boasting the rather grand title of 'House of Culture', Robert quickly located his mother's home. Lying on the outskirts of the village it appeared to be, by East German standards, quite a decent property, a fair sized two-storey house standing alone a little way back from the road and surrounded by a tiny but neat garden. Next to the house was a small garage.

Nervously, Robert approached the front door and knocked loudly. After what seemed like an interminable wait his mother came to the door. She was already wearing her nightclothes.

"Heinrich!" she said in amazement.

"Mutti, I had the weekend free, so I thought I'd come down."

She stood back from the door to let him pass.

"Well, come in. It's very cold outside tonight. How did you get here?"

Robert stepped into the warm hall and closed the door behind him.

"I came by car, but I'm afraid it was a bad mistake!"

A frown passed over her face.

"A mistake? Did you have some trouble with the police?"

"Not the police. The roads. My car crashed into a bank of snow up the hill towards Oberhof."

She looked at him in amazement.

"You came down that little road in this weather! No one comes down there when it's like this."

He looked at her rather sheepishly.

"I did," he muttered.

"What did you do?"

"Came here. Walked."

"You mean the car's still up there! Still sitting in a snowbank!"

"I'm afraid so. I thought you might be able to help me get it out."

"Get it out! But how?"

"Well, it doesn't appear to be damaged. I just need a little pull from another car and I think maybe I can get it back on the road. I thought you – or maybe Ingrid – might possibly have a car."

"Well, you're in luck, it just so happens Ingrid has got a car. But she's not in yet. She had to go to a special Party meeting tonight."

Robert stared at his mother.

"She's in the Party!"

"Of course. Didn't I tell you? She couldn't possibly do her job if she wasn't in the Party. But she'll be back soon."

Robert fell silent for a moment. After his experiences with Sonja and her friends, the idea that his own sister was a member of the Party came as something as a shock to him. But his mother did not seem to notice his surprise.

"Come into the kitchen," she said, "and I'll get you something to eat."

They went through into a small but tidy kitchen and she busied herself at the stove.

"I've got some soup," she said. "It'll warm you up."

She was just ladling out a large bowlful of steaming potato soup when they heard the sound of the front door opening. A few moments later his sister appeared at the open kitchen door. She was a tall, elegant woman, with flowing black hair and a long angular face, but it was her dark green eyes that immediately struck Robert: they somehow seemed so serious, as if his sister never laughed.

"Hallo, Mutti ..." she began, and then noticed Robert sitting at the table. He got up and approached her.

"I'm Robert . . . Heinrich. Your lost brother."

She moved gracefully towards him and held out her hand.

"Mutti told me you had found her. I'm so pleased."

Her voice was not cold, and her welcome sincere enough, but as Robert took her hand he could feel a certain reticence about her manner. His mother watched them together for a moment before speaking.

"I'm afraid Heinrich tried coming down the hill!"

Ingrid looked up at her in astonishment.

"Not by car?"

"Yes," Robert interjected, "and it's got stuck in a snowdrift."

Ingrid turned to her brother.

"Nobody goes down that hill in winter. We all go round the long way."

"Next time I'll remember," he muttered. "It's a pity someone can't put up a little sign somewhere to tell those of us who aren't from these parts."

135

A cloud passed over Ingrid's face.

"Have you reported it to the police?" she asked.

"No. It's a bit awkward. You see, I'm not really supposed to be here tonight. I'm supposed to be staying at the Interhotel in Oberhof, but I wanted to come and see you both while I had the chance." He threw a quick glance at his mother and then turned back to Ingrid. "And I gathered it might be better for you too if I didn't contact the police."

"Yes ... yes, you're right," she said anxiously, "but I really don't see what we can do."

"Heinrich thought you might be able to get him out of the drift with your car," her mother interjected, "just by pulling him."

Ingrid thought for a moment.

"Well, it's just possible, I suppose. But I'll need to put the chains on."

"I'll come with you," Robert volunteered, following her out into the snow.

"Mine's not a powerful car," she said, pointing to her little Trabant as she opened the garage door, "and I'm not sure whether it'll have enough acceleration."

Robert touched her arm and stopped her.

"I'm sorry I had to meet you like this," he said, "it's not quite what I intended."

She turned.

"It's not your fault," she said calmly as she began to attach the snow chains.

As soon as she had finished, Ingrid slung some rope from the garage into the back of the car together with a few old pulleys that were hanging on the wall.

"I used to play with these as a child," she explained. "Maybe they'll come in useful."

Robert got into the car beside her and they set off, the chains clanking noisily over the ancient cobbled surface of the village streets.

Before long they had arrived at the site of the crash and Ingrid brought the car to a halt. They both clambered out and peered over the edge of the road at the rear end of Robert's car, which was still sticking up out of the snow like a discarded child's toy.

"I'm surprised you didn't hurt yourself as you went into that lot," she said in a rather dour voice.

"I jumped out before I got there."

She looked at him but said nothing.

"It's really not going to be easy getting it out," she said at last.

"I can't pull you on this snow, even with the chains on."

Her comment did not seem to invite a reply and Robert watched her anxiously as she paced nervously about carefully analysing the situation.

"Can you start it?" she asked.

"Yes," Robert replied.

She fell silent again and then clambered down onto the snow behind his car, fixing the rope quietly to the rear of the bodywork before pulling it up behind her so that the free end was lying on the road.

"I'm afraid you're going to have to dig," she said, indicating the snow at the front of the car. "The front's got to be free of snow right down to the tyres."

Robert did as she had asked, pulling his driving gloves out from the car and shovelling the snow away with his hands. It took him a long time, and when he had finished he clambered back up the bank to the road.

"My God!" he exclaimed in English, and he could see Ingrid turn in surprise at sound of the alien tongue in which he had spoken. She had moved her car off the road onto some snow lying in the forest and had attached the rope by a series of linked pulleys to her own car. Under the wheels of her car she had spread a large amount of accumulated debris from the forest floor to improve the grip of her chains.

"You see what I've done here," she said, pointing at her wheels, you've got to do the same with your car."

Robert scrambled down the hill and obeyed, leaving Ingrid watching expressionless from the road above.

"Have you got any carpet in the car?" she asked.

"Yes."

"Then get it out and put it under the wheels. You'll need all the grip you can get on that bank."

With some regret, Robert ripped out the carpet from the car and shoved it under the tyres.

Finally Ingrid nodded.

"O.K., that'll do," she said. "Now get into your car, put your seat belt on and start the engine. When I sound my horn try and reverse slowly up the slope. I'll be pulling you from behind. If you start to skid or you're simply not making any progress you must sound your horn and concentrate on trying to stop yourself sliding back down again. O.K.?"

Robert nodded.

He climbed into his car, waiting for the sound of her horn. Finally it came, and just before he started reversing he could feel the steady pull of her engine helping him up the slope.

Slowly his car started to rise up the hill, creeping backwards inches at a time. Soon Robert was having to push against the dashboard with his free hand to prevent himself falling forward. Then, suddenly, the wheels started to skid uncontrollably and he hooted, ramming on the handbrake with his free hand. There was a long silence and he wondered whether he should try to get out of the car.

"Thank goodness you didn't try to get out," came a voice from outside, and he looked up to see Ingrid clambering around examining his wheels. She moved the piece of carpet to a new position and started taking off her coat. Robert looked at her in horror.

"You're not going to put that under it, are you?"

"I am," she said drily, "and I'm going to put yours under it as well. We need the grip. You'll have to take it off."

Robert was in no position to argue. He wriggled out of his coat and handed it to her through the window. Ingrid positioned it carefully under one of the tyres.

"Right," she said, "we'll try again and this time with any luck we should make it up to the top."

Robert waited for the hoot and reversed again. This time the wheels gripped and he could once again feel the car edging imperceptibly up towards the top of the bank.

Finally it reached the road. Robert pulled on the handbrake and started climbing out of the car.

"Don't get out yet," Ingrid shouted, "or you'll end up right back where you came from. Just keep reversing until you're right off the road amongst the trees."

Chastened, Robert did exactly as he was told.

"O.K?" he asked out of the window.

She looked at him, and for the first time since he had met her a hint of a smile passed across her face. Then she nodded.

"O.K." she said.

They got out of the cars and walked towards each other.

"Thanks," Robert said with relief. "It's a pretty impressive arrangement you've set up here." He paused. "I really am sorry that we should have to meet like this."

She looked at him.

"To tell you the truth," she said in a soft voice, looking round admiringly at the complex arrangement of pulleys and ramps she had assembled, "I haven't enjoyed myself so much for years."

There was silence for a while.

"It's strange having a sister," Robert said quietly. "I always knew I had a mother, even if I was thinking about the wrong woman, but I always thought – well, until three years ago I thought – that I was an only child."

The rather distant look he had seen before returned to her face.

"Yes," she said quietly, "it must be very strange."

* * * * * *

There was an odd sort of scraping noise which seemed to repeat itself over and over again. Robert opened his eyes. Through the drawn curtains he could see that the morning sun was shining brightly. He lay still for a moment and thought how odd it was to be surrounded by his own family again after all these years.

He got out of bed to investigate the sound, which seemed to be coming from outside in the garden. Pulling the curtains apart so that the sunlight streamed into the bedroom, he could see Ingrid hard at work with a shovel, clearing the garden path of a deep layer of fresh snow which must have fallen during the previous night. He watched her for a long time from the window as she laboured: she was a unusual woman, he thought, and she seemed to carry with her an aura of numbed sadness that he found hard to pinpoint; perhaps his mother was right to be concerned.

He glanced at the clock on the bedside table and saw that it was nearly nine o'clock. Gathering up his clothes he quickly went to the bathroom to wash and dress.

When he came downstairs he found that his mother had laid a breakfast table ready for him in the kitchen.

"Good morning, Heinrich, have you slept well?" she said when she caught sight of him.

"Very well, thanks, but now I'm feeling guilty because I see that Ingrid has been shovelling snow while I've been asleep."

His mother laughed.

"Don't worry about Ingrid," she said with a smile. "She's been shovelling snow every winter since she was five years old."

Robert came over and held his mother's arm.

"Only because I wasn't here to do it," he said, kissing her gently on the cheek, "but today it just so happens that I am."

He left the room and went outside into the garden.

"Ingrid," he called, "leave the rest for me."

She looked up at him in surprise.

"Oh. Good morning, Robert," she said, her deliberate attempt at pronouncing his English name rather forced. "It's all right, I don't

139

mind doing it."

Robert walked up to her and held out his hand for the shovel.

"I know," he said quietly, "ever since you were five. So I reckon that means today is my turn."

"I suppose you've got a point," she said, handing him the shovel.

She stood watching him while he worked.

"Do you have a lot of snow in England?" she asked.

"No, not a lot. And anyway, if we did your nephews would insist on clearing it away. I wouldn't get a look-in."

Ingrid remained silent.

"How old are they?" she asked at last.

"Justin's thirteen and Timothy's eleven." He took out a photograph from his wallet. "Here. This is them."

Ingrid took the picture and looked at it. For a long time she said nothing, and although he couldn't be sure, Robert sensed that the sight of his sons had somehow upset her.

"They're nice," she murmured, handing him back the picture. "They look like you, particularly the older one."

Robert looked at the picture. People always said he bore a resemblance to Justin, although frankly he could never see the likeness himself. He looked up at Ingrid.

"Do you suppose we look alike?" he asked.

She thought for a moment, leaning her head slightly to one side as she did so.

"Perhaps we have a certain angularity of face in common. I don't really know."

Robert cleared the path all the way to the front door.

"Is that it?" he asked.

"That's it," she said. "Shall we go inside? Mother will never forgive me if I monopolise you."

Robert tramped through the snow to the garage and put the shovel away. At Ingrid's suggestion, he had parked his car there the night before so as not to attract unnecessary attention, and now the sight of it made him feel rather edgy.

He returned to the kitchen and sat down to eat his breakfast. His mother had gone to a great deal of trouble to turn the usual dreary assortment of East German groceries into something appetizing.

"I've got to get back to Oberhof after I've eaten," he said. "Do you want to come?"

His mother looked up sharply.

"Will you be coming back?"

"Yes, if I may. I don't have to go back to Berlin until tomorrow.

But I've hung a 'Do Not Disturb' sign on the door. I just have to hang around there until the domestic staff have had a chance to fix the room, then I'll ruffle the bed again and come back." He could see them staring at him in amazement. "Yes, it's a bit ridiculous, isn't it. I only want to visit my mother and sister but it's illegal, isn't it?"

Ingrid looked at him.

"Not if you apply correctly," she said.

"I know," Robert replied quietly, "but as you know my circumstances are a little unusual."

His mother poured him another cup of coffee.

"If you're coming back then I won't come, if you don't mind. Why don't you go with Ingrid?"

He turned to his sister.

"I'd love to. Will you come, show me around a bit?"

Ingrid nodded.

"If you want," she said, her voice subdued.

Robert finished his coffee and stood up.

"Shall we go, or they'll begin to think I've strung myself up in the hotel bathroom."

Ingrid rose to her feet.

"O.K. But Robert, let's go in my car, it's less trouble."

Robert looked at her for a moment and nodded.

Ten minutes later they were sitting together in the car and the last houses of Rittershausen were disappearing into the distance.

"The way we're going is the best route to Oberhof in winter," Ingrid observed. "No steep hills."

Robert let the remark pass.

"Do you work near here?" he asked, trying to make conversation.

"Not far," she said.

"What sort of thing do you do?"

Ingrid was silent for a moment.

"I'm afraid I can't talk about it, Robert. I'm not trying to be rude."

Robert was shocked by the finality of her remark.

"That makes two of us," he said. "I can't talk about my work either."

They drove along without speaking for a while.

"Mutti said you're in the Party?" he said eventually.

"Yes, that's right."

"Did they make you join?"

She glanced across at him.

"No, I joined at university. Before that I was in the League."

"The League?"

"Yes, the League of German Youth."

"Oh them, Sonja said she was in that crowd too. She thought they were the natural successor to the Hitler Youth."

"Who's Sonja?" Ingrid asked, clearly irritated by Robert's remark.

"Someone I know in Berlin," Robert muttered.

"She must be a rather stupid person."

"Why?"

"To make such stupid comparisons. The League is nothing like the Hitler Youth."

Robert thought of Sonja cleaning the toilets on the platform over-looking the tower-blocks of West Berlin.

"You're not really a communist, are you, Ingrid?" he said quietly.

"Of course I'm a communist. That's what the Socialist Unity Party is, you know, it's the East German name for the Communist Party."

Robert looked at her incredulously. It was one thing Lechner at the Ministry of Trade or that idiotic little station-master in Berlin being a communist, but this was his own sister.

"You can't be serious. I mean, you're just saying you have to be a communist because of your work, aren't you?"

Ingrid leant down and turned on the car radio, adjusting the controls until she had found some light music.

"Why don't we talk about something else, Robert? I'm not attacking your politics, am I?"

He fell silent. It seemed incredible that his own sister, an intelligent, university-educated woman, could actually believe in a system so utterly bankrupt that it had to fence in its own people with dogs and barbed wire. They didn't talk again until they had arrived in the town and Ingrid had pulled up in a car park not far from the hotel.

"The hotel's over there," she said. "I've got to do some shopping. Can we meet later?"

"Yes, where do you suggest?"

She pointed at a large cafeteria away to their right.

"In there. Can you give me an hour?"

Robert nodded and got out of the car.

"See you in an hour," he said, and started walking briskly towards the hotel.

Robert arrived outside the main entrance and glanced again at his watch. Ten-thirty, and if the cleaning staff were like those elsewhere in the world they would no doubt be fidgeting because they hadn't been able to get into his room yet. He ambled around to the side of the hotel until he found a side-door where he could slip inside without encountering the prying eyes of the reception staff.

The 'Do Not Disturb' sign was exactly where he had left it, hanging on the door handle, and he quickly slipped it off and went into his room. Nothing had been disturbed, and he dived into the bathroom and sprayed some after-shave around before going down to the restaurant. He strolled casually over to the reception.

The girl at the desk smiled politely.

"Good morning, sir, can I help you?"

"Yes, can you tell me where I can get my breakfast, please?"

She glanced up at the clock on the wall opposite.

"I'm afraid breakfast has finished, sir, but you can get some coffee in the lounge."

Robert thanked her and walked across to the lounge with a feeling of relief; after the large meal provided by his mother he really didn't want anything to eat. He sat down in a comfortable armchair and ordered some coffee.

There was a copy of the 'Morning Star' lying on a table near to where he was sitting. He picked it up and started idly flicking through the pages. In England the paper had always struck him as an indigestible rag, but in comparison to the East German press it had quite a lively style.

"Herr Stanton!"

With a shudder Robert looked up from his paper. There, bearing down on him fast from the other side of the lounge, was the large and rotund figure of the dreadful Herr Lechner. The timid Frau Lechner was in her usual position about five paces behind.

"May we?" he asked, indicating with a flourish of his hand the chairs beside Robert.

There was no escape.

"Certainly," Robert replied. "What a pleasant surprise!"

"Indeed a pleasure!" grinned Herr Lechner enthusiastically. "We've come for the weekend. Nothing like the good mountain air of Thuringia for clearing those musty Berlin cobwebs away."

"My thoughts entirely," Robert muttered, wondering if he could quickly make his excuses and slope off back to his room without appearing impolite. But just then his coffee arrived and he knew he was caught.

"Waiter!" Herr Lechner ordered crisply, in the manner of one used to giving commands. "Bring two more coffees please."

He turned to Robert with a broad smile.

"This is indeed a piece of exceptionally good fortune! We'll be able to get to know each other much better this weekend." He looked around the room. "But tell me, where is your charming wife?"

"She's in England - she had to go back for the Christmas holidays."

"Oh dear! What a pity! Such an endearing lady."

There was a brief lull in the conversation. Robert tried drinking his coffee, aware that he could not possibly make his excuses until his cup was empty, but was forced to abandon the attempt after badly burning his tongue. His companion picked up the copy of the 'Morning Star' from Robert's lap.

"A good paper?" he asked.

It crossed Robert's mind that he ought to restrain himself. But he didn't.

"Actually it's a bloody lousy paper and nobody reads it in England," he said with a friendly smile, "but it's the only English-language paper you can get hold of out here."

Herr Lechner looked perturbed.

"Really! I must speak with my colleagues in the periodicals section at the Ministry and get them to look into the situation. Perhaps there are some technical difficulties with procurement."

There he went again. Robert remembered the man's yarn about people applying for permission if they wanted an exit visa. It was obviously a favourite tactic of his.

He smiled sweetly at Herr Lechner.

"An excellent idea. Wider availability of English papers might give a real boost to English teaching in East Germany."

Herr Lechner looked askance at Robert.

"You will have lunch with us today, of course," he announced. "As our guest."

Robert tried sipping the coffee again, but it was still too hot.

"It's very kind of you, but I can't," he said.

"But why not? You are all alone here, are you not?"

"Yes, of course." Robert replied, rather too quickly.

"Then that is settled," Herr Lechner concluded with an air of absolute finality.

Before Robert could reply, the waiter had reappeared with the Lechners' coffee.

"I know a very good place to eat not far away from here," Herr Lechner continued after the waiter had departed. "It has, I think you will see, a certain measure of local colour."

Robert braced himself.

"Really, I'd rather dine alone today. You know I was rather unwell last week and I'm trying to rest up. But it was very kind of you to invite me."

Herr Lechner looked away, clearly affronted by the blunt manner of Robert's refusal.

"As you wish," he muttered drily.

Robert returned to his coffee and found that it had cooled sufficiently so that if he blew hard on the surface before sipping he could force it down his throat without too much pain. In next to no time the cup was empty.

"You must excuse me," he mumbled, rising from his chair, "I have a few things to do. I hope you both have a most enjoyable weekend."

Herr Lechner nodded frostily. Robert turned away, heading quickly for the nearest lift. When he returned to his room he saw to his relief that the cleaning staff had finished their work. Immediately he set about systematically undoing everything they had done, so that within several minutes it looked as messy as it had appeared a quarter of an hour earlier. Then he quietly replaced the 'Do Not Disturb' sign on the door and slipped discretely out of the hotel by the side-door through which he had entered.

By the time he arrived at the cafeteria his sister was already waiting for him, sitting sipping a small cup of coffee at a long trestle table crowded with other people. There was a stark contrast between the quiet ambience of the first-class hotel from which he had just come and the mean and crowded surroundings of the building in which he now found himself; for despite the fact that the cafeteria was designed for the efficient delivery of essential sustenance to as large a number of people in as short a space of time as possible it was still hopelessly overcrowded, with a long queue of sullen-faced East Germans stretching away from the serving hatches into the snowy world outside. It was only a quarter past eleven, yet most of these people appeared to be waiting for their lunch.

He walked past the passively waiting queue and over to Ingrid.

"How did you manage to get that?" he said, pointing to the coffee. "It seems like there's half of East Germany queuing up."

Ingrid looked up.

"They seem to all turn up just after eleven. If you get here before that it's not so bad."

"You certainly like taking your lunch early in this country," he said with a grin. "In England we're only just getting to coffee-break time."

"They don't want to eat now," Ingrid explained, "they've just come early to beat the rush."

Robert stared at the enormous queue snaking its way outside.

"You mean it gets worse than this?"

"Oh yes. Much worse. You should see it here at one o'clock."

Robert nearly made a derogatory remark but thought better of it. His sister clearly did not enjoy such conversations and there seemed no point in gratuitously offending her.

"Do you eat here often?" he asked.

"No. Not often. Usually I eat at the Institute."

"Look, Ingrid, I'd intended to invite you to lunch with me at the hotel but I've just bumped into a boring old idiot I know from the Ministry of Trade. It might be better if we go somewhere else."

"That's all right," she smiled, "I don't mind. I'd invite you to the Institute restaurant, but I'm afraid visitors aren't allowed."

Robert looked with distaste at the queue. The people seemed to be pushing up closer and closer to one another, as if the ones at the back were trying to squeeze forward into the building in order to escape the freezing conditions outside.

"Does that mean we eat here?" he asked glumly.

"No, Robert, you don't need to worry. I know a place in the woods. It's a bit off the beaten track and you need a car to get there, so it's generally much less crowded."

Ingrid drank up the remains of her coffee and they returned to the car, leaving the seething mass of increasingly miserable-looking lunch-hunters behind them. Ingrid had fallen silent again, and Robert felt increasingly uneasy as they started to drive away from town. There were so many no-go areas, so many things about which his sister seemed unwilling to talk.

"I asked Mutti about our father," he asked finally, "but she wasn't very forthcoming. Do you know anything about him?"

"He died before I was born."

"I know he did. But surely Mutti must have told you about him?"

Ingrid threw him a sideways glance. "I think his death must have upset her a great deal, because she never speaks about their last years together during the war. But she once told me about how she met him, if you're interested?"

"I am."

"It was when she was staying at Aunt Katherina's before the war. Mutti's own parents died when she was quite young and Katherina acted as a kind of mother to her when she was in her teens."

"I knew that. I even met a man in Berlin who knew them when they lived there."

"Did you? Anyway, at that time father was apparently quite a frequent caller to the house, even when Mutti was still barely more than a child. Mutti said he used to be wildly in love with Katherina but that her sister had rejected him in favour of the man who finally became her husband. But the point was, all the time Mutti was growing up she was secretly and passionately in love with father.

"Then, one day shortly before the war broke out, Mutti had come home from work and father had been there alone waiting for her. She had supposed that he had come to see Katherina, but then, right out of the blue, he had begged her to marry him and go with him to East Prussia. So of course Mutti accepted, and that was how it all started."

"But she never remarried?"

"No. I don't know why not. It might have been good for her to remarry; she's often so terribly lonely."

Robert paused for a moment before continuing.

"Are you going to get married, Ingrid?"

She drove along in silence for a while before replying.

"I don't know, Robert. Perhaps. I've never met anyone."

"Mutti worries about you, you know?"

"I know she worries about me. But then I worry about her too. It must run in the family."

They fell silent again until Ingrid turned off from the main road onto what seemed like little more than a forest track.

"It's a little way down here," she said as they bumped along. "I hope you approve."

After about a hundred yards they arrived at a rustic timber-framed building set in a large clearing in the trees. The building itself was certainly picturesque, although the overall effect was rather spoiled by the crowded car park, and the place looked moderately promising until Robert spotted the tail of a queue snaking out from the main entrance.

"It's nice," he said with a smile, "but it looks like we're not the only ones to have had the idea."

Ingrid pulled up sharply and they got out of the car.

"It's all because the area's being developed for winter sports," she explained tersely. "The last five-year plan underestimated the demand for eating facilities in this region by roughly fifty percent. Now we're told it'll take a few years until the imbalance is rectified."

They joined the queue and waited patiently for a table. Every now and then a party would leave the restaurant and the queue would patiently shuffle a few inches further forward.

"How long do you think it'll take to get to the front?"

Ingrid looked at her watch.

"It's slightly worse than usual today," she said, "perhaps half an hour."

"Oh well," said Robert, settling in for a long wait, "at least it gives us a chance to work up a really good appetite."

Just then they became aware of a commotion behind them and turned round to see what was happening.

"Someone's pushing through," Ingrid muttered in disgust.

Robert stared in disbelief as the queue-bargers approached. For the second time in as many hours he was helplessly trapped.

"Well, what a surprise!"

Robert took the proffered hand and shook it.

"Herr Lechner. We seem to keep on bumping into each other."

"We do indeed." Herr Lechner replied with an understanding wink, "and you seem to know the good spots to eat just as well as the locals do."

Robert waited, hoping he would move on. But he didn't. Instead he turned to Ingrid.

"Since we're all here together after all, aren't you going to introduce us?"

"Oh. Yes. Er ... Ingrid, may I introduce Herr and Frau Lechner. This is Ingrid, a friend of mine."

The look of anxiety on Ingrid's face was plain to see despite her determined attempt to conceal it.

"Delighted," she said politely, nervously shaking their hands.

Herr Lechner looked up and shouted imperiously at a stumpy little waiter who was supervising the front of the queue rather in the manner of a traffic policeman. The man looked up and scuttled forward obediently at the command. Taking him aside by the sleeve, Herr Lechner whispered a few words into his ear before returning.

"Come on," he said, taking Robert by the arm and almost pulling him past the by now silent queue of people. "You don't need to wait here with this lot. I booked ahead. You can eat with us."

They were swept forward into the dining-room where a portly-looking head waiter came scurrying towards them.

"Herr and Frau Lechner!", he smiled obsequiously. "How pleasant to see you again." The waiter looked with concern at Robert and Ingrid. "We were expecting only yourself and your wife," he said humbly, bowing his head slightly.

"That's correct. But I'm sure you can accommodate my two guests in such an excellently-run establishment as this."

Suitably rebuffed, the head waiter's head sank even lower.

"Of course, Herr Lechner, if you could just wait one tiny moment."

He moved away slightly and clicked his fingers urgently at two young waiters serving other tables. They immediately put down the dishes of hot food that they were carrying on a side-table and came quickly over to receive their orders. The head waiter returned.

"All has been arranged, sir. If you would like to come with me ..."

He directed them to a large round table by the window where the junior waiters were bustling around laying two extra places.

When they had settled into their seats, Herr Lechner turned to Ingrid with his usual obsequious grin.

"If I am to call you Ingrid you must call me Hans. And my dear wife's name is Lotte."

He looked expectantly at Robert.

"Oh, I'm Robert," he said, trying to look gracious.

"Robert," he repeated with an atrocious attempt at an English accent. "A very fine English name. I like it."

The junior waiters were still arranging the finishing touches on their table and Robert glanced around at the place where they had left the dishes they had been carrying. The plates of food were still lying exactly where they had been left, presumably getting increasingly cold.

Herr Lechner smiled at Ingrid.

"Are you from East Germany?" he asked, offering her a bread roll.

"Yes," she replied, accepting the proffered roll and starting to butter it.

"From Berlin?"

"No. From near here."

"How nice." He paused, then turned to Robert with the bread rolls.

"I did not know you had friends in our country. I had erroneously supposed it was your first visit here."

Robert glanced cautiously into his eyes in an attempt to ascertain exactly what he was driving at. But his face gave little away.

"Yes, it's nice, isn't it," he said with a broad smile before turning purposefully to Frau Lechner.

"Lotte, do you have any children?" he asked without giving her husband time to ask any further questions.

Frau Lechner's first reaction on being addressed was one of complete bewilderment, as if Robert was the first person who had spoken to her in her entire life. But as soon as she had got over the initial shock her eyes lit up.

"Why, certainly I do. I have three."

Robert smiled at her warmly.

"Do please tell us about them. How old are they?"

To his immense relief, the ploy worked admirably. Frau Lechner, once let loose, was easily capable of out-talking even her verbose husband. In her exposition, she decided to take the children one at a time and start with a detailed description of her pregnancies. Her husband glared at her with a look of pronounced irritability and from time to time made a determined attempt to turn the conversation onto something else, but every time he tried to do so Robert would ask eagerly for further details. How were East German push-chairs designed? What did she feel about breast-feeding? What was her general attitude towards whooping-cough vaccinations?

At first Ingrid sat silently munching her bread roll and looking at Robert's enthusiastic talk about babies with a look of dull exasperation. But then she must suddenly have realised what he was attempting to do because she too started asking questions, encouraging the by now blissfully happy Lotte to give yet further snippets of information about her offspring. By the time the main course had arrived Herr Lechner had given up all attempts to converse and was silently eating his dinner with a sullen look on his face, washing his food down with generous quantities of the rather fine Hungarian bulls' blood he had ordered.

After what seemed like an interminable wait the sweet trolley arrived, with Lotte now describing her second child's experiences at the League of German Youth summer camp. This part of her narrative was taking some considerable length of time because Ingrid had persuaded her to review the relative difficulties of obtaining all the different kinds of badges that the children could obtain.

Frau Lechner paused to examine the sweet trolley with her husband and Robert took the opportunity to smile conspiratorially at his sister. For a moment she returned his smile, but then, quite suddenly, her eye fell on something beyond the window and her face froze rigid.

A few moments later she pushed her chair back from the table and rose to her feet.

"I'm sorry," she said, her face ashen, "you must excuse me. I've suddenly come over feeling unwell."

Robert glanced over his shoulder out of the window towards the car park beyond but could see nothing unusual.

"What's the matter, Ingrid?" he asked anxiously.

"I'm having one of my funny turns, Robert. I'll be better outside in the fresh air. You don't need to hurry your meal." She turned to the Lechners. "I've so enjoyed meeting you."

And with that she hurried towards the door, picking up her coat from the hanger as she went.

"Poor girl!" exclaimed Frau Lechner when she had gone. "I hope it wasn't anything I said."

They watched through the window as Ingrid walked briskly out into the car park. A middle-aged couple had just arrived and she paused to talk to them for a while before walking on towards her car.

Herr Lechner finally picked up his spoon and stuck it into the large plate of trifle that the waiter had placed in front of him.

"Your friend seems to be feeling better now she's outside," he commented, depositing the first consignment of trifle into his mouth.

Robert put his hand in his pocket and pulled out his wallet.

"All the same, I'd better go and see if she's all right," he said, opening up the wallet.

Herr Lechner touched his arm.

"Of course," he said, "but you must put the wallet away. I will attend to the bill."

Robert thanked him and hurried outside to join Ingrid in the car. Out of the corner of his eye, he could see Herr Lechner's puffy face watching his every move.

It was obvious that something had gone seriously wrong. Ingrid said nothing as he joined her in the car, but her face was tense with what looked like a combination of fear and anger. She rammed the car into gear and accelerated out of the car park, along the bumpy track and back onto the main road towards Oberhof. For a few minutes they drove in silence, but then she swirled the wheel around to the right and swung the car off onto another little track into the woods. As soon as they were out of sight of the main road she jammed on the brakes and got out, hurrying off alone into the trees.

Uncertain of what to do, Robert watched her for a while before leaving the car and approaching her. She was standing with her back to him by a large fir tree with long branches that hung down under the weight of the snow so that they nearly touched the ground. Robert said nothing. He could hear that she was crying bitterly.

After a few minutes her tears started to subside and she turned to face him.

"Why did you have to come here?" she said, her voice bitter and angry.

Robert looked at her in bewilderment.

"Why? I don't know why. I wanted to meet you, I suppose. I'm sorry about that idiot at lunchtime."

"Don't you see, you're threatening everything I've ever worked for! Do you know who that man was I met back there in the car park? He's the chief of security at the research station where I work. He's a decent enough chap, you might even call him a friend of mine, but if he finds out that I've got a brother working for a Western Embassy – even if he finds out that I'm talking to a Western national without reporting it, then I'm going to lose my job, I'm going to lose everything I've got."

Robert was silent, watching with horror the anguish written all over his sister's face.

"Is the work you do so very sensitive, Ingrid?" he asked quietly.

Ingrid picked up some snow from the branch and wiped it over her tear-stained face. It seemed to help her calm down.

"Listen, Robert, I'm sorry. It's not your fault. I suppose you deserve a bit more honesty than you've had from me since you arrived here."

"You frightened me back there. When you saw those people out of the window and reacted like that I just didn't know what the hell was going on."

She paused.

"I'm a mathematical physicist, you know that?"

Robert nodded.

"Mutti told me. She said you were very good."

"I am. But did she tell you where I work and what I do?"

"No."

"I'm a ballistics expert. The centre where I work is one of the most important research stations in the Warsaw Pact and I know pretty well everything there is to know about the scientific work that's going on there. My particular field of expertise is the development of new trajectory systems that will effectively by-pass Western defence computers."

Robert closed his eyes, trying unsuccessfully to block out the meaning of her words.

"I see," he said finally, "I . . . I didn't realise."

Ingrid looked at him, her eyes like those of a frightened animal.

"As soon as mother told me she'd found you at Katherina's funeral I was terrified. I knew you might come down here or write to us or something crazy. And then you actually turned up on our doorstep; but when I found out that you too were nervous about being discovered I realised you'd be careful. I thought the worst of the danger had passed."

"Mutti warned me to be careful on your account. I thought she was being paranoid, but clearly she wasn't."

"Anyway, when we went out today I knew you'd have the sense to keep your mouth shut about who you were if someone came up to talk to me. I was going to introduce you as an old friend from university if anyone met us and I knew you'd take the cue from me."

"But you weren't reckoning on Lechner, were you?"

Ingrid shook her head.

"He's a monster. But worse still, he's a loud-mouth. If Kurt – that's the security chief at the Institute – if Kurt had come into the restaurant while I was sitting with you I knew for certain he'd have come straight over and started chatting. He's like that. And then Lechner would probably have asked him to join us at dinner and we'd have had to do the rounds with the introductions. I couldn't have done anything; I'd have been helplessly trapped."

She fell silent. Robert looked at her for a long time, trying to find the courage to speak. For he knew that when he did speak, there was only one thing he could say.

"I'll go, Ingrid," he said quietly, "I'll go tonight. I'd go right now but I can't do that to my mother. I've got to say good-bye to her."

Ingrid looked at him for a moment with that strange distant look that Robert had noticed several times before.

"Thank you," she said quietly, and without a further word started slowly retracing her steps towards the car.

* * * * * *

Robert threw himself heavily onto the bed: it was nearly midnight and he felt utterly exhausted. Yet as he lay on the comfortable hotel bed and gazed out through the window across the moonlit range of snow-covered hills beyond, he could not help but feel a growing sense of relief. Ingrid's words had forced him to do something which he should have done many days earlier; they had finally forced him to turn his back on the unreal fantasy world he had entered since coming to East Berlin.

In his mind, he could see again the two young people trying to break across the Wall at Checkpoint Charlie. They had found it impossible to break through and Ingrid had helped him realise that it was equally impossible for him to break across in the opposite direction. She was absolutely right; he had no place amidst these people: back in 1945, a young British officer called John Wilberforce Stanton had carried him across Europe on a one-way trip to a different world. It was a world from which he could never return.

The afternoon and evening had been difficult. After leaving the clearing in the woods Ingrid had driven him back in silence to his mother's house. She had been there to greet them, coffee and home-made cake all ready to serve, and Robert had not had the heart to tell her straight away. Just for a while, even if only for a few short hours, he had allowed her to play at being the mother she had once been. And so they had sat in the home that could so easily have been his own, eating cake, drinking coffee, and talking about a past and a future in which he had no part.

Most of the time Ingrid had remained silent, sitting quietly in the corner of the room, and when Robert had tried to smile at her, to reassure her that he understood and respected her reasons for asking him to leave, she had been unable to meet his eyes.

Yet eventually he could bear the pretence no longer. He had risen from his chair and held his mother in his arms and told her quietly that he would never be able to see her again. He had been expecting her to cry, perhaps even to be angry with him, but she had instead remained quite still, almost as if she had been expecting the moment to arrive. She had held him for a last long embrace before releasing him and wishing him well in his future life. And then she had simply left the room and gone quietly upstairs to her bedroom, telling him to come up and see her one more time before he left.

He had packed his things together and gone to her room as she had asked. When he entered, she was stooping low over a small cup-board beside her bed, sorting through the things within. Eventually, she had turned to face him and had pressed into his hand two small black-and-white photographs and a little blue box.

Sitting up on the hotel bed Robert put his hand into his pocket and pulled out the two photographs; one of them must been taken a few years before at Ingrid's doctoral graduation ceremony, because his sister was dressed in her full academic garb; the other was much older and showed a proud-looking man in wartime German military uniform holding a little baby; it was his mother's only photograph of him together with his real father.

He carefully put the photographs onto the bedside-table before putting his hand into his trouser-pocket and pulling out the box. Inside was a small silver spoon, and on it, engraved in old-fashioned German script along the handle, were the words: 'To our darling baby Heinrich, to treasure all your days, from your ever-loving parents – Friedrich and Frieda.'

Clipping the spoon back into its box, he placed it carefully next to the photographs on the bedside-table before rising quietly to his feet. The curtains were still wide open, and as he drew them shut to lock out the night beyond, he realised that another chapter in his life had drawn to a close and that this time there could be no turning back.

Robert yawned and went into the bathroom to get himself changed for bed. Even though it had ended like this, he knew he would never regret his decision to search out his family. For even though he could never see them again, he knew that they had helped him bury the ghosts that had haunted his life ever since that distant June day when he had discovered the death certificate in St Catherine's House.

He returned to the bedroom and climbed wearily between the covers. Then, after one final glance at the photographs lying beside his bed, he turned out the light and fell fast asleep.

* * * * * *

There was a rhythmic knocking that refused to stop. Robert finally opened his eyes and became aware that the sound was coming from the bedroom door. He switched on the bedside light and glanced at the clock; it was nearly two o'clock in the morning!

"I'm coming," he called, getting out of bed and pulling his dressing-gown around him. It was probably just some drunk turning up at the wrong room.

The knocking stopped and Robert opened the door.

"Ingrid!"

His sister was standing at the door, her coat pulled around her shoulders, her face distraught.

"Can I come in?" she said, glancing nervously around her at the empty corridor. "I don't want anyone to see me."

Robert stepped back quickly to let her pass.

"Are you all right?" he asked as soon as he had closed the door.

As he spoke she was standing with her face away from him, but when she turned he could see that tears were rolling down her face. He had seen her cry before, earlier that day in the woods, but those had been tears of anger, an anger directed primarily at him. Now her face showed no sign of anger, only an abject sense of near total despair.

He went over to her and held her close to him.

"It's all right, Ingrid. It's all right. You're safe now."

After what seemed like an eternity her sobbing began to subside. Robert reached over and picked up a handkerchief from beside the bed.

"Here," he said, "use this."

She took the handkerchief and wiped her eyes, slowly beginning to regain her composure.

"I had to come," she said, her voice still unstable, "I just had to come and see you again before you left."

"I thought you didn't want to see me any more," he said gently. "That's why I did leave, Ingrid."

"I know you did, and that's precisely the point. You'd come to see your own mother, the woman who gave birth to you, for Christ's sake. I'd no right to ask you to go away. I'm so terribly ashamed of myself."

She started sobbing again, sitting down on the edge of the bed.

"What's the matter with me, Robert? How could I have behaved in such a way?"

Robert sat down beside her and watched her cry. It was as if the protective outer coating that she had worn since his arrival at her house had suddenly fallen away and left her utterly exposed.

"You didn't do anything wrong, Ingrid, it's just the situation we're in. It's not your fault, it's not my fault, in fact it's nobody's fault. It's just the way it is."

"What kind of a crazy world is it where you can't even see your own mother and sister without all hell breaking loose?"

Robert smiled wryly.

"I've wondered that myself more than once over the last three years. For three years I've been going round like a kind of criminal - telling lies to just about everyone I know including myself. During the last few days I've almost got used to it: dodging in and out of hotels to avoid the reception staff; deliberately evading the police; undertaking all sorts of subterfuges to prevent the security staff at my own Embassy getting wind of what I'm up to. It's almost becoming a second nature to me. For the last couple of weeks I've been taking the most absurd risks with a pretty promising career in order to track you and my mother down and see you. But I realised today that there's one immense difference between my deceits and the deceits I've imposed on you."

She looked up at him enquiringly.

"I consciously chose to go down this path and you didn't."

Ingrid stopped crying and stood up.

"May I use the bathroom?" she said suddenly.

He watched her through the open door as she took off her coat and splashed cold water on her face. He had never noticed it before, but there was a hidden kindness about Ingrid's face, a sensitivity which she generally made extraordinary efforts to conceal. And as he watched her he suddenly knew that here at last was someone he could trust.

"How did you get past the reception?" he called.

"There's a late bar," she said. "And I often come here. They know me."

Robert lay back on the bed with his head propped up on a pillow.

"Actually, Ingrid, you chose a good time to come. I was having a terrible nightmare when you knocked."

She came back into the bedroom again and sat down on the bed.

"I had a bad nightmare last night," she said flatly. "It's been one of the things that's been eating away at me all day. I dreamt I'd programmed a warhead at work – I even did all the basic mathematical calculations in my head while I was asleep. But as soon as I'd finished, instead of just filing it away as we really do at work, we got an order to actually fire the thing."

She paused for a moment.

"Sounds like a predictable sort of dream for a weapons expert," Robert said grimly.

Ingrid nodded.

"It is," she muttered. "I've often had nightmares about a real war and what it would mean. I suppose it's an occupational hazard. But this one was different. Nastier."

"Nastier? I can't think of anything much nastier."

"In the dream I was actually flying with the missile, rather like a bomber pilot. And so I saw where the thing was going."

She looked up at him and a strange, agonised look came over her.

"I suddenly knew it was going straight for you. It was an idyllic summer's day and you were playing in a garden full of bright flowers with your children. They were playing a game with pulleys, pretending to pull a car out of a ditch, and you were telling them about an aunt in a faraway country who they could always rely on even if they could never meet her. And all the time I was flying closer and closer with the missile I'd programmed. I desperately tried to change the controls, to alter the flight path so that it wouldn't touch you, but I'd programmed the thing failsafe so I couldn't break in. And then it was coming out of the sky, straight down towards you, but you still couldn't see it coming. I screamed at you to run away, to take cover. At first you didn't hear me but then, only seconds before it exploded, you suddenly looked up and stared at me. And in that second, I knew you could see exactly what I'd done."

She stopped.

157

"That's a pretty bad dream, Ingrid."

"Didn't you hear me call out?"

"No. I didn't hear a thing."

"When I woke up Mutti was in my room. I'd been screaming your name out loud and she'd come in to see what was happening. When she told me I was terribly embarrassed in case you'd heard me."

She paused for a while before continuing.

"As soon as I was dressed I went straight out into the garden to dig the snow, to try and shake off the memory of the dream through physical exertion. I'd almost succeeded when you came out into the garden and showed me the photographs of your children."

Robert looked at her, uncertain of the significance.

"I don't follow."

Ingrid looked away from him, nervously picking at her fingers.

"Don't you see, I'd never seen your children; I didn't know how many you had, what sex they were, what ages they were. For some reason neither Mutti nor you had got around to telling me. But when you showed me the photographs they were exactly like the children I'd seen in the dream."

There was a long silence. The memory of the dream was clearly painful to Ingrid, and it occurred to Robert that he ought to make light of it in some way, to avoid the awful significance of what she had imagined. But as he thought about it he realised there was no way to belittle the experience she had been through; her nightmare was only the gentle press of a button away from reality.

"Surely you've always known that the missiles are aimed at ordinary people, Ingrid," he said finally. "You must have known that."

"Of course I did," she said quietly, "but in the past it's always seemed so absurdly abstract. Like a kind of intellectual game. We always talk of 'targets', never of people, and I've never in my life known anyone who was a part of one of those targets."

Robert looked at her with surprise.

"Never? But surely . . ."

"I tell you never," she interrupted. "They wouldn't employ me in a job like mine if they thought I was unreliable. When you're selected, they give you a ferociously strict security vetting and if you've got friends or relatives in the West they just don't select you. It's as simple as that. And you are forbidden to have any sort of relationship with people from the West."

Robert laughed drily.

"Sounds familiar, Ingrid. Do you think it's any different for me?"

She looked at him thoughtfully for a moment.

"No, I don't suppose it is."

"It's a joke, isn't it. We both happen to find ourselves in influential jobs on opposite sides of the Wall. You might suppose that it would be particularly important for us to know and understand people on the other side. But the one thing our respective governments are apoplectically terrified of is that we get to know each other."

"You're right, it doesn't make any sense."

"It makes bloody good sense. It suits your establishment and mine equally well to make out that anything and everything on the other side of the great divide is utterly evil. It simplifies the issues tremendously."

Ingrid got up and walked over to the window, gently pulling aside the curtain and looking out into the night beyond.

"You said you had a nightmare too," she murmured.

Robert joined her by the window.

"I'll tell you if you want, Ingrid, but in some ways mine was even worse than yours."

She looked at him, her dark eyes fixing him in a searching gaze.

"Tell me, Robert. Tell me what you dreamt."

"I was lying on the bed in this very room. But I couldn't move, I was completely paralysed from the neck down. My wife was standing just there, by the side of the bed. She was furiously angry with me and kept screaming at me that I was sleeping with a younger woman. I tried to calm her down, to stop her, but I found I couldn't speak."

Ingrid smiled.

"Is it true?" she asked.

Robert looked at her with a wry smile.

"It's funny," he said, "Kate really did accuse me of being unfaithful just before she left for Christmas. When she did, it wasn't true. She was the only woman I'd ever slept with."

"But now it is true?"

"Yes. The very next day I slept with someone else, a girl in East Berlin."

Ingrid looked at him with disbelief.

"You slept with an East German girl! You're a diplomat and you slept with an East German girl!"

"Yes. Like I said, I've been doing some pretty silly things lately. Her name's Sonja, and she's only twenty-one years old."

Ingrid's face turned white.

"What did you tell her?"

"Listen Ingrid, I know exactly what you're thinking. But I really don't believe she's State Security. I might be wrong, but I just don't believe it. It was a friend of hers in the Ministry of the Interior who helped me trace you.''

Ingrid walked away from the window and returned to the bed. She kicked off her shoes and lay down.

"I just hope you're right," she said.

Robert knew there was nothing he could say. It was perfectly obvious that everything Sonja had said to him could have been part of an elaborate act.

"Robert," Ingrid said quietly, "it sounds to me as though your dream was like mine – just a guilty conscience at work."

"Of course it was, but that's precisely what was so disturbing about it. You see, the dream didn't just end there with Kate's accusations. She finally tired of screaming at me and swept melodramatically out of the room, slamming the door furiously behind her. I lay back exhausted, thinking I was alone, but then I became aware of another figure in the room, the figure of a girl hunched up and all alone. It was Sonja.''

Robert looked at the place where she had been, crouched down between the central heating radiator and the armchair. In the dream she had seemed so incredibly real.

"She was completely naked, her slender body curled up about her as if she was making an unsuccessful attempt to fight free of her own thoughts. And as I watched her I could see that she was sobbing to herself, tears of infinite self-pity rolling down her cheeks. At first she didn't seem to be aware of my presence, but I could tell that it was I who was the cause of her distress. You can't imagine how much that girl loathes this country, Ingrid, and how much she wants to get out. And in the dream it suddenly became obvious to me that just by being with her, by letting her start a sexual relationship with me, I had stirred up within her a kind of desperate subconscious hope that she might escape with me to my world. Yet now she knew I was going to leave her and the awareness of that reality had driven home the full extent of her misery.''

"Is that why she slept with you?" Ingrid asked gently, no trace of censure in her voice. "Because she thought you'd help her?"

Robert looked sharply at his sister.

"No, she isn't like that. Sonja's not like that at all. If you met her you'd see at once that she can't abide the idea of using people. In the dream, she suddenly became aware of my presence and the fact that I had glimpsed right into the depths of her despair. She rose from the corner and approached me, begging me to forgive her for allowing me to see how miserable she felt about my departure without her. But it was all too late, and nothing she could say or do could shake the overwhelming feeling of guilt and shame that swept over me. But then, before I could find a way to comfort her, she simply faded away from view, leaving nothing but her memory behind. Once again I was left all alone."

Ingrid looked at him with sympathy.

"Your conscience has been giving you a bad night, hasn't it?" she said.

"But that's the whole point, Ingrid. Both Kate and Sonja were utterly justified in everything they were saying and thinking. I even knew they were at the time, when I was actually experiencing the dream. So what really threw me was when you appeared."

Ingrid sat bolt upright on the bed and stared at him.

"In the dream?"

"Yes. This is the second time you've been here tonight. You came in my dream as well."

There was a long silence.

"Look, Ingrid, I really don't think it's a good thing for me to start telling you all this. It was only a silly dream."

But Ingrid's face was deadly serious. "Tell me, Robert. Tell me what happened."

"Suddenly I was no longer alone and you were standing by the bed. But you didn't look like you do now; you were gaunt and drawn, as if you hadn't eaten properly for a long time. And for some reason you were not wearing your normal clothes but a kind of drab blue overall, as if you were living in an institution. You looked down at me with dull and lifeless eyes and told me quietly, with absolutely no trace of emotion in your voice, that I had killed my own mother. I tried to speak, to ask you to explain what you meant, but my voice didn't work. And then you slowly turned around and walked out of the room, quietly pulling the door closed behind you."

Ingrid said nothing. She just lay on the bed, motionless, staring at Robert with a strange confused expression. And as he watched her lying there, he suddenly became aware of an overwhelming desire to hold her in his arms.

His sister looked at him for a long time before she spoke.

"Hold me, Robert," she murmured, her dark green eyes looking at him with a pleading expression. "I'm so terribly frightened I don't think I can bear it much longer."

Robert lay quietly down beside her and took her head in his arms. And then, ever so gently, he started stroking her thick dark hair.

"I'm so sorry, Ingrid, I'm so sorry any of this ever happened."

She didn't reply, but he could feel her shudder beneath his touch. When eventually she did speak, her voice was scarcely more than a whisper.

"I lied to you when I came here tonight. I told you I came because I felt guilty about sending you away from Mutti."

There was a long pause.

"I've always been so unbearably lonely. It doesn't hurt too badly most of the time, I just push the feelings away. But I've never felt really close to anyone. And now you've walked into my life out of nowhere, and it has to be you of all people whom I know I can trust. In the woods today, when you stood there like that and told me you'd go away and never return, I suddenly knew that I . . ."

She stopped, searching for the right word.

"That you love me."

Ingrid lifted her head up from his chest and looked at him for long time.

"Yes. That I love you."

Robert closed his eyes. He had not expected the words, but now that she had uttered them he realised that there was a growing sense in which they were true for him too. Why else would he feel so strongly that he wanted Ingrid to share every one of his innermost thoughts and fears?

He opened his eyes again. Ingrid was still looking at him, tears rolling slowly down her cheeks. He wiped them gently away with the sheet.

She put her head back down on his chest and they lay together for a long time listening to the gentle rhythm of each other's breathing. And then they both fell fast asleep.

* * * * * *

She stirred and he opened his eyes. For a moment he felt disorientated, unsure of exactly who he was holding in his arms, but then the memory of the previous night flooded back and he remembered that it was his sister. It was morning, and the crisp winter sunshine glinting through the cracks around the still closed curtains served as evidence of the frozen world beyond. But inside the centrally heated hotel bedroom it was stiflingly hot and Robert lifted Ingrid's sleeping head gently onto the pillow so that he could slip into the bathroom and fetch himself a glass of water.

When he returned he sat down in the armchair by the bed, sipping the water and gazing thoughtfully at Ingrid's face. In her sleep she looked so tranquil, so content, and Robert dreaded the moment when she would awake and have to face reality.

The previous night didn't make leaving any easier but leave he would undoubtedly still have to do.

Robert smiled bitterly at the thought of his own insufferable arrogance. He had thought of himself as so big, so important, as if he was the only one putting his future on the line by all this extraordinary subterfuge. But in reality he was just a nothing, a miserable little pen-pusher of a civil servant who happened to know a few lousy secrets about what the Secretary of State thought about negotiations with Eastern bloc countries over trade in textiles. The secrets he knew were trivial small change compared to the devastating mass of Warsaw Pact data that his sister carried around within her head.

And if it were just too awful for his conscious mind to contemplate what the bastards would do to her if they found out that she was deceiving them, a dream had forced him to recognise the truth.

Robert rose quietly to his feet and walked slowly over to the desk. There was some writing paper embossed with the name of the hotel arranged carefully in a little rack. He pulled out a clean sheet and started to write.

'Dearest Ingrid,' he began, 'I will be gone when you have read this note, because I know that if we speak again I might weaken in my resolve. Somewhere within you you must know, as I also know, that we cannot ever see each other or communicate with each other again, however much we may both wish to do so. In order that you understand my reasons for leaving I will first tell you what to do when you have read this letter. When I go I will pay the bill and leave the hotel immediately, saying I have to return urgently to Berlin on business. I will, however, leave the 'Do Not Disturb' sign hanging on the doorhandle so that the cleaning staff will not come in before you leave. This should not give rise to any great risk since I very much doubt that the cleaners liaise with the reception staff about who has left until much later in the morning. In case you oversleep I have left my own travel clock on the bedside-table with the alarm set for eight o'clock. When you awake you should take the clock and leave the hotel by the side-door to the left of the main lift; you will find it cannot be seen from the reception desk. This letter you should of course destroy immediately.

'Ingrid, you must understand that this kind of action is typical of what I have come to regard as normal during recent weeks. Yet neither of us is a spy and neither of us has any particular wish to become a spy. I can tell you from bitter experience that this kind of subterfuge is no way for decent human beings to live and I cannot see that it would ultimately be possible for either of us to find any kind of happiness in perpetuating a relationship surrounded by such behaviour.

'Do not misunderstand me, Ingrid. I know that there is a growing bond between us and it is not just you who feels the strength of that bond. I do not pretend to know or understand why it exists, whether it is because we are brother and sister or for some other reason altogether. But I do know that it does exist and that I love you too.

'I wish you every future happiness. Although our crazy world will not allow us to be together, we will always be with each other in our thoughts. Goodbye, my little sister. Robert.'

* * * * * *

Robert kicked off his shoes as he came into his flat and nervously checked the floor to see if any visitors had left notes for him during his absence. But there was no visible evidence that anyone had called round while he had been away so he ambled through to the lounge and dropped into his favourite armchair with a recent copy of 'The Times'.

He put his feet up on one of the other armchairs in the room and tried unsuccessfully to concentrate on reading the newspaper. But eventually he gave up trying and put the paper down: it was becoming abundantly clear that he would not be able to think clearly about anything until he had forced his increasingly complicated life back into some kind of order.

His dream had pointed the way; that much was obvious. If only he would listen to the wise councils of his conscience then perhaps he would yet be able to recover his equilibrium. That morning he had taken the first and most difficult step, and had cut and run from Ingrid before it became too late, but the problems posed by the other women in his life remained as yet unresolved.

Kate was relatively easy, because in some ways the dream had already been overtaken by reality. When he had last spoken to her it had been Kate who was seeking his forgiveness, and as long as he responded to her overtures in a spirit of generosity there seemed to be no logical reason why they could not resume their relationship as before. By a strong effort of will he succeeded in pushing firmly into the nether regions of his subconscious the awkward question of whether he really wished to resume that relationship.

It was Sonja who presented the real dilemma. He could cut and run, as he had done with Ingrid, but whereas Robert had left his sister in the certain knowledge that it was in her best interests, he could use no such justification in the case of Sonja. He shuddered. She had been so kind to him at a time when he desperately needed that kindness, and he now knew that if he just walked out on her the guilt would haunt him for the rest of his days.

It was not the first time that the thought of trying to get her out had occurred to him. Earlier, while he had been crossing over to the West at Checkpoint Charlie, he had found himself carefully eyeing the border defences to see whether there was the remotest chance of getting her across in his car.

There was undoubtedly a chance he could succeed. It would have been unthinkable for ordinary visitors, but he had an unfair advantage: as a fully accredited diplomat to East Germany he was in possession of a fancy set of diplomatic papers. Normal motorists leaving the country, unless travelling across the heavily policed transit routes from the West, would as a matter of routine have their cars thoroughly searched to establish that there were no undocumented human beings tucked away somewhere in the vehicle. But diplomats were different and the East German border police would only dare search a diplomatic car if they had certain and positive proof that a human being was concealed within.

Robert thought carefully about the mechanics of such an operation. His car was fairly large, with plenty of room for a small girl like Sonja in the boot. He would simply have to drive over to East Berlin, tell her what he was proposing to do and bundle her straight into the back of the car before driving back over the border. Assuming that Sonja really was honest about her purpose and not a member of the Security Police, he should be able to manage it without any trouble.

Robert took out his car keys and fingered them nervously. If he was going to do it, he should do it now before his nerve broke. He looked at his watch and saw that it was just gone midday. If he left straight away, he could have her out by two o'clock. He rose from his chair and moved slowly towards the door, but then he checked himself and sat down again: impulsive though he might have been becoming of late, it was absolutely ridiculous to embark on such a venture without at least trying to plan in advance for all the eventualities that might arise.

The trouble was, the longer he thought about it, the less straightforward the plan became. Sonja herself was the first problem; she would probably simply refuse to go with him. It was not hard to imagine what would happen: she would look at him with those big baleful eyes of hers and simply tell him it was too risky and that she would never forgive herself if he ended up serving ten years in an East German labour camp on her account. And if he persisted she would laugh and make light of her situation, pretending that she was sure they would agree to her leaving soon in any case. What on earth was he supposed to do if that happened, tie her up and physically force her into the boot of his car?

But even if he did persuade her to come, there were other objections to the plan. For example, if the State Security Police had worked out that Sonja had developed a close relationship with a senior Western diplomat they would in all probability have placed a tail on her. If that was the case, and he had to accept that it was a distinct possibility, then he would probably be detected picking her up and stopped as he crossed the border.

Which brought him to the next problem. What exactly would he have achieved if he were caught and ended up in a labour camp because, as was quite likely, the British authorities refused to bail him out by pleading diplomatic immunity? He would have got Sonja and himself locked up, and also left his wife and children without any means of support.

He put the car keys back in his pocket and helped himself to a large Scotch. Surely if he sat there long enough and thought about it hard enough there must be a better solution.

* * * * * *

"Come along in, sir, we've got some very exciting girls in the show tonight. I'm sure you won't be disappointed."

"No thanks," Robert muttered, pushing past the sleazy little man who had scuttled out from what looked superficially like a bar into the night-time bustle of the Kurfürstendamm. Not in the least upset by his rebuff, the man began to retreat to his lair in order to wait for the next single man who chanced by. But then a thought occurred to Robert and he turned.

"Excuse me!"

The man looked round.

"Yes."

"I'm looking for a bar called the 'Pussy Cat'. Do you know where it is?"

A smile spread slowly over the man's face.

"Oh," he said with a wink. "Now I can see why you weren't interested in our little entertainment. The 'Pussy Cat' is about two hundred metres down there, on the other side of the road."

"Thanks," Robert muttered, unsure of the precise meaning of the man's remarks.

"Hope you have a good night!" the man sniggered before shuffling away.

From the outside, the 'Pussy Cat' looked like a pretty typical sort of city centre disco, with flashing neon lights and an array of plastic pot plants arranged just inside the window fronting onto the street. The loud music throbbing deep within was spilling out into the cold night air, luring passers-by with the promise of warmth and excitement within.

Robert pushed open the door and went inside. The disco was not particularly large, with low tables and a small bar tastefully arranged around a compact dancefloor towards the back of the room; and the rather claustrophobic atmosphere created by the cramped surroundings was magnified by the sheer volume of the heavily amplified music. With the exception of the crowded dancefloor, over which bright multi-coloured strobe lights were playing, the place was dark and gloomy, lit only by small candles on the tables and some dull red background lighting. But the striking thing about the disco was neither the noise nor the gloom, for Robert realised with a shock that the room was full of homosexual men.

He looked around and shuddered. Unlike the men of his father's generation, Robert had never been openly hostile to homosexuality, yet the scene that now met his eyes he still found hard to accept. At the tables and on the dancefloor, men were openly embracing and kissing other men, as if suddenly released within the confines of the bar from the artificial restraint under which they continually laboured in the heterosexual world beyond the doors.

A man who appeared to be some kind of waiter approached, and somewhat to Robert's surprise he spoke with a perfectly normal voice.

"Good evening, sir. Are you here on your own?"

"Yes," Robert mumbled, "I'm alone."

"Well, sir, why don't you come and meet some of the boys over by the bar?"

Robert followed obediently towards a group of three pleasant-enough looking young men sitting on high stools by the bar. When he first saw them they were talking animatedly to each other but as they saw him approach they fell silent.

"This gentleman's by himself, boys," he waiter explained. "I wonder if you'd like to look after him."

One of the young men smiled broadly at Robert.

"Hallo," he said. "I'm Fritzy. This is Helmut and he's Hans. What's your name?"

"Heinrich," Robert replied. "Nice to meet you."

"Want a drink? It'll warm you up."

The one called Hans seemed amused by this.

"We're good at warming people up," he sniggered.

"Shut up, Hans!" Fritzy snapped. "Don't take any notice of Hans, he's got no manners."

Robert looked at the three and realised that he had no choice but to get straight down to business if things were not to get rapidly out of hand.

"I would like a drink," he said, "but I haven't come here for a night out. I saw the sheet of paper stuck on the observation tower near the Brandenburg Gate."

The three men fell silent, the flirtatious look on their faces suddenly transformed into one of extreme caution.

This time it was Hans who spoke, but now his voice was serious and controlled.

"And what would you like to drink, Heinrich?"

"I'll have a Scotch."

He called over to the barman.

"A Scotch for the gentleman, and tell Michael not to disturb us."

Then he turned and stared straight into Robert's eyes for a long time, as if trying to form an instant judgement of how much he could be trusted.

"Who is it?" he said finally.

"A friend. A close friend of mine."

"Male or female?"

"Female."

"Where does she live?"

"East Berlin. Köpenick. In a shared flat."

"Job?"

"She cleans the toilets on the S-Bahn."

Hans flicked a sharp glance at the other two.

"So what did she do to deserve that?"

Robert shrugged and said nothing, uncertain what he meant. Hans leant closer to him, and Robert recoiled at the strong scent of perfume that filled his nostrils.

"She's in trouble with the Security Police, isn't she? That's why she's doing that crummy job. It might mean they've got a tail on her."

"She's not important. She just put in a request to leave the country, that's all."

Hans looked at the other two with a grim smile.

"O.K. How old is she?"

"Twenty-one."

Hans looked at him with surprise.

"Twenty-one. Who is she anyway? A relative?"

Robert looked at him irritably. Hans was beginning to annoy him with his stupid monosyllabic questions.

"Does it really matter who she is?" he said brusquely.

Hans sat back in his chair and slowly lit up a cigarette.

"You don't know anything about this game, do you?" he muttered softly. "So you'd better listen to what I say real good because I don't like repeating myself."

Robert began to regret his earlier remark.

"It's just money to you, isn't it? You pay the money just like if you want a new car. But you've got to understand that this business ain't no game. People are going to have to go over there and risk their lives to get your girl out of that stinking hole. So when I ask you a question, you just answer it, and you answer it straight."

Robert nodded.

"I'm sorry," he said, "the girl is a close friend of mine. I had an affair with her a while ago but now it's finished. You might call it a debt of gratitude."

Hans smiled.

"That's better," he said. "Now give me your I.D. please?"

"My what?" Robert said, playing for time. He had been expecting to be asked for money, not identification papers.

"Your identification papers. I have to see your identification papers."

Robert sighed. These people were professionals; there was no point in lying to them. If he did, they'd just chuck him straight back out on the street where he came from. And anyway, Hans was right, somebody would be risking a lot to get Sonja out.

Robert pulled out his diplomatic papers from his jacket.

"I lied to you before. My name's not Heinrich, it's Robert Creighton Stanton, and I work for the British Embassy in East Berlin."

He handed Hans his papers and for a long time the three men studied them carefully.

Finally Hans looked up and handed Robert back his passport. When he spoke, he spoke in fluent English.

"I'm sorry, we just can't risk it. It's too dangerous."

Robert looked at him in consternation.

"What do you mean?"

169

"I'm sure your friend is very sweet. But you've been conned, Mr Robert Stanton. That little innocent you know over there is ninety-nine percent certain to be a fully paid-up member of East German State Security. I'm very sorry, but we just can't touch her."

* * * * * *

'British Airways regret to announce that flight number 7159 from London to Berlin has been delayed by approximately two hours due to fog at Heathrow. British Airways regrets any inconvenience caused.' Robert cursed and turned away from the arrivals area. What a way to spend New Years Day!

There was a coffee bar on the far side of the concourse and he walked disconsolately towards it. It wasn't that he was so enthusiastic about his impending reunion with Kate, in fact quite the opposite, but he had been bracing himself for her arrival all day and now he'd have to do so for another two long tedious hours.

He walked into an antiseptic-looking airport coffee bar. Half Europe must have been covered in fog because the room was crowded with people apparently awaiting flight arrivals. But eventually a table came free and he lowered himself gratefully into a chair before ordering himself a large pot of coffee and a pair of frankfurters.

There was what looked like a group of students sitting at the next table chatting away to one another. They were all about the same age as Sonja, and Robert frowned as he remembered the total blank he had drawn in the Kurfürstendamm bar the previous night. Sonja was an intelligent girl, she had a right to be there with these young people, studying at some university or other for a career that would match her obvious talents. Yet instead she was serving out an indefinite punishment for no other crime than that of wishing to be free.

One of the students, a young chap in a scruffy shirt and jeans, seemed to be having a heated but friendly argument with the others about the status of the Allied powers in West Berlin. The concensus around the table was that the status quo should remain, but this particular young man seemed to feel passionately that Britain, America and France should tear up the post-war agreements with the Russians and allow West Berlin to become a fully integrated part of West Germany.

"Damn the Russians," he was saying, "I don't for the life of me see what it's got to do with the Russians."

A girl sitting opposite him started laughing.

"You must be stupid, Helmut, you really must be. What about 1948? What about the Wall? They'd be in here like a shot if we gave them half a chance. You should thank your lucky stars the Allies are prepared to stay here rather than trying to push them out."

Robert smiled to himself as he listened to the young man trying to convince himself and the others around the table that there really was nothing to be afraid of. He was so incredibly naive.

He picked up the frankfurter that had appeared in front of him while he was listening to the conversation and lifted it mechanically to his mouth. But then, without taking a bite, he slowly lowered it to his plate again and looked thoughtfully at the young man. Perhaps he had found just what he needed: an incredibly naive young man.

* * * * * *

Sonja opened the door of her flat.

"Hallo, stranger," she said with a smile, "I've been waiting for you. I thought you'd be back days ago."

Robert looked at her anxiously.

"Can I come in, Sonja?"

She stood back to let him pass before closing the door.

"Is your flat-mate here?"

Sonja looked at him with concern.

"No, she's out tonight. What's the matter, Robert?"

"Oh, nothing. Fancy a walk?"

"No way. It's all right for you lazy bureaucrats, but I've been on my feet all day except for when I sneak a little sit down on one of the toilets to read a book when nobody's looking."

Robert frowned.

"All the same, Sonja, I think a walk would do you good."

Without a word, she disappeared to another room and collected her coat.

"On second thoughts, I'd love a walk," she mumbled, opening the door and following him outside.

They walked in silence until they came to the local park. The fresh snow that had been there on their last visit had largely melted, replaced by an unpleasant mixture of sludge and mud.

"O.K. Robert. What's up? You didn't bring me out here because the weather's so inviting, did you?"

"I'm sorry, Sonja. Something about this country makes me paranoid."

She looked at him with an amazed expression.

"You don't really think they're bugging my flat, do you?"

"Probably not, but I didn't see any reason why we should take

171

the risk, not with what I've got to say to you."

Sonja looked at him for a long time before she finally spoke.

"This is the last time I'm going to see you, isn't it?"

He stopped and took her slender hands in his.

"We both knew it wouldn't last, didn't we, Sonja? My wife came back to Berlin yesterday. I'm probably going to be sent back to London in a few days time. It's got to finish."

She looked away, and for a fraction of a second Robert could see that everything he had imagined in his dream was true. But then she smiled again, leaning up and gently kissing his cheek.

"I've no regrets," she said. "No regrets at all."

He looked at her, trying to work out how she was going to react to what he was about to say.

"Sonja, I'm not going to leave you here when I go."

It took her a few moments to grasp what he had said. But then she suddenly did.

"What do you mean?" she said nervously.

"If you want to go, I've arranged to get you out to the West."

Sonja froze.

"But how?"

Robert laughed.

"Even if I'd asked them that, which I didn't, I'm sure they wouldn't have told me," he said, "but you can be sure they'll let you know when they're ready."

Sonja was trying to keep her cool, but he could tell that she was soon going to crack.

"Robert, will you please tell me what you are talking about."

"I'm sorry, Sonja, I'm not being very clear, am I? Over the weekend I've been doing quite a lot of thinking. About me, and about how I've got to lead my life from now on. I've been trying to straighten everything out. But I decided I can't straighten everything out while you're rotting away in this dump. So I decided to do something about it."

He could see her flinch.

"You don't owe me anything. Nothing at all. I didn't have sex with you so that you'd help me."

He put his arm around her shoulder and started to steer her gently along the path.

"I knew you'd say that, Sonja. And what's more I know it's true. In point of fact, if it weren't true, I probably wouldn't have done what I have done."

She looked at him plaintively.

"But I still don't know what that is!"

"Like I say, I decided to try and get you out. At first I thought I'd come and bundle you into the boot of my car and smuggle you out under diplomatic cover. I nearly did it a couple of days ago."

She looked at him in horror and Robert immediately realised that he had been right in thinking that she would never have agreed.

"But despite my cover it's still too risky." He glanced around at the other people in the park. "Look at them all," he said. "If the Security Police have worked out that I'm seeing you, and that shouldn't have been too difficult for them if they're as efficient as everyone always says they are, then any one of these people in the park might be keeping an eye on us to see what's going on."

Sonja remained silent, waiting for him to continue.

"The next thing I did was stupid. So stupid that I frankly surprised myself at my own lack of intelligence. I'd heard about escape organisations that smuggle people out for money, and I tracked one of them down . . ."

Sonja was starting to look frightened. "Do you have any idea what it costs, Robert? You're talking about big money. At least forty thousand marks. West marks. You can't even think about spending that on me."

"It's no big deal, Sonja. I'd only be lending you the money. Before I went to see the escape people I visited a rather sleazy firm of money lenders and arranged a loan over ten years for the money. It was dead simple. I told them I was a British diplomat and that I'd been having a run of bad luck at a West Berlin casino without my wife or my employers knowing. They took one look at my passport, took a photocopy of it, and lent me the money. DM40,000 in grubby used banknotes, with my reputation as a diplomat as security. They agreed I needn't start the repayments for a year. If you get out, you can get a job and pay them back. You can think of the repayments as the price of freedom."

She smiled.

"And if I don't get out?"

"Then it's my problem, Sonja, but I can afford it."

She said nothing.

"Anyway, I went to see the escape people. I thought that if I had the money they'd agree to do the job, but then they asked to see my identification papers."

Sonja laughed drily as she suddenly realised the implications.

"And they told you that you were being led a merry dance by a sexy little tart from the State Security Police and that you could take your business elsewhere."

Robert laughed.

"Right in one."

"So what did you do then?"

Robert grunted. He didn't particularly want to be reminded.

"Got drunk and saw in the New Year all by myself on the Kurfürstendamm."

"That must have been fun."

Robert didn't reply. It had been a miserable evening.

"For a while I really thought I'd have to leave you here. But then I had a brainwave, or perhaps it was simply a stroke of good fortune. I was in a little coffee bar at Tempelhof, waiting for my wife's plane to come in from London and idling my time away listening to this student at the next table. He seemed to combine extreme gullibility with naive idealism in roughly equal measure, and then I realised that here was exactly what I needed – an idealistic and gullible young man of about your age who was in possession of the right papers."

"So you've been telling lies, have you, Robert?" she said with the impish grin that had so attracted him on the day they first met. For a moment he wished their affair was not yet over.

"Listen, you do want to get out of this place, don't you?" he said angrily, pushing his memories of her naked body firmly aside.

Sonja's face froze, her smiling face replaced by a look of silent desperate hope.

"Yes," she said simply. "Yes, I do."

"Well, the gullible student finally went off on his own and I approached him. I started off by telling him about the night just before Christmas when I saw those two young people trying to get out across the Wall. I told him how one of the two had run up and spoken to me before being led away by the police. All that was true. But then I dropped the lie. Instead of saying that the man had given me his own name, I said that he had given me the name of a girl – a close friend of his – and had begged me to help her escape."

Sonja looked at him with a strained expression.

"He didn't believe that, did he?"

"I can look very honest when I want to, Sonja: it's my diplomatic training – the trick is to believe the lie when you say it. Anyway, I told him that I'd only had a few moments to speak to the man before he was pulled away and that I'd agreed to do what he asked."

Sonja could not resist smiling.

"By this time I could see he was eating out of my hands. I told him I couldn't help you myself because of my diplomatic status but that I really couldn't live with myself if I didn't at least try to do what I'd said I'd do. I told him how he could help and he agreed to act as your lover."

"My lover!"

"I'm afraid so. Why else would anyone want to buy a one-way ticket across town for forty thousand marks?"

"But I don't even know his name, this lover of mine."

"He's called Helmut. But you've got to do more than know his name, you've got to know him. In fact, in about two hours time you're going to meet him at the Rosenkranz Cafe in the Alexanderplatz. You'll be carrying a copy of 'Crime and Punishment' by Dostoyevsky and be sitting alone drinking coffee. He'll come over and start chatting to you. And later on he'll come back with you to your room."

Sonja's mouth dropped open.

"Hang on a minute."

"I'm sorry, Sonja, but we've got to do it this way, I'm afraid. I've burnt my fingers with these escape people and I can assure you that they're pro's; we have to reckon that they'll check on absolutely everything they're told, including establishing whether you really are having an affair with my Helmut."

Robert could see that Sonja was reeling, unable to absorb all the myriad implications and dangers in what he was proposing.

"But there's another reason why I want you to meet the man, Sonja. It's not for me to decide whether or not to trust him. All I'm risking is money whereas you're risking a pretty hefty labour camp sentence doing much worse things than clean toilets if you get caught."

Sonja looked at him and nodded.

"I understand," she said quietly. "Tell me what to do if I trust him, and tell me what to do if I don't."

"If you want to go ahead, then tell him that the deposit required for the escape organisation is held in a safe-deposit box at the Spandau branch of the Potsdamer Bank and that he can get access to it using the code name 'Trumpton' and the code number 89375. I've already told him how to make contact with the escape organisation."

"And if I don't trust him."

"Then it's up to you, Sonja. I'll leave the money there for one year from today and you can find someone else – someone you do trust – to do the job. Or if you'd rather not risk it, then you can stay here."

Robert could see that tears were beginning to roll down Sonja's face.

"I trust you, Robert, but don't know how to tell whether I trust anyone else. I just don't know."

He put his arm around her shoulder.

"I think you'll know when you find someone," he said eventually. "Everyone keeps telling me you're a member of the State Security Police, and logically they're all correct, but the funny thing is that I'm prepared to stake everything on the fact that you're not. Sometimes you just know."

"What book did you say I should carry with me?" she asked, wiping her tears away.

"'Crime and Punishment'."

"Very apt," she laughed, pulling out a large handkerchief and loudly blowing her nose. "Very apt indeed."

"There's one more thing, Sonja."

"Yes."

"When you see Helmut, and assuming you want to go ahead with it, tell him to leave it a few months before approaching the escape organisation. If the Security Police are by any chance watching you because of me, they'll soon get fed up with doing so once I've gone back to Britain. So don't forget – the word is 'Trumpton' and the number is 89375. And if you do get out, remember you'll need the balance of the money to pay the escape organisation. It's in an account coded 'Upper' with the number 89376 where you'll also find all the details about repaying the loan. Helmut doesn't need to know about that bit."

Robert looked at his watch; it was nearly seven o'clock. Kate would be expecting him for a dinner that she had no doubt spent all day preparing.

"I've got to go, Sonja," he said gently.

She looked at him again, her slender face pale and drawn in the early evening moonlight. Yet Robert could see that deep down within her he had lit a candle to help her through the difficult months ahead.

"Robert," she said, "if I get out, can I come and see you – see you in England, perhaps?"

Robert took her hands in his and looked into her eyes. For the second time in less than a week, he was forced to say good-bye.

"No," he said finally, "don't ever try to contact me again, Sonja. I owe that much to my wife."

She nodded quietly.

Robert leant down and kissed her gently on the cheek. And then he turned and walked away across the park, his feet squelching noisily through the dirty sludge.

* * * * * *

Eventually he turned a street corner and Sonja was gone. Reluctantly his thoughts turned to his wife. The previous day, when her plane had finally arrived, she had seemed so incredibly pleased to see him. She had not spoken again of their row, and Robert could see in her face that during her time in England she had decided simply to ignore any extra-marital affair he might be having. It was not that she was condoning the existence of such a relationship, but rather that she could see no alternative way of coping with a situation in which, as she supposed, he was being unfaithful to her. It was as if she had calculated that her future was inseparably linked with his, and that if she detached herself from him she would have nothing left.

The problem was that as soon as Robert tried to analyse the reasons for her reactions, he found himself increasingly annoyed by them. As in everything else Kate had ever done, she was simply trying to please him, to satisfy the partner with whom she would be able to achieve the acclaim that she so desperately sought and that she was so patently unable to achieve in her own right.

The streets were nearly deserted and Robert glanced around, wondering for some reason whether Sonja might have followed him. If she had been there he would probably have weakened in his resolve and gone back with her there and then to her room. But behind him there was only a young man in a long grey greatcoat shuffling along with his collar pulled up around his neck to fend off the cold.

Robert crossed the road and trudged on towards the car. He tried to remember why his relationship with Kate had seemed to work so well in the past. He had lived with her for over ten years and never in that time had he really questioned the notion that he loved her. He tried to work out if she had changed in any way, but there was nothing he could put his finger on. But if she hadn't changed, the only logical conclusion he could draw was that it was he who had changed. Robert frowned with the realisation that if that were true, it did not augur well for the success of his determined attempt to turn the clock back in his life as if nothing whatsoever had happened.

He finally arrived at his car and quietly unlocked the door. But as he did so he froze. For behind him, no more than two hundred yards away in the direction from which he had come, he had caught sight of the young man in the greatcoat whom he had seen earlier.

He was standing in the doorway of a rundown tenement block, staring straight at Robert and talking discreetly into a small black object in his hand.

Robert pulled the car door open and quickly clambered inside. For weeks he'd been acting on the assumption that unless he was careful it would happen, but the shock of actually seeing the State Security Police observe his movements was deeply disturbing.

He turned the key and the engine hummed into life. Trying hard to retain a grip on his emotions and think clearly, he swung the car out into the street and started heading slowly back towards the city centre. He glanced in his rear mirror, wondering if one of the cars behind him could be a tail, but as soon as he had done so he realised that even if they were following him they could do him no harm because of his diplomatic status. Yet he still shuddered as he contemplated what would have awaited him at the border if he had tried stuffing Sonja into the boot as he had originally planned.

As it was, Sonja was probably going to be all right. As far as he was aware, she hadn't broken any laws by talking to him or even by having an affair with him. Even if they picked her up for questioning, he was confident that she would have the sense to say nothing. They would have to let her go, and within a few months, by the time she made her move to escape, they would probably have forgotten all about her.

It was not Sonja who was in danger, but rather Ingrid. For if they had by any chance followed him to Thuringia then despite his precautions they would almost certainly have become aware of his connection with her. In his mind he could see his sister again as she had been in the dream, gaunt and sallow as if she had been in prison for a long time. Yet the harder he tried to convince himself that they were unlikely to have followed him down there, the greater the burning sense of guilt within him seemed to become.

For a fraction of a second Robert wondered whether he should try in some way to warn his sister, to alert her to the fact that he was being followed, but it only took a few moments for him to realise that any such course of action could achieve nothing and perhaps only serve to lead them to her if they had not yet established the link. There was nothing he could do but pray that they had not detected her.

The traffic thinned as he pulled away from the main thoroughfares in the centre of East Berlin and drove through the drab, silent streets near to Checkpoint Charlie. Few East Berliners came to this area, constant reminder as it was of their imprisoned status, and the semi-derelict buildings by the side of the streets reinforced the dismal impression that the war had only just finished.

Robert slowed cautiously as he approached the border itself. Despite his diplomatic status he could feel his heart pounding as he drew the car to a halt and waited for the East German officials to come and inspect his papers. If they had decided that he was spying, perhaps carrying classified documents with him to the West, there was at least a possibility that they would stop and question him.

A smartly dressed East German border guard approached his car and Robert wound down the window and handed over his papers. The guard seemed to study them more carefully than usual, and Robert fought hard to control the feeling of panic growing within him. He glanced ahead, wondering for a fraction of a second whether he should put his foot on the accelerator and try to swerve around the myriad obstacles that lay between him and the fluttering line of Allied flags that marked the demarcation line itself.

The guard bent down and peered through the window at him. Putting on the haughtiest diplomatic face he could muster, Robert stared directly at the man and purposefully held out his hand.

"Please. I'm in a hurry."

Suddenly flustered, the guard hurriedly handed them back and saluted. The officious little man must have been new to this game, more used perhaps to tyrannising helpless tourists or West Berliners than to dealing with the East Berlin Diplomatic Corps. Breathing a deep sigh of relief, Robert pulled the car forward and drove slowly towards the border.

The road thinned to a single lane as it passed through the Wall itself, and Robert could see the thin black line drawn on the road that marked the exact position of the Iron Curtain. It seemed ridiculous that a line painted on a road could mean so very much, but Robert could sense the tension flowing out of his body as his car passed across the line and back into the familiar world of the West.

The usual bored cluster of American servicemen were standing around a run-down hot dog stand by the side of the road near to where the Allied flags fluttered gently in the breeze, but other than that there was little sign of life. Robert slowed the car as he approached the West Berlin customs post, glancing at his watch and trying to estimate how late he would arrive home for dinner.

He drew the car to a halt by a low building where a bored G.I. normally sat and yawned behind a pane of glass as he waved people backwards and forwards across the border, confident in the knowledge that his opposite number on the East German side would do sufficient checking for them both. Robert held up his papers, expecting to be waved through as usual, but this time the American, who wasn't looking bored at all, took his papers from him and started carefully examining them.

Robert looked at him with curiosity, wondering whether he too was new to his job, and waited patiently for their return. But then, instead of handing them back, the soldier stood silently up and disappeared from view into a small room at the back.

Robert's heart skipped a beat and he glanced around, trying to make sense of the situation. But what he saw offered little comfort, because three armed American soldiers had emerged from the shadows behind him and were purposefully blocking the road back to East Berlin while three more were taking up positions just in front of his car.

This time Robert couldn't control the panic. Surely this had to be some kind of stupid mistake. He pushed open the door and started to get out of the car, but as he did so the soldiers tensed and lowered their guns.

"Get back in the car," one of them commanded, his broad Texan drawl permitting of no misunderstanding, and Robert hurriedly did as he was told.

A little way away a door opened, and three men in civilian clothes emerged. Two of the men Robert didn't know, but there was no mistaking the third: it was Angus MacPhearson, British Ambassador to the German Democratic Republic.

The two men with the Ambassador held back and he approached alone. Robert braced himself. Whatever it was they thought he had done, he must at all costs avoid looking guilty. The soldiers seemed more relaxed now and he got out of the car.

"Angus, can you tell me what's going on, please? What's the welcoming party all about?"

Angus looked utterly miserable.

"I'm sorry about all this melodrama, Robert. I told them it wasn't necessary but I'm afraid I was overruled."

"Overruled?"

"I'm afraid so. These two gentlemen would like a little word with you, that's all. They've flown in specially from London."

Robert looked behind him at the three soldiers barring the road back to East Berlin and suddenly it all became clear. Somehow or other M.I.5 had managed to convince themselves that he, Robert Creighton Stanton, was working for the communists. The soldiers were there to make sure that he didn't make a dash for safety back to the East.

Robert looked directly at Angus, his eyes pleading.

"I'm not a spy, Angus. You know that."

The Ambassador squirmed.

"Why don't you answer all their questions honestly and openly, Robert, and I'm sure you'll be able to sort everything out."

One of the two men from M.I.5 was speaking to one of the soldiers and the American approached them. Without saying anything, he got into the driving seat of Robert's car, turned on the engine and started to drive away.

"What the hell are they doing with my car?" he asked, but Angus just frowned.

"I've already phoned Kate and said you won't be back yet," he muttered, and then turned and walked away.

The two men approached. They were both middle-aged, perhaps in their mid-forties, and were soberly dressed in dark suits and ties. Robert had on several occasions had dealings with members of the security services, and it had always struck him that although they looked superficially like any other Whitehall bureaucrats, there was a strange hidden reserve in their faces, as if they were constantly aware that they were players in a deadly poker game in which people's lives were the stake-money.

It was the taller of the two who spoke.

"Mr Stanton, will you get in the car please," he said, indicating a large black limousine parked nearby. His voice seemed devoid of emotion. Robert looked at him glumly.

"I don't seem to have a lot of choice, do I?" he said quietly, walking slowly towards the car.

* * * * * *

The room was far from uncomfortable. There were no windows, but on one wall there was a large photograph of the Queen resplendent in military uniform while on another there was a painting of open moorland and sea that reminded Robert of a childhood holiday he had once spent at a remote cottage in the Scottish Highlands. There were several armchairs, a rather ornate writing table with an equally ornate chair tucked neatly underneath it and, more ominously, a bed. Through a discreet door just next to the picture of the Queen was a small but well-appointed bathroom.

Robert sat in the most comfortable of the armchairs and gazed at the image of the moorland view. It crossed his mind that the picture was somebody's idea of a joke, since the wild and open sense of space conjured up by the painting stood in such stark contrast to what was, despite the relative comfort of the room, quite clearly a prison cell.

The building in which the room was located was of a modern construction and stood deep in the thick forest which lies on the western fringes of West Berlin. His two besuited companions on the journey from Checkpoint Charlie had ignored all his attempts at starting a conversation and on arrival they had brought him straight up to the room. As they had left he had thought he could detect the crisp click of the door being locked behind him, yet for some reason he had not tried the doorhandle to find out.

He glanced at his watch. It was nearly ten o'clock in the evening, nearly two hours since he had been brought to the room, and he was gradually becoming aware of a nagging sense of hunger. For a brief moment he wondered whether they were proposing to leave him there without food until the next morning, but no sooner had the thought occurred to him than he heard the sound of a key turning in the lock.

He looked up, expecting to see one of the two men enter, but instead found himself staring at a tall, elegantly-dressed woman of about his own age. She was struggling with a heavily-laden tray of sandwiches and two large cups of coffee.

Robert rose as she approached.

"Hallo," she said in a remarkably friendly voice. "I've brought you something to eat."

"Thanks," Robert replied, uncertain of the woman's status, "I was getting a bit peckish."

His visitor smiled broadly.

"I'm sorry," she said apologetically, putting the tray down on the desk and handing him a cup of coffee and the plate of sandwiches, "but I've only just arrived."

Robert was tempted to express some surprise that neither of his silent companions on the journey had been capable of making some coffee and sandwiches but he decided to restrain himself.

"Don't mind me," the woman said cheerfully. "Eat up!"

She lowered herself gently into one of the armchairs and watched as he started munching mechanically through a cheese sandwich.

"I should introduce myself," she said just as he had placed a particularly large piece of food into his mouth, "I'm Dorothy Peterson from M.I.5."

Robert tried to dispose of the cheese sandwich as quickly as possible in order that he could reply without appearing rude.

"I would say I'm pleased to meet you," he said as soon as he had cleared his mouth, "but my parents always taught me not to lie."

"A very good principle, Mr Stanton," she said with a disarming smile, "but is it one by which you've always abided?"

Robert looked away, angry that he had left himself exposed to such an obvious jibe. He had been expecting some tough treatment from the two jollies who had driven him over from Checkpoint Charlie and now he found the woman's pleasant and relaxed manner distinctly disconcerting.

He slowly placed the remains of the cheese sandwich on the plate and looked up.

"Let's get down to business, shall we, Miss Peterson! Perhaps I should start by telling you exactly what I know?"

She looked at him with what appeared to be surprise.

"It would save some trouble," she said sympathetically.

"You have clearly formulated the view that I am involved in some kind of spying activity for the communists. Moreover, you appear to hold this view with some considerable degree of conviction, because you have made no attempt whatsoever to dress up bringing me here for this interrogation as anything other than an arrest. Am I correct so far?"

Miss Peterson smiled. "Absolutely correct, Mr Stanton."

"What I am less sure about is how it is you have come to form your exceedingly negative opinion of me. For the last two hours, apart from getting increasingly hungry, I have been sitting here trying to work out a satisfactory answer to that question."

Miss Peterson looked at him with feigned sympathy.

"I'm sorry, Mr Stanton, have I come too soon? I could easily pop back tomorrow if you'd prefer to get a good night's sleep before we talk."

She started to rise from her chair and Robert could feel his nerve beginning to break. Difficult though the conversation was likely to be, the last thing he wanted was to be left alone.

"I'm not in the least bit tired," he interjected rather too quickly, "and I don't require any more time to think about it. It's just that if you feel you have information that suggests I am involved in spying the very least you can do is tell me the evidence against me."

Miss Peterson allowed a sly smile to spread across her face as she slowly sat down again, as if to show him that she knew full well she had gained the upper hand. But the smile faded quickly and she fixed him with a penetrating gaze.

"You left the Embassy at five-thirty tonight and yet you didn't arrive at Checkpoint Charlie until gone seven. But the Embassy is only a short drive away from the border. Would you mind telling me exactly what you did during the intervening period of time?"

Robert flinched. If only he knew how much they knew, it would be easier to construct a suitable cover story to explain his movements. But the devious Miss Peterson was not going to oblige.

"I went for a drive."

"I wonder if you could be a little more specific?"

Robert took a deep breath. Too few lies were dangerous, but then so were too many.

"Since you must know, I went to see a girl I have become friendly with. An East German girl."

He could see Miss Peterson relaxing in the armchair opposite, as if she was relieved to have broken the ice.

"I see," she said non-committally. "An East German girl. You are presumably having an affair with this girl?"

Robert looked her straight in the face.

"I was. It's over now."

"Over? So why are you continuing to see her?"

"I broke it off tonight."

Miss Peterson balanced her coffee cup delicately on the wing of her armchair.

"And that is what you told her in the park?"

Robert stared at his interrogator incredulously.

"How did you know I told her in a park?" he asked sharply.

She looked at him sternly.

"Mr Stanton, you must realise we are not in the habit of arresting senior and highly respected members of the Foreign Service on hearsay. You have had some powerful voices speaking up on your behalf."

Robert tried to restrain the excitement he felt growing within him.

"So it was your man with the walkie-talkie. The young man in the greatcoat."

She looked surprised.

"You mean you saw him?"

"Of course I saw him. He was standing not two hundred yards away from me talking into it. I could hardly fail to see him."

She sat back in her chair and sighed.

"I told them he was useless," she said with irritation. "It's so hard to get good people for street work these days."

Robert sank back in his chair with relief. If it was the British who had been watching him and not the East Germans, then Ingrid and his mother were safe after all.

"And what did she ask you to do, this pretty young girlfriend of yours?"

Robert tried to smile.

"I know exactly what you're thinking," he said, "but you're wrong. The girl has nothing to do with the Security Police."

"And you I suppose are presuming that she is a sweet little kid with a great body who thinks you are the most wonderful man she has ever met."

Robert could feel himself relaxing. If this was the best they had on him then they'd find it hard to make a spying charge stick in court.

"Miss Peterson, I realise that I have broken the normal rules of the Diplomatic Service by having an affair in this manner in an Eastern Bloc country. And to be honest I can appreciate your suspicion of me under the circumstances. But I can assure you that even if the young lady in question is a member of the State Security Police, which I don't believe for a minute to be true, she never asked me for any information relating to my work."

Miss Peterson looked at him intently for a few moments. Then she reached quietly into a pocket hidden in a fold in her dress and produced a small brown envelope.

"I wonder," she said calmly, "if you could take a glance at the photograph in this envelope and tell me who you see."

He took the envelope from her and pulled out the photograph from within. It had clearly been taken from a considerable distance and then magnified, because the image was blurred and indistinct. But despite the lack of clarity there was no mistaking the face in front of him.

It was that of his sister.

LONDON, JULY 1980

The summer sunshine was streaming in through the window onto the wall opposite. Robert lay on the bed and watched as the vertical shadows thrown up by the bars crept slowly along the white painted surface of the wall. A wry smile passed across his face as he realised that in his earlier life, in his life as a busy man of affairs, he had never been aware that you could see a shadow move. It was like watching a flower grow, or seeing the hour hand on a clock move round. It was an occupation that required time.

In his present circumstances time was the one thing that was certainly not in short supply, especially now that the prison warders had started this ridiculous work-to-rule and the inmates were locked away in their cells for many hours at a stretch. Normally the prisoners were only locked up at night, but now – apart from the relative excitement of slopping-out, mealtimes and exercise periods – there was nothing to disturb the tranquility of the endless days.

The shadows of the bars crept relentlessly onwards, as they did every day when the sun shone, and he felt a growing sense of excitement as the leading bar approached a little mark on the wall where some of the paint had been chipped away. The passage of the first bar across that little mark had assumed a special importance to Robert, rather as some people find a particular passage in a Beethoven symphony particularly exhilarating. It represented a triumph over fate, and signified more clearly than anything else in his present life the passing of yet another wasted day.

The cell was designed for only one prisoner but such was the general state of overcrowding in the prison service that it contained two beds. For the last year, Robert had been forced to share with a numskull of a young man who had been locked away for failing to appreciate that helping yourself to the contents of your employer's safe without permission was contrary to the spirit of the free market economy. Two weeks ago he had been released, no doubt to commit a similar crime again, and Robert was finally able to feel some sense of amusement for the absurd quasi-intellectual way in which he had continually tried to justify his crime as a logical extension of Thatcherite economic values.

He became aware of the ringing metallic sound of shoes on the iron walkways outside his cell. The shoes grew louder and louder, until eventually they stopped outside his door and the heavy sound of a bolt being drawn back and a key being turned brought his reverie to an end. The door swung open and a thickset warder by the name of Turnbull entered the cell, closely followed by a rather frail-looking elderly man with horn-rimmed spectacles perched on the end of his nose.

Robert rose to his feet as they entered.

"Afternoon, Stanton, we thought you might like some company."

The warder's rugged face cracked into a friendly smile. It was obvious that he liked Robert, who was never any trouble, and despite the man's superficially gruff manner Robert couldn't help but reciprocate the feeling.

"That's very kind of you, Mr Turnbull. As it happens I was getting a bit lonely. It's nice to meet you, Mr ..."

"Smithson," the elderly man replied, his voice as frail as his looks, "but you can call me Peter."

The warder turned to leave.

"I'll give you some time to get to know each other, then," he muttered, pulling the door closed behind him and gently turning the key.

Robert waited until he had gone and then sat down on the bed again.

"That's Turnbull," he said. "He's one of the most decent warders here."

"Is he?"

"You can tell by the way he closed the door."

His companion looked surprised.

"How?" The man's accent was superficially upper class, but somewhere deep down there was a faint echo of an East End drawl.

"He didn't slam it. Most of them bang the door closed when they leave and lock the door as loudly as they can. Must make them feel powerful or something. But Turnbull was making a special effort not to remind us we're locked in. It's that kind of little touch that makes me think he's O.K."

Peter sat down wearily on the bed and Robert looked at him sympathetically.

"You look tired. Would you like me to shut up and let you rest?"

The new arrival looked at him and smiled.

"No, that's all right," he replied, "I don't mind talking. What did you say your name was?"

"I didn't, but it's Robert, Robert Stanton."

Peter looked at him sharply.

"How long you been in here, Robert?"

"Year and a half come next week, but it seems like longer."

Peter lay back on the bed and stared at the ceiling for a long time.

"I've heard of you," he said finally, turning his head to look at Robert, "but I can't quite place where."

Robert laughed.

"I suppose I did attract a certain amount of notoriety at my trial, even though I pleaded guilty."

Peter sat up and peered at him, his hitherto tired eyes suddenly alert and probing.

"You're that K.G.B. spy, aren't you? The one who got caught while you were working at the British Embassy in Moscow."

"Well, actually it was East Berlin and the East German Security

Service. But let's not split hairs."

Peter looked utterly delighted, all trace of his earlier exhaustion vanished from his face.

"What a bit of remarkably good fortune!" he grinned.

Robert looked at him with a puzzled expression.

"Why's it good fortune?"

Now it was Peter's turn to laugh.

"Oh, I just mean that it's my good fortune to share a cell with a real live spy, that's all. I thought I'd get some sort of thug – you know, someone who got caught beating all hell out of a little old lady somewhere – but instead I've got myself a real intellectual to keep me company. You really have made my day."

Robert smiled.

"Well, I'm pleased I've cheered you up," he said.

A frown passed over Peter's face.

"If you're a spy, why are you still here? I mean, why haven't they swapped you for one of our spies?"

"Maybe they don't want me back. I wasn't a very important spy."

Peter's face lit up.

"That's right, it's coming back to me now. You were blackmailed by them, weren't you? They got you ensnared with some sexpot while you were working over there and then started pumping you for all they could get. That's right, isn't it?"

"Yes. I'm afraid I was rather stupid."

"So you're not really a proper spy at all, not like Philby or Maclean?" He looked almost disappointed.

"No, not in that sense," Robert replied. "Sorry."

Peter looked at him for a few seconds and then laughed.

"I'll bet you wished you could get your hands on the girl who framed you now."

Robert thought of Sonja, and wondered as he had wondered many times since his arrest whether she had managed to escape to the West. In recent months he had imagined that she must have managed it, since nobody had come to ask him why a shady firm of money-lenders in West Berlin was writing to the Foreign Office enquiring when the first instalment of their loan repayments would arrive.

"Yes, I'd love to get my hands on her," he replied truthfully enough, although his meaning was quite different to that supposed by his companion. After a year and half without sex thinking about any woman's body was hard to endure, let alone thinking about Sonja's.

"How did they catch you, then?" Peter asked, obviously enjoying the conversation tremendously. "If you don't mind me asking, that is."

Robert shook his head. The funny thing about his previous cell-mate, the one who couldn't resist putting his hands in the till, was that during his many months of close confinement with Robert, and despite a tedious propensity to talk from morning till night, he had never once asked Robert anything about his past. To find someone prepared to listen to his story, even if it was a complete pack of lies, was quite a refreshing change.

"They filmed me in bed with the girl, the bastards. And not only in bed, but in all sorts of other places as well. They'd probably have preferred it if I'd been gay, but that girl managed to get me so utterly compromised in the space of a few evenings that they had the squeezers on me good and proper."

Once again, watching Peter's eyes light up at the yarn he was unfolding, Robert could only wonder at the ease with which it was possible to make people believe in a story they wanted to hear. He had fooled M.I.5, he had fooled the courts, he had even fooled the press and television with his lurid stories of sexual adventures with Sonja recorded for posterity on closed circuit television by the East German State Security Police.

Robert grinned.

"If you like, I'll fill you in on all the grisly details one evening."

Peter pretended not be overly concerned, but Robert could tell that he was already looking forward eagerly to an excellent evening's entertainment.

"Anyway, one day the bastards picked me up and showed me the films. They told me they'd pass them over to a couple of Western television stations and the British Foreign Office if I didn't co-operate. They explained that they didn't expect me to pass any very high-grade information, just some background material on political attitudes and so on. The worst thing about it was that the girl who'd compromised me then became my control – she even offered to carry on doing the things with me that she was doing on the films if I co-operated."

"That must have been quite an incentive."

Robert grunted.

"I'm afraid I couldn't see her in quite the same light any more."

"So how did the British catch you?"

"A bloody double-agent told my employers that the East Germans had recruited a new spy in the British Embassy. I'd just turned up in Berlin and they worked out the rest for themselves."

Robert paused. The strange thing was that the bit about the double-agent was true if the delightful Miss Peterson was to be believed. He could only suppose that a real spy had been recruited in the Embassy at about the time of his posting or that the British had made up the story in order to be sure of securing a conviction.

"So they picked you up."

"Yes. Right under the noses of the East Germans as I came across the border one evening. I thought it was a bit odd at the time that they'd done it that way rather than more discreetly but it seems they wanted to send a clear message to the Politburo that they were wasting their time with such ploys."

Peter pulled out a packet of cigarettes from his pocket and offered one to Robert. He shuddered inwardly at the thought of endless months breathing in the disgusting fumes.

"Want one?"

"No thanks, I don't smoke."

Peter looked alarmed.

"Mind if I do?" he asked anxiously.

"No," Robert replied reassuringly. "I don't mind at all."

It was extraordinary how well engrained the habit of lying could become.

* * * * * *

Robert finally gave up trying to sleep. For hours he had been trying to switch off his mind, to recover the sense of passive acceptance that he had felt the night before, and the night before that, and all the other nights for the last year. But Smithson's arrival had somehow managed to stir up once again all the secret fears he carried within him. Perhaps, after all, it was better not to sleep and risk exposing himself once more to the terrible nightmares that had plagued him to the verge of suicide during his first few months in prison.

Robert knew from bitter experience that there was only one way to combat the sense of panic and despair that came over him on nights like this. There was no point in running away, no point in trying to distract himself with thoughts of other things. The only way to cope was to address the sources of his misery head on.

The twin emotions of sorrow and anger jostled for primacy in his mind as he thought about Kate. Whatever he had done to her, however much he himself had wronged her, he surely hadn't deserved the savagery with which she had treated him since his arrest and public disgrace. A bitter smile spread slowly across his face as he remembered that he had intended to go back to her for good on that last cold winter night of freedom in Berlin.

He had neither seen nor spoken to her since then. At first, while he was still under interrogation in West Berlin, he had thought that it was his interrogators who were denying him access to his wife. Every time he brought the subject up and asked if he could see her or speak to her on the telephone, Miss Peterson had muttered that she would look into it and had moved swiftly on to other topics of conversation. But then, one day about two weeks later, she had come into the room and asked him to sit down and prepare himself for a shock. Then she had handed him a brief and formal letter from a firm of solicitors in England saying that his wife was seeking a divorce and asking for his consent. The letter explained in forthright terms that Kate had no desire to speak with him ever again and that she would be seeking absolute custody over the children.

In that moment, as he had read and re-read the letter, he had come to understand the nature of his relationship with Kate, or at least of her relationship with him. He had always assumed, even when he was himself being unfaithful to her, that she was utterly loyal to him. It was precisely because he thought she was so deeply attached to him that he had felt so guilty about his infidelity. Yet in that moment he had understood that she had never loved him at all, she had only loved the façade that was seen by the outside world, the façade of a successful diplomat whose sole role in life was to make her the wife of a rich and influential man.

There had been absolutely nothing he could do. There was no point in contesting the divorce, and it soon became clear that in view of the charges against him it would be equally fruitless to seek any legal rights of access to his children. So he had agreed to all her demands without a fight and had even given her absolute title over their home in England so that she would at least have some capital to help her bring up the family while he was unable to work.

He had thought that she would at least be grateful to him for not forcing her to go through lengthy and distressing court proceedings. But she had promptly sold the house and left for Australia with the two boys, presumably intent on escaping the shame of his public disgrace and starting again in the New World. Before her departure, she had instructed her solicitors to write and inform her former husband that she was leaving England for good and that it was her wish that he have no further contact with his children.

He slipped out of bed and fetched a small leather wallet from his drawer before sliding back under the covers. Opening the wallet, he pulled out the photograph of his children that Kate had sent him two weeks earlier, peering at their image in the dim light cast by the weak prison nightlight overhead. They were standing on a sunny beach in their bathing costumes, their young bodies bronzed by lengthy exposure to the Australian sun. Justin had his arm protectively around his younger brother's shoulders, and Robert wondered whether his older son had managed by some extraordinary effort of will to help replace his father in Timothy's eyes as a male figure to look up to and admire. But other than by looking at the photograph he had no way of knowing, because Kate had not sent any accompanying letter.

For over a year he had heard nothing, and then this photograph of the two boys had turned up out of the blue. He wondered why she had sent it to him after all this time? Was it possible that she was finally feeling some sense of remorse for the brutal way in which she had terminated their relationship? He looked again at the photograph and immediately discarded the theory. If she had felt even the slightest scrap of compassion she would have written a covering letter to say how they were all faring in their new life. But she had sent nothing and he fought back the feeling of despair growing within him as he realised that the photograph served no other purpose than to magnify the bitter torment she knew he would already be suffering at his separation from the boys he loved so much.

He lay back on the bed and closed his eyes, trying to imagine that he was there on that sunny beach. In his mind, the dull grey outlines of the prison cell were transformed into silvery white sand shimmering in the hot Australian sun. In his nostrils he could smell the fresh breeze as it swept in from the brilliant blue sea stretching away to the distant horizon and in his ears he could hear the sound of giant waves breaking and shattering into thousands of tiny white droplets before their energy was finally spent.

The boys were shouting as they played with a football, throwing it between each other as they ran backwards and forwards on the beach. Robert ran towards them, calling out first to Timothy, then to Justin, telling them that they should throw the ball to him. But however loudly he shouted, however much he gesticulated, they took not the slightest bit of notice of him. It was as if he were simply not there.

From the distance there was a call from a woman's voice and the boys stopped playing and dropped the ball, as if the woman had suddenly made them aware of his presence. For a moment they stood absolutely still, apparently unsure that it was really him, but then they started to run towards him, slowly at first but then increasingly desperately. He knelt down as they approached, and as they fell sobbing into his arms he could see with crystal clarity how sorely they had missed him during his absence.

For a long time he held them close to him as the sounds of their sorrow and relief mingled with the rhythmic crashing of the waves against the shore, but then he remembered the woman's voice, the voice that had made his boys realise that their father had not deserted them after all. And as he remembered the voice he became aware that the woman was kneeling by his side, holding him and comforting him as he in turn held and comforted his children.

He looked up and found himself staring into the face of his sister.

Robert awoke with a shudder and opened his eyes. Ingrid was gone. The boys were gone. Even the beach was gone. There was nothing but the usual drab surroundings of the prison cell and the rhythmic sound of Smithson quietly snoring in the neighbouring bed.

Robert got up and crept over to the washbasin, angry with himself that he had fallen asleep and allowed the nightmare to return. He splashed cold water over his face before putting the photograph safely back in its drawer and returning to bed. Why oh why did he always have to dream about Ingrid?

As so many times before, his thoughts returned to that night they had spent together in the hotel room high above the snow-laden pine trees of the Thuringian forest. She had come to him and held him as if he had been all that she had ever possessed and as he had held her in his arms and comforted her he had felt a feeling growing within him, a feeling of absolute trust and companionship, perhaps even a feeling of love, that he had known full well could have no future. So he had crept away in the morning without saying good-bye, hoping beyond hope that he would be able to put the memory of his mysterious sister behind him and console himself with the thought that he had saved her life from ruin by running away.

In the excitement of the days that had followed his hurried departure from her side, right up until the day of his final conviction on spying charges, he had really believed that he had pushed her memory and his feelings aside. It was only in the days and months that followed, during those first long months in prison, that she had returned to haunt him in his dreams. Always they were in each other's arms as they had been that night, never speaking, never moving, but always he could tell that with her and only with her was he safe.

It was a strange but terrible kind of nightmare, quite unlike any other he had experienced. Robert remembered other nightmares, especially one particularly terrifying one he had had as a small child in which he had been pursued by a grisly monster with huge bloodstained teeth. Just as it was about to tear his flesh apart he had awoken in terror, screaming so loudly that his parents had come running in alarm into his bedroom. But when they arrived they found him laughing, tears of joy running down his cheeks. The monster didn't exist. It was only a silly dream. And for weeks he had gone around in a kind of euphoria, so great was his happiness at simply being alive.

Ordinary nightmares could be bad, yet you awoke from them and realised how lucky you were that it was only a dream. But in his dream with Ingrid he was always serenely happy, and it was the bitter pain of waking to the sad and empty loneliness of reality that was almost too much for any human mind to bear.

He wondered what Ingrid was doing now and whether she had been able to continue living her life as before. He had paid – was paying – a high price for his determined attempt to keep her connection with him hidden from the East Germans, and yet he could only hope that his deceit had not been in vain.

The plan had occurred to him during that first night under interrogation in West Berlin. The suave Miss Peterson had shown him the photograph of Ingrid and he had been left with little choice but to think fast. He had had to assume that M.I.5 had been keeping a close tail on him during his entire weekend with his family. There was absolutely no point in his trying to pretend nothing had happened.

He had asked Miss Peterson for time to think and somewhat to his surprise she had agreed. She had left him alone until the following morning, and by the time she returned he had handed her a full written confession, explaining how Sonja had blackmailed him and how he had passed classified information to the East German authorities in exchange for their promise that they would keep quiet about his indiscretions. For good measure he had provided her with a full list of the material he had supposedly passed across.

By the time she had finished reading his confession he had been able to tell from the expression on her face that Miss Peterson was actually beginning to feel sorry for him. Here was no hardened spy, not even a traitor in any satisfying sense of the word, but a pathetic little man approaching middle-age with a failing marriage and a taste for bizarre sexual activities in which his wife was not prepared to indulge. Yet not only was she feeling sorry for him, she was feeling exceedingly pleased with herself, because she could return to her superiors with a full confession in a potentially difficult case in the space of less than twenty-four hours.

Only then had he known that the time was right to spring the only lie that could save his sister from certain discovery. He had told his interrogator that the woman in Thuringia was completely unconnected with the whole spying episode and that he had simply been looking up a family that his father had known at the end of the war. He had explained that on his arrival he had found that the woman in question was working in a highly sensitive field and was likely to be in very serious trouble if it was ever discovered that he had been in contact with her. He had appealed to Miss Peterson to keep Ingrid out of her internal report and out of any material that she submitted to the court when he came up for trial.

For several minutes she had studied his crestfallen face, and he had known that Ingrid's fate lay in her hands, but then she had quietly nodded her head and left the room. And so far as he knew that was the last that had been said or written about Ingrid by the British.

Had he really been left with no choice but to confess to a crime he had never committed in order to protect his sister? He had often lain in bed at night and run over the reasoning behind his hurried decision that night. But with what other choice had he been left? It was clear that M.I.5 had staked everything on a public conviction and a public disgrace. They had twisted arms in high places to get him arrested in the first place and they had even chosen to do so in full view of the ever-watching East Germans at Checkpoint Charlie. If he had not confessed, they would have pushed the case to a public trial at which they would have produced the offending photographs and reported on every aspect of his movements during his last weekend of freedom in Thuringia.

There had been another option. He could have tried telling them the truth, directing them to the fateful black volumes at St Catherine's House and revealing that Ingrid was really his sister. They would then have seen the death certificate of Robert Creighton Stanton for themselves and known that at least some of what he had said was true. But in all likelihood they would still have pressed for a conviction, and even if they did not, and had decided to drop the case, there was a always a danger that somewhere down the line, amidst the exhaustive enquiries that would undoubtedly have taken place as he tried to clear his name, the story would have fallen into the hands of some double-agent at M.I.5 and filtered back into the hands of the East Germans.

So he had gambled on a lie within a lie, throwing his interrogators the story they wanted to hear in exchange for their silence about a truth he wanted to repress. And so far as he knew, the plan had worked.

Robert lay back exhausted on the bed. Once again he had faced his living nightmare head on and won. Ingrid was safe. He had made her safe. And confident in that knowledge he could close his eyes and sleep through what remained of the long prison night in peace.

* * * * * *

Smithson gingerly pushed the knight forward.

"Checkmate!"

Robert stared at a move that looked blindingly obvious after the event.

"A good move, Peter. In fact I'd go so far as to say an excellent move. If you're as good at forging things as you are at chess I'm not surprised you made a good living at it."

Smithson looked downcast.

"The trouble is," he muttered, "chess and forging are the only two things I am good at, and making a living from playing chess is hard, whereas making a living from forging is easy."

Robert looked up with a smile.

"Easy but illegal!"

Smithson nodded sombrely.

"It's not my fault it's illegal," he grumbled. "In the war it wasn't illegal. I used to work for the Admiralty forging papers for the special units they sent over to the continent. In those days there was a good solid demand for honest forging work."

Robert laughed. "You should have gone and worked for the secret service. I'm sure they still needed some help after the war."

"I bloody well applied to the secret service. Both M.I.5 and M.I.6, in point of fact. After the war they came nosing about looking for people with the right talents and so it didn't take them long to find me."

He stopped talking and slowly started to pack the chess pieces away in their box.

"So what was the problem? Wasn't the pay good enough?"

"I don't know whether it was or it wasn't. They never got as far as telling me about the pay."

He paused and Robert looked up at him with a perplexed expression. From the tone of his voice it was clear that his rejection by Her Majesty's Secret Service still rankled after nearly four decades.

"So why didn't they want you, then?"

Smithson looked at him cautiously, as if trying to decide whether to say.

"Because I am what used to be called rather quaintly in those days a queer."

Robert looked at him in astonishment. There was no way anyone could have guessed from his looks or his manner.

"Are you?"

"Yes. I hope you don't mind."

"Mind? Me? Not at all."

Smithson laughed. "You're a decent chap, Robert. You really are a decent chap."

"Why?"

"You mind like hell if I smoke and you really do find it a bit hard to stomach that I prefer men to women. But you pretend you don't mind either prediliction so as not to upset me."

Robert looked away. Despite their totally different external appearances, there was a striking similarity between Smithson and Sonja. Both of them seemed to share not only the ability to remain cheerful in adversity but also the knack of seeing right through Robert Creighton Stanton.

"I'm sorry it's so obvious."

Smithson smiled.

"That's all right. As it happens I'm sorry that I can't give up both habits. They're bad for me in equal measure. I tried many times when I was younger and always failed, so now I've given up trying."

"So you've never been married or had children?"

Smithson lay back on the pillow and smiled.

"I've been married to many different women and I've had countless children, but only ever on paper."

Robert smiled. "Forged paper?"

"I'm afraid so. Forging fresh sets of papers becomes something of a habit. Rather like smoking, I suppose. But it probably accounts for the fact that I escaped the long arm of the law for so long."

"This is your first time inside, isn't it?"

"I fear it is. I'm no more of a jail-bird than you are."

"So how did they catch up with you?"

"I decided to retire. Start living a clean life on the right side of the law."

"That's hardly a reason for getting arrested."

"That's what I thought. I must have been getting sentimental in my old age but I claimed a state pension in my own name. I just wanted to use the name my parents gave me for a change. It was the first time I'd used it for years. A fatal mistake, I'm afraid. It turned out they'd been looking for me under my real name ever since the early 1950's when some clever bastard in Special Branch had done a piece of handwriting analysis on a false document I'd done and matched it up with some work I did for the Admiralty during the war."

Robert laughed.

"Bad luck, but if you ask me I'd say you were having the last laugh. They're paying a damn sight more to keep you in here than they would be if you were just getting a lousy state pension."

"It wasn't even as if I needed the stupid pension," he grunted. "I'd stashed plenty of cash away for my old age. I just liked the idea of going down to the Post Office with all the other old grandpas to collect it."

Robert looked at him with curiosity.

"Tell me, what sort of things did you forge?"

For a moment Smithson glanced at him suspiciously, wary of his line of questioning.

"Sorry," Robert muttered hastily, "I shouldn't have asked."

But Smithson's face was already relaxing.

"There's no reason I shouldn't tell you. After all, when they picked me up I asked for all my many other crimes and misdemeanours to be taken into account." He paused for a moment before continuing. "In the fifties I was mainly involved with business fraud. You know, legal documents and that sort of thing. But then in the sixties the government must have been feeling that the forging business was in the doldrums, because they decided to give us a legislative boost."

"Let me guess," Robert interjected. "Immigration controls?"

"Yes. A real forgers' charter, that's what immigration controls were. It's not just boring old passports, you know. It's birth certificates, marriage certificates, even driving licences. You'd be surprised at the variety of work involved."

Robert picked up one of the chess pieces and started fingering it absent-mindedly.

"I met some people who must have been involved in forging when I was in West Berlin," he said. "Gays actually, like you. And their job was probably pretty similar to yours, except that they were more concerned with trying to get people out of a country than getting them in."

"From East Germany, you mean?"

"Yes."

"Personally I don't think there's any moral difference between a government stopping people leaving and a government stopping people coming in."

Robert looked at him sharply.

"Don't you?"

"Nope. When you're staring someone in the face who has a burning desire to get over a man-made border both policies seem pretty barbaric and inhumane."

It was certainly a novel idea. Robert had never before heard anyone openly suggest that British immigration controls could be compared with the Berlin Wall.

"But surely the East Germans have got a better right? A right to leave is surely more important than a right to enter?"

"What good is a right to leave when there's nowhere to go?"

"But there's always somewhere."

"So what about the Jews. The Jews who wanted to get out of Germany before the war because they were clever enough to read the writing on the wall. Many of them couldn't get out because nobody would take them in. Are you really saying the borders that shut them out were just and fair?"

"No. Of course I'm not, but modern British immigration controls aren't like that. We always let in people who are refugees."

"You really are a funny sort of traitor," Smithson grunted. "You're so touchingly British, so seemingly incapable of believing that dear old England can do anything brutal or nasty. But in order to do so you have to walk around with your eyes so tightly closed that I'm surprised you don't keep bumping into things."

"But why?"

"Think, man. Across this planet there are human beings living on diets as low in calories as anything ever experienced in Belsen and other equally innocent human beings dying of abject poverty and starvation in ways that are just as disgusting as the gas chambers of Auschwitz. Yet all we do is put up barricades to keep these people out of our country and out of our minds in exactly the same way as we did with the Jews in the 1930s."

Smithson stared aggressively at him, challenging him to deny the truth of the remarks he had uttered. Robert stared at the old man, trying to find a suitable reply, trying to find some way of justifying his country's actions in any other terms than those of brute selfishness. Yet no words came to him and he remained silent.

Smithson's eyes softened and a smile spread slowly across his face. But he didn't take his gaze off Robert for a second.

"Why don't you tell me the truth, Robert? You'd feel a whole lot better for it if you did, you know."

Robert stared at him in astonishment.

"What do you mean? What do you mean tell you the truth?"

"All that junk about sado-masochism in East Berlin bedrooms and spying for the communists. It's the biggest load of old twaddle I've heard for a very long time. I didn't think it sounded quite right when you told me in the first place but I wasn't quite sure. But now I am sure, and I just think it might save your sanity if you unburden yourself of what's eating away at your soul before it's too late."

LONDON, MAY 1981

It was the first time he had shaken Turnbull's hand.

"It's a pleasure to be able to call you Mr Stanton at last," the warder said with a smile as he moved towards the last door before the main gates and started to unlock it.

Robert smiled warmly at him.

"If you ever meet me again you can call me Robert," he replied. "And I want you to know how much I've appreciated your civil behaviour towards me. It was kind of you."

Turnbull shrugged.

"Everyone who comes into this place is a criminal, but you're all still human beings. And I like to make my own mind up about what kind of human beings."

He opened the door and stood aside for Robert to pass.

"Just walk across the courtyard and the officer will let you through the gate."

Robert glanced one more time at the kindly face of the warder who had done so much to make his stay in prison tolerable and then walked briskly past him into the warmth of the bright summer's day. About a hundred yards ahead, across the courtyard, the huge arch of the main prison gate loomed before him and, beyond, the freedom he had been so painfully denied for more than two long years. Yet as soon as Turnbull had closed the door Robert found his pace slowing until he was standing completely still.

It was hard to adjust. Hard to accept the simple fact that beyond that huge gate lay freedom. He glanced nervously behind at the closed door through which he had just come, remembering the security of his prison routine. But there was no way he could go back, even if he had wanted to, so he had no choice but to start walking towards the little wooden door set into the bottom of the gate.

Outside, his father would no doubt be waiting with the car as they had arranged when they had spoken on the phone the previous week.

John Wilberforce Stanton had been to visit on several occasions since Robert's incarceration, but they had never felt able to talk freely in the public confines of a prison visiting room. Yet during those visits, while they had been chatting about Robert's mother's health or the latest gossip from the golf club, Robert could tell that his father was fully aware that his adopted son was concealing something important about the time he had spent in Berlin.

He had had every right to demand an explanation. Robert had lost his children, but his parents had lost their only grandchildren with the same sudden brutality. It must have been almost as hard for them to endure the separation as for him. There was no doubt about it, his father deserved at long last an honest account, and that was exactly what Robert intended to give him as soon as he had the chance.

An officer was waiting by the gate and opened it silently as Robert approached. Clutching the customary brown paper package containing his few personal possessions, he stepped over the threshold into the street beyond.

He looked around. There was little apparent sign of life, and although there were some cars passing up and down the road, there was no sign of his father or a waiting car anywhere to be seen. Robert looked at his watch, which suddenly seemed to have taken on a new significance now that he was released from the tightly regulated regime of the prison, and then looked around again. If anything he was a little late, and it was strange that his father, who as a military man was normally so proud of his punctuality, was not yet there to meet him.

He was just wondering what to do when a taxi-cab pulled sharply to a halt at the kerb nearby. The door swung open and an ageing, rather portly-looking gentleman got out and started to fumble in his pocket for some change.

Robert shrank back, suddenly wishing he could crawl back through the little wooden door into the security of the prison. For the man who had emerged from the taxi was not his father; it was none other than Sir George Burberry, Member of Parliament.

But there was no escape. Sir George had finally succeeded in paying his taxi fare and was striding towards Robert with his usual purposeful air.

"My poor chap," he exclaimed, grasping him firmly by the hand as soon as the opportunity permitted, "my poor old chap!"

Robert was suddenly aware of the shabbiness of the brown paper package under his arm. He tried to smile.

"Sir George," he said, "how nice to see you. But I was expecting my father."

"Yes, young fellow, I know you were expecting your father and I'm sorry to disappoint you, but he asked me to come and pick you up since he couldn't make it."

"He couldn't?"

"No. He's gone and done his back in. Did it on the fourteenth, silly man?"

"But I spoke to him only last week. That was after the fourteenth."
Sir George grunted.

"I didn't mean the fourteenth of May. I meant the fourteenth hole. It's a particularly long fairway, you know."

"You mean while he was playing golf?"

"That's right. Taking a swing with the wood. Just goes to show you what a dangerous game golf can be." A sly smile spread over Sir George's rotund face. "Rather like spying, I suppose!"

Robert looked at him, wondering how to reply, but Sir George's mind had already switched to the task of attracting the attention of a passing taxi.

"I'm a stupid fool to have let that other one go," he said gruffly. "I really must be losing my marbles."

A taxi slowed to a halt and they got in.

"56, Berkshire Street," Sir George replied crisply to the taxi-driver's enquiring look, as if he were surprised at the man's apparent inability to read his mind.

"Are we going to your flat?" Robert asked.

"Spot of lunch before you set off down to Upper Trumpton, that's all." He hesitated. "I'd take you to the Club, only it's a bit difficult. I'm sure you understand."

Robert nodded silently. Sir George didn't show it, but the public disgrace of his erstwhile protégé must have come as a terrible shock. Robert wished he could explain, wished he could at least reassure Sir George that he was no traitor to his country, but of course he couldn't.

It was strange. He had trusted Peter Smithson with the truth, even though the man had spent his entire life deceiving people, but for some reason he wouldn't trust this kindly old M.P. who ever since his schooldays had been prepared to take his side at every turn.

"Tell me how you are, Robert. I mean, are you still the same person, or have you changed?"

Robert looked at him for a moment. There was a look of deep pity and concern in Sir George's face that somehow didn't make sense. He had always assumed that his political benefactor would have reacted to his conviction on spying charges with complete revulsion. Yet he obviously hadn't.

"I'm still the same person. I'll always be the same person," he said quietly, "only perhaps I now know a bit more about the kind of person that I am."

Sir George nodded sympathetically.

"It's hard to be not what you seem, isn't it?" he muttered quietly, almost as if he were speaking to himself.

* * * * * *

The lunch had been excellent, a welcome change from the dreary routine of prison catering, yet despite the quality of the food and the plentiful supply of claret that had accompanied it, Robert felt miserable and depressed as he left Sir George's Berkshire Street flat and headed off on foot for Waterloo Station and the train to Upper Trumpton.

Sir George had told him some disturbing truths about his parents. His mother, in particular, had gone downhill fast since his arrest. She was much frailer than she had been of late, and Sir George had warned Robert that he would have to be very careful how he handled her. Sir George did not mince his words: Robert's mother was close to despair primarily on account of her abrupt and total separation from her grandchildren. In Sir George's view, Robert should do his upmost to track Kate down in Australia and demand some proper rights of access.

As Robert walked slowly over Waterloo Bridge, watching the murky waters of the river making their slow progress down towards the sea, he reflected that it was hardly any wonder that his mother was so upset. She had lost her own child when he was only two years old and had replaced him with another, bringing the replacement up as if he were her own. Yet now, thirty-five years on, she was having to endure the grief of separation from children she loved for a second time – and again as a result of events that were entirely beyond her control.

Robert stopped walking. He could feel a sensation of raw, cold anger growing up within him. It was a strangely intense feeling, a feeling he had never felt before, but he suddenly knew how it was possible to knowingly hurt someone. Whatever he had done, Kate had no right to behave as she had done since his disgrace, and if she valued her life she was going to grant him and his entirely innocent parents some kind of civilised access to Timothy and Justin.

Within seconds he had resolved how to act. The anger was still burning within him, still just as strong as before, but it had now been overlaid by a layer of cold, calculating logic.

A taxi swung into view round the corner and he hailed it. There was just a chance, even if only a fairly slim chance, that Kate had been stupid enough to leave a forwarding address at their old London home when she had sold up and left the country.

* * * * * *

The road looked so reassuringly familiar. The ornamental cherry trees on the broad grass verge lining the pavement had only just finished blooming and the new leaves were still green and crisp, full of the tantalising promise of a long warm summer ahead. It had been the same time of year when they had first moved into the house when the children were small, and Robert could remember so well teaching them to ride their bikes at the weekend on the grass verge adjoining the pavement. The boys had tried to dodge in and out of the trees, rather as though they were an obstacle course, and every now and then there would be floods of tears as one little boy or the other would fail to complete the prearranged course without falling off.

The taxi deposited Robert outside his old house. It was a large, rambling, semi-detached property which had always had a garden that was too large to maintain properly, particularly in view of the lengthy periods of time that they had had to let the place when he was posted abroad. The tenants had never bothered with the garden, and they had invariably been faced on their return from overseas with a jungle to clear.

The garden at least seemed pleased to have new owners, because everything was in good order, with new roses lining the long path to the large wooden front door. Robert carefully put his brown paper package down behind one of the rose bushes and walked up the path to ring the bell.

Eventually the door opened and an elegant, well-dressed Asian lady approaching middle-age appeared.

"Can I help you?" she enquired, her accent showing absolutely no signs of her Asian ancestry.

"Yes, I hope so. I was wondering if you had a forwarding address for some people who used to live here. In fact, they were probably the people from whom you bought the house."

"I'm sorry," she said, "they didn't leave one. The lady who lived here was emigrating, I believe, and she did say she'd send us a forwarding address, but she never did."

Robert cursed inwardly. Why was it that he seemed destined to spend his entire life running around trying to track down various members of his family?

"Oh," he said politely, "well, thank you anyway."

He turned to leave, but then a thought occurred to him and he turned to face the lady again.

"Er . . . I don't suppose you kept the letters that came, did you?"

"Of course I did. They're not mine to throw away, are they?"

"Well, perhaps you should give them to me."

She looked at him suspiciously.

"Why should I give them to you? You don't know her address either, do you?"

"No, but I'll be speaking to some people who probably do. You see, I'm an old schoolfriend of hers but I've been abroad for some time. Since you don't have the address, I'll look up someone else from school who I'm sure will have kept in touch and then I can send the post on to her and remind her to send you a forwarding address. You know, Kate was always very well-organised; she probably did send you the address and it got lost in the post. You know what the post's like."

The woman nodded her head sagely. Everyone knew what the post was like. He could see her beginning to relent.

"All right," she said finally, "I suppose they're not doing much good here, are they?"

She turned and disappeared for a moment, reappearing with a sizeable bunch of letters stuffed into an old cardboard box.

"Here you are," she said, "but if you do manage to trace her, do please tell her to send us a forwarding address. You're the second person who's been round asking this week!"

"Am I?"

"Yes," she said, "but you must excuse me, I've got to go and pick up my kids from school and I'm late already."

The woman grabbed her coat from a nearby peg and left the house, pulling the front door closed behind her.

"Bye," she smiled as she walked briskly down the path.

Robert stood on what had once been his own front doorstep and watched her climb into her car and drive off down the road. Then he walked back slowly down the path, picking up his brown paper package as he went, and set off towards the Underground station.

He had only gone a few paces when he recognised someone walking towards him along the street. It was Mrs Watkins, their erstwhile next-door-neighbour, a sweet little old lady who had often done some babysitting for them as a favour when the kids were small. She had obviously been shopping, because she was burdened down with two heavy bags piled high with groceries, and because her eyes were lowered to the pavement she had not yet seen him. Robert approached her.

"Mrs Watkins!" he said with a smile, pleased to see a familiar face.

She put down her bags and looked up at him. But instead of the warm look of recognition he was expecting, he was met by a stare of complete disgust.

"Oh, it's you, is it?" she snarled.

Robert looked at her in horror.

"I just thought I'd say hallo."

For a moment Mrs Watkins was silent, as if trying to decide whether or not to speak her mind. But then she resolved that she would.

"I don't see any reason to say hallo to the likes of you, Mr Robert Stanton. Not only do you betray your country but you cast off your poor wife and children without so much as a second thought. Quite frankly, the words that I think are fit to describe a man like you are not the sort of words it's right for a lady to use."

And before Robert could reply she had picked up her bags and shuffled off past him down her garden path.

Robert looked after her as she went with a sinking feeling in his stomach. Was that typical of the kind of reaction he was going to get from the people he knew? Mrs Watkins really was as nice a woman as you could ever hope to meet, a warm, kind-hearted old soul who was never quick to criticise others. Yet even she now held him to be a leper, a person not fit to walk the streets. It was a depressing thought.

Robert stepped up his pace, eager to escape any further chance encounters with shadows from the past. The whole street was full of memories of a happier life, a life when he had felt so profoundly optimistic about the future, and the sooner he was away from it the better he would feel.

* * * * * *

Before long he arrived at the Underground and boarded the first train to Waterloo. He thought of taking a taxi, but it occurred to him that he was no longer a successful civil servant on a substantial government salary. Now he was an unemployed ex-spy, and money was going to be a commodity in distinctly short supply.

The familiar clatter of the Underground was somehow reassuring and he sat for a few moments watching the faces of the other people in the carriage. Here at least he was unknown, a man without a past or a future, just another ordinary nondescript passenger occupying a place where no-one else could sit.

He looked disconsolately at the cardboard box on his lap containing the letters delivered to his old address. He wasn't really sure why he had asked for them since they couldn't really help him in his search for Timothy and Justin, and he certainly didn't want to stir up yet more painful memories of a happier past. It occurred to him that he should simply deposit the letters unread into the nearest litter bin, but he resisted the temptation and started slowly undoing the string that held them together.

There were about twenty or thirty envelopes and he started to flick through the pile. Most of them appeared to be official letters of one sort or another, computer-generated reminders to pay subscriptions to periodicals and that sort of thing, but a few of them were personal, with handwritten addresses. There was one in particular that caught his eye. It was a plain, rather poor-quality envelope, and he didn't recognise the handwriting on it; yet the strange thing about it was neither the envelope nor the handwriting, it was the fact that it had been posted in Hungary, a country he had never visited and with which he had never had any contact.

Robert put the other letters back in the box and carefully studied the envelope. From the post-mark, it was apparent that it had been posted about a year before in Budapest. He tore the envelope open and pulled out the letter within. It was written in German.

'My dear brother,' it began, and Robert could feel his whole body tensing inwardly as he realised the letter was from Ingrid. Other than in his recurring dream in prison, he had managed to avoid thinking of her for most of the time he had spent in captivity. However much he might have sub-consciously regretted it, he had sincerely believed that his encounter with his sister was a closed chapter in his life.

'You must believe me,' the letter continued, 'when I tell you how hard I have tried to prevent myself from writing this letter, just as I tried once before to prevent myself from coming to your room in the hotel at Oberhof. But just as I failed on that other occasion, so I have failed again. I simply do not know where else to turn for help other than to you.

'I have often wondered what happened to you after you crept away from my side that night. I hope that you are happy, although I suspect that you are not. I have no way of knowing one way or the other.

'When I awoke and found your note a part of me knew that you were right to run away. As we each understood perfectly well, your contact with me was dangerous for us both. Unfortunately, however, your decision to cut and run came too late for me, because when I left the room and tried to leave the hotel as you had suggested, I found two officers from the State Security Police waiting for me at the bottom of the lift.

'They bundled me into a car and took me straight to a large building in Berlin that I think must have been their headquarters. At first they were straightforward in their manner of questioning, asking me why I had been holding clandestine meetings with a senior Western diplomat. I couldn't think of any convincing way to lie, so I told them the truth, that you were my brother and that I hadn't even known you were alive until you had turned up out of the blue.

'Then they started getting nasty. There were two men, big burly brutes who didn't seem to have a scrap of compassion between them but who shared a foul and disgusting sense of humour. They collapsed into laughter at my explanation, and then one of them got up and came over to me. With a snigger, he reminded me that since incest was anyway a serious offence I might just as well admit that I was passing high-level military secrets to the West via my secret meetings with you.

'At first I couldn't accept what was happening. I tried to persevere, to make them believe me, but the more I tried to convince them the more brutal their manner became. They clearly knew how I had tried to conceal my connection with you at the restaurant when I met my security chief and they asked why I had done so if I was innocent and why I had failed to report my knowledge of your existence to the authorities as soon as I had became aware of it. I floundered, and then one of the two, the one who had made the gibe about incest, started screaming at me, his face so close to mine that I could feel his warm spit on my face.

'I was a slut, a traitor, an agent for the capitalist imperialists. Even if it were true that you were my brother, that fact combined with my proven lies and deceits about my contact with you only served to confirm that I was a hardened spy. I had been spying for many years, concealing the truth under a carefully-maintained pretence of political loyalty and Party membership. Dirt like me, he shouted, could expect no mercy from the Party or from the People's Courts.

'Suddenly my whole world collapsed about me. I knew that whatever happened there was no way I could clear my name. And I also knew that with the secrets I carried within my head there was no possible way that they would ever risk letting me free again.

'Robert, I do not want to burden you with the details of all that happened to me during the days and weeks that followed. Suffice it to say that I was held in custody for many weeks and that I was very poorly treated during all of that time.

'The frequent "interrogations" were hardly that. They were opportunities for my persecutors to write a script for me to learn by heart so that I could recount my crimes in open court with total fluency. Many weeks passed, and by the end of that time I was more than ready to sign anything. In the final version, no mention was made of the fact that you were my brother, which they persisted in regarding as utterly unimportant, simply a long rendition of the way in which I had been accepting substantial payments in Western currency into a Swiss bank account over many years. It was also stated that the Western security services had promised to arrange my removal and that of my mother from East Germany as soon as my spying services were completed or the authorities appeared to be becoming suspicious.

'After I had signed the paper I was sent back to my cell. For days I was left alone, as I had rarely been left alone during all my time under arrest, and at last I had time to think.

'I thought of you, Robert. As you yourself feared, you had swept into my life from the other world that lies over the border and had destroyed everything that I had ever held dear. I should have hated you for that, hated you as I hated you before I ever met you, when our mother first told me of your existence. But my feelings were not those of hatred, they were feelings of intense closeness, a closeness that I knew we both shared on that last night together in the hotel. And even though you were far away, even though I knew that I would probably never see you again, it was that feeling of kinship that helped me survive those long and lonely days awaiting my trial.

'But then a miracle happened. It was the middle of the night and I was fast asleep in my cell. I was awakened suddenly by the sound of a key turning in the lock and saw an elderly man enter. This in itself was strange, because although the police building housed both male and female prisoners, the corridor on which I was held was reserved for women only and was staffed exclusively by female warders. But there was something else about him that was unusual; he seemed to exude a sense of quiet authority that was markedly different from the nervous, hectoring tone of the other police staff that I had met.

'Despite the fact that I was only wearing my nightdress, I stood to attention at the end of my bed as was the normal practice in the cells. I was frightened and had no idea what was in store for me, particularly in view of the fact that he had come to me in the middle of the night.

'The man came in and quietly pushed the door of the cell closed behind him. My heart was pounding, and the thought passed through my mind that he was going to rape me. But then he looked at me with a strangely distant look and said, so quietly that I had to ask him to repeat it, that I was going to be given a conditional release and that I was free to leave.

'I looked at him in bewilderment, trying to work out if this was some kind of bizarre practical joke that the prison warders played on the inmates facing long sentences. But his face seemed perfectly serious and I sensed that he was not joking.

'I asked him why, after the authorities had spent so many weeks trying hard to persuade me to sign a confession, they had decided to release me now that I had finally agreed to admit to the crimes of which I had been accused. But he looked at me sternly and shook his head, telling me that it was none of my business and that I should simply be grateful that the state had resolved to deal with me so leniently.

'He told me to sit on the bed and started to pace quietly up and down the room. Life was not going to be the same as before, he warned, because I was no longer going to be allowed to work at my old job. A new job would be found for me when I returned home. He pointed out, rather unclearly, that there would also be other changes in my domestic affairs, changes that I would find rather inconvenient. Finally, he told me that I would not be permitted to travel overseas and that I would have my identity card endorsed to indicate that I would need special authorisation from the police if I wished to travel away from the district in which I lived.

'I sat on the bed and stared at him, hardly listening to what he was saying. He spoke with the quiet authority of one used to power, and every now and then he paused and looked at me with an odd, non-committal stare. And then, when he had finished speaking, he suddenly turned on his heel and left the cell.

'A few moments later one of the female warders came to me carrying my normal clothes, the clothes I was wearing when I last saw you. She was a monster, not afraid to use both physical and mental techniques in order to undermine the confidence of her charges when the occasion arose. But this time she was polite, almost obsequious, as she lay my clothes on the bed and asked if I would like to shower before I left.

'I turned down the offer of a shower and hurriedly dressed since I was afraid they might change their minds. They escorted me to an outer office where my handbag and identity card were returned and another strangely subdued policewoman explained in more detail the restrictions that had been placed upon my movements. It was only when they had finished all this that I was taken to the street and told to return home by the first available train.

'It was wonderful to be outside, to be free again, and I felt a tremendous sense of elation as I walked though the dark streets of Berlin towards the station and then again as I boarded the early morning train bound for home.

'But my elation didn't last for long. As soon as I arrived back I knew that something had gone seriously wrong. It was early Sunday morning, and I was expecting mother to be at home in the kitchen. But when I called for her in the house there was no reply. I called again, a feeling of panic growing within me, and then I went up to the bedroom to see if she was upstairs. There was nobody there either, but by now I was sure that something bad had happened, because the bed was unmade. In all the years I lived with her, I had never once known a time when she had gone out without first making the bed.

'I rushed out into the garden and through the gap in the fence that led to our neighbour's house. We knew the neighbours well and I was sure that they would know exactly what was going on. I feared that mother was ill, perhaps that she had been taken to hospital.

'As soon as Frau Schneider opened the door I knew that mother was dead. Her kindly old face had pity written all over it as she took me inside to tell me how it had happened. It had been only a few days before, and she had gone round to cheer up mother, who had been very depressed since my arrest, but when she had arrived mother had simply been lying there on the floor, her lifeless body still wearing the apron in which she had been preparing some cakes to share with her neighbour.

'Apparently her heart had failed. I had known for years that she had a weak heart, and I can only assume that it had all become too much for her.'

Robert stopped reading. His eyes glazed over as he pictured in his mind the dead body of the woman at whose breast he had been raised. Was it possible that somewhere within him, far beneath his conscious mind, a memory lay embedded, a memory so strong and so powerful that it could account for the fact that he now found it almost impossible to accept the reality of her death?

For a long time he sat motionless, watching the empty blackness of the tunnel walls flash past, but then his eyes returned once again to the the letter in his hand.

'This news will, I know, come as a great shock to you. Although you never knew her as I did, she was as much your mother as mine, and you must have shared many experiences together before your conscious years. But her death is a simple fact, and there is nothing either you or I can do about it.

'Mother was dead, but I was still alive. In one sense I was free but I soon began to realise that my freedom was an illusion. That man who came to my cell had been right in saying that my life would never be the same again.

'Shortly after the funeral I was summoned to the local employment office. My job at the research station had of course been terminated and I had been found alternative work as a production line worker at a local paper mill. I couldn't believe it when they told me, thinking that there must have been some mistake. I told them that I was a physicist, perhaps one of the most highly qualified physicists in an entire country that is desperately short of good scientists, and that even if I couldn't work at the research station there must be some sort of useful civilian work I could do. But they just shook their heads blankly. The paper mill was the job that was allocated to me and the job I would have to do.

'I have worked there to this day. It is not particularly strenuous, but it is frustrating to spend so many hours each day doing the same repetitive work. At first I tried to keep my brain alive by thinking up ways to improve the technical operation of the mill. It did not take long to think up several, because both the working practices and the equipment are extremely antiquated, but when I went to see the plant's managers with my ideas they reacted with outright hostility, telling me bluntly that no changes were needed. They seemed to be afraid of change, although perhaps they were simply afraid of me.

'I am left with my free time – precious little of it because the shift hours are long and hard. But my free time too has gradually turned into a nightmare. Not only is the pay far lower than before, but I was told by the accommodation office that since I was now single I could no longer live in the house in which I had grown up. They have found me a place in a crumbling block of flats which I have to share with another woman from the paper mill. My flat-mate is a hopeless alcoholic who seems to spend her entire time drinking or having drunken fights with one or other of her many boyfriends. I have applied several times for a transfer but no action has ever been taken.

'On my release I tried keeping up with my acquaintances from the research station. Some of them I'd even counted as friends of a sort. But although most of them were polite, I could tell that they were afraid of any close contact with me for fear that they would be tarred with the same brush. Before long, I gave up any attempt to see them.

'Every week I have to visit the police station and endure a lengthy and humiliating cross-examination about my movements over the previous week. I have to sleep at my flat every night and have thought more than once that my flat-mate is also keeping an eye on me. The strange obsequiousness of the police officers at the time of my release has turned out to be a passing phase, and I can sense that the local police are just waiting for an opportunity to report me to their superiors in Berlin on account of some minor infringement of the regulations and restrictions which seem to surround my every move.

'For months now I have tried to endure all this alone, to suffer without complaint and be grateful for the fact that I am not in prison, but I know I cannot endure it much longer. I have been condemned without trial to a cruel form of internal exile from which there is apparently never to be any escape. The machinery of the state has me firmly in its vice-like grasp, and I fear it will hold me there until I can breathe no longer.

'I now know I have to leave this country for ever. Please help me, Robert, please try to help me before it is too late.'

Ingrid had signed the letter and then a thought must have occurred to her, because she had added a postscript.

'P.S. You may notice the letter is posted in Hungary. I have persuaded a colleague at the paper mill to post it there while on holiday in order that it will not be intercepted by the local police, who will presumably have your address on their files. It is hopeless to try and send me a letter because the Secret Police are bound to be intercepting all my incoming mail. But if you can, you must find a way. With all my love. Ingrid.'

Robert sat and looked at the letter for a long time, reading it over and over again. It was just as he had dreamt that night in the hotel: his mother was dead, his sister weakened by her experiences to the point where she was prepared to beg him for help. And although she did not hold him responsible for what had happened, he knew deep down within himself that it was a responsibility he could never evade.

There was, however, another emotion, an emotion that surprised him by its intensity as he read the letter through yet again. He could feel a sense of relief that she had written to him. More than two years had passed since their last encounter, yet he could remember her face as if it were only yesterday. And he could also remember the feelings he had experienced that night, the feelings he had pushed violently aside in his futile attempt to protect her.

She may still be a prisoner, but he at last was set free. No longer did he have to pretend, even to himself, that she was an unimportant interlude in his life, a fading memory that would become ever fainter as the years rolled slowly by. Now at last he could accept the simple fact that he loved her.

LONDON, NOVEMBER 1981

The infrequent streetlights cast a luminous yellow haze over the street of aging terraced houses in which Smithson had said that he lived. It was late November, and the cold London air made Robert shiver as he searched through his overcoat pocket for the piece of paper on which he had written the address.

"Robert! Are you looking for me?"

He looked up and saw the smiling face of his old cell-mate beaming down at him from an open first floor window on the opposite side of the road.

"Peter! As a matter of fact I was."

It was a pleasure to see the old man again after so long, and particularly pleasant to see him in the freedom of the world beyond the prison gates. As he shuddered at the memory of the many months of their shared existence, even the damp November air seemed fresh and invigorating.

"What are you standing about for, then?" Peter called. "Come on over and I'll open the door for you."

Before long Robert found himself sitting in the old man's comfortable living room and sipping a large glass of a rather fine Scottish malt. Although the house itself was of fairly modest proportions, the interior had been lavishly decorated, the result Robert supposed of a lifetime of substantial illicit earnings that could hardly be declared to the tax authorities. Particularly striking were a series of fine eighteenth century watercolours adorning the walls which seemed to reflect a more cultured side to his companion than he had previously perceived.

"Do you like them?" Smithson asked, indicating his paintings with a sweep of his glass.

"Actually I do. I like them very much indeed. You'll probably think me very ignorant, but who are they by?"

A sheepish look came over the older man. "You mean who actually painted them?"

Robert nodded. The question had seemed straightforward enough.

"Well, I did, actually." Smithson paused for a moment before continuing, clearly very proud that somebody had been moved to admire his humble work. He took a large swig of his malt. "But they're only copies, I'm afraid."

Robert looked at him in amazement and then a grin spread slowly across his face. It was the first time he had smiled in several months.

"You old devil," he muttered, "you clever old devil."

Smithson could hardly contain himself with pleasure.

"I've been doing it ever since I was at school. Always been good at drawing, you see, but absolutely no imagination. I can only copy things. A sort of flesh and blood equivalent of a camera, I suppose."

He stopped speaking and for a moment their eyes met, exchanging in seconds more than could be expressed in many hours of verbal conversation.

Smithson rose slowly from his chair and poured out two more drinks.

"Something's wrong, isn't it, Robert?" he said slowly. "That's why you've come."

Robert sipped the proffered drink and nodded.

"You're just too good at smoking out the truth, Peter."

Smithson eased himself gently back into the soft cushions of his armchair.

"It's a damn good thing somebody is. I really thought you were going to crack up on me when we were in prison together, what with your vanished kids and that mysterious sister of yours."

Robert peered into his glass, wondering where to start. The temporary lift to his emotions that he had felt at his reunion with his old companion was fading fast, only to be replaced by the same nagging depression that had followed him around like a shadow for weeks.

"So is it the kids," Smithson asked quietly, "or is it the sister?"

Robert looked up into his eyes. There was a deep honesty about the man that was hard to square with his chosen profession.

"At first I thought it was the kids. I just couldn't make contact with them, couldn't make contact with my own bloody children, for heaven's sake. And when I came out I soon realised it wasn't just me that was going crazy. My mother – my Engish mother that is – she was getting dangerously close to a mental breakdown."

"Did you manage to trace them, then?"

"I didn't, but someone else did. An old friend of the family with some pretty powerful connections managed to get their address and also managed – God knows how – to persuade my ex-wife to allow me to correspond with them. So now I write to them regularly and they write to me. I've agreed not to go out to Australia but they're to be allowed to fly over and see me and their grandparents at Christmas."

Smithson smiled.

"And you call that trouble. Sounds like manna from heaven if you ask me. Are they all right?"

"Under the circumstances. I think the older one – Justin – has adjusted to it better than Tim. But you can't really tell the truth from letters so I guess I won't know for sure until they come over at Christmas."

Smithson sank back even further into his armchair.

"So welcome to the club, old son," he said quietly.

Robert looked at him with a puzzled expression.

"What club?"

"The club of those who cherish forbidden desires."

Robert stared at him.

"You love that sister of yours, don't you? And not quite in the way that God intended."

Suddenly there was no point in lying.

"I kept trying to deny it, even to myself. But the first day I met her she caught my imagination as no other woman has ever done. Although she was distant, hostile even, I knew that I couldn't ignore her. She was important to me."

He paused for a moment, remembering once again his emotions at their first encounter as she had tried to budge his stupid car from the bank of snow.

"I knew it was foolish, suicidal even, to react like that. It promised nothing but mutual destruction. And within days I'd decided to clear out, to escape a path in life that could bring nothing but suffering in its wake."

Smithson grunted but said nothing.

"She seemed so cold towards me that I thought the attraction was one-sided. But then when she came to my room that night I suddenly knew that she felt it too, that the bond between us was mutual."

"You should have stayed, Robert. You really should have stayed and faced it out. Running away never helps."

"I see that now, although I don't see that things would have worked out any better if I had stayed. You see, it was already too late."

Smithson looked alarmed.

"Too late?"

"Yes, they picked her up only hours after I left."

Smithson mouth fell open.

"You mean it was all in vain. All those lies to protect her from being detected. All those months you rotted away in that lousy prison cell."

Robert smiled bitterly.

"Yup. What a fool, eh?"

"So what happened to her?"

"That's just it, Peter, that's actually why I've come to see you. I'm worried senseless about what's become of her and yet I've absolutely no way of finding out."

He recounted how he had discovered her letter shortly after his release from prison six months earlier. The old man listened quietly to the story, only stirring to light an old pipe that lay on the table beside his chair.

"And that's all you know? You haven't had any communication since then – not for one and a half years?"

Robert could feel the claustrophobic sense of frustration rising within him again as it regularly did several times a day.

"There's no way I can contact her. Don't you see, I'm absolutely stuck."

Smithson puffed slowly on his pipe for a while before speaking.

"I think I see. One, you can't write to her, because they'll detect it and either stop it getting through or make trouble for her. Two, you can't go there, because they won't let you in. In short, they've got you over a barrel and you're burning up inside."

Robert nodded. Smithson looked glum.

"Which is where I come in, if I'm not mistaken."

Robert looked at him with pleading eyes. He hated doing it, but he really had no other choice.

"I've tried everything. Absolutely everything. You know I paid to get someone out before. Well, I tried that again. I even managed to raise the money, which isn't easy when you're working as an insurance salesman. But they're all too bloody cautious, they won't touch someone like Ingrid with a bargepole."

"Don't blame 'em. Their whole system could be blown."

"Exactly. Anyway, since I drew a blank on that front I tried talking to some people I used to know in the West German ministry – people who are involved with buying out political prisoners for hard currency. But again, no go. They simply told me the East Germans would refuse to play ball in a case like this because of who she is."

Smithson slowly fingered his pipe.

"Have you tried M.I.6?"

"M.I.6?"

"Yes. They might conceivably be interested in her as an intelligence asset."

"Sure thing. A convicted East German spy turns up at British Intelligence and suggests they abduct an East German scientist and you think they'll simply jump to it. More likely they'll go out there and start pumping her for all they can get with some vague promise of eventual help. And then she's really going to be for the chop if the other side finds out."

"Hmm. Perhaps you're right." Smithson paused, as if playing for time. "So you want to go in yourself to pay her a visit and see what's going on. And you want me to provide the requisite paperwork."

"I don't like asking you, Peter. I know you've only been out of prison a few days and I also know you're trying to go straight."

Smithson said nothing. He sat for a long time in his chair, slowly puffing at his pipe and gazing quietly into the fire.

"I did say I was retiring," he said finally, "but that only meant I wasn't going to do any more paid employment."

Robert could feel his heart pounding.

"You mean you'll do it?"

"Yes, Robert, for you I'll do it."

GERMANY, JANUARY 1982

The windscreen wipers effortlessly flicked the little flurries of snow away from the glass in front of him. Robert threw his passport onto the empty passenger seat and moved away from the relative security of the slick West German customs post onto the empty road that snaked away into the pine forest beyond. He shivered as he wound up the window and turned on the car heater, trying as he did so to brace himself mentally for the deception that lay ahead.

A roadsign indicated a speed limit of thirty kilometres per hour. Robert slowed the car down to a crawl as he passed the large concrete column adorned with a red hammer and sickle which marked the exact line of the border. On either side of the road a sturdily-built metallic fence now appeared, its fine mesh surmounted by high tension cables of which the function was all too clear.

As he rounded a bend he saw ahead a small building by the side of the road which looked rather like an airport control tower. From the observation platform at the top, two guards were busy watching his slow passage as though he were a light aircraft coming in to land. Next to the tower, straddling the road between the two fences with a small gap just wide enough for a car to pass, was a sturdy concrete barrier, about as high as a man and several metres thick. As Robert drove cautiously through the small gap, he noticed what appeared to be a sliding concrete gate set into the barrier to the side of the road; this could presumably be slid into position to block the road at the touch of a button by the gentlemen watching his progress from the tower. The barrier was the final hurdle for anyone, including the customs officials and border police themselves, who was foolish enough to make a dash for it to the bright lights of the West.

He passed the barrier and crawled on down the empty road. At first there were no other buildings to be seen, only the two menacing fences rising up on either side of the road and the distant snow-covered pine trees beyond. But then, after what must have been nearly a mile, a large area of single-storey buildings came into view.

Robert slowed his car to a stop as he approached two men in uniform standing by the first of the covered sheds. Forcing his nerves under control, he wound his window down and smiled at the waiting soldiers, offering them his passport and hotel reservation.

The older of the two guards took the papers and started to examine them. He was clearly bored, but Robert noticed to his relief that he was also shivering slightly under his inadequate greatcoat.

"Thank you," the man replied in broken English as he handed the papers back. "Lane number three please."

In front there appeared to be several lanes, as if the desolate and empty border had been designed to accommodate a veritable explosion in East-West travel. With Robert's car as the only one in sight, it all looked faintly ridiculous.

Robert moved his car forward into the designated lane and presented his papers to another equally bored-looking official. More alarmingly, however, this one appeared to be wearing appropriate clothing for the season and was not shivering at all.

"Your papers please," he said.

Robert silently handed them over, remembering that it was supposed to be foolish to talk too much in such situations. The guard studied them carefully for a few moments, bending down several times to examine Robert's face.

"You are going to Suhl?"

The question was stupid. The hotel reservation was clearly marked for Suhl.

"Yes."

The guard eyed the skis attached to his roof-rack with suspicion.

"Why are you going to Suhl?"

Robert looked at him in feigned surprise. Suhl was a large town set in a wooded valley well below the main skiing area around Oberhof.

"I'm going skiing," Robert said, indicating the skis on his roof with his finger.

The guard looked even more suspicious.

"The best place for skiing is Oberhof, high up in the mountains. Suhl is right down in a valley."

Robert gulped hard. He could hardly tell the guard that he was afraid the hotel reception staff at Oberhof would recognise him from his previous visit.

He forced a grin.

"They didn't tell me that in London. I'll remember it next time."

The guard shrugged, obviously satisfied by the explanation offered.

"Is it your first trip to our country?"

"Yes."

The man looked genuinely puzzled.

"But why do you come skiing in East Germany?"

Robert could see what was going through the man's mind. East

Germans might flock to Oberhof for winter sports. But then they could hardly go to the Alps.

Robert forced a smile.

"For a change. The Alps get boring after a while."

"Do they?" the guard asked with surprise.

Robert flicked a glance in his rear mirror, hoping that the appearance of another vehicle would distract the man. But the road stretching away behind him remained completely deserted.

"I too am a skier," the guard continued, warming to the subject, "but I have never been to the Alps, only to Oberhof and once to the Tatras in Czechoslovakia. But I would love to go skiing in the Alps one day. Tell me where you have been skiing in the Alps."

The guard was smiling, the question well meant. But Robert could feel the tension rising within him. He had never been skiing in his entire life.

"Oh, I prefer the Austrian resorts – particularly the older ones like Seefeld." Seefeld was one of the few Alpine skiing centres Robert could think of, although he'd never actually been to it.

The guard smiled again and handed Robert back his papers.

"Perhaps I will see you on the slopes while you are on holiday, Mr Brown. I wish you a pleasant stay."

* * * * * *

Robert nodded in greeting to the elderly lady on the reception desk as he slipped out of the hotel. By East German standards the establishment, although somewhat shabby, was not a particularly bad place. Despite an economic system which appeared to have been specially designed to ensure thoroughly appalling service, the hotel manager seemed to take considerable pride in his duties and had even found the time to come and introduce himself to Robert over dinner.

It was icy outside and he pulled up his coat around his neck to give himself some protection from the biting wind that was sweeping down from the nearby hills. Glancing about himself to gain his bearings, he strode off purposefully toward the centre of town. Although the most direct route from the hotel to Ingrid's address did not pass though the centre, he reckoned it might surprise the staff if he were just to plough off into the back streets without any apparent reason.

East Germany hadn't changed a bit in the three years since he had last seen it. The buildings looked just as grubby, the roads and open spaces as poorly maintained and the air still reeked of the ubiquitous brown coal – a kind of cross between real coal and peat – that issued forth in winter from every chimney in the land. It almost made him feel at home.

After he had been walking for about half a mile he threw a glance over his shoulder to check that no one was interested in his movements before turning into a dingy side street. The pavement was fronted with tumble-down buildings, their tile-lined walls in desperate need of repair, and he peered through the windows where the curtains had not yet been drawn. In stark contrast to the uniformly shabby exteriors, flat after flat appeared immaculate, as if the entire effort of its inhabitants had been devoted to improving the defensible space behind their front doors – the inner sanctum of people's individuality where not even the long arm of this ferociously powerful state dared to reach.

He stopped walking. Glancing through a large ground floor window covered by trim net curtains, he could see a family sitting down to start their evening meal. There were four of them, two parents and two boys in their early teens, and he could almost sense the human bond that drew them together as they prepared to share their simple meal. He watched as the man of the family smiled at his wife before pouring out some water from a large jug and joining his family at the table. It could so easily have been him within that room, sitting down to share a meal with a wife who loved him for himself rather than for his prospects and two children growing up happily without the emotional torture to which his own two children had been so cruelly subjected since his divorce.

And suddenly, despite the long working hours, despite the stench of the brown coal, despite the political repression, despite the long military service, despite the lack of freedom to travel, despite the queues, despite everything that was catastrophically wrong with East Germany, he could feel a sense of overpowering jealousy welling up inside him as he compared his lot with that of the man he could see behind the net curtains.

But the man had noticed him. He rose from his chair and came towards the window, a suspicious frown on his face. The curtains were drawn and Robert was once again alone, listening to the sound of the wind and the rhythmic clanking of a loose drainpipe as it banged repeatedly against the side of a nearby house.

Robert stepped out with a new sense of urgency. If only he could find her – if only he could find Ingrid they would just possibly be able to help each other live. Together there was at least a chance that they would be able to make some sense of a world that seemed determined to conspire against their happiness.

He turned a corner and arrived at the street where she had said in the letter that she lived. Here the apartment blocks seemed even drabber, even more dilapidated, and his pace slowed as he peered at the doors and tried to identify the numbers.

There it was – number 79! But he didn't stop – he just made a mental note of the building and carried on walking as before. He was undoubtedly playing a dangerous game. She had warned him in the letter to be careful, and if by any chance they were watching her it would be madness to enter the building and simply knock at the door of her flat.

About a hundred yards past the entrance to her block he noticed an alley-way leading between two high buildings on the opposite side of the street and slipped quietly into the protection of the narrow passage. Since there were no street-lights in the alley, he could observe the comings and goings from Ingrid's block without himself being observed.

An hour passed. Every now and then someone would hurry down the street, staying close to the tile-lined walls in a futile attempt to escape the wind. Each time Robert would cower back into the relative shelter of the alley-way, fearful he might be observed, but the passers-by were far too intent on making their way home to waste any time looking around for loitering strangers.

The biting cold was developing into a serious problem. Robert glanced at his watch again and decided that even if his sister were still living there, she had almost certainly gone to bed. He had almost resolved to return to the hotel and try again the next day when the sound of shattering glass made him freeze. Looking anxiously across the road, he saw that a large object of some kind had been hurled through one of the first floor windows of Ingrid's block. For a few moments silence returned, but then a man's voice could be heard, shouting hysterically at someone deep within the building. A door banged, then another, and finally a fat young man wearing filthy clothes emerged into the street, tucking a grimy shirt into his trousers as he did so.

A naked woman appeared at the broken window. She was young and may once have been beautiful, but although her body was still attractive enough, her face was crumpled and drawn. The fat man looked up at her in a white fury.

"You bitch!" he shouted, unable to speak clearly because of the excess of alcohol and emotion under which he was suffering. "That'll teach you to mess with me."

He stormed off, leaving the naked woman sobbing plaintively at the window above. Crossing the road, he swept straight past Robert without seeming to be aware of his presence and vanished into the dark alley that lay beyond.

Robert looked up in alarm, wondering what would happen next. It occurred to him that he should disappear as quickly as possible in case the police arrived to investigate the disturbance. The woman was no longer to be seen at the window. A few seconds passed, and then she too rushed out onto the street, an old coat and a pair of shoes her only protection against the winter cold. Without a moment's hesitation, she dashed across the road and down the alley-way, clearly intent on pursuing her angry lover to his destination.

The commotion had drawn many people to their windows, their puzzled faces peering out to see what was happening, but as silence returned to the street he could see them retreating once more to the security of their private worlds, pulling windows shut and drawing curtains closed. Within minutes everything had returned to normal, except for the smashed glass lying on the pavement and the empty shattered window above.

Yet as he watched, another woman appeared at the broken window. She was wearing a long white nightdress which fluttered gently in the cold evening breeze and was carefully examining the broken pane of glass. And as soon as he saw her he knew that it was Ingrid.

He wanted to rush towards her, to shout and draw her attention. But he knew he dare not risk it, so he quietly left the safety of the alley-way and walked casually but briskly down the street in her direction, hoping against hope that she would recognise him. But instead she left the window and retreated into the interior of the flat.

Now he was opposite the window. He stopped, pretending to do up his shoe-laces but continuing to watch the window out of the corner of his eye. Within seconds she was back, clutching a large piece of hardboard in one hand and a box of nails in the other. Robert swore to himself as she placed the hardboard across the window, but then she lowered it to the floor and started to fumble in the box of nails.

He had to act.

"Excuse me, miss," he called in German, trying to copy the accent of the locals as closely as possible, "but can I help you with that?"

She looked out of the window towards him but with no hint of recognition, and for the first time he could see how different she appeared to the last time they had met. Three years before she had been alert and full of a kind of continual nervous energy, yet nowshe seemed crushed and subdued, as if resigned to a fate over which she had lost all control.

"Thank you, but no," she said, her voice as listless as her looks. "I can manage."

She had found the correct nails and leant down to pick up the piece of wood from where it was resting. Robert looked at her with desperation.

"You ought at least to sweep up the broken glass," he called gruffly. "Someone might get hurt."

She looked at him again, and slowly – ever so slowly – life seemed to flow back into her hitherto lifeless face.

She leant out of the window and examined the mess on pavement.

"Oh yes," she replied, her voice still showing no sign of the fact that she had recognised him, "I suppose you're right. I'll come down with a broom and deal with it."

Robert was ready for this. Walking casually across the road, he quietly pulled a crumpled piece of paper from his coat pocket. Glancing up one more time to check that she was watching him he quietly dropped the piece of paper amongst the pile of shattered glass and continued briskly on his way.

* * * * * *

Robert eyed the greasy, unappetising Bockwurst on his plate with scarcely-concealed disgust and decided not to risk it. Looking up, he noticed the sullen-looking waiter who had informed him that it was the only hot food on offer that evening eyeing him with bored curiosity from his perch on a stool in the corner of the room, as if he were wondering whether the well-dressed visitor from the West was actually going to eat the enormous sausage.

"Waiter!" Robert called to him, and the man rose slowly to his feet and ambled over.

"Yes?" he said when he eventually arrived at the table, his voice as sullen as his looks. "What do you want?"

"Another coffee, please. And can you tell me what time you close tonight?"

The man looked at his watch. "In about an hour, at ten o'clock," he replied before shuffling off to the kitchen.

Robert looked at the three empty coffee cups on the table in front of him and wondered why the waiter didn't take them with him while he was making the journey. But clearly the extra burden would have been too much strain.

He glanced around at the other people sitting in the crowded room.

Unlike him, they were all eating their Bockwursts with remarkable relish, sinking the fat, greasy sausages into little mountains of strong German mustard on the sides of their plates before taking a large bite.

After a few minutes he tired of watching the other customers and his eye returned to his watch. It was gone nine o'clock. He had told Ingrid in his note that he would be in the café from seven until closing time and that she should meet him there if she could. Yet she had still not shown up.

The coffee arrived and Robert had begun to raise the cup of steaming liquid to his lips when he caught sight of her coming into the room. She was alone, and as she entered he could see her glance nervously around looking for him. For a second their eyes met, but then she turned purposefully away and went to sit at an empty table in the far corner of the room, well away from where he was sitting but so that he could watch her without turning his head.

As she lowered herself into a chair the waiter moved over to her and smiled. From the way in which they greeted one another it was clear that she knew him, although there was no indication that she was acquainted with any of the other people present. After a while the waiter disappeared and returned to bring her yet another Bockwurst before disappearing to serve some other tables.

Robert watched as she mechanically devoured her meal. She didn't look up at him once, and he realised that his cautious approach on the previous evening must have been fully justified. After about half an hour she finished her meal, paid the bill, and left the café. Trying not to appear over-anxious, he rose from his chair and walked briskly over to the waiter, stuffing a note into his hand and mumbling some words of thanks. The waiter stared down in astonishment at the size of the tip, but by the time he had looked up to express his thanks his generous customer had vanished.

Outside on the pavement, Robert could see Ingrid walking away towards the centre of town. He started to follow, careful to remain several hundred yards behind her. Every now and then he would flick a glance over his shoulder to check that they were not being followed. Yet there were no other people to be seen, and he began to wonder whether the precautions they were taking were not becoming slightly absurd.

Ahead of him, his sister was walking along a street next to a park. Throwing a quick glance over her shoulder to check that he could see, she suddenly turned off into the park, following a path that led away between some tall bushes.

Robert followed. There were no lights in the park and within a few paces it was hard to make out where he was going. On either side of him, the dark outlines of the bushes loomed up like mighty beasts poised to pounce. There was no sign of Ingrid now, but he followed the path's twists and turns deeper and deeper into the undergrowth, confident that she would stop him when she was ready.

"Robert!"

Her soft voice called him and he turned and saw her standing beside one of the bushes, almost hidden from view. He went over to her and they stood in silence for a moment, looking intently into one another's eyes.

"You've come," she said weakly, and as he enfolded her in his arms he could feel violent sobs shaking her body as if the mental restraint of many long months of waiting had suddenly collapsed.

For a long time he held her to him, saying nothing because nothing needed to be said, until finally her sobbing began to subside.

"I knew you'd come. I just knew you'd come one day," she murmured, taking his face in her hands and pressing her cheek against it.

Helplessly, uncontrollably, Robert pushed her back into the darkness of the bushes, slowly lowering her down onto the damp undergrowth. Her body was beneath him now, eager, desperate, and as he started undoing the buttons on her coat he could tell that she was helping him, her slender fingers easing the tiny buttons free of their holes. There was no time for foreplay, no need perhaps, and as he lifted her long dress up about her he could feel her hands about him, urging him forward as if she feared that he might disappear again as he had disappeared before.

And then at last they were together, the secret desire of many long months abated, and as he thrust deep within her he could see with sudden clarity the absurd yet beautiful nature of human existence. She was breathing more deeply now, clutching his shoulders and pulling his coat around them both for warmth. He could so easily have ended it but there seemed to be no need; better to linger, better to savour a moment for which they had both waited so very long. For this was no mere gratification of a basic human desire, it was something else, something profoundly different, and also something infinitely better.

Finally their breathing slowed, all energy spent, but for a long time they remained entwined, their interlocked bodies covered by his warm winter overcoat. Neither wanted to move, neither wanted to face up to a reality that had already given ample proof that it was a mortal enemy to them both.

She stirred beneath him and he lifted himself gently from her, lying beside her and pulling her coat back around her to protect her from the cold.

"I love you, Robert," she murmured, her penetrating eyes gazing tenderly into his.

"I know," he said, gently stroking her face. "I know you do."

For many minutes they were silent, but then she rose slowly to her feet and started straightening out her clothing.

Robert stood up and pulled her to him.

"Is there anywhere we can go together," he asked, "anywhere that is safe and warm? We have to talk."

She thought for a moment.

"Yes," she said, "But it's too far to walk; you must bring your car. I'll wait in the bushes by the entrance to the park while you fetch it."

Her face had changed again. The look of fear he had seen in the restaurant had returned.

"Are you being watched?" he asked.

"I don't think so, not tonight. But they do watch me often and you must be careful. If you see any police or anything strange as you drive by the park, go on and return to wherever you are staying. I'll meet you here tomorrow evening at the same time. Only stop if all is clear."

Robert nodded and started to walk away. But then he paused and turned to face her once again.

"Ingrid," he said quietly, "I love you too."

* * * * * *

When he returned with the car the road was still as deserted as it had been on his departure, so he drew to a halt outside the park and leant across to flick up the lock on the passenger seat door. As he looked up, he could see Ingrid slip out from behind the cover of the bushes and approach the car, but instead of getting into the front seat she signalled to him that he should unlock the rear door. As soon as he did so she clambered quickly in, crouching down low on the floor of the car.

"I'm sorry," she said as he drove off, "but they all know me. The police in this town all know my face."

Robert nodded silently.

"Where do I go?" he asked.

"To the left at the next crossroads, and then keep straight on until you're out of town and the road starts to climb up into the hills."

"Where are we going?"

"There's only one person who I'm sure I can trust, an old forester who lives alone in the hills. We'll go to him."

They were reaching the outskirts of town when Robert noticed they were gaining fast on a squat little East German car with the distinctive markings of the Volkspolizei.

"Stay down," he whispered, "there's a police car crawling along in front of us."

He was already driving slowly, well within the speed limit, yet he was still gaining on the police car. He braked gently, hoping it would pull away, but the more he braked the more it too slowed until they were both crawling along at no more than ten miles an hour.

"Ingrid, I'm going to overtake it. There must be something wrong with the stupid thing."

Flicking his indicator switch, he pulled gingerly out and drove slowly past the creeping car, but no sooner had he done so than it accelerated past him again and once more started to slow. A policeman leant out of the window and gestured to Robert that he should pull over.

"What's happening?" Ingrid asked anxiously from the floor of the car as Robert started to slow again.

"They're stopping me for some reason," he answered, trying unsuccessfully to hide the fear in his voice. "Pull that blanket on the back seat over you and lie still."

He pulled to a halt behind the police car and waited while a smartly dressed policeman climbed out and approached them. The two other policemen in the car remained inside. Robert wound down the window.

"Good evening," the man said politely, "may I see your papers, please."

Robert pulled out his passport and handed it over. The officer examined it carefully.

"And your car papers please – your registration document and your driving licence."

Robert handed them over.

"Have I done anything wrong, officer?" he said, deliberately speaking German with a heavy English accent. "I wasn't driving too fast, was I?"

The officer looked at him sternly.

"Wait here," he said, and walked slowly back with Robert's papers to the police car to rejoin his colleagues.

Robert waited silently until he was out of earshot.

"Christ knows what he's doing," he muttered softly. "I don't think he saw you, but I hope to God he's not found something wrong with my papers."

"Should there be anything wrong with your papers?" Ingrid whispered in surprise, the sound of her voice muffled by the blanket.

"Not much. They're all bloody well fake, that's all."

After what seemed like an eternity, all three policemen got out of the car and started walking towards them. They circled the car several times without saying anything and appeared to be paying particular attention to the controls, taking it in turns to peer down and examine them.

"Is something wrong?" Robert asked, deciding he had nothing to lose by adopting a more forceful tone.

The officer who had spoken to him before seemed to jump, as if he were surprised by the authority in Robert's voice. But then he quickly handed the papers back and saluted.

"No, nothing is wrong, Mr Brown. I wish you a pleasant stay in our country."

And with that they were off, piling back into the police car and screeching off down the road with scant regard for a speed limit that other drivers would have been very foolish to ignore.

Robert fought to recover his nerves.

"What the hell were they up to?" he said, glancing round to see if Ingrid was all right.

She pushed the blanket aside and peered out.

"Just fighting boredom, I expect," she said, the relief obvious in her voice. "Ostensibly they're checking to see whether you've left the motorway transit routes to West Berlin without permission. But in reality, they're probably just curious to see an English car with the steering wheel on the wrong side."

Robert looked at her grimly.

"I hope it's not too far to this friend of yours," he said, forcing a smile as he started the engine up.

As they climbed higher into the wooded hills of the Thuringian Massif, the visibility on the road became poorer and poorer. It had started to snow, although whether this was simply due to the altitude or represented a general change in the prevailing weather conditions was impossible to tell.

"You can sit up if you like," Robert said, sitting forward in his seat in a futile attempt to get a better view of the road ahead. "Since I can hardly see a thing I very much doubt anyone will be able to see us."

Ingrid eased herself gratefully up from the floor of the car and leant forward so that her face was just near his.

"I love fog," she said, leaning forward and kissing him gently on the back of his neck.

Robert sank back in his seat, comforted by her close proximity.

"You mean you don't like seeing where you're going?"

"No," she chuckled, "because I don't like other people seeing where I'm going."

Robert threw her a glance.

"Ingrid, I think that's the first time I've ever heard you laugh."

"Perhaps I've never had anything to laugh about before."

"And now you have?"

"Yes, and now I have."

"Ingrid," he said suddenly, "you haven't asked me why I didn't come to you sooner – as soon as you wrote."

He could feel her tensing behind him.

"I knew you'd come when you could," she said. "I supposed you might be abroad on a posting with your family and that you couldn't get back."

"I didn't come because I was in prison. I only got your letter six months ago when they let me out and I went to fetch the mail from my old address."

For a moment she was silent.

"Prison?" she asked eventually, her voice uneven. "But why?"

He laughed the dry cynical laugh that seemed to be his only defence against the memory of those two wasted years.

"Because my government formed the opinion that I was spying for the East Germans. They found out that I was having an affair with that girl in East Berlin and decided I'd been blackmailed by State Security."

"And they convicted you on that?"

He paused.

"No," he said at last, "I confessed."

He could hear her take a sharp breath behind him.

"No, Ingrid, it's not what you're thinking. I confessed because they knew about you too. I think they knew all about us but I persuaded our security services to suppress what they knew about you in exchange for the confession."

For a long time there was silence. Finally it was Ingrid who spoke.

"Then you did it for me. You confessed to try and protect me."

He glanced at her and saw the look of horror in her face.

"I'm sorry it didn't help," he said gently.

"How the hell are we going to get out of this mess, Robert?" she murmured.

He thought for a moment.

"I don't know, Ingrid, I really don't know."

* * * * * *

The burning logs crackled in the old stone fireplace, driving the winter cold out beyond the thick walls of the little wooden cottage. The old man rose laboriously from his chair and moved towards the door.

"I'll get that coffee I promised," he said, shuffling out of the room and closing the door behind him.

When he was gone Ingrid rose from her chair and moved to the fire, warming her hands in the shimmering glow.

"What do you think of him?" she said without turning.

Robert smiled.

"It's easy to see why you like him. You know, he reminds me of someone I shared a cell with when I was in prison."

"Franz has been through a lot," Ingrid said, staring at the open door through which he had just vanished, "which I suspect is why he understands so well how I feel. In the 1920s he was active in the Socialist Party, happily married with two young children. As things went in those days he reckoned himself to be pretty happy. But then the Nazis came to power and he became involved in the resistance so before very long he found himself in a concentration camp where he remained incarcerated until the end of the war. By the time he came out both his sons had been killed on the Russian front."

Ingrid paused, picking up a long iron poker and carefully rearranging the logs on the fire.

"After the war he was encouraged to join the Communists and develop a career in the new administration," she continued eventually.

"But he didn't."

"No, he refused. He was never a communist."

"They must have liked that."

Ingrid shrugged.

"They just gave him a job as a forester which he did until he retired. Nobody's ever bothered him – I think they know he's harmless."

Robert listened to the old man moving around in the neighbouring kitchen. After what he had seen of human society, it was hardly any wonder that he preferred the company of trees.

"So how long have you known him?" he asked.

"Since shortly after I wrote that letter to you. I started walking up here in the woods a great deal; I suppose I found it a kind of mental escape. And then one day we started talking and we've been talking ever since. He's probably the main reason I haven't gone mad."

The door opened and the old man returned. He was carrying a tray laden with coffee things which Ingrid hurried over and collected, placing the tray on a small table by the sofa.

"Thank you, Franz," she smiled as he sat down wearily in his armchair, "and thank you for letting us come here tonight."

He looked at her fondly, fingering his short grey beard as he did so.

"You look like a brother and sister," he said softly.

Ingrid looked away.

"Do you mind?" she asked quietly.

"I don't think so," he said. "Why should it matter to me if that's what you both want?"

She started to pour out the coffee.

"I hope other people are as generous in their attitudes," she murmured.

The old man smiled, the deep furrows on his face becoming even deeper as he did so.

"They won't be," he said flatly.

Ingrid passed round the small coffee cups and sat down next to Robert on the sofa, slipping her hand into his.

"However, I wish that incest laws were the only laws we were up against," she said grimly.

Franz picked up the little spoon on his saucer and started slowly stirring his coffee, staring down into the swirling liquid as if it would reveal some important insight into their dilemma.

"What are you going to do?" he said.

"Any ideas?" Robert asked.

Franz's thin lips cracked into a dry smile as he fixed Robert with a penetrating stare.

"There's only one way. We all know it. With what she knows, they'll never agree to let her out. She's got to go out over the Wall."

There was a long silence. They sat and stared at the burning logs, listening to the crackle of the sparks as they flew up the chimney towards the open sky above.

"It's impossible," Robert said finally. "I've seen enough of that border to know it's utterly impossible."

"Nothing is impossible," the old man retorted angrily, rising again from his chair and stabbing at the logs with the poker. "You just have to be determined enough."

Robert watched him and knew better than to contradict words that were based on bitter personal experience. Eventually the old man satisfied himself that the fire was bright enough and turned to face them.

"I'm going to bed. You're not staying the night, are you?"

"No," Ingrid replied quickly. "We can't. But we'll let ourselves out quietly when we go."

The old man moved to the door. But before he left he stopped and turned.

"You'll find a way," he said again before closing the door behind him. When he was gone they listened silently to the sound of his heavy footsteps fading slowly into the distance as he climbed the ancient wooden staircase to the tiny bedroom in which he had slept alone ever since his wife had died.

Ingrid lay down along the sofa with her head on Robert's lap.

"Do you think he's right?" she whispered. "Do you think I will be able to get out?"

Robert looked at her and smiled, pretending to a confidence he did not possess.

"Perhaps he's right. Perhaps it can be done if we're determined enough. Now that I've found you and I'm certain you want to come, I'll try and work out a way of getting you through when I'm back in the West."

She looked up at him enquiringly.

"How?"

Robert shrugged.

"I can't use any of the existing escape organisations: they simply won't touch you. I'll just have to go and find a place where I can get you through myself."

She looked at him with disbelief.

"To West Germany."

"Yup. After all, it's only a couple of fences."

Ingrid sat up again, the by now familiar fear again in her eyes.

"Robert, it's not so easy. In Berlin you can walk right up to the inner Wall. Actually touch it if you want. It's not like that with the border with West Germany proper. You need a special authorisation permit stamped in your identity card before you can go anywhere near it."

Robert looked at her with interest. "And how do they check

whether you've got this authorisation?"

"Round the clock roadblocks on all the approach roads to the closed border zone and a local reporting system."

"A what?"

"I've heard that everyone who lives near the frontier is paid a fee when they report strangers to the police. Just like my alcoholic flatmate with the tempestuous love-life is paid every time she reports to the authorities on my movements."

Robert looked at her grimly.

"Is she?" he said, feeling more depressed by the minute.

Ingrid closed her eyes.

"They don't even seem to care if I know about it," she said. "She works at the mill, like I do. So I know perfectly well what she earns. And I also know she gets through more than her pay in booze alone. I'm pretty sure it's the Security Police who are supplementing her income."

Robert put his arm around her, trying to ease the fear and tension in her face.

"You're terrified of them, aren't you?"

She looked at him silently for a long time before replying.

"When they arrest you, you quickly realise they are possessed of absolute power. They decide when you sleep, when you go to the toilet, how warm you are. They control every single thing that affects your life. And they are masters at manipulating that total control of your environment in order to gain control of your mind itself.

"It took me quite a while to realise that 'truth' was a fiction within the walls of a Security Police prison. If it was not for the prisoners to decide when they should sleep or go to the toilet, then it was self-evidently not for the prisoners to decide what crimes they had committed. If permitted sleep patterns and access to the lavatory were the proper concern of the prison authorities, then crimes were the proper concern of the prosecutor's office. The prisoners' only duty was complete obedience to decisions passed down from above."

Robert pulled her closer to him. It was clear from the way that she was shaking in his arms that it had not been an easy point for her to grasp.

"But I was a slow learner. What they were saying about me was patently absurd. I had told them the truth, hiding nothing, and I was convinced that they would come to believe me as soon as the facts became clear to them. But my total honesty was only interpreted as cheeky deceit, so they decided to teach me a lesson I'd never forget."

She was silent.

"You've never told anyone this before, have you?"

She looked up at him for a long time before continuing.

"They put me in a small empty whitewashed cell with no bed and no chair. I think it must have been underground, because there were no windows – only a small vent set into the ceiling which made a strange mechanical clanking sound as it pumped air into the room. The cell was so brightly lit that even with your eyes tightly closed you couldn't block out the light. They put me in that room and told me to stand and wait until it was time for my next interrogation. Sitting on the floor, I was informed, was in contravention of the regulations. And then they left.

"I don't know how long I was in there. Perhaps three days and three nights – it was hard to tell. Every now and then I was brought some food, which I had to eat standing up. Eventually I was so tired that I sank down to the floor despite their warnings, but minutes after I had done so the door was flung open and two burly female guards appeared. One of them pulled me up while the other told me that if I sat down again I would be punished severely. As they stood there lecturing me about the importance of total obedience to the security organs of the East German people they seemed to find the whole performance tremendously amusing.

"I stood up and managed to stay standing for what must have been several more hours. I was terribly frightened of what they might do to me and I had become aware of the fact that they were peering at me every few minutes through a tiny peephole set into the door, as if waiting patiently for a further transgression. But eventually my desire to rest overcame even my fear of the guards and I let myself sink to the floor again. I just didn't care any more what they did as long as I could rest. Or at least that's what I thought.

"Before long they were back, setting to work on me with such obvious relish that I'm sure they'd just been waiting for the opportunity, surprised perhaps that I had taken so long to give way to the inevitable exhaustion."

There was another silence.

"Tell me, Ingrid," Robert said. "You've got to tell me."

She laughed the bitter laugh that is all that remains to those who are beyond tears.

"I suppose they must at least have pretentions to be civilised in this country – at least in the eyes of the world. I'm convinced they'd been trained, Robert, because they knew exactly how to hurt a woman in a way that left absolutely no outwards signs that could afterwards be shown to a doctor. But although they left no visible marks, it was enough to make me stand again and not sit down. That day, I discovered that fear is a stronger emotion than even the strongest physical desires."

Robert pulled her closer to him, and she seemed comforted by his presence.

"But it didn't last for ever. Eventually they let me out and took me to an ordinary prison cell. But my time in that little room was more than enough to start me firmly on the road to total obedience. It took some time until they were satisfied with the small print of my confession, but I never really risked another outright confrontation with them. From being an enemy of the people, I seemed to become more like a schoolgirl who was slow at learning her lessons. It was only a matter of time until my confession was complete in every detail."

There was a pause.

"So why did they let you go, Ingrid?"

She was silent for a while.

"I don't know," she said. "First they humiliated and tortured me until I agreed to confess to crimes I never even dreamt of committing, and then they let me go. It didn't seem to make sense at the time and it still doesn't."

"Do you think it had anything to do with what happened to me? With the publicity surrounding my trial in the West?"

She shrugged her shoulders.

"Possibly. They must have been a bit confused about why you were confessing to spying charges that they knew perfectly well were untrue. Maybe they realised they'd made a stupid mistake."

"But even if they did realise they'd made a mistake, they were crazy simply to let you go like that after what they'd put you through. Even if you hadn't been a security risk before the interrogation, they must have known you would have become one after your experiences with them. They must have known you'd be likely to try and defect, if only to get your own back, and they've certainly not done anything since releasing you to discourage you from trying to leave."

She shrugged again.

"I know all that, Robert. Even if they realised they'd made an error, they should have gone ahead with the trial anyway or simply disposed of me."

From her voice it was clear that she was angry, angry with herself because however many times she went around the problem she could not come up with any satisfactory explanation for her fate. Robert rose from the sofa and moved towards her, putting his arm gently around her as she stood by the fire.

"Don't talk any more, my love," he whispered softly.

She turned to face him, slowly unhooking her long dress and letting it fall softly to the floor. And as he looked into her eyes he could sense that she was filled with a strange discordant mixture between happiness and sorrow.

GERMANY, MARCH 1982

Robert stepped out of the warm Gasthaus into the crisp morning air and looked about admiringly at the market square. There was no denying that the small West German town of Allendorf was a pretty little place, rather like something out of a tourist brochure, with street after street of the brightly painted half-timbered terraced houses that were so typical of central Germany. If you kept your eyes firmly above the ultra-modern shop fronts on the ground floor and ignored the sound of the Audis and Mercedes on the streets, it was not difficult to pretend that this was the seventeenth century rather than the twentieth.

Robert lingered, pretending for a precious moment that he really was a tourist enjoying a well-earned break, but then he pulled a small street map from his pocket, examined it for a moment, and started walking briskly towards the object of his visit.

It was late March and the daffodils made a handsome display in the large flowers-boxes placed on either side of the street. Over two months had passed since Robert had been to see his sister and it was his first trip to Germany since then. On his departure from East Germany he had returned to London to earn some badly needed money, devoting most of his free time to seeking out sources of information about the Wall and the various methods of escape that had been attempted over the years. He had even resorted to reading spy books in case these might throw some light on unusual methods of escape. Yet little if anything had come of these researches other then a growing conviction that the task was utterly beyond him.

Exactly as arranged, precisely one month after his departure from East Germany, the old forester Franz had telephoned Robert's former cell-mate Peter Smithson from a call box in East Germany and asked casually whether the two old men could meet up. Ingrid had argued that another trip by Robert over the border on false papers would be too dangerous and at her request the forester had agreed to act as a go-between. Since he was a pensioner, and therefore economically useless to the East German state, he was permitted to travel freely to the West provided that he required no foreign currency. The old man was therefore pretending that he had struck up a friendship with Peter Smithson a few years before and that they were trying to renew their acquaintance for a few days in West Germany. In reality, of course, any meeting arranged would be with Robert, not Peter, and the purpose of the meeting would be to transmit the detailed instructions for Ingrid's forthcoming escape.

On the last occasion that Franz had phoned, Robert had been forced to explain to Ingrid via this circuitous route that he was as yet unable to propose any clear plans and had asked Franz to telephone again in exactly a month's time. Yet that last phonecall had been over six weeks ago, and as Robert walked towards the edge of town he tried to push firmly into the back of his mind the various possible explanations of that unexpected delay.

As he reached the outskirts of the town the old timber-framed buildings gave way to the modern detached houses so characteristic of the post-war German recovery. Each house was set within its own large immaculately-kept garden, the opulence and individuality of each property providing a clear indicator of the determination and dynamism that had transformed and revitalised the shattered remnants of the Western half of Germany in the decades since the war.

But before long even the newly-built houses began to peter out and a little yellow sign at the side of the road confirmed the obvious fact that Allendorf had indeed come to an end. Ahead lay broad grass fields and beyond, no more than one kilometre away across the meadows, a small village by the name of Wahlhausen which appeared to be full of timber-framed houses identical to those found in neighbouring Allendorf.

For centuries the little country road along which he was walking had connected these two adjoining settlements with one another. Children had run backwards and forwards to visit their friends and play; girls from one village had married boys from the other; carts and later cars, trucks and buses had carried people about their daily affairs along the little road. Yet all these people had undoubtedly been totally ignorant of the extreme privilege they were enjoying by so doing. For in the sophisticated world of the 1980s nobody ever travelled along the road between Allendorf and Wahlhausen, since cutting across it, separating with a brutal finality the lives of the ordinary human beings on either side, lay the crazy human construct of the Iron Curtain.

Robert's pace slowed as he ventured out down the empty road towards the outer fence. As he went, the ghosts of pre-war traffic seemed to echo around the empty fields to either side of him, as if defying the barrier which lay ahead. He glanced behind him at the last row of houses on the outskirts of Allendorf, wondering how the people who lived in those houses felt in the morning when they woke up and pulled open their bedroom curtains to gaze upon this scene. But there were no clues to tell him how they felt and he could only suppose that they had long before become totally immune to living at the edge of the world.

The border was much as he had described to Ingrid, just a couple of fences, but he knew from the careful researches he had undertaken in London that the system with which those fences were used had been designed by some of East Germany's best brains in order to achieve almost total impregnability.

The westernmost fence, stretching away on either side of him as far as the eye could see, appeared to be a rusty grill about three metres high that reminded Robert of the kind of fencing used to prevent large kangaroos from jumping out of their enclosures at zoos. He approached until he arrived at an innocuous line of small red and white posts running through the fields to either side of him about fifty yards distant from the fence and then stopped. At the side of the road was a sign that reminded him of a fact of which he was already well aware – if he went one step further he would be on East German soil and the two East German soldiers already eyeing him suspiciously from the other side of the fence would be quite within their legal rights to lift up their rifles and shoot him dead.

Robert reached into the shoulder-bag he was carrying and pulled out a large pair of binoculars through which he carefully observed the two guards as they studied him through their own binoculars from the other side. He waved at them, not so much because he wanted a jolly exchange of greetings but rather to confirm something he had read in a book written in the West by a border guard who had recently defected. In the book it had explained that the guards were under firm instructions not to respond to any friendly human gestures from the West.

"They won't wave back, you know!"

Robert jumped and swung round to find himself face to face with a well-built man sporting a long rugged black beard and wearing a grey uniform. Accompanying the man was a large alsatian which looked as if it would take great pleasure in devouring Robert's leg if only it were given permission by its master.

"Hallo," said Robert in a voice that was trying hard to sound casual despite the alsatian.

"They never wave back," the man repeated.

"Oh," Robert muttered, noticing that the man was wearing the insignia of a West German customs official.

The man was silent, watching the guards on the other side of the border with a morose expression.

"I shouldn't think you get a lot of business here!" Robert said, trying to make conversation.

"Not a lot," the man replied in a miserable voice and Robert wondered if a posting to patrol the wastelands of the East German border was some kind of punishment duty imposed on indolent West German customs officials who managed to upset their superiors.

"Ever get any escapes?" Robert said cheerfully, playing the role of the curious tourist.

"Nope," said the man, warming to Robert now that he offered the promise of a conversation to wile away a few minutes. "Just look at it all, it'd be suicide trying to get over that lot."

Robert looked and nodded grimly. It was not the answer he had been hoping for.

"So what do you do here all day?" Robert asked.

"My job's to prevent border violations."

"What!" Robert exclaimed, genuinely surprised. "You mean from our side."

"Yes," the man continued, his enthusiasm growing. "You get all sorts of cranks who want to go up to the fence and touch it. People like you, tourists. And that gets them very excited over there." He jerked his head in the general direction of the two guards on the other side.

"Don't they shoot?"

"Not if I'm here," he said, "they just let me deal with it. But they'd be within their rights to shoot, if that's what you mean."

Robert looked at the two East Germans. It was true that they seemed to have relaxed somewhat now that their Western colleague had arrived. Instead of peering through the field glasses, they seemed to be exchanging jokes with one another.

"What a creepy place!" Robert muttered.

The customs official shrugged. "You get used to it," he said, "but I suppose it is."

"Is this the only fence?" Robert asked, not wishing to appear too knowledgeable.

"Oh no," the man replied, "this isn't the proper fence at all. The real fence is further back. You can't even see it here because it's too far away, but if you look up on that hill in the distance you can see it running along well inside the outer perimeter."

Robert looked through the binoculars towards a distant rise over which the border ran. Well over a hundred yards inside the outer fence lay another, tall and modern and obviously in a good state of repair. In between the two fences lay a road, a wide strip of raked sand and a deep ditch. Overlooking the hill and the valley where they now stood was a large modern watchtower.

"The principle of the thing is really very simple," the guard explained. "It's all based on delay. On the other side of the border, beyond both fences, is a kind of security zone several kilometres wide. Nobody's allowed within that zone without proper authorisation. And then that inner fence is quite an obstacle in itself – if you look at it carefully you can see that it's well over three metres high and is surmounted by stakes protruding at an angle on either side. Running along those angled stakes at the top are high tension cables which I suspect would make a bit of a mess of you if you touched them. And in case that wasn't enough to put people off, the whole fence is wired so that anyone who so much as brushes against it sets off all the alarms and gets everybody running about."

Robert nodded, straining to make out the features the official was describing through his binoculars.

"So that's why the fences are set so far apart," he observed, "to give them time to catch up with anyone getting through the first fence before they have time to escape over the second."

"Exactly," the guard replied. "They don't have the personnel to have a couple of guards standing every few metres along the entire border – so they give themselves a good long lead time to allow the troops to get out from the watchtowers if anything happens."

Robert looked at the two guards, who had now lost all interest in him and had started walking casually off along the border between the fences.

"What about them?" Robert asked. "What about the guards? Don't they ever try and get over?"

The customs official looked at them and nodded.

"If those two wanted to come, they'd probably manage it, simply because they're already past the inner fence," he said, "but the East Germans are well aware of that danger and have another strategy to deal with it."

"Do they?"

"Yes, they do. They make them patrol in twos, so that the one who tries to escape can be shot by the other one. And they're not allowed to patrol for very long with the same person so as to prevent them from building up too close a relationship with one another."

Robert shivered, imagining for a moment that he was in the shoes of one of the two young men patrolling on the other side. It would certainly take a great deal of courage to suggest to a complete stranger that you both take a run at the fence – a terrifying gamble between freedom and a ten-year prison sentence for attempting to flee the Republic.

Robert looked through his binoculars at the edge of the village on the other side of the border.

"What's that kind of screen thing?" he asked, pointing to a tall solid barrier around the western side of the village that looked rather like the noise breaks erected by the side of urban motorways.

"Stops the villagers looking out at the border as they go about their business," the official replied. "Maybe they think simply looking at us will pollute their minds."

"Curious," Robert muttered.

"Have you got a map?" the man asked, as if he had just had an idea.

Robert pulled one from his bag and gave it to him.

"I'll show you somewhere where you can get a really good view of a village on the other side of the border. You'd never find it if it wasn't pointed out to you."

He opened the map and pointed at a tiny village called Lindawerra that lay a little way further down the river valley in which they were standing.

"Drive down the main road in the direction of Kassel until you get to this village," he said, pointing on the map, "and then turn off down this little track to your right near the church. The track follows the river round a long bend for about two kilometres until it peters out at the remains of a bridge which the communists blew up after the war. You'll see the East German village immediately opposite and slightly below you on the other bank, with the border defences packed close together right under your nose between the river and the village streets."

Robert made a mental note of the place as the guard handed back the map. He was still thinking about the delay factor the guard had spoken about.

"What would happen if someone blew the outer fence from this side," he said quietly, "while someone else blew the inner fence from the other side? Surely the delay factor wouldn't work quite so well then."

The alsatian started growling menacingly, aware that his master had suddenly tensed.

"What are you doing here, anyway?" the guard asked, all trace of friendliness in his voice suddenly vanished.

Robert looked away, aware that he had gone too far.

"I was just curious," he said, putting his map and his binoculars away. "But I must be going now."

And with that he turned and started to retrace his footsteps towards Allendorf, wishing to the very core of his being that curiosity had really been his only motive for the questions he had asked.

* * * * * *

As he walked back through the trim streets of Allendorf towards the hotel, Robert found his nagging fears about the forester's unexpectedly long silence returning with renewed vigour. Perhaps it was the grim reality of the border defences he had just seen, or perhaps it was simply his encounter with the dour customs official and his equally dour alsatian, but the misery that Ingrid was being forced to endure for as long as she remained within the borders of the East German state somehow seemed even more vivid than it had appeared first thing that morning.

And if all was indeed well, why on earth had Franz not telephoned over two weeks earlier as he had promised?

As soon as he arrived at the hotel, he headed straight for his room. Without even stopping to remove his overcoat, he picked up the phone and dialled Smithson's number in London. There was a long wait and he cursed inwardly at the thought that the old man might be out. But then there was a faint click as someone lifted the receiver.

"Hallo. Smithson speaking."

"Peter, it's Robert."

He could hear a deep sigh of relief at the other end of the phone.

"Thank Christ for that," the old man exclaimed, "I've been ringing hotels near the wretched border all morning trying to find out where you're staying. Your friend rang."

Robert sank gratefully to the bed.

"That's the best news I've heard all day, Peter. Did you tell him to ring back in a month's time?"

There was no reply.

"Peter?"

"Yes, I'm here. Listen carefully, Robert, there's been a change of plan."

He tensed.

"The reason I've been spending all morning trying to get hold of you is that he's coming out to the West. He'll be at the main station in Bebra at eleven-forty on Thursday morning. You're to meet him there."

"But there's no point in meeting him yet. I still haven't got the foggiest idea how I'm going to do it."

There was a pause before Smithson replied.

"You know I couldn't talk freely to him on the phone, but from his voice I'd say that something serious has cropped up."

* * * * * *

The muffled sound of the station tannoy echoed mechanically around the station buildings.

"Bebra Hauptbahnhof. Bebra Hauptbahnhof. The train from Eisenach is now arriving on platform three."

With a great deal of squeaking and rasping, the train ground slowly to a halt, as if breathing a deep sigh of relief at finally being permitted to rest. For a second or two nothing happened, but then doors started flying noisily open. Relatively few people seemed interested in alighting at Bebra, and it did not take long before he spotted the thin figure of Franz at the far end of the train. Another passenger had taken pity on him and was helping the frail old man down the steep steps with his luggage, which seemed to comprise little more than a shabby brown suitcase and an equally shabby string shopping bag.

Robert started to hurry towards the distant figure, dodging round the small groups of people still lingering on the rapidly emptying platform. Franz was alone now, peering around anxiously to see if anyone had come to meet him. He seemed to look directly at Robert without showing any obvious sign of recognition, and it occurred to him that the old man's eyesight might possibly be failing.

Franz turned and looked the other way, clearly perplexed at finding nobody to meet him in the alien Western world to which he had never before travelled. Robert approached and tapped him on the shoulder.

"Franz!"

The frail old figure turned and for a fraction of a second Robert could see with dazzling clarity the young and active man he had once been. But then the brightness in his eyes faded and the familiar look of numbed sorrow returned.

"Thank you for coming," he said quietly, holding out his hand.

"It's me who should be thanking you," Robert replied, taking the proffered hand and finding himself as surprised as he had been on the occasion of their first meeting at the strength of older man's handshake.

"She's all I've got," Franz said, fixing Robert with a searching look.

There was a long silence as the two men's eyes met. Then Robert picked up the bags and they started slowly walking down the platform towards the station exit.

"Something's wrong, isn't it?" Robert said at last.

The old man paused, the effort of simultaneously walking and talking clearly too much for him.

"She asked me to say something to you before I tell you what's happened," he said, still wheezing from the exertion.

Robert steered him to a nearby bench and they sat down. A whistle blew and as they watched the express began slowly heaving itself forward along the tracks. Gradually Franz's breathing steadied.

"She wanted me to tell you that she's very happy," he said at last.

Robert nodded. Franz looked him straight in the face.

"She's pregnant," he said.

"Pregnant?"

Franz could see the perplexed look on Robert's face.

"Yes, it's definitely yours," he said, answering a question that had never been asked even within the privacy of Robert's mind.

"But . . ." he began, the sentence trailing away into nothing.

"Are you angry?" Franz asked. "She thought you might be very angry."

"No. Of course I'm not angry. But it means there's more urgency than I'd supposed. It means I've got to get her out quickly, before she's completely incapacitated by the pregnancy."

"No, Robert, I'm afraid it means quite the opposite. That's what I've come to explain to you."

"What do you mean?"

"She's ill. The pregnancy has made her ill. For the last three weeks she's been in hospital. They say it's her only chance of keeping the baby."

Robert could feel a familiar yet uncontrollable fear rising within himself, a fear that despite all his efforts life was running out of control.

"What's the matter with her?" he asked anxiously.

"Shortly after she missed her period she began to bleed heavily. When she went to the clinic for tests they told her that she was pregnant and that she should try to rest as much as possible or she'd miscarry."

"And they sent her to hospital?"

The old man laughed drily.

"You don't know our country. They didn't even write her off sick."

"But I thought you said she was in a hospital."

"That came later. At first she carried on struggling to work every day, trying to rest as much as she could when she was off duty, but it didn't do any good. After a few weeks the bleeding started to get worse. She was close to despair, terrified she would lose the child you both shared. On several occasions she went back to the doctors and asked for a sick note, but each time they refused."

"But why did they refuse? They'd told her themselves that she needed rest."

Franz looked at him quietly.

"Don't ask me questions, Robert. Just listen. One day, completely out of the blue, someone telephoned the mill while she was at work and told her an ambulance was coming to pick her up. When it arrived, it took her straight to hospital."

Robert looked at the old man in astonishment. Franz nodded.

"Yes, it is odd, isn't it? But wait, it gets odder. When the ambulance arrived it took her to a little hospital tucked away up in the hills not very far from my cottage."

"Why's that odder? You said they were going to take her to a hospital; it sounds like where she should have been in the first place."

"I know the hospital well because I used to tend the trees in the grounds before I retired. Most East Germans would give their right arms to be in a place like that when they fall ill."

"Why?"

"Because they can't go, that's why. It's strictly reserved for people with connections, people who are used to getting the very best a communist state can provide. From being the scum of the earth, it seems your sister has suddenly and for no apparent reason become a valued member of our most privileged élite!"

* * * * * *

Robert swung the car off the main road onto the unlit track running besides the rapidly flowing waters of the River Werra. On the opposite bank, the dim outline of a high range of hills could be seen against the bleak night sky, a solid reference point against the dark clouds scudding past overhead. High above the river a modern railway bridge soared over the valley floor, its graceful arches blending delicately with the natural curve of the surrounding hills.

Franz peered dismally out of the window.

"Is that my homeland?" he asked, looking across the river towards the hills on the opposite bank.

Robert flicked a glance to see where the old man was looking.

"No," he replied, "not any more. It seems the Russians occupied the whole of this valley at the end of the war, carefully slicing a few kilometers out of the main north-south rail route through this part of the American zone. Then, when the cold war started, they tried using their stranglehold over this stretch of the rail route to blackmail the Western powers. For a few days there was a political crisis which looked as though it might get nasty but then the local Russian and American military commanders arranged a swap and the Americans got this bit of the valley together with their precious railway line."

Franz said nothing, staring vacantly out of the window into the dark rushing depths of the river below.

The valley narrowed and started to curve sharply round to the right. On either side the hills seemed to close in menacingly while beneath them the river flowed swiftly past in the opposite direction to that in which they were travelling, as if urging them to return towards the safety from which they had come.

They swung round a final twist in the narrow road and saw ahead of them a small village lying just below them on the opposite bank of the river. From the windows of the ancient timber-framed houses the yellow glow of countless electric lights seemed to beckon towards them, as if offering a safe haven from the dangers of the night, but as Robert brought the car to a halt it rapidly became apparent that this was no safe haven for strangers from the West. For just ahead, where the road had once crossed over the river and joined the main village street, the bridge over which it had passed for many long years had been blown up by East German border troops, and the track along which they were travelling came to an abrupt end.

"That," Robert muttered, switching of the engine and the lights, "is your country."

Franz said nothing. He pulled his coat about him and climbed clumsily out of the car before walking slowly out onto what remained of the long vanished bridge and peering over into the heart of the village.

Since it seemed that Franz wished to be alone with his thoughts for a while, Robert remained in the car and carefully studied the opposite bank. The customs official had been right; the village of

Lindawerra was an excellent place to observe the border fortifications. To his left, on the opposite bank beyond the sharp bend in the river around which they had just driven, the double fence could clearly be seen sweeping down from a tall watchtower at the crest of a high hill towards the village, the wide empty swathe of the death strip forming a stark and violent contrast with the quiet beauty of the heavily wooded slopes to either side. As they cut through the forest, the inner and outer fences appeared o be at least half a kilometre apart, but as the border approached the river and had to squeeze between the village houses and the water's edge, the two fences drew closer and closer together until at one point, where a ramshackle old wooden building had been left standing only yards from the river-bank, the two fences came to within less than six feet of each other, separated by nothing more than a thin grass strip.

Robert leant over onto the back seat and grabbed his binoculars, peering at the place where the two fences converged. The water was separated from the rusty outer fence by nothing but a steeply rising bank covered with thick scrubby undergrowth. Beyond the outer fence came the narrow grass strip, its lawn as carefully trimmed as if it were under the charge of the Royal Horticultural Society. And there, rising gracefully from the closely-cropped lawn, lay the silvery form of the high-tech inner fence, the fence that really mattered. It glistened menacingly in the yellow glow cast by the lights in the village street beyond, the delicate tracery of its thin wire mesh surmounted on either side by the angled posts that carried the high tension cables.

Robert swung the field glasses a hundred yards along to the right, towards the eastern end of the bombed-out bridge. On the remains of the approach road the East Germans had erected a tall concrete watchtower: it appeared to serve as some kind of guardhouse for as he watched it two young border guards emerged from a small door at the base of the tower and mounted a small Army motorbike on which they set off to patrol the village. At the top of the control tower, two more guards were carefully observing their visitors through their own field glasses, no doubt grateful to have found some brief relief from the tedium of their long night shift.

Robert quietly opened the car door and walked over to where Franz was leaning against the crumbling parapet which was all that remained of the western side of the bridge.

"I always knew it would come to this," the old man murmured, as if transfixed by the scene that met his eyes. "Even on the day in 1945 when the Russians came to liberate us from our camp I knew deep down that it would finally come to this."

Robert looked at him and saw that tears were streaming down his face. The old man wiped them away with his handkerchief and turned to look at Robert.

"I'm sorry," he said quietly, "but you see we have all lived with this thing for so long that you finally start to accept it as normal, as if this is how people are supposed to live. But when you see it from the outside, like an observer, then you can no longer even pretend that it is anything but totally obscene."

Robert took hold of his arm.

"Why don't you leave for good, Franz? You're a pensioner; you're free to go. And the West Germans will give you enough money to live on."

"I've always been afraid to leave. Before today I'd never even visited the West, and even though you know in your heart of hearts that the Party is lying when it speaks of the horrors of life in the capitalist world for the old and infirm, there is always a part of you that is secretly fearful they may be right."

"And now. Now that you've been out to see for yourself."

He looked down at the fence for a long time.

"Maybe," he murmured. "Maybe I will."

Franz took a deep breath.

"So how are you going to get them out?" he asked, staring down into the dark waters sweeping by beneath the parapet. "How on earth are you going to get Ingrid out now that she's going to have a tiny baby with her?"

Robert looked once again at the place where the two metal fences almost seemed to touch each other as they skirted the old wooden building near the water's edge.

"That," he said eventually, a wry smile spreading slowly across his lips, "is a question to which I think I may have just found the answer."

GERMANY, DECEMBER 1982

Robert slipped quietly into the icy water in his black wet suit and felt a strange sense of relief engulf him. After so many months of interminable waiting and painstaking preparation, it was good to find himself on the verge of action. He looked at the waterproof watch on his wrist and saw the second hand moving inexorably round. In exactly half an hour it would be midnight, the start of a new year, and he would be reunited forever with Ingrid and the little girl they both shared.

Or they would all be dead, shot down in the act of escape by a bunch of pathetic East German teenage conscripts who would then have to live with the guilt for the rest of their mortal years.

The thought forced him to concentrate on the matters in hand. He pulled the heavy black case under the water, grateful at the reduction in its weight. And then, carefully adjusting his snorkel, he took one last look around before letting his head sink slowly below the surface.

The water swirling around him was dark and murky, but it was easy enough to follow the riverbank by crouching low in the shallows and pulling himself along by grabbing the underwater plants with his free hand. He started mentally counting the yards as he moved forward, aware that every time he raised his head above the water's surface he was running a quite unnecessary risk.

"One, two, three . . ."

It was important to run through the plans again and compose himself. He had already confirmed that Ingrid and the baby were waiting by the old wooden building next to the fence, and therefore that the first part of his plan had been a success. That in itself had been a high risk gamble. If she had followed his advice as transmitted by Franz, Ingrid would have avoided the control points along the approach roads to Lindawerra by walking through the woods after dark, carrying her small baby strapped to her front and a rucksack on her back. Then, just before leaving the relative security of the forest and entering the built-up area, she would have changed her clothes into those befitting one of the many New Year's Eve visitors to friends or relatives in the village, discarding the dirty clothes and rucksack before casually walking away from the cover of the trees and onto the streets. That must have taken guts, but he knew from experience that Ingrid was perfectly capable of rising to such an occasion. Then all she had to do was amble along the village roads towards the border as if she was taking an evening stroll to try and settle the child before midnight. She would have had nothing with her except her warmly wrapped infant and nobody would have suspected that she was about to make an attempt on the Wall. Nor would anyone have been able to see that in place of her underclothes she was wearing a wet suit. In the unlikely event of anyone querying her movements, she would have researched the name of a family living in the village from the telephone book with whom she could claim that she was staying.

"Ninety-eight, ninety-nine, one hundred ..."

It was strange to think that he now had a daughter. For so long he had assumed that his family was complete, that Justin and Timothy were going to be his only real attack upon mortality, but now they were nearly grown up and here he was starting all over again with a new family. It was something he could never have imagined in his earlier life, but then perhaps that was because he had been an entirely different person in that earlier life.

"One hundred and eighty-one, one hundred and eighty-two, one hundred and eighty-three ..."

His arms were beginning to ache and his chest to heave at the exertion of pulling against the current. From the surface, the flow of the River Werra had looked strikingly similar to the current in a river that ran through the woods near his childhood home in Upper Trumpton. So for the last few months he had combined weekend trips to see his adopted parents with solitary night-time training sessions. He had thought he was ready for anything the river could throw at him, yet now the current seemed far stronger than anything he had experienced before, the water pulling savagely at his body, threatening to sweep him back towards the West if he lost his grip of the underwater plants. And yet, despite the ache in his arms and the pounding in his chest, he found the force with which the water attacked him reassuring. Soon, with luck, it would be his closest ally against a greater danger.

"Two hundred and ninety-eight, two hundred and ninety-nine, three hundred ..."

Three hundred yards. The river should be beginning to turn the bend now, passing the trim white post on the bank that marked the beginning of East German territory. But there was no way of knowing, because in the swirling, murky depths there was no possible way of telling in which direction he was moving. There was nothing to do but keep on counting and hope that his calculations had been correct.

"Three hundred and forty-five, three hundred and forty-six, three hundred and forty-seven ..."

Getting the case constructed had been by far the hardest part; it had to be both waterproof and bulletproof, with just the right degree of buoyancy to keep it beneath the water's surface without becoming unduly heavy. In other words, it was not the sort of suitcase it was possible to order from your local department store. But it had seemed that the great British underworld could do almost anything for a price, and an old friend of Smithson's had cheerfully constructed the thing from first principles in exchange for the outstanding balance of Robert's already much diminished building society account.

"Four hundred and ninety, four hundred and ninety-one, four hundred and ninety-two ..."

It had been a long and difficult year while Ingrid had lain in her privileged Thuringian clinic and rested. He had agreed with Franz that there would be no contact except for a brief coded telephone message to inform him of the baby's birth and a further message to confirm that the escape was on. Other than that, he had no knowledge of developments in Ingrid's life. But the two telephone messages had come exactly as planned, and now he knew that they were there, waiting for him a few hundred more yards along the riverbank.

"Six hundred and fifty-three, six hundred and fifty-four, six hundred and fifty-five ..."

Robert stopped and took several deep breaths through the snorkel. He drew his watch up to his face and saw from its glowing hands that he had only fifteen minutes left until the New Year dawned. For weeks now a nagging fear had been growing within him, a fear that the timing of the escape was flawed. Standing on the opposite bank with Franz all those months ago, the idea of an attack on the border at exactly the stroke of midnight on New Year's Eve had seemed brilliant; not only would the presence of a relatively large number of strangers in the village significantly improve Ingrid's chances of reaching the border without challenge, but there was a good chance that the border guards themselves would have succumbed to the temptation of joining in the festivities by having a quiet drink or two in the privacy of their watchtower. At the very least it was unlikely that any of the guards would be out patrolling when they could be up at the top of the watchtower enjoying the traditional German burst of fireworks that greeted the arrival of the New Year. And amidst the general noise of the firecrackers, there was even a chance that the guards might waste valuable seconds eliminating the possibility that the explosion was a firework gone wrong before they realised they were confronted with a full-blown attack upon the border defences. But despite all these perfectly good reasons, he found he could not calm his misgivings and had to content himself with pushing them firmly into the back of his mind.

"Eight hundred and ninety-eight, eight hundred and ninety-nine, nine hundred . . ."

One hundred yards to go. Robert tried to calm his nerves and check through the order of operations. Split-second timing would be required if the plan was to succeed, with even the slightest miscalculation likely to result in disaster for them all.

"Nine hundred and ninety-eight, nine hundred and ninety-nine, one thousand."

Robert stopped. Looking at his watch, he realised that the crawl had taken him longer than he had expected. If he had misjudged the distance to any significant extent, he would have no chance of being ready by midnight.

He lifted his blackened face quietly above the water's surface and peered cautiously around. From so close the bank seemed steeper and higher than he had imagined, but far above him he could just make out through the undergrowth the angled roof of the wooden building by which he knew that Ingrid and his little daughter were waiting.

Glancing along to his right towards the eastern remnants of the bombed bridge, he could clearly make out the dark silent shadow of the huge searchlight surmounting the watchtower through the undergrowth, but with relief he noted that if he crouched low on very edge of the river, the guards in the viewing platform just beneath the searchlight would be unable to observe his actions.

Pulling himself silently out of the water, he started mechanically unpacking the case. Before long a large pair of pliers, an explosive device with a timer, six smokegrenades and a small yet deadly pistol were lying on the damp ground in a neat row. Taking care to keep his head low to avoid any prying eyes from the watchtower, he started adjusting the balast weights in the case to ensure that it was ready to receive its precious consignment of human flesh.

He finished his work and glanced anxiously around before picking up the pliers and explosives and starting to crawl gingerly up through the thick undergrowth towards the top of the riverbank. In stark contrast to the swirling current in the river beneath him, the bushes through which he now moved lay still and calm in the cold night air. Any vigilant guard observing that particular part of the bank through his field glasses would be sure to notice the unusual rustling of the bushes; yet there was nothing he could do but pray that the guards had better things to do as they made their final preparations to welcome in the coming year.

Suddenly the bushes ahead of him cleared and there, no more than two feet away, lay the rusty grid of the outer fence. He looked up and saw that Ingrid had seen his approach, because she smiled a grim smile and raised her hand slightly to indicate that she was ready. To her chest she was clutching her sleeping baby in a tight sling, her passive little body heavily drugged to prevent her from awaking, and for a fraction of a second Robert found himself wondering if he had any right to impose such extraordinary risks on one so very small and helpless. But the thought vanished and Robert motioned to his sister that she should take cover.

Placing the explosives carefully on the ground beside him, he started to cut the wire mesh of the outer fence. Despite its rusty appearance, he was fearful that the first cut would trigger some sort of alarm and was relieved when none sounded. The ageing mesh was broadly spaced, and before long he had cut a hole big enough to crawl through.

He moved back to the cover of the bushes and waited as the final moments ticked by, carefully checking the explosive timer to ensure that it would allow him exactly one minute to retreat from the inner fence to the safety of the lower part of the riverbank so that he could avoid the full force of the blast.

Exactly two minutes to go. With a quick glance around to make sure nobody except Ingrid was watching, he pulled the wire back from the hole he had cut and crawled stealthily through into the death strip beyond. Now there was no turning back. He crawled across the grass to the fence, carefully laying the explosives exactly midway between two concrete support posts for maximum impact. Then he quietly pressed the button which activated the timer and hurried back through the gap in the outer fence.

There was no time to lose and little more point in stealth. But he nevertheless kept low as he clambered back hurriedly down the bank and grabbed a smoke grenade in each hand, checking that the others were close by. Behind him he could hear the distant cheers of the village folk as they welcomed in the New Year and, shortly afterwards, the sound of the rockets screaming high into the night air from the village gardens.

He thought of Ingrid and his child cowering for shelter as they waited for the explosion and suddenly it all seemed such a farce.

They didn't want to hurt anyone, they didn't want to threaten anyone's precious political system. All they wanted was to live together and love each other and bring up a child in peace and quiet; yet here they were, forced by a crazy idiotic world into attacking metal fences with high explosives.

An almighty explosion cut short his thoughts and without further delay Robert lobbed the smokegrenades as far as he could in the direction of the watchtower before picking up two more and throwing them in the same direction. Then he picked up the last two grenades and held them in his hand, ready to throw up the bank towards the place where the hole had been cut after Ingrid had reached him.

Seconds passed and dense clouds of smoke started to rise up from the place where the smokebombs had exploded. A high-pitched scream came from the general direction of the fence where the alarm had been triggered but as yet the searchlight remained inactivated.

Looking up, he saw Ingrid's silhouette appear in the darkness at the top of the bank and start clambering down. Robert lobbed the last of the smokegrenades high over her head, and as they exploded behind her he became aware that the beam of the searchlight had started sweeping along the bank where Ingrid was still climbing down, its normally sharp light diffused by the spreading clouds of dense white smoke.

As she reached him the guards in the watchtower had started firing at random into the mist, but although their aim was wild he sensed that some of the bullets were far too close for comfort.

"Give me the baby!" he shouted above the sound of the gunshot.

With a terrified look, Ingrid started fumbling with the catch holding the baby's harness in place. Robert watched her with impatience, trying to estimate how quickly the guards would be able to reach the riverbank on foot from the watchtower.

"I can't get it free!" she screamed.

She was close to panic. Robert picked up the revolver and thrust it into her hand.

"Let me," he said, trying hard to control the fear growing within him with every passing second. "Take this and shoot anyone you see coming out of that smoke."

Ingrid took the gun without protest and turned to face the hole in the fence. Within seconds, Robert had released the catch on the halter and grabbed the baby, quickly strapping the sleeping child into its place in the case and slamming the waterproof lid closed. They would have to be quick; the sound of gunfire had ceased, which must mean that the border guards were now approaching on foot.

He leant over and picked up the two snorkels from the damp ground, thrusting one into Ingrid's waiting hand and pushing the strap of the other one over his own neck.

"Swim out into midstream and let the current carry you round past the bend in the river. And for Christ's sake keep your head underwater until you're out of their range."

Ingrid pulled her shoes off and threw herself into the water. Robert picked up the case and started to follow.

"Halt or I'll shoot!"

Robert shuddered. He turned and saw standing high above him in the swirling mist at the top of the bank a young man in military uniform, his rifle aimed straight at Robert's chest. Although the water's edge was only a few feet away, it might just as well have been a thousand miles.

"Put down the case!" the soldier ordered, his voice trembling with a fear that showed that this was no hardened soldier but rather a terrified conscript, a lad scarcely older than Robert's own boys.

If only he had still had the gun, but Ingrid had slung it away into the undergrowth before jumping into the water and it was nowhere to be seen.

Robert stared at his terrified young adversary and knew at once that everything had been lost. The soldier was going to kill him if he took another step. A sinking feeling of despair started to seep through his body as he began slowly lowering the case to the ground. The young man, sensing his victory, took a cautious step forward.

Suddenly, in the distance, a single shot rang out. For a fraction of a second Robert wondered if the guard had taken fright and fired, but as he looked up he saw that the soldier had dropped his weapon. He was standing at the top of the bank as he had been before, but now the look on his face had turned from fear into a kind of blank non-comprehension. And then, without so much as a whimper, he sank slowly to his knees and disappeared from view.

There was no time to seek explanations. Grabbing hold of the case, he plunged into the safety of the water's depths.

* * * * * *

As soon as he judged it safe to do so, Robert swam to the side of the river and dragged himself and the case out of the water. Looking around, he saw Ingrid some two hundred yards further down the bank; she had caught sight of him and was running quickly towards him.

Without waiting for her to arrive, he carefully lifted the lid of the case and unstrapped the tiny drugged infant within. Lifting the baby girl gently into his arms he was able to concentrate for the first time upon his daughter's little face. He sat down on the ground, rocking her slowly back and forth.

Ingrid had reached him now.

"Is she all right?" she asked anxiously, taking the infant from his arms and holding it gently to her.

"She's breathing," Robert said, realising as he handed the child over how exhausted he felt.

Having satisfied herself her baby was well, Ingrid sat down beside him on the grass and quietly kissed his face.

"We made it," she said.

Robert looked up at her.

"I nearly didn't," he said. "After you jumped into the water, an armed guard popped up out of nowhere and challenged me."

"So you jumped?"

"No. He was pointing his rifle straight at my chest."

"But . . ."

"Someone killed him. Someone shot him dead from behind. Then I jumped."

Ingrid looked at him in horror for a few moments.

"Are you sure?" she said, her voice unstable.

"Yes. I can't make it out. One moment he was standing there ordering me about, the next moment he was dead."

For a long time Ingrid was silent, gently rocking her sleeping infant backwards and forwards in her arms. Finally, she spoke in a whisper.

"It must have been Franz," she murmured, so quietly it was hard to make out her words.

"Franz!" Robert exclaimed. "Why Franz?"

"He came with me as far as the edge of the village. I thought he'd turned back then, but he must have followed me so that he could give me covering fire if I needed it. It must have been him who shot the guard."

Robert looked back down the river. There was nothing either of them could say, nothing either of them could do.

For what seemed like a long time they sat in silence, listening to the sound of the river rushing by beneath them. But then their reverie was broken by the approaching sound of a siren as a modern white van carrying the insignia of the West German Customs Service screeched to a halt on the narrow road above them.

A young man in his mid-twenties jumped out and scrambled down the riverbank towards them.

"What the hell is going on?" he shouted as he approached.

Robert rose to his feet, his dark wet suit gleaming brightly in the light from the man's torch.

"This woman and child have just escaped from the East," he explained.

The young man looked at them in silence for a moment.

"So what was that bloody great explosion? We could hear it in the village, despite the fireworks."

"I used explosives to blast through the fence."

A frown passed over the young man's face.

"Who did you say escaped?" he asked.

"She did – and the baby."

"So who was it who blew up the fence?"

"I did. You wouldn't stand a chance blasting it from the other side."

"Come up to the van, please," the young man said. Although his voice seemed friendly enough, there was something insistent about his tone.

They clambered up through the scrub to the road. An older man had climbed out from the driver's seat and was staring at Robert.

"It's you!" he exclaimed, and Robert immediately recognised the customs official to whom he had spoken when he had been snooping around the border the previous spring.

At first Robert didn't reply. He realised with a shock that he had been so obsessed with the border itself that he had failed to plan any suitable explanations of his actions for officialdom in the West.

The younger customs official opened the rear door of the van and asked them politely to climb inside. As they did so, they could see him climbing back down the bank to retrieve the empty case. After a few moments, the older man joined them in the back of the van.

"I thought at the time you were more than just a tourist," he muttered, a strained look on his face. "Perhaps you'd better tell me exactly what's been going on."

Robert explained in detail how he had executed his plan, carefully omitting any reference to the fact that an East German border guard had been killed in the process.

"A pretty impressive escapade, Mr Stanton," the customs official commented drily when he had finished. "But I'm afraid you'll have to come with us until our enquiries are complete."

Robert nodded his head as the official clambered out and slammed the door closed, leaving them alone in the back. A few seconds later, the engine hummed into life and the van jolted into motion.

Robert wondered where they were going, but there were no windows in the back of the van so there was no way of telling. He lay back on one of the benches that ran along the sides of the van and closed his eyes. For months he had supposed that he would be elated if his plan succeeded, yet now he found that he simply wanted to sleep.

"What happens now?" Ingrid asked, and from her voice it was clear that she was as exhausted as he was.

"I don't really know," Robert murmured. "I suppose we go to the police station and make a full report and then we can go to the hotel and rest. I booked a double room with a cot."

Ingrid sat down by him and stroked his hair.

"What shall we call our daughter?" she asked quietly.

Robert opened his eyes and looked at the sleeping infant in her arms.

"Haven't you decided yet?"

"I wanted to wait, I wanted to wait until we could decide together. The name I used on her official East German papers doesn't matter."

His tiredness suddenly vanished, Robert sat bolt upright.

"What do you mean it doesn't matter?" he asked sharply.

"I mean we can call her something else now."

He looked at his daughter for a moment. Slowly, almost imperceptibly, the drugs seemed to be wearing off. She was still asleep, but her sleep seemed somehow more normal.

Finally Robert's face broke into a smile.

"Tell me what you called her, Ingrid – tell me what you called her on her East German papers."

"Margit."

"Then I think we will call her Margit."

At last he could feel himself slowly relaxing, and he pulled Ingrid and the baby towards him.

"So we made it," he said, "after all this time we finally made it."

For a long time they sat in silence, taking it in turns to hold their still drowsy baby, until finally the van drew to a halt and they could hear the sound of the front doors opening.

"We must have arrived at the police station," Robert said, rising to his feet ready to climb out of the van. "I hope to God this doesn't take too long."

They waited for somebody to come and open the rear door of the van but nobody came.

"What's the matter, Robert," Ingrid asked. "Why don't they come and let us out of here."

Robert tried releasing the catch on the door from the inside.

"It's locked," he said, "they've bloody well locked us in from the outside."

Ingrid looked at him with a perplexed expression.

"I don't understand, Robert. They surely can't have just forgotton about us."

Robert moved to reassure her, but no sooner had he done so than the catch was released.

"Oh no ..." Ingrid gasped in terror as the door swung open, and she seemed to shrink back with her baby into the farthest corner of the van.

Robert turned around and saw the older West German customs official appear at the door. His face looked grim, but that was not why Ingrid had recoiled. For next to him, standing with an equally grim look on his face, was a middle-aged man dressed in the unmistakable uniform of a senior East German army officer.

The West German beckoned to them to climb out of the van.

"Where are we?" Robert asked, trying to hide the fear in his voice, but in reality the question needed no answer. The West Germans had driven them straight back over the border to an East German army base.

As soon as they were out of the van it was the East German officer who took control of the situation.

"You will please go with these two soldiers," he ordered, the courtesy in his voice clearly intended to appease the visiting West German officials.

The two young conscripts he had indicated moved forward briskly. Robert flung a last desperate glance at the customs official. The man was supposed to represent a government that despised the communists; surely it wasn't possible that he could betray them like this. But he was standing with his head bowed so as to avoid Robert's gaze, a look of deep shame indelibly engraved on the wrinkled features of his face.

"You can't do this to us!" Robert yelled, but one of the soldiers had already grabbed him by the sleeve and was pulling him forcefully along towards a low wooden hut some distance away.

Before long the soldiers had pushed them through the door of the hut. There was nobody inside, and one of the soldiers indicated that they should sit down on two chairs placed to one side of the small desk in the middle of the room. The soldiers themselves stood on either side of the door, effectively precluding all thoughts of escape.

Ingrid sank slowly down onto the chair clutching her baby, rocking the still sleeping infant gently to and fro. There were no tears in her face, just a look of inconsolable dread at what she knew was bound to come.

Robert looked about him with the eyes of a trapped fox.

"Ingrid," he whispered sharply, "Ingrid, we've got to think fast. They'll separate us soon."

One of the soldiers tensed and raised his gun.

"The prisoners will not talk!" he ordered. With a shudder Robert sensed that his initial guess that these soldiers were conscripts had been wrong. The voice was that of a hardened soldier of the regular army.

He sat back in his chair, trying frantically to think of a way of avoiding the inevitable, but before he could do so the door swung open and the army officer who had first met them entered the room. He was carrying a large black briefcase which he threw roughly down on the floor before lowering himself into the chair on the other side of the desk and silently observing his prisoners.

After a while he picked up the phone.

"Sergeant, send in Frau Grumpel, please," he ordered crisply.

He put down the phone and resumed his silent observation of his prey. Robert glanced sideways at Ingrid. Margit seemed finally to have recovered from the drugs and was gazing lovingly into her mother's eyes while Ingrid tenderly rocked her back and forth.

The door swung open again. Robert turned and saw a burly lady in late middle-age enter. She was wearing civilian dress.

The officer rose politely from his chair as she entered.

"Thank you for coming so quickly, Frau Grumpel," he said, shaking her hand.

The officer moved round the desk and approached Ingrid.

"You must hand over the child to this lady," he said firmly.

Robert stared at Ingrid. But she continued to sit there rocking her baby just as she had done before. It was as if the officer had not spoken.

The officer repeated his order, this time more forcefully. But again she took no notice. Then he turned to the waiting Frau Grumpel.

"Frau Grumpel," he said politely, "please take the baby."

The woman approached. Her face seemed so cold, so completely lacking in any kind of human emotion. She leant over Ingrid and placed her large puffy hands firmly around the baby's tiny form. And then, with one sharp tug, she dragged it free of Ingrid's grip.

"Mutti . . .!"

He awoke, the scream still echoing on his lips, and tried to control his jarring emotions. But there was nowhere to go; neither backwards into the nightmare from which he had just emerged nor forwards into the reality from which he had prayed in vain that sleep would give him some temporary respite.

He realised with a shock that he had never before dreamt of his own childhood separation from his mother. For over thirty-five years he had managed to bury all recollection of his early life and it had taken the terrible screams of his own innocent daughter as she was dragged away from her own mother to stir up memories of those distant events.

Robert rose stiffly to his feet and started to pace up and down the empty cell. There were no windows to relieve the dull monotony of the crumbling paint on the walls and the only furniture, other than an old metal bucket, was the decaying mattress from which he had just arisen.

He wondered what they were doing to Ingrid. She had been separated from him shortly after Margit had been taken away and he had no idea what had become of her since. For himself, he had had little choice but to make a full statement to the interrogating officer describing the circumstances of the escape. Then he had accompanied the officer to an adjoining room and had formally identified Franz's lifeless body, his bloodstained corpse riddled with countless bullet-marks.

Subject to the constraints of his job, the interrogating officer had not been overly unpleasant. He had informed Robert that Frau Grumpel was in charge of the orphanage in the local town and that the baby would be well cared for. When Robert had asked what sentence Ingrid and he could expect to receive for their crime, the officer had explained that a great deal would depend on the view that the court took of where the responsibility lay for the young soldier's death. His guess was hard labour for between fifteen and thirty years.

As soon as the preliminary interrogation had been completed, Robert had been taken to the cell where he now found himself and been left alone. For over twelve hours, he had heard nothing.

The sound of footsteps became audible outside in the corridor and Robert tensed inwardly. Having only just awoken, he didn't yet feel in good enough shape to withstand another session with his interrogator. The door clanked open and a smartly-dressed soldier appeared.

He was clutching a pile of clean clothes which he threw on the mattress, motioning to Robert that he should get dressed. When he had done so the soldier secured his hands behind his back with handcuffs and left the room, indicating to Robert that he should follow.

Before long they emerged from the guardhouse into the open air. There was an empty army jeep pulled up immediately outside and the soldier motioned to Robert that he should get into the back seat. Then, without saying a word, the soldier climbed into the front and they drove off.

Robert looked around anxiously as the guard swung the jeep round and headed straight for the road barriers at the entrance to the camp. As they approached, the barriers were silently raised by the watching guards and the jeep accelerated out onto the open country road beyond. Soon the army camp was completely lost from view. The jeep was trundling along an empty road through deep pine forest and Robert found himself without any guard whatsoever except for the young soldier sitting in the front.

He leaned forward in his seat.

"Where are we going?" he asked.

The guard threw a glance in his direction, his face expressionless.

"You'll soon see," he replied, "it's not very far."

The jeep swung off the road onto a small track that led away through the woods. For a long time the vehicle seemed to jolt along the bumpy track, throwing them first to one side, then to the other.

It was hard to make any sense of what was happening. For a dreadful moment, Robert wondered whether he was being taken out into the woods to be shot. Yet if the East Germans wanted for some reason to dispose of him they had little reason to do so in the woods rather than in the privacy of an army cell.

After several minutes the jeep swung round a bend and shuddered to a halt. Blocking the road ahead, not twenty yards away, lay the thin metallic grid of the innermost border fence, its design identical in every way to the fence he had blown up only the previous night.

The guard sprung nimbly from the jeep and spoke briefly into his walkie-talkie before opening the gate in the fence and returning. Then he drove speedily through into the death strip beyond. Away in the distance, a tall watchtower soared up above the treetops, and he could make out a tiny figure carefully observing their progress through binoculars from the viewing platform near the top. Before very long the jeep came to a halt again and the driver jumped out and opened the rear door.

"Come with me," he said in a voice that sounded somehow different from the usual crisp military tones of a soldier.

Robert climbed out and looked uncertainly around. Several hundred yards away he could make out the familiar rusty grill of the outer fence, and beyond that the red and white posts that marked the border of East Germany, but between where they were standing and the final barrier lay a long strip of smooth raked sand that looked suspiciously like a minefield. But the raked sand did not seem to bother his minder, who started walking briskly across it towards the perimeter fence. Robert followed, trying as best he could to follow exactly in the man's footsteps.

As they approached the outer fence, Robert could see that they were heading for a small metal gate. As soon as they arrived the guard lifted a bunch of keys from his pocket, casually unlocked the padlock and pushed the little gate open. Fifty yards beyond, the neat little row of posts marked the exact location of the West German frontier.

"Just keep walking through the forest and in about half an hour you'll get to a village," explained the guard dispassionately as he selected another key from his bunch and undid Robert's handcuffs. Robert walked through the open gate, which the soldier then carefully relocked before starting to saunter back towards his jeep.

"Excuse me," Robert suddenly called after him, angry that he had failed to enquire about Ingrid's fate earlier, "but do you know what is going to happen to my friend. To the woman."

The man stopped and looked at him for a moment, clearly uncertain of whether to reply. But then he returned to the fence and fixed Robert with a humourless gaze through the bars.

"If you take my advice," he said in a whisper, "you'll simply forget the woman!"

* * * * * *

Before long he emerged onto an empty road which led into a trim West German village that he had never before seen. At the heart of the village was a large Gasthaus. It must have been lunchtime, because the sounds of many voices could be heard spilling out from within.

He felt despondently in the pockets of the clothes he had been given at the camp, realising that he didn't have any money with which to buy something to eat, and found to his surprise a crisp new DM50 note. But for the moment hunger overcame curiosity and he entered the Gasthaus, sat down at a table in the corner and ordered himself a beer and a large plate of food. It was only when the beer had arrived and been consumed and a second one ordered that Robert became aware of the conversation amongst the regulars sitting at the neighbouring table.

"I went down to look at it myself this morning," one of them, a middle-aged gentleman with a large pot-belly, was explaining to the others. "The place was overrun with photographers."

His companions fell silent, eager for more details.

"It's just like they said on the radio this morning – a damned great hole right there in the middle of the fence – I guess it must have been a good three metres wide."

"Whoever it was, it's a pity they didn't make it through," one of his friends commented, washing down his remark with a generous swig of beer as if by way of offering his condolences.

"Apparently there was quite a shoot-out," the fat man continued. "I saw Herbert this morning – he and the hound were down there briefing the press; Herbert saw the whole thing while he was on duty last night."

"So what did he say happened?"

"Well, there was this explosion at exactly midnight – just as the fireworks were going off. It seems a man from our side had blasted through the fence to try and rescue a girl from over there, because shortly after the explosion Herbert saw a woman trying to get through the gap. They didn't stand a chance, of course, although it seemed the bloke managed to gun down one of the border guards before they got nabbed."

Robert's meal arrived and he mechanically started to push the food into his mouth. By now the conversation at the next table had moved on to other matters, and as soon as he had finished eating he quietly paid the bill and left.

It was turning cold outside, heavy clouds moving low overhead and bringing the promise of snow. Robert cursed that the East Germans had not equipped him with a better coat as he started to walk slowly down the main village street, wondering exactly what he was going to do next. By now the police would no doubt have removed his car from the riverbank and his possessions from the hotel room in Allendorf. There seemed little to do except return to England and try to think, yet with no passport and little money even that did not seem altogether straightforward.

A car swung out of a nearby turning and drove slowly down the street towards the Gasthaus. At first Robert took little notice, but then – as he caught sight of the driver of the vehicle – he felt his whole body tense. For the driver was none other than the corpulent figure of Herbert, the customs official with the alsatian, the very man who had turned them over to the East Germans. He was off-duty now, no doubt coming for a quiet drink with his friends to help him relax from the exertions of the previous night.

Now fully alert, Robert glanced up and down the empty street before walking swiftly towards a side-road adjoining the Gasthaus where Herbert was busy parking the car. The customs official was just clambering out of the vehicle when he spotted Robert walking purposefully along the street towards him.

He froze, unable to believe his eyes.

"Good afternoon, Herbert," Robert said, trying hard to control and direct the anger seething within him. He thought of Ingrid silently rocking their little baby in her arms as the woman from the orphanage had dragged it away.

Herbert took a step backwards.

"But ..."

"You're surprised to see me, aren't you?"

Herbert didn't move.

"I just want a little word," Robert said, "so I suggest you climb quietly back into the car and we'll go for a jolly little drive together."

Herbert glanced quickly around at the empty street and then back at Robert.

"Get in the car, Herbert!"

Realising that resistance was pointless, he climbed slowly back into the car. Robert joined him in the passenger seat.

"Just drive. Drive out of the village."

They drove in silence until they were clear of the village streets and then Robert ordered him down a narrow track that led off into the woods. When they had lost sight of the main road, Robert instructed him to stop the car and switch off the engine.

"Now get out."

Herbert climbed nervously out of the car.

"Put your arms up on top of the car."

Herbert did as he was told as Robert frisked him thoroughly. Then he leant menacingly over Herbert's corpulent form and whispered coldly into his ear.

"Give me one good reason why I shouldn't kill you here and now."

Herbert flinched.

"I ... I was just following orders."

"Whose orders?"

"The Ministry's."

"Tell me about your orders."

The man was terrified. That was plain to see.

"I ... We have standing instructions that in the event of an armed attack on the border from our side in which the perpetrators are apprehended we are to immediately ring the incident room at the Ministry in Bonn. When we called them from the van we were told to arrange for your immediate transfer to the relevant East German authorities."

Robert closed his eyes and cursed inwardly at his own inept stupidity.

"What's happened to my things?" he asked, the steely edge in his voice gradually beginning to subside.

"They're with the customs," he said. "A full report will be made to the British Consulate which the East Germans will corr ..." He stopped before finishing the word 'corroborate'.

"But ..."

"Yes, Herbert, the word is 'but'."

Herbert turned to face him, curiosity finally overcoming fear.

"How the hell did you get out?"

Robert smiled grimly.

"Your guess is as good as mine, mate, but you're going to be in a big pile of trouble if I go down to Lindawerra and start chatting to all those journalists and photographers, aren't you? All that stuff you fed them about how you saw it all and how we didn't stand a chance."

"But it was orders... orders from the Ministry. It's not my fault."

Robert stared straight into his eyes.

"Yes, Herbert. But you haven't got any evidence that they gave you those orders, have you? You just phoned them on the van radio."

Herbert looked at him in horror, suddenly realising the implications of Robert's words.

"What are you going to do?" he said, his voice barely audible.

Robert turned away and walked slowly back to the passenger seat.

"Get back in the car, Herbert, and I'll tell you while we drive."

* * * * * *

Robert walked briskly into the thickly-carpeted entrance hall of the Spandau branch of the Potsdamer Bank. The carpet itself was new, but everything else about the place, including the rather pretty young woman sitting a few yards away from him at the reception desk, was exactly as he remembered it from his last visit nearly four years before.

"Can I help you, sir?" she asked in the familiar business-like tone of the retail banking sector.

"Yes, miss, I'd like to check the contents of my two safe-deposit boxes."

"Certainly sir, can you give me the box numbers and the passwords, please."

Robert offered up a silent prayer of thanks for the excellence of his memory in such matters.

"One of them is 'Upper' and has the number 89376 and the other is 'Trumpton' and has the number 89375."

Robert watched nervously as the girl typed the details into the computer terminal on her desk and studied the screen. He was normally such a calculating man, yet this was nothing but an instinctive hunch.

"I can only find a record for one of the boxes, sir. The one called 'Trumpton'."

Robert's heart jumped. That made sense; it would be idiotic to pay for two boxes.

The girl led him down a corridor, past several automatic doors and into a small room containing nothing but endless rows of small silvery-coloured safe-deposit boxes. She quietly keyed some numbers into the small electronic control panel on the front of one of them and left the room.

As soon as she was gone, Robert pulled the door of the box open and pulled out the little piece of paper within. It seemed that his hunch had paid off.

* * * * * *

He pushed open the main door of the modern apartment block and entered the waiting lift. Her flat was on the tenth floor, and as the lift started rising silently upwards, Robert began wondering exactly what he was going to say when he saw her. But before he had had time to reach any firm conclusions the lift drew almost imperceptibly to a halt and the doors opened to reveal an elegant communal corridor. Immediately in front of him was the door of her flat.

He rang the bell and waited. After a few moments the door swung open and a well-dressed young man in a dark suit appeared.

For a second they stared at each other, each double-checking in their minds his recollection of the other.

"Hallo," the young man said in surprise. "It's you, isn't it?"

"Yes," Robert managed to say, finding it hard to collect his thoughts. The young man seemed to have changed beyond all recognition from the last time they had met four years before. Then he had been a scruffy student, scarcely more than a boy, his whole manner revealing a kind of dogged determination to remain innocent against all the odds. Now, as he faced Robert across the threshold of the door, only his eyes showed that nothing had really changed.

"Come in," he said in a friendly voice.

Robert stepped into the interior of the flat and the young man closed the door behind them. When he turned Robert held out his hand.

"So you stayed with her," Robert said quietly.

"Yes," he said. "In fact, I did more than just stay with her – I married her. Sonja's a very special girl, as you know."

Robert nodded drily.

"Is she here?"

"No. She's out at the shops. But she'll be back soon. Why don't you come and sit down and wait for a while."

The young man went to the kitchen and fetched two glasses of beer.

"Your plan worked like clockwork," he said as he handed the beer to Robert.

Robert tried to smile. "At least something's worked out all right," he said.

Helmut looked at him askance.

"Sorry?"

"Oh, nothing." He wondered if they knew what had happened to him in England; Sonja would still have been in the East at the time of the publicity surrounding his trial. But he decided to say nothing until she returned.

"Tell me how you got out?" Robert asked.

"I didn't do anything, really. Sonja and I pretended to start up a relationship just like you said. It was a bit difficult at first, but then it sort of developed a life of its own. After about six months we decided to approach the escape people as you suggested; they did the rest."

"Which was?"

"They got her out using false papers through Czechoslovakia. A real professional job."

The sound of a key turning in a lock interrupted their conversation and a few moments later Sonja appeared at the door of the living room, clutching a huge paper bag piled high with groceries. As soon as she caught sight of Robert she dropped the bag and rushed over to him, flinging her arms around his neck.

"Robert!" she exclaimed. "I don't believe it!"

Embarrassed by her display of enthusiasm in front of her husband, Robert kissed her gently on the cheek and tried to step backwards.

Sonja broke into a sudden laugh.

"Still the same old Robert, I see." She released him from her grip and pulled Helmut towards her.

"As you see," she said proudly, "I've made it to the promised land."

Robert looked at her fondly. Despite the traumas of the past few days, it was good to see her again.

"How are you, Sonja?" Robert asked.

"Come with me," she said, pulling the two men with her towards the living room window. "Look over there. You can see the beastly border, and just beyond you can see the railway line and some of the stations where I used to work. Every morning I get out of bed and look through my window at that railway line and the little trains puffing along it – and believe you me nothing can depress me after that."

It was true; away in the distance – beyond the border – Robert could see a dumpy S-Bahn train just pulling away from a station platform.

"That's the station where that crazy station-master worked, isn't it?" he asked.

Sonja laughed.

"Yes," she said, a cheeky look spreading over her face. "I know I shouldn't have, but I wrote him a little letter after I left. I wrote and told him exactly where I was living and that I'd wave to him every morning when I got up."

Robert tried hard to laugh. For a few moments he had almost felt able to share in her happiness, but now his own feelings of confusion and despair were slowly returning.

"What's the matter, Robert?" she asked, all trace of humour vanished from her voice.

He looked at her with a glazed expression.

"You don't know anything about what's happened to me in the last four years, do you, Sonja? You don't about my divorce and my separation from my children. You don't know about the two years I spent in prison on spying charges in a futile attempt to try and protect a sister in East Germany with whom I'd fallen hopelessly in love. You don't know that I've had a child by that sister and that I finally managed to get them both out of the East only to have them handed straight back to God-knows-what fate . . ."

He sank slowly down to the floor, tears streaming down his face.

For months the tension had been growing inexorably within him, as he had planned and executed his intricate plans for Ingrid's escape. Yet now he had to accept that all his cherished dreams lay in tatters. There was no longer any way forward, no longer any hope; he had reached the end of the road.

* * * * * *

"Drink the coffee!"

There was an edge in Sonja's voice that told him it would be unwise to refuse.

"You've got to think, Robert. You've got to shake it off and start thinking." She grinned impishly. "It's the only thing you ever were any good at."

The joke was lost. "I've told you what's happened, Sonja. Is it any wonder I feel like I do?"

"No," she said sharply. "But letting despair take over isn't going to help you, is it? You're amongst friends now. We'll find a way."

Robert took a sip of the coffee.

"There's a lot about what's happened that doesn't make sense, Robert. For example, I can see why the West German government handed you back to the East but I'm blowed if I can see why the East threw you back again. It's not their style to be lenient."

"They wanted me to do something, I suppose. They didn't just hand me back, they even gave me some money."

"But why?"

"The only thing I can think of is that they wanted me to go to the press. To embarrass the West German government about handing me over."

Helmut leaned forward in his chair.

"So why should they want to do that?"

Robert shrugged.

"It doesn't make perfect sense, I know. Public exposure would weaken those elements in the government here that are in favour of appeasing the East."

"So are you going to go to the press?" Sonja asked.

"I don't think so. From my point of view I can't really see what it would achieve."

"Besides which it might be dangerous," Sonja added.

Robert looked at her and nodded.

"Exactly. Some people's political reputations are going to be on the line if they know I'm on the loose. They just might try and silence me."

"Do you think that customs official will say anything?" Helmut asked.

"Not a chance. I told him I'd keep my mouth shut if he did – and I also mentioned that I'd personally string him up from a tree if word got out that he'd met me – if, that is, somebody else didn't get to him first."

Sonja sipped her coffee before speaking.

"You know, things could be worse. Frankly I'm surprised your little sister is alive at all – with what she knows I'd have thought the East Germans would have arranged a little accident for her years ago. In some ways you've both been quite lucky, almost as if you had a sort of part-time fairy godmother keeping an eye on you."

Robert stared at her for a moment, his mind racing.

"Jesus Christ!" he exclaimed abruptly, all trace of tiredness suddenly gone from his voice. "I wonder if you're right!"

* * * * * *

It was good of Sonja and Helmut to give him their car since hiring one without any papers would have been virtually impossible. He tensed as he saw a smart blue sign by the side of the motorway informing him the border was only one kilometre away and reduced his speed. The sheer volume of transit traffic flowing out of West Berlin had meant that a short queue was building up on the Western side of the border even though the bored officials were making only the most cursory of checks prior to waving the vehicles on to the East.

Robert waited patiently as the cars ahead of him were cleared through the Western control point, trying hard to steady his nerves for the ordeal ahead. Now there were two cars ahead of him, now only one, and now the road ahead was clear, stretching away towards a large East German flag by the side of the road about a kilometre away that marked the exact position of the border.

"Your passport, please," came a metallic voice from a little grill by the side of Robert's car.

Robert's foot pressed down hard onto the accelerator and the car shot forward, soon leaving the slick Western control point far behind. Here at least there were no tank barriers to be seen, nothing to stop him from reaching his goal.

As soon as he had passed the flag marking the border he slowed down to the crawl required by the East Germans, taking his place in the queue of cars waiting to pass through the first East German control point. Glancing nervously into his rear view mirror, he was relieved to see that the West Germans were making no attempt to follow him.

The first control point comprised two uniformed East German border guards standing by a small wooden shelter. As Robert was well aware, their only job was to make a preliminary examination of the passports and other paperwork and split the arriving vehicles into transit traffic and traffic wishing to enter East Germany proper.

After a lengthy wait, the car in front of him was finally cleared through and his turn arrived. One of the two guards beckoned him forward with an imperious wave and indicated that he should wind his window down.

"Turn off your engine, please," the officer muttered mechanically.

Robert did so.

"Your documents please."

Robert braced himself.

"I'm here on special business. I have instructions to see Ferdinand Brand."

The officer looked at him with a bemused expression, as if he were dealing with some kind of moron.

"Give me your papers, please. Your passport and your car registration document."

Robert stared him straight in the face. Surely the man had heard of Ferdinand Brand.

"I have already told you, officer, that I am here on special business. You are to tell Ferdinand Brand, the Head of the Security Service, that Heinrich Obermann is here to speak with him."

The man looked hard at Robert and then turned away to consult his colleague. After a few moments it was the colleague who returned.

"Please give me your papers," he demanded.

"I've already told the other officer that I'm here to see Ferdinand Brand on special business. Please will you tell him I am here."

"But where are your papers? You must have papers!"

Robert looked at him with exasperation. It seemed that the very concept of a human being without papers was too much for an East German official to grasp.

"I don't have any papers," Robert said finally, hoping that the official would begin to get the idea. He did get the idea.

"If you don't have any papers, you'll have to go back! Turn the car round over there."

The officer started to walk away.

"Officer!" Robert called after him. The officer turned.

"Will you please telephone for instructions from higher authority."

The guard's face started to turn red.

"I already have my instructions. People without papers are to be turned back. The instructions permit no exceptions."

Robert moved the car slowly forward as if he intended to turn round as the official had instructed and as he did so the man's attention switched to the car immediately behind. But then, before anyone could stop him, he suddenly accelerated forward.

In his rear view mirror he could see the officials with whom he had just spoken running frantically towards the little wooden sentry box to report his actions. Ahead, the motorway split into many lanes as it passed underneath the sheds where the detailed passport and customs checks were undertaken. Carefully avoiding the relatively heavy traffic in the lanes marked for transit vehicles, Robert swung the car into one of the empty lanes reserved for traffic entering East Germany.

By the time he arrived they were waiting. As he pulled the car to a halt six armed soldiers had run out of a nearby hut and were aiming their rifles straight at him. One of the soldiers pulled the car door open.

"Out of the car!" he barked.

Robert obeyed, trying to appear as confident as possible.

The guard pushed him up against the side of the vehicle and frisked him thoroughly. By the time he had finished a more senior officer had arrived on the scene.

Robert turned around to face him.

"Officer . . ." Robert began, but it was as if he hadn't spoken.

"Take him inside," the officer snapped at the waiting soldiers, "and clear the car away for thorough inspection."

The soldiers frogmarched Robert into the guardhouse where they pushed him into a small cell and slammed the door closed. Outside, he could hear their animated conversation as they discussed the circumstances of his arrest.

About half an hour later the cell door opened and yet another officer entered the room clutching a bunch of papers.

"Why are you trying to enter East Germany without papers?" he asked as soon as he had sat down.

"I have already explained several times that I have to speak with Ferdinand Brand, the Head of the Security . . ."

"I know perfectly well who Ferdinand Brand is," the officer snapped. "And why do you wish to speak with Herr Brand?"

"That is something I cannot discuss with you," Robert replied, trying to sound as self-assured as possible.

The officer flicked through some of the papers he had brought into the room, pausing for quite a long time on one particular sheet before speaking again.

"Why have you come here, Mr Stanton?" he asked.

In the corner of the sheet of paper held by the officer he caught sight of a small, passport-sized photograph of himself. It looked as though it had been taken in his Foreign Office days.

"I have come to see Herr Brand. You will please tell him that I am here."

A look of cold anger suddenly passed across the man's face. He rose from his chair and silently left the room.

About an hour passed. Outside, Robert could hear the guards eating their dinner, but no one thought to bring him anything to eat. There was nothing to do except wait. Finally the door was opened and two soldiers entered the cell. After securely handcuffing Robert they led him out of the cell and along a corridor to another room.

At first glance the room they entered appeared to be rather like a dentist's surgery. There was a large padded chair with a high back in the middle of the room surrounded by various pieces of what appeared to be scientific equipment.

One of the two soldiers undid his handcuffs.

"Take everything off except for your pants and sit on the chair," he ordered.

Robert looked at him.

"Do it!" the man shouted.

He did as he was told, and as soon as he had done so they strapped him securely to the chair by his arms and legs using thick leather thongs.

Just as they were finishing their work three more men entered the room. One of them looked like a doctor, because he was wearing a white coat. The other two were wearing military uniform and appeared to be senior officers of the Security Service.

The older of the two officers spoke first.

"Doctor, you will please give this man a full examination and ensure that he is fit for interrogation."

Robert tried to lift his head as far as it would go but found it hard to look dignified in such circumstances.

"Excuse me . . ." he began.

"The prisoner will remain silent," snapped the second officer, and Robert lay back quietly while the doctor completed his examination.

After about fifteen minutes the doctor finished his work and nodded to show that he was satisfied. Then he quietly left the room.

The older officer approached the chair.

"Mr Stanton, my colleague tells me that you refuse to give him any satisfactory reason for smashing your way yet again onto the sovereign territory of our state."

Robert looked up at him. It really did remind him of being at the dentist; even as a child he'd hated going.

"I did tell him."

"Oh ..." The officer looked surprised. "Perhaps you would repeat what you said."

"I said I'd come to speak personally with Ferdinand Brand."

"And why exactly should Herr Brand wish to speak with you."

"I can't tell you that."

The officer smiled a grim smile.

"And I suppose you think that will suffice, Mr Stanton. You think I will simply go and telephone the Head of the Security Service of the German Democratic Republic and tell him that a double-murderer wishes to pop in and have a little chat with him."

Robert flinched.

"What did you say?"

"You heard perfectly well what I said."

"A double-murderer?"

"Surely you don't deny it."

"Of course I bloody well deny it. I've never murdered anyone in my life."

"We know everything about you, Mr Stanton, so there's no point in playing games with me. Fact one, you blew up the frontier defences near a small village called Lindawerra several weeks ago in an attempt to secure the illegal removal from East German territory of a known spy. Fact two, when you were challenged by the border authorities you shot and killed a guard before you were able to escape. Fact three, when you were arrested in the West you were handed back under the terms of our agreement with the West German government. Fact four, while you were under arrest, you overpowered and brutally killed a guard who was accompanying you and managed to escape over the border to the West."

The man turned away, satisfied with his summary.

"But ..."

"Surely you don't deny these simple facts, Mr Stanton," the officer yelled. "They are all written down on this report. We know perfectly well that you are a British agent and what your game is. All we want to know is what you're doing here now."

Robert waited quietly for the man's anger to subside.

"I've told you what I can," he said quietly.

The man looked at him again, his eyes now showing a deadly tranquility.

"When I was a young man in the 'fifties," he said slowly, "we knew how to deal with the likes of you in a fitting manner. Now all we can use is this." He jerked his finger disparagingly at the equipment beside the chair to which Robert was strapped.

The second officer was fiddling with some electrodes.

"What is it?" Robert asked. Somehow the officers words had failed to reassure him.

The officer looked at him with contempt.

"A lie detector, Mr Stanton. We'll just see how you fare up to examination with a lie-detector."

Robert looked at the other officer, who had finished preparing the electrodes and was now carefully adjusting the settings on the machine itself. He only had seconds left in which to think. He braced himself for a final attempt.

"Just think before you do it, you stupid idiot," he said.

For a fraction of a second, the man hesitated. It gave Robert his chance.

"My name is not really Robert Creighton Stanton," he said. "It is Heinrich Obermann and I work for exactly the same Security Service as you do, only my rank is somewhat higher than your own. And I am under instructions to report in person to Ferdinand Brand. If you will only telephone his office all this will be confirmed."

It was clear that for a few seconds doubts had entered the officer's mind, but now he seemed to make a determined attempt to push them firmly to one side.

"A clever trick to delay the inevitable, Mr Stanton, but nevertheless a pack of lies. If you really worked for Herr Brand you would not have appeared at this border in such a dramatic fashion with no papers. You would have had papers, even if they had been false papers." He turned to the other officer. "Attach the electrodes so that we can start," he barked.

The more junior officer, who had quietly backed away during the earlier exchange, started to approach the chair again.

"You've said it yourself, you bloody idiot," Robert shouted as the officer began to attach some small electrodes to his chest. "If I was really a British agent, would I have come crashing across the border like that without any papers! I came across the border without papers because the bastards were on to me. I didn't have time to get my papers."

Again the hesitation. The officer's defences were palpably beginning to crumble.

"And one more thing before you turn on that damned machine, officer. If you think that you can check out what I'm saying with the lie detector, just remember that the information I possess is for the ears of the Head of the Security Service only. If you inadvertently find out too much, you know perfectly well what will happen."

Suddenly the struggle was over. The senior officer touched his colleague's arm to indicate he should stop what he was doing and fixed Robert with an icy glare.

"Very well," he said through clenched teeth, "I will go and telephone Herr Brand's office and see what they say. But if it turns out you are lying to me I can personally promise that you will spend the rest of your days wishing you had never been born!"

And with that he swept angrily out of the room.

It seemed that he was gone for an eternity but it was probably no more than twenty minutes. When he returned his previously stern face was sallow and drawn. As he approached the chair he stood rigidly to attention and saluted.

"Please accept my apologies, sir," he barked, his military bearing struggling to overcome the fear he clearly felt.

Robert eyed the little man with a sudden pity. It was exactly the same pathetic hierarchical response he had encountered so often before; the greater the fear of the one above, the greater the unpleasantness to the one below.

"I will feel more like accepting your apologies, Colonel, if you would be so kind as to disconnect me from this ridiculous machine."

The officer turned angrily to his subordinate, who was standing to attention in the corner of the room and trying to pretend that he didn't exist.

"Well, then, what are you waiting for, disconnect the machine."

Robert smiled reassuringly at the junior officer as he approached.

"Don't worry, officer," he said to the man as he carefully started disconnecting the electrodes from his chest. "I do appreciate that you were only following the direct orders of your immediate superior." He looked straight at the older man and enjoyed watching him squirm. He was still standing rigidly to attention.

"And now, my dear Colonel, I would be pleased if you could organise for the return of my clothes. I would not wish to report to Herr Brand wearing nothing but my underpants!"

* * * * * *

The secretary lifted his head from the computer terminal at which he was working and peered over his spectacles at Robert.

"Herr Obermann?" he enquired.

"Yes," Robert replied.

"Herr Brand is expecting you. Would you just wait for one minute, please."

He picked up the phone and spoke briefly into it. Then he turned to Robert again.

"Herr Brand will see you now," he said politely, indicating with his hand a large door on the opposite side of the room.

Robert walked towards the door and pushed it firmly open.

The room he entered had been designed to impress, and seemed more suited to a stately home than a functional office block. The wood-panelled walls were draped with delicately-woven tapestries and the vast expanse of the deep burgundy carpet was dotted with ornate pieces of eighteenth-century furniture. The room itself was rectangular in shape, and at its far end was a large mahogony desk behind which sat an elderly man.

The man rose slowly to his feet as Robert entered the room. There was an intensity about his eyes, but when he spoke his words bore no relationship to his expression.

"Herr Obermann! Welcome back!" he said, his tone majesterial. "You have done your work very well."

Robert looked at him and knew better than to speak the truth. It seemed that even here, even at the very pinnacle of power in this most totalitarian of totalitarian states, fear and suspicion festered in every corner.

"For me too it is a pleasure to be back amongst friends, Herr Brand," he said.

The old man moved to a small cocktail cabinet by the wall and pulled out two crystal tumblers.

"May I offer you some Scotch? I seem to remember that it is your preferred drink."

Robert accepted the drink and the remark in silence.

"To better times!" the old man continued, raising his glass to his lips, and as he did so his hitherto stern face seemed gradually to mellow. But as soon as the drink was gone he walked swiftly to his desk and spoke briefly into the intercom before turning back.

"Herr Obermann, I have a car waiting for us downstairs. We shall go to my home to speak further."

Gulping down his drink, Robert followed as the old man led the way through endless corridors to a large black Mercedes that was waiting for them in the yard outside. A smartly-dressed chauffeur in military uniform saluted crisply and opened the doors.

They drove in silence through the drab streets of East Berlin for what seemed like many miles. People turned to stare as they passed, sometimes putting down heavy bags of shopping on the pavement to pause and take a better look. As they approached the suburbs Robert noticed that the character of the houses was beginning to change: no longer were the streets lined with the crumbling, bullet-scarred tenement buildings of the city centre; here the houses were set apart, each surrounded by its own small plot of land.

A road barrier blocked the way ahead, but as they approached it rose silently to let them pass and they entered a broad tree-lined avenue. Now the houses were even more imposing, each set far back from the street and surrounded by extensive grounds and high metal security fences. Before long the car swept through the open gate of a particularly large mansion and pulled to a halt outside a high front door. Behind them, Robert caught sight of the gate through which they had just passed as it swung silently closed.

The chauffeur held open the doors while they both got out of the car.

"Kurt," Herr Brand said to him, "you can take the car back to town now. I won't be needing it any more today. And when you get back, tell my secretary that I am not to be disturbed other than in a dire emergency."

The driver nodded silently and was gone.

Robert looked at the old man standing by his side as he watched the car disappear from view. He seemed different now to when they had first met, as if his spirit had finally been crushed after a long, hard struggle.

"How did you know?" the old man said at last, avoiding Robert's gaze.

"I worked it out," Robert said quietly. "It took me a while, but eventually I managed to piece it together."

The old man turned and looked at him.

"You are truly your father's son, Heinrich, and I am proud of you for that."

He turned away and walked slowly up the steps into the silent house. Robert followed a few yards behind.

The interior of the house was gloomy and oppressive, the curtains drawn as if to keep out the freshness of the daylight beyond. The old man led him to a large book-lined study and lowered himself stiffly into a deep leather armchair, indicating another for Robert.

"We can talk here," he said. "I don't trust the Ministry building:

there is always a danger that someone might be listening. But here the walls have no ears."

Robert had been expecting to find his father as a man at the height of his powers, and so indeed it had seemed when they had first met in his office. But now he looked frail and drawn, as if he had lost the will to live.

"How long have you known of my existence?" his father asked.

"It first occurred to me several weeks ago. Then I had to fill in the details."

"And have you done so?"

"I think I know the salient points."

"And what are you going to do now?"

"I haven't decided yet. I wanted to talk to you first."

His father seemed to sink deeper into his chair.

"Even your mother didn't know I was still alive."

Robert rose from his chair and walked over to the heavy damask curtains.

"Do you mind if I open them? It's rather dark in here."

His father nodded his assent and Robert pulled the curtains back. Then he turned to his father with a strained look.

"I can't understand how you could have done it. I can't understand how my own father could have been involved in such things."

His father sighed deeply.

"It was all a very long time ago," he said, his voice so quiet that it was barely audible, "and it was a different world, a world you will never know."

Robert turned away and looked through the window at the immaculate garden beyond. He didn't really have the stomach for a long recitation of excuses for the inexcusable.

"You must think me a very evil man, Heinrich," his father continued, "but I will tell you what took place and then you must make up your own mind about it. What has happened has happened, and nothing you or I can do now will undo the past."

Robert remained silent, his gaze still resolutely fixed on the garden outside. Having come this far, he had no choice but to hear his father out.

"I will start at the very beginning. It was just before the war and I was a young and ambitious man. I wanted to get on, I wanted to make progress, to influence things in my country. I suppose you could even say that I was an idealist."

He paused, and Robert remembered that he had probably not spoken of his past, his true past, for nearly forty years.

"But the Germany in which I lived was a fascist state, a state dominated by the overpowering attraction of one man, of Adolf Hitler. There was only one way in which it was possible for a young man like myself to develop any kind of career and influence his country's destiny. So I accepted the inevitable and joined the National Socialists.

"Shortly before the war I had a chance encounter with Hitler at a garden party; I had been invited through the influence of a friend of mine who was the son of one of the leading Nazis and Hitler came up and started chatting with me. He was interested in my opinions on the political situation in Russia, a topic on which I happened to be particularly well informed, and seemed greatly impressed by my analysis of the situation. At the end of our encounter he asked if I would like to go to East Prussia in order to undertake some important work for the Party.

"I accepted immediately, of course. In those days the offer of a paid party post from the Führer himself was like a dream come true. But then, before he wandered off to talk to someone else, Hitler turned and asked if I was married. When I explained that I was still a bachelor, a frown passed across his face and he muttered that it was unhealthy for a strong young German like me to remain single. He suggested that I quickly find a wife who could bear me some children.

"It was not a remark to be ignored, or at least so I thought. That very evening I asked your mother to marry me. I had known her sister Katherina for some years and knew that Frieda had long been infatuated with me. So when I asked for her hand it came as no surprise to me that she accepted."

Robert's mind drifted back to the day of Katherina's funeral and suddenly he realised that this was not the first occasion on which he had seen his father's face.

"It was you, wasn't it? You were the man sitting next to me that day, the man who pointed out to me where my mother was sitting."

His father nodded quietly but made no comment.

"Frieda came with me to East Prussia and life went smoothly for a while. I was working in a special Nazi policy unit on Eastern Europe, a unit charged with keeping abreast of contemporary political developments in the Soviet Union. It was interesting work, and by the standards of the day well paid: I met Hitler on several more occasions and his personal patronage remained a powerful factor behind my rise within the ranks of the Party machine.

"Everything started going wrong in the summer of forty-three. By that time, we were not only fighting the Russians but also losing the fight, with the humiliation of Stalingrad still fresh in our minds.

And with the Americans also in the war, everyone who had a brain on their head knew that it was only a matter of time before Hitler's 'Thousand Year Reich' would be consigned to the dustbin of history. Yet if you wished to avoid incarceration by the Gestapo you had at all times to pretend to hold precisely the opposite opinion.

"But as I and many other Germans were becoming all too well aware, the most terrifying events in 1943 were not taking place on the Russian front, but behind the lines in occupied Poland. Knowledge of those events infinitely magnified the overwhelming atmosphere of fear and revulsion that was slowly descending on Germany in those closing months of the war."

Robert had been standing quietly by the window all this time, fingering a small book that lay on a finely-engraved table beneath. Suddenly, without warning, he raised the book and brought it slamming down onto the table.

"I can see all that!" he exclaimed angrily, turning to face his father for the first time since he had started speaking. "I can see and understand why you tagged along with the Nazis for all those years. And if I'm really honest with myself I can see that I might well have done the same. But that doesn't excuse what you did later, nothing can excuse you for that and it scares all hell out of me that I come from your blood."

His anger suddenly subsided and was replaced by a strange feeling of emptiness.

"Why did you do it?" he asked quietly.

His father looked at him for a long time without replying. And when he finally spoke, his voice was scarcely more than a whisper.

"I did it for you, Heinrich."

At first Robert thought he must have misheard his father's words.

"For me?"

His father remained crumpled in his armchair, and now Robert saw that his hands were shaking with an emotion that was too intense for tears to show.

"It was known that I was one of Hitler's blue-eyed boys in the policy unit and I'd already trodden on a few influential toes amongst Himmler's cronies. I thought I was safe because of Hitler's personal patronage, but then word reached me from a friend that the S.S. had begun to take an interest in my wife's Aryan ancestry. When I spoke to Frieda about it I discovered to my horror that there was a closely-guarded rumour circulating in her family to the effect that her long dead maternal grandfather may have been of Jewish descent."

He paused for a while before continuing.

"Do you know, Heinrich, what would have happened if those rumours had been substantiated?"

Robert said nothing.

"Answer me, Heinrich," his father demanded.

Robert sank slowly down into an armchair. He didn't want to reply, but his father was leaving him no alternative.

"She and I would have been sent to the camps."

His father nodded.

"There was still a chance I could prevent it happening, however. It wasn't always easy to prove these things. Many of the Jews in Germany had been fully integrated into the wider society in which they lived for many years. In a case like Frieda's it was more a matter of slur and innuendo; but I knew full well that such rumours could easily escalate into a one-way trip to an extermination camp.

"Yet despite their obvious wish to do so, the S.S. were frightened to move against me and my family because I had Hitler's personal support. They had sometimes tried that kind of thing before with people they didn't like and it had backfired badly on the individuals responsible when the Führer found out. So they needed some sort of proof, some evidence that I was soft on the Jews, something they could take to Hitler to support their argument that I was intimately linked with Judaism.

"One day when I was sitting in my office I received a visit from the senior S.S. medical officer. He started off by pointedly asking me about the health of my new-born son. Then he told me that there was a secret project that had been authorised in the very highest circles – the usual code for referring to Hitler – and that I had been selected as the right person to lead the team.

"He explained that the Reich was to start preparatory work for the reconstruction of Eastern Europe after the war. Since the Germans required more living space, it was self-evident that the Slavs would have to be correspondingly reduced in number in order to prevent undue pressure on resources. The doctor explained that the approach being applied to the Jewish problem was not considered appropriate for the much larger Slavic population on the grounds that it would be likely to lead to serious public order problems. A better solution had to be found. So a team of S.S. scientists were to work on developing a chemical product that could be selectively and secretly introduced into the public water-supply; the product would have the effect of preventing the population conceiving but carry no other immediately visible side-effects.

"At the end of the interview, he asked me whether I would be interested in accepting the post. I could have refused, but I knew full well that Hitler would have taken a very dim view of such a course of action. Yet without Hitler's personal support, I knew that my family's chances of escaping the gas chambers were slight indeed. But even knowing that, I thought long and hard about whether or not to accept the offer: I knew in my heart that possibly, just possibly, my family's lives were not worth saving in that way.

"But the more I thought about it, the more I realised that there was absolutely no logical reason why I should refuse. The experiments were to be undertaken on young Jews of child-rearing age brought from the extermination camps. If they had not come to my research station they would simply have been killed. For the men and women who were sent to me, I was able not only to prolong their lives, but also to make their living conditions much better than they were in the camps, since I was able to insist on perfectly good scientific grounds that they live as normal a lifestyle as possible under the prevailing circumstances, with adequate nutrition, shelter and exercise.

He paused and buried his head into his hands. Robert stared at him.

"But what if you'd succeeded? What if the products you'd developed had really been used on the Slavs?"

Suddenly, without warning, his father looked up. The deep anger on his face was plain to see.

"If you are really my son you should try not to be so stupid, Heinrich! I would never have agreed to participate in such a programme if I had not been one thousand percent certain in my own mind that we had lost the war. You look at life from the blinkered perspective of one who has lived through four decades of peace in Europe – do you not realise that at other times and in other places the whole framework within which we must operate is totally different?"

His anger subsided as quickly as it had arisen; he slouched back into the depths of his chair and closed his eyes.

Robert looked at the old man's crumpled form and wondered if he would have acted differently. It seemed that nothing was ever black or white; everything always turned out to be a nondescript shade of grey.

"I have not come here to stand in judgement on you," he said. "I have no such right. All I want to know is the truth; the truth is more important to me than anything else."

His father's eyes opened and he looked wistfully at his son.

"I remember when you were a tiny child so very well," he said softly. "You were the only thing in my life that has ever brought me real happiness. My hopes, my dreams, my world – everything I held dear was collapsing at the end of the war, but when I came home in the evening and held you in my arms the look on your face and the sound of your voice would always give me the strength to know that one day a better world would arise again from the ruins."

For a while he remained still. But then his face cleared and he continued.

"In fact the end came sooner than even I had expected. After Stalingrad the Axis armies in the East rapidly started to disintegrate. I knew the time had come to act. The research station in East Prussia where we lived was about to be overrun by Russian troops: if the Russians had captured me and discovered the kind of work I was directing, I would most certainly have been shot. And it didn't take a great deal of imagination to suppose that they would do exactly the same to my immediate family out of sheer revenge. Frieda was pregnant again but I told her to pack some things and travel west; I said that she should try and reach the Americans or the British and that I would find her later, after the war had finished. But when I kissed you good-bye that day, I knew – or at least I thought I knew – that it would be the last time that I would ever see you.

"As soon as she had left I set my plan in motion. Using my extensive contacts in the upper ranks of the German armed forces, I managed to obtain some important strategic information that would be of use to the Russians in their advance. Then I threw away my uniform and contrived to surrender to a Russian infantry unit, pretending to be an ardent underground member of the German Communist Party, and handed over the information I had obtained. Unusually for a German in those days, I spoke pretty fluent Russian as well as having a good knowledge of the way in which the Stalinist system operated, and my plan worked exactly as I had envisaged. By that stage in the war Stalin knew perfectly well that he wished to annex Germany to the Soviet system and he also knew that some politically reliable Germans would be required to administer the puppet régime he planned to build on German territory. Within weeks of my capture the Soviet army command sent me to Russia for a period of intensive political indoctrination.

"It was always a huge gamble, of course. If they had undertaken any serious checks on my assumed identity they would have quickly discovered that I was not who I said I was. And if they had systematically checked the photographs of untraced war criminals as these became available after the war they would have noticed that my face bore a remarkable similarity to one of the particularly notorious ones. But I had been right in my hunch that they never really would check, that they didn't actually care which Germans served their puppet state, provided that they displayed a blind obedience to Stalin's purposes.

"After the end of the war I became one of a large number of political re-education officers working in the Russian sector, administering a wide range of activities that were too menial for the Russians to perform. But after a few years I came to the attention of the new Russian-controlled German security service that operated in the Eastern sector and was recruited to its ranks. As you can see, I have worked for it to this day."

He rose slowly to his feet and seemed much revived by his reminiscences. It was almost as if the telling of the tale had lifted a heavy burden from his shoulders, a burden that he had carried alone for far too long. He walked over to a small glass table by the side of the room and poured out two more glasses of Scotch before walking over to join Robert by the window.

"You have come for Ingrid, have you not?" he asked, handing Robert one of the glasses.

Robert took the glass and lifted it thoughtfully to his lips.

"I have come for Ingrid and I have come for your granddaughter. We have called her Margit."

His father nodded.

"Margit. That is a very good name. I had a great-aunt once called Margit."

Robert waited. Despite his age, it was clear that his father was thinking fast.

"I never meant to hurt you as I have," he said finally, "so perhaps before we talk about Ingrid and your little girl you will let me explain some more things to you that you may not know."

Robert nodded. If his father valued his own future within the East German state, he would have no choice but to hand over Ingrid and Margit in the end. The evidence about his past that had been left behind in West Berlin would see to that.

"However much I wanted to, I knew I couldn't see my family again after the war. If I had revealed my identity I would have been tried as a leading war criminal and probably hanged. And even if I had only been sentenced to a long term of imprisonment my family would have been blighted by my wartime activities. But just because I couldn't let my family know of my continued existence didn't mean

I didn't care about their fate. Quite the contrary. I resolved that I would do everything within my power to assist them during the course of their lives."

As his father said this Robert tensed and almost interrupted, but then he thought better of it and waited for the old man to continue.

"My wife and daughter were easy enough to help. By the mid-1950s I had already risen sufficiently high in the Service to pull a few strings on their behalf. Early on I got them a house, then I ensured that Ingrid received an excellent education – although it was she herself who excelled at the work – and finally I secured for my daughter a post at one of the Warsaw Pact's leading scientific research stations."

He turned to Robert.

"But you were more difficult. For a long time, I simply couldn't trace you. It was as if you had simply vanished. For many years I thought you must have died in the ruins of Berlin with Katherina's children, as I suspect Frieda believed until you found her. But then, in about 1952, I was charged with compiling a comprehensive list of all known infringements by the Western powers of the detailed rules governing the administration of the eastern sector of Berlin. The purpose of the exercise was to compile material which could be useful for propaganda purposes, but amongst the huge mountain of obscure reports that passed across my desk there was one in particular that caught my eye; it was written in Russian and described how a young British army officer had for no apparent reason abducted a two-year-old child from an orphanage in the eastern sector. I normally wouldn't have looked at it twice, but clipped to the report was a photograph of all the children at the orphanage with one particular face ringed in ink: the face was yours!

"I didn't immediately know what to do with the information, but eventually I persuaded my superiors that if we could trace the child who had been abducted then we might one day be able to make some political capital out of it against the British. That was how I managed to track you down, despite your extraordinary change of identity."

"You mean you've known about me all along? Since 1952?"

His father didn't reply. He walked slowly over to a tall wall unit behind his desk and pulled opened a small drawer from which he extracted a leather-bound photograph album.

"Come and see for yourself," he said quietly.

Robert could feel himself shaking as he walked over to where his father was standing. He had already guessed that his father had learnt of his true identity, but had supposed that he had only discovered

289

it since his arrival in East Berlin four years before.

The old man placed the photo-album open on the table and Robert stared down at two pictures of himself as a child. In one he was only about nine years old, swinging happily backwards and forwards on an old swing in his garden at home. In the other he was a little older, perhaps eleven or so, leaning against a fence just near his old school. He turned the pages and saw other childhood shots of himself, then yet others of his wedding, then some of his own two boys Justin and Timothy as babies. And as he turned the pages in the book he already knew with sickening certainty how his father had been able to keep track of his life so closely.

"Uncle George..." he mouthed silently, and all of a sudden he saw in his mind's eye the distant look on Sir George's face in the taxi as they had driven together from the prison to George's flat for lunch. He saw his face and he heard his words – 'it's hard to be not what you seem.' All the photographs in the album had been taken by Sir George.

"He's always been one of my best people," his father said. "I'll be very sorry to have to lose him."

Robert could feel the room swimming beneath his feet. Now even his childhood in England was being ripped away from him by this man who was the flesh from which he came. He sank heavily into the chair by the desk and looked in horror through the photos in the book.

"It's sick," he said, "it's utterly sick."

His father said nothing for long time. When he spoke, it was in a whisper.

"Is it really sick to love your child?"

There was another silence. Then it was Robert who spoke.

"And all that business about going into Parliament, was that your plan too?"

"Yes. George was getting too old and I thought it would be what you'd want. I'm sorry it didn't work out."

Robert looked up at him, a cynical look in his eye.

"How the hell did you get George to do it? I'd have sworn he was far too incorruptable to succumb to either blackmail or bribery?"

A look of immense sadness came across his father's face.

"There is no need to either blackmail or bribe the likes of George Burberry, Heinrich: he is a far more committed communist than I'll ever be."

"Is he?" Robert said in astonishment.

"Ever since he was at Cambridge before the war. Always was,

and no doubt always will be. Despite everything, you British always seem to insist on thinking that communists go around wearing grubby raincoats and clutching copies of the 'Morning Star'."

Robert looked back glumly at the photographs. It still seemed hard to accept.

"And what would you have done if I had got into Parliament and risen to a position of power? Would you have blackmailed me then?"

His father picked up Robert's glass and moved over to the drinks cabinet.

"I can't entirely make my mind up about you, Heinrich," he said drily. "One minute I think you're incredibly clever, and the next minute you say something that makes me think you're incredibly stupid."

He quietly handed Robert another Scotch and returned to his armchair. Robert gulped the drink down at one go.

"I'm sorry," he said eventually, "you didn't deserve that remark. Maybe the strain of the last few weeks is beginning to tell."

Perhaps it was simply the drink, or perhaps it was something about his father's manner, but Robert had to admit that he was actually starting to rather like the man. His father's face softened.

"It is really me who should be apologising," he said, "for despite the best intentions I have brought nothing but misery to both my children over the last four years."

Robert looked into his empty glass and cast his mind back to Sir Percival Sotherby's imposing Whitehall office four years previously.

"And was it you who arranged for my posting to East Berlin?"

His father smiled.

"No," he said, "I'm afraid I didn't have what your American cousins call the 'capability'. But when I heard about your posting to East Berlin I was overjoyed: for many years I had been receiving regular photographs from George but here at last was my chance – probably my one and only chance – to see you again in the flesh, perhaps even to talk with you on some pretext or other. My great fear was that you would resign from the Service before you came."

"So you told George to decide to remain in Parliament for another term."

His father nodded.

"I'd miscalculated badly, though. I didn't realise that you'd found out you were not Robert Creighton Stanton, so you can imagine the shock I got when I saw you sitting next to me at Katherina's cremation. All that night I lay awake, trying to find a way of squaring

291

the circle, trying to find a way of preventing you and your East German family from destroying one another.

"At the end of the day I could not avoid the conclusion that I had to choose between you. Thanks largely to my help, Ingrid was in a job of incredibly high security classification; she was and still is under intense surveillance by not just my own security service but also those of the other Warsaw Pact countries whose secrets she shares. There was no way I could protect her and indirectly her mother if a clandestine link with a foreign diplomat was to be firmly established. For their sake I knew I had to get you out of East Germany, and get you out fast."

"So it was you who tipped off the British about Sonja!"

His father looked glum.

"You didn't seriously think they worked it out for themselves, did you?" he muttered. "And for good measure I pushed in a bit of discrete disinformation about low level security leaks since your arrival at the Embassy."

"It certainly worked," Robert grunted, remembering all too clearly his two wasted years in a prison cell. "You certainly got me out of the way."

"The British screwed it all up by overreacting in a most uncharacteristic way," his father retorted angrily. "I could tell you of literally hundreds of precedents over the last forty years to suggest that you would have been immediately recalled from East Berlin and either posted to some obscure consular backwater or else quietly asked to resign without fuss. And since I knew you had decided to resign and enter Parliament anyway, I really didn't think it mattered all that much."

"What did you tell them I'd leaked?"

"Oh, nothing important – just a few indiscretions about what people thought and so on."

Robert remembered the long confession he had signed for M.I.5 in which he had admitted passing all manner of highly classified material to the Eastern Bloc. He was on the point of telling his father, but the old man seemed to have read his mind.

"Yes, you did go rather over the top with that yarn, didn't you," he grunted, "although I can see from your point of view what you were trying to achieve."

A thought occurred to Robert and he looked at his father with a frown.

"Since you were so keen to protect Ingrid, why did you order her arrest as soon as I'd gone?"

His father looked at him sharply.

"Did you think I was joking when I said it was dangerous, Heinrich? I didn't order Ingrid's arrest, I used my power to prevent her immediate liquidation."

Robert looked at him in astonishment.

"You obviously think I've got far more power than I do in fact have," his father continued. "It was the K.G.B. who got wind of Ingrid's liaison with you in Oberhof that weekend. The night she came to you at the hotel, someone high up in Moscow woke me up and told me the circumstances of your meeting. They suggested that I terminate Ingrid forthwith in view of the obvious security risk that she represented to the Warsaw Pact.

"It was an extremely dangerous position for me and for her. I had to retain my own credibility or Ingrid would have had no chance of surviving. But in order to do so I had to passify the K.G.B. That is why I ordered her arrest and full interrogation by my own people.

"But then you released her."

"It was a risky decision, but I couldn't bear the thought of incarcerating my own daughter for the rest of her days. To cover my action I used the argument with my colleagues that I was trying to expose an extensive spy ring operating in East Germany through the British Embassy in Berlin and that I needed her as bait. My long-term plan was to let her sweat it out for a while in the paper mill and then slowly rehabilitate her."

Robert walked over to the drinks cabinet and carefully poured himself another Scotch. Slowly, inexorably, everything that had happened was falling into place.

"But you hadn't reckoned on us falling in love."

His father held out his empty glass and Robert brought over the decanter and filled it.

"How the hell was I supposed to guess you'd fallen in love with your own sister. People aren't supposed to fall in love with their sisters, are they?"

"She's no more my sister than you are my father," Robert retorted angrily.

For a moment he could see a look of deep sadness, almost of despair, pass across the old man's face.

"You did me the goodness of not passing judgement on me earlier, Heinrich," he said, "so it seems only reasonable that I now reciprocate."

He paused for a moment before continuing.

"After your release from prison I found it increasingly difficult

293

to follow your movements. You started behaving like a professional spy yourself, hiding away in little nooks and crannies. I knew of course that you were trying to find your children ..."

"Oh my God!" exclaimed Robert. "That was you, too, wasn't it? It was you who forced Kate to let me have access to the boys."

"Don't sound so angry about it," his father snorted, "it was what you wanted, wasn't it? And it wasn't even particularly difficult: she had settled in a small Australian town and told everybody including her new husband a complete pack of lies about her past in England. Once my people had traced her, all they had to do was intimate to her that they would tell the local press about her true identity if she didn't co-operate."

"But you didn't think I'd come back for Ingrid?"

"I thought it unlikely," his father replied. "Conceivable, but unlikely. I didn't realise you'd come back for her until I heard that the West Germans had handed you back after that brave but idiotic attempt to break through our border fortifications a few weeks ago."

"And it was you who ordered my release the following morning, using as a pretext the possibility of seriously embarrassing the West German government."

A thin smile passed across his father's lips and for a fraction of a second Robert could see that it was only the fact that he was this man's son that tempered his habitual ruthlessness.

"Did you think so, Heinrich, did you really think so?"

"I wasn't sure. I couldn't quite see why it would be in the interests of the East Germans to alienate the faction within the West German government that thought it right to passively hand us back."

"Exactly. But I wanted you out, so I arranged for you to 'escape', killing another border guard on the way out. The man who released you was working directly for me, as was the border guard in the nearby watchtower. The man in the jeep is now officially dead and will assume a new identity. The official version is that you forced him to trick the border guard into releasing you and then shot him in cold blood when you became frightened that he was attempting to prevent your escape."

"And what if I had gone to the press? I might have done, you know."

"We would have publicly confirmed the West German account of events and demanded your instant return to face a double murder charge. Nobody would have believed your version, particularly in view of your previous spying conviction, but with the attendant publicity the West German government would not have dared to pass you back again. After a few days, the whole incident would almost certainly have been forgotton."

His father paused.

"You have clearly gone to an extraordinary amount of trouble to keep me away from your prisons," Robert said at last, "but why did you not arrange the release of Ingrid and Margit at the same time."

His father rose slowly from his chair and moved over to the window.

"You have listened to my story with great patience, Heinrich," he said. "And you are right; now it is time we spoke of Ingrid's fate."

He stood a long time by the window before he continued, staring out glumly through the glass.

"As you should already have divined, Ingrid's involvement with you has placed her in a position of great personal danger. As I have already explained, if it had not been for my immense personal influence within the security apparatus she would long ago have been liquidated, because I can assure you that had I not been her own father I would have instantly agreed to Moscow's request for her termination."

He rose to his feet and moved slowly to his desk.

"Can you read Russian, Heinrich?" he asked.

Robert looked surprised.

"A little," he replied.

"Then read this," his father said, handing him a small sheet of paper that he had removed from one of the drawers, "and tell me what you think I – we – should do. I received it yesterday."

Robert took the sheet of paper. It was a decoded transcript of a telegram, and was covered with various symbols that Robert took to indicate some kind of restricted security classification.

"To Ferdinand Brand. Attention immediate. Reports have arrived that Omega has made unsuccessful escape bid. Please confirm. If true, we strongly advise immediate liquidation of same. Please communicate proposed response. Fraternal Greetings. Comrade General Leon Axelrod."

Robert re-read the telegram several times.

"Have you replied?" he asked.

"Not yet," his father muttered. "As I'm sure you're aware, their advice is perfectly sensible in the circumstances. The material Ingrid developed is still the basis for much of the Warsaw Pact strategic defence programmes. She could still inflict great damage on our security, particularly if she reached the West and was fully debriefed by specialists in her field."

Robert sank into a chair and stared at the note in horror. Only hours before he had thought of his father as an adversary, as the man who possessed the power to release Ingrid and little Margit if only he could be blackmailed into so doing. Yet now he could see they were actually on the same side, both pitted against a larger danger that lay beyond.

"So now perhaps I think you see my dilemma," his father continued. "If I had engineered her release with you – or indeed if the West Germans had not handed her back to our custody as they did, Ingrid would by now be dead. A K.G.B. hit team would have tracked her down within days and killed her – probably with you and the baby if you'd been with her. In the West the Russians would have had absolutely no scruples about acting without my consent ..."

"But provided she's on East German territory," Robert continued, "the K.G.B. won't harm her out of deference to you."

His father nodded.

"Now I think you understand," he said. "There is a kind of code that operates between the security services of the Warsaw Pact countries, just as there is between the security services of N.A.T.O. members. I am ninety-nine percent sure that the K.G.B. will not kill Ingrid while she is on East German territory."

Robert was hardly listening to his father's words; if what his father had said was true there was nothing more he could do. It seemed that only by remaining within an East German prison could Ingrid have any chance of staying alive.

"Heinrich!"

Robert looked up at the old man blankly.

"Heinrich, are you listening?" he repeated in a stern voice.

Robert tried to shake himself together and nodded.

"There's more, Heinrich. I'm afraid there's more bad news."

"I don't know for sure," his father continued, "but I think I may be under investigation myself."

Robert sat bolt upright.

"You!" he exclaimed.

His father nodded and took the telegram from Robert's hand.

"I can't be sure," he murmured, fingering the little sheet of paper, "but I think this is a final test – just like the test arranged by Himmler's people forty years ago."

There was little outward sign of emotion on his father's face, but deep down Robert could sense the strength of the conflicting emotions with which he was struggling. His father caught his gaze.

"It's not me I'm frightened for, Heinrich," he said quietly. "Can't you tell that I'm tired of all this?" He waved at the house around him, the empty trappings of his external success. "I just want to get you out of the hole you've both dug yourselves into before I die."

As he spoke Robert could hear the tremendous fear in his father's voice and knew he had spoken the truth. He had chosen a path and lived a life and now he realised that it had all come to nothing. And now, from the catastrophic failure that was his own life, all he wanted to do before he died was to rescue the only people he had ever really loved from the wreckage – he wanted to rescue his own children.

Robert suddenly found that the man he was with was no longer a stranger to him. It was as if they had always been together, as if the world had never come and torn them apart. And for the first time since he had arrived, he let his hand touch his father's arm.

"What are we going to do?" he said. "There must be some way out."

His father looked at him and tried to smile. It would probably have been better if they had embraced, if they had released the bitter emotion that fate had thrust upon them, but try though they might, neither of them could find the strength to do so.

"Perhaps there is a way," his father said at last, his voice heavy and tired. "Perhaps it is the only way."

He moved to his desk and sat heavily down in his chair. Without speaking, he pulled a little memo pad out of his drawer and wrote for a few moments. Then he quietly handed the note to Robert.

"To Comrade General Leon Axelrod. Your report confirmed. Omega to be eliminated forthwith. Fraternal greetings. Ferdinand Brand."

Robert stared at him, knowing better than to enquire.

"I must arrange for her death," his father continued, "just as I arranged for my own half a century ago. Sometimes death is the only way to survive."

"But can you do it?"

"Yes," he said flatly. "Because there is someone I can trust completely."

"Are you sure?"

"Yes. The person is you."

Robert stared at him with a look of blank non-comprehension.

"How was it that you got to me today?" his father asked.

"Why... as one of your agents, I suppose."

"So who better to undertake a discreet liquidation?"

Robert's brain was spinning, trying feverishly to keep up with a man who had a lifetime's experience of deceit.

"But it won't wash. I mean, surely everyone knows it was I who tried to smuggle her out in the first place."

His father smiled grimly.

"But that's the whole point," he continued. "I will say that you were working for me all along. I will explain how I was convinced that there were extensive security leaks from our defence complexes involving not just Omega but also other even more senior people in the defence establishment. It was imperative that I identify the full extent of the leaks and the only way to do so was by finding out exactly who was running these damaging operations. It was for this reason that I had decided to use one of my most able sleepers in the British Diplomatic Service, a young man operating under the name of Robert Creighton Stanton, a man who had himself been cultivated from an early age by one of my best men in the West – the British Conservative M.P. George Burberry."

Robert watched him in amazement: as he spoke it seemed as if he actually believed the whole story.

"I arranged for Robert Stanton to make contact with Omega and try to gain her confidence by pretending to be a member of the Western Security Services. But although she was drawn to Stanton personally, Omega refused to reveal the information I wanted. Then the K.G.B. stumbled clumsily across my operation and suggested that I liquidate Omega, a policy which would of course have ended all chance of bringing the operation to a successful conclusion. I therefore refused to eliminate Omega as requested, but did not offer any further explanation on the basis of 'need-to-know.'

"But my plan was now under threat from another direction. Stanton had been activated in East Berlin by another of my own agents – a young girl operating under the name of Sonja – but the British had obtained evidence of their clandestine meetings and had decided to prosecute Stanton. In order to conceal his connection with Omega, Stanton cleverly admitted to passing British secrets to Sonja and was jailed for two years.

"After Stanton had been released from prison, I attempted to reactivate the Omega file, which seemed to have gone dead in the intervening months. Despite her release from prison and intensive surveillance, Omega's true contact had not reappeared on the scene – an ominous fact which suggested that she had been sacrificed by the Western security services in order to protect other more senior people in the defence sector. But Omega then wrote to Stanton, with whom she had clearly fallen in love, and asked for his help in securing her escape to the West. I decided that Stanton should play her along.

"Stanton therefore arranged a clandestine visit to East Germany to see Omega and try to win her full confidence, but still she resisted, insisting that Stanton arrange for her to leave the country. This Stanton then agreed to do in the hope that her successful removal to the West would finally convince her of his trustworthiness and loosen her tongue. As soon as he was sure Omega had no further information, Stanton would immediately terminate Omega in an arranged accident before any further security risk could arise from her presence in the West.

"A serious unforeseen problem then arose, however. During his visit, Stanton had seduced Omega and made her pregnant; even more seriously, she had become dangerously ill during the early stages of the pregnancy. Since her death would have ended all chance of a successful conclusion to the Omega operation, I ordered her immediate hospitalisation and shifted the escape operation forward until the following year. Thanks to expert medical support, Omega survived the pregnancy and everything then went according to plan until the West Germans handed Stanton and Omega back following their successful escape. I then arranged for Stanton's speedy release under the guise of a further escape, planning to use him again in the future to break Omega's silence.

"A critical point has now been reached in the operation. Stanton is under acute danger from the West German security services, since they fear he will cause political damage to the government by revealing their decision to hand back Omega and Omega's small baby to the communists. He has therefore abandoned his cover completely and made a dash for it to safety."

He stopped, and looked thoughtfully at Robert.

"Now do you see what I'm driving at?" he said.

Robert was standing by the window.

"No," he said with a frown, "not entirely."

"On my instructions you are going to make one final attempt to extract the information you require from Omega before killing her."

"But Omega doesn't have any information. She never did."

"That hardly matters, Heinrich, because this time you yourself are going to be killed before you can tell anyone what it is."

"Killed? But how?"

"That," his father explained, "will soon become clear."

* * * * * *

Despite the shelter provided by the surrounding pine forest, a biting wind lashed across the deserted grass strip that served as a makeshift runway. A small light aircraft was completing its final descent, and as it touched down Robert and his father exchanged a final glance before leaving the relative warmth of the large black limousine, watching silently as the plane slowed gradually to a crawl and taxied over towards them. Moments later the engine fell silent and the single occupant clambered cautiously out of the cramped cockpit. The new arrival, a puffy-looking man of advanced years, strode forward enthusiastically to greet his friend.

"Leon!" Robert's father exclaimed in greeting as the two older men embraced each other with what gave every appearance of being a genuine show of emotion.

"Ferdinand! It has been far too long since we have spoken in the flesh."

"Alas, yes," Robert's father replied, "it must be nearly two years. Life is short, and we are both far too busy."

The two men embraced again and then, almost simultaneously, turned to Robert.

"Leon," Brand began enthusiastically, as if he were proudly showing off a prized possession, "may I present Comrade Heinrich Obermann. Comrade Obermann, this is Comrade General Leon Axelrod of the K.G.B."

Robert stepped forward and shook the General's outstretched hand, trying hard to avoid the thought that it was the very hand that had on at least two occasions attempted to order Ingrid's assassination.

"Comrade Obermann," the General began, "I extend the fraternal greetings of the Soviet people to one who has struggled so hard for our cause. Comrade Brand has already explained to me the dangerous and onerous duties you have so diligently and selflessly performed to protect our common security."

"It was my duty," Robert relied crisply.

Robert's father took the General by the arm and steered him towards the waiting car. The two old men climbed into the rear seats while Robert took his place in the front and drove away from the silent airstrip, leaving the lone plane rocking from side to side in the wind.

"I hope you enjoyed your flight from Berlin, Leon? I thought you would appreciate the opportunity to do a little solo flying in German airspace again."

"Except for the wind, Ferdinand," he laughed. "It is a while since I have done much flying. But at least the planes are better now than they were in the war."

For a long time the two old men reminisced about their early experiences in the Soviet Union. It seemed that they had spent several years together in their younger lives learning the basic survival techniques required to become competent field agents, and it was only after some considerable length of time that their exchange of old memories momentarily lapsed.

"It was good of you to ask me down to witness the closing stages of your operation, Ferdinand," the General remarked, his face growing serious, "but I have to confess I will be most relieved when Omega is no longer with us."

Robert's father smiled.

"I am only sorry that I did not feel it correct to tell you what I was up to earlier," he said.

The General laughed.

"It is true that there were many people in Moscow who were puzzled by your actions. But I repeatedly assured them that Comrade Ferdinand Brand was not a man to make an error of judgement in these matters." He paused for a moment and then continued, his voice quieter than before. "It was nevertheless a good thing that you asked me here today."

There was no trace of unfriendliness in the General's words, but Robert sensed that his father's intuition that he himself had fallen under suspicion by the K.G.B. had been well-grounded. It was almost as if the General felt some sense of personal relief that by agreeing to liquidate Omega, Robert's father had passed the test that had been set for him by his enemies in Moscow.

"Do you think you will succeed?" the General asked bluntly, turning to Robert.

"I don't know," Robert replied, staring blankly at the road ahead as it twisted through the deserted pine forest. "Omega is not easy to handle. She is very frightened, like an animal in a trap. She may simply freeze."

The General laughed a cynical laugh that instantly revealed the impenetrable barrier of ice that lay behind the friendly exterior.

"A frightened animal, you say," he grunted, "but I have heard it said that animals are renowned for protecting their offspring even when it must be at the cost of their own lives."

In the rear view mirror, Robert could see his father tug at the General's sleeve.

"Leon," Brand muttered under his breath, "you should remember that the child in question is also the daughter of Comrade Obermann."

The General fell silent for a moment.

"I must apologise, Comrade," he murmured. "It was a foolish and tactless thing for me to say."

For a while they drove on in silence down the empty road, until at last they arrived at a clearing in which was set a large single-storey concrete building surrounded by a high security fence. The guard at the gate saluted crisply as they entered.

"Is Omega here?" the General asked.

Robert's father nodded.

"We use this centre for special operations of this kind. In view of the media interest in the West, I felt it particularly important to maintain the highest security. That is why we moved her here."

The General smiled broadly.

"You have always displayed the characteristic efficiency of your country to the highest degree," he commented approvingly.

Robert pulled the car to a halt outside the low single-storey building as several soldiers ran forward to hold open the doors.

A senior officer hung back until they had all emerged from the car and then came forward.

"Is everything ready?" Brand asked.

"Yes, Comrade Brand, everything is arranged as you ordered. The baby arrived while you were at the airstrip."

They stood silently for a moment, listening to the wind whistling through the trees surrounding the clearing. But then, from somewhere deep inside the building, Robert gradually became aware that he could hear another sound, a sound totally alien to a military camp – the sound of a small baby's plaintive cry.

They entered the building in silence and the officer who had greeted them showed them down a long corridor to what appeared to be a small control room. Two walls were completely covered with modern communications equipment of various descriptions, and three chairs had been carefully positioned around a small screen mounted on a low desk. As they sat down the officer quietly flicked a switch on a control panel to activate the screen before leaving the room.

For a long time the three men watched the image that appeared in silence. Ingrid was sitting on a small metal-framed bed in what seemed to be a windowless whitewashed cell, her head bowed low and her body rocking slowly back and forth. Closing his eyes for a second to block out the painful image, Robert braced himself for the extraordinary performance that lay ahead.

"Does she know the baby is here?" he asked eventually, turning to face his father.

"No," the old man replied curtly. "That is for you to tell her when you are ready."

"And I have the personal assurance of you both that irrespective of the outcome of the interview no lasting harm will come to the child. Absolutely no lasting harm."

His father nodded silently.

"It is quite unnecessary to injure the child permanently and it will not be done," the General said grimly, looking down at the floor.

Robert rose silently from his chair and, with one further look at the picture on the screen, quietly left the room.

* * * * * *

The cell door swung open and his sister raised her head. For a moment hope flashed across her face, but then the hope seemed to fade as fast as it had arisen and her head sank forward again onto her hands. Robert remained motionless as the guard closed the door, leaving them alone together in the tiny room. In his pocket he could feel the outline of the small revolver with which he had been provided.

He took a cautious step towards her.

"Are you all right?" he asked. There was no recognition, no reply.

"When did they bring you here?" Again no reply.

"Ingrid, we've got to talk. There isn't much time."

Ingrid looked up at him with a bitter smile and jerked her thumb at a video camera high up in one corner of the room.

"What's the point?" she said, but then a note of curiosity entered her voice. "Why have they sent you here, Robert?"

He approached her and sat down on the bed.

"They think you know something. They're convinced you know about some kind of high-level spying operation within the Warsaw Pact defence establishment."

Ingrid shrugged.

"I've already told them that I've never spied for anyone in my life. I've told them all that before and it's their problem if they don't believe me. But if they want me to sign another piece of paper you can tell them I'll do it."

Robert looked at her with exasperation.

"It's no good, Ingrid, they don't want any more stories. This time they want the truth."

Ingrid shrugged again. "Then I can't help them," she said flatly.

Robert braced himself.

"They've got Margit here."

It was as if she had been subjected to an electric shock. From being morose and resigned, her whole body became alert and tense.

"What did you say?"

"You heard what I said. And they intend to use her to get what they want."

"They're lying!" she said, but it was clear from the fear in her voice that she knew they were not.

"I don't know, maybe they are, but I'm to tell you that the only way you can prevent harm coming to our child is by telling them the truth about your work for Western Intelligence."

Ingrid shook her head violently.

"But I don't know anything," she pleaded. "I'll sign anything they like, but I can't tell them anything more because I've got nothing more to tell."

Robert grabbed her arm. His voice was shaking with emotion.

"It's no good, Ingrid, it's no bloody good. They know you were spying. I don't know how, but somehow they've worked it out. There's no point in pretending any more."

He looked frantically at his watch and turned to face the video camera.

"Give me some more time," he begged. "Please give me some more time to talk to her."

The video camera stared at them passively from the corner of the room, but suddenly the cell was filled with the amplified sound of a baby's cry.

"Margit!" Ingrid cried, rising from the bed.

"Jesus Christ!" Robert swore in English. He grabbed Ingrid by the shoulders and started violently shaking her. "Tell them! For Christ's sake, tell them!"

But before she could reply the nature of the sound that filled the room changed. No longer was it the whimpering cry of frightened baby, now it was the uncontrolled scream of a baby in pain.

Ingrid froze, her face white with terror.

"Stop it!" she yelled at the camera. "Stop it and I'll tell you everything you want!"

Without warning the crying ceased.

For a long time there was silence. Then Robert turned to face the camera.

"You can interrogate her now," he said, his voice devoid of all emotion. "She'll tell you everything you want to know."

For several minutes nothing happened, but then the door of the cell opened and the officer who had first met them appeared.

"Comrade Brand requests you both to follow me," he said crisply.

Without a word, the officer led them back to the room where the two old men were waiting. As Ingrid entered she stopped dead, staring at Brand.

"It's you," she said numbly, as if remembering his night-time visit to her prison cell.

"Yes," Brand began in a small voice as they listened to the sound of the officer's retreating footsteps in the corridor outside. "Last time I tried to discover the truth by releasing you. Now I am obliged to try less subtle methods."

"You bastards," Ingrid muttered, her voice barely audible. "You evil bastards."

Brand looked at her sharply.

"That attitude will get you precisely nowhere," he murmured. "You have agreed to tell us what you know and I would suggest that you start to do so straight away."

Ingrid stared down at her feet for a long time.

"And you'll leave the child alone?" she said. "I have your word on that."

Brand nodded silently.

"I was passing information, but it was always for the Americans, never for the British as your people always believed. I don't think the British knew anything about it."

General Axelrod, who had previously been slouching passively in his chair, suddenly sat bolt upright.

"The Americans!" he said. "And when precisely did they recruit you?"

"Shortly after I arrived at the research station."

"And who recruited you?"

"A businessman. An American businessman at the Leipzig Trade Fair. We were ... He became my friend and told me that the Americans were prepared to pay me a great deal of money for the information I could provide them with. He promised that the C.I.A. would help me start a new and better life in the West when my work for them was finished."

General Axelrod picked up a pen and started fingering it nervously.

"And this was your only contact, your only control?" he asked.

"No. He just made the initial contact. Over the years I was contacted by quite a few other people. At first the contacts were always foreign – American, I think. But then I was handed over to a local control, another scientist in a different branch. It was through him that I transmitted most of the technical information. When he was a little drunk once, he told me that he sometimes felt like a busy telephone switchboard, because so much technical information flowed through him to the West."

The General flicked an angry glance at Brand.

"So you were not the only filthy German spy at work in our research establishment," he snarled.

Ingrid stared at him with a look of scarcely concealed contempt.

"A German! It wasn't a German. The man I always dealt with was a Russian."

At this General Axelrod sprang to his feet and approached Ingrid with a menacing look.

"A Russian! Who?"

"He was a scientist, but I'd always thought he worked for the K.G.B. Many of the Russian scientists worked for the K.G.B."

Axelrod face was rapidly turning red.

"What use is it to talk to me about Russian scientists! There are hundreds of Russian scientists! Tell me who you are talking about this instant or I will personally bring your child in here and tear its limbs apart while you watch!"

The General glared at Ingrid with a look of profound loathing. Had his old friend Brand perhaps sensed that it was a Russian who lay at centre of this evil ring? Had he suspected that the Russian was somehow linked to the K.G.B? Was that the real reason why he had not informed Moscow years earlier about operation Omega? And had he – Comrade General Leon Axelrod – been summoned all the way from Moscow so that he could be publicly humiliated by the upstart security service of a tiny satellite state?

"Speak woman!" he yelled.

Robert knew the time had come to act.

"It's enough!" he said suddenly, pulling the revolver from his pocket and aiming it straight at Axelrod's chest.

"Drop it!" Robert shouted at Brand as he tried to pull something from his jacket pocket. The old man slowly removed a small gun and let it clatter noisily to the floor.

"You bastards must really think I'm made of stone to listen to all this crap. Get up against the wall with your hands up high and don't even let me hear you breathe."

Ingrid was staring at him in horror.

"Robert!" she mumbled, her voice confused and uncertain.

"Never mind what's going on, Ingrid. Just go over and pick up the gun on the floor for yourself. Then search them thoroughly for any others."

Ingrid fell silent and did as she was asked.

Robert approached his father and pushed the barrel of the revolver hard into the back of his neck.

"You really thought I'd do it, didn't you?" he snarled. "You really thought that I'd trick her into telling you everything you wanted to know and then use this revolver to put a bullet through her chest. Just like that!"

His father said nothing, but it was clear that his whole body was shaking with suppressed emotion.

"I know this room is secure," Robert continued in a calmer voice. "Nobody knows what's going on in here and that's the way it's going to stay. Got it!"

His father nodded.

"Now listen carefully, Brand. The first thing you're going to do if you want to stay alive is to press the buzzer on the intercom and order one of your men to bring the child here."

His father hesitated and then did as he was told. A few moments later there was a polite knock at the door.

Robert pushed the revolver into his pocket.

"Come in!" Brand barked, and the officer stepped briskly into the room, clumsily carrying Margit in his arms.

"Give the baby to the woman and then leave us," his father ordered.

Ingrid grasped the child and held her with one arm, but she didn't let her concentration waver for a moment.

"Right," Robert said slowly as soon as the officer had left, "now listen carefully. First we're going to walk to the car, and then we're going to drive to the airstrip. I will take up the rear and if either of you act in any way strangely you have my word that I will shoot you both dead."

"There is no escape for traitors," Robert's father muttered, at last finding the words to express himself.

"Perhaps," Robert replied. "But now pick up the telephone and order the car to be made ready."

* * * * * *

"Out!" Robert snapped as the limousine drew up at the deserted airstrip.

As soon as they were outside, he motioned to the two old men that they should walk towards the aircraft in which the General had arrived.

"Now we all get in the plane!"

The General's head twisted in horror.

"You're not planning to try and go up in that thing with all four of us on board, are you?"

Robert looked at him and looked at the tiny seats in the cockpit.

"Maybe you're right," he said. "It's too small. You're the fattest, General, you'll have to stay here." He turned to Ingrid. "Give me the baby and tie him up."

Ingrid looked around with a flustered expression for a moment.

"Take off your trousers and lie on the ground," she said to the General, handing Margit to Robert and taking the Swiss army knife that he had produced from his pocket.

With a look of immense relief, the General quickly removed his trousers and let Ingrid bind his hands and feet behind him with strips of material cut away from his trouser legs. When she had finished, the previously dignified spy bore more resemblance to a Sunday joint about to be placed into the oven.

Leaving Ingrid to stand guard over the two old men, Robert walked briskly back to the car, swiftly immobilising the engine and the radio transmitter.

"You may rest assured, Comrade General," he said as soon as he had returned, crouching low so that he could whisper into the man's ear, "that we will all assume new identities after we have completed our mutual de-briefing in Washington. Please do not bother to organise a search for us."

The General made a strange kind of snorting noise which was all he could manage through the gag which Ingrid had made with his belt.

Robert rose to his feet and walked over to his father, thrusting the revolver roughly at his throat.

"Get in the plane! You're flying!"

His father looked at him with a surly expression as the General watched from the ground.

"No!" he retorted.

"I said get in the plane! Do it now!"

"No! You can shoot me if you wish. But I will not betray the cause I have worked for all my life by aiding your escape."

They stood and stared grimly at one another for an instant. Then Robert took a step back and glanced at Ingrid.

"Give me the knife!" he ordered, handing her back the baby.

She did as she was asked. For a few moments Robert adjusted the blades, carefully selecting a small serrated carving knife. Then, ever so slowly, he pulled off one of the Russian's socks.

"You are a brave if heartless man, Brand, and so we will not start with you. We will start with your Soviet friend. What do you say, should we begin by sacrificing a toe – or perhaps even a whole foot – to the noble cause of the Revolution?"

His father squirmed. So did the Comrade General.

"We are both brave men," his father said. "The Comrade General will willingly lay down his life."

Robert flicked a glance at the General.

"Shall we ask him?" he said with a grim smile, removing the belt from his mouth. "Shall it be a finger, a toe, or perhaps even an ear?"

The General stared up in horror at Robert's father.

"For Christ's sake don't just stand there," he shouted. "Get in the plane if that's what they want."

Robert's father looked at him with a scathing look.

"We cannot allow this woman to escape. You know that as well as I."

"In the name of the Soviet motherland," he snarled, "I categorically order you to get into that plane and take off."

For a moment, Robert's father looked as if he were going to refuse. But then a thought seemed to occur to him and he climbed into the plane. As he did so, a look of infinite relief spread across the General's face.

Robert climbed up into the passenger seat and Ingrid clambered up beside him with the baby. As soon as they had slammed the door, Brand started the engine and the plane started to crawl slowly forward towards the end of the runway.

"My God!" exclaimed Robert as soon as they were out of Axelrod's earshot. "That was bad."

"A most impressive performance by us all," his father commented drily. "I know Axelrod well. He is an effective operator, but I do not think there will be any doubt in his mind that your escape is a genuine one."

The plane was now facing the runway.

"Hang on," the old man said, and the plane surged forward. Moments later, they had left the ground and were climbing up above the tops of the trees, leaving the still squirming figure of the General watching them from far below.

The plane stayed low, Brand allowing no more than several metres clearance above the trees. They flew for several minutes, until the plane was well out of earshot of the Russian, and then a small forest track appeared ahead of them, snaking its way through the densely packed pine trees.

"That's it," their father said sharply. "Now hold on!"

The plane dipped below the tops of the trees and they clung on as best they could as the old man brought it to a standstill on a straight section of the track just where it crossed a small clearing. At the edge of the clearing, carefully hidden under several large trees, they could just make out the large white Mercedes with West German numberplates that Robert had left there first thing that morning.

"Hurry up!" the old man ordered brusquely, taking the baby from Ingrid. "We haven't got much time."

Robert and Ingrid jumped free of the plane and rushed towards the waiting vehicle.

"Brace yourself, Ingrid," Robert warned, as he pulled open the rear door of the car to reveal the inert bodies of a man, a woman and a baby, the last remains of a family killed in an East Berlin road accident only the previous evening. Robert had collected the bodies in the night from the morgue under the written authority of the Security Police. They were already dressed in identical clothes to Robert, Ingrid and Margit.

Within minutes the corpses were slumped clumsily next to Brand in the cockpit of the tiny plane. The old man handed his grandchild to Ingrid and gazed silently for a few moments at his family standing on the track beneath him. And then, without saying a word, he turned back to the controls and the plane began to accelerate.

For a few moments Robert and Ingrid watched in silence as the small plane rose into the sky and resumed its journey west.

"Do you think he'll make it?" Ingrid asked at last.

Robert said nothing until the plane had disappeared from view.

"He told me he was going to climb steeply and then parachute out, saying that he had overpowered us and managed to clamber free, but somehow I didn't . . ."

His words were cut short by the thunderous roar of a mighty explosion in the distance. And then, above the tops of the pine trees at the edge of the clearing, they could just make out a thin trail of black smoke snaking its way slowly towards the sky.

GERMANY, JUNE 1995

The man who had been born as Heinrich Obermann, had lived for many years as Robert Creighton Stanton, and had for the last twelve years been known as Hans Peter Schmidt, finally reached the top of the spiral staircase and pushed open the rusty metal door. It had taken him quite a long time to find out who possessed the key to the building, but eventually he had tracked it down with the owner of the small but friendly Gasthaus round the corner, a delightful gentleman who also turned out to be the secretary of the local history society. It had been only with considerable difficulty that he been able to dissuade the man from giving him a full guided tour.

The small circular room in which he now found himself had been lovingly preserved for posterity. In the centre was a wooden table with several objects neatly arranged on it – an old East German telephone, several pairs of high resolution binoculars and a weighty book that appeared to be some kind of instruction manual. On every side of the room, instead of walls, large panes of glass made it apparent that he had reached the top of the observation tower, the vantage point from which the border guards would have maintained their constant vigil. Robert picked up one of the pairs of binoculars from the table and moved silently to the edge of the room.

A wry smile spread over his face as he looked down at the little village of Lindawerra where he had made his premature attempt to blast away the barriers of history so many years before. For although the control tower itself had been preserved for future generations, there was little other visible evidence to suggest that the Iron Curtain had once passed through this place.

Where the bombed-out remains of the pre-war bridge had once stood, a brand new bridge had been constructed, its sweeping modern arch forming a somewhat incongruous contrast with the quiet rural charm of the village. Between the riverbank and the first houses, where previously the twin fences of the border had passed, the village council had carefully constructed a small park, complete with mini-golf, a bandstand, and an oversized outdoor chess set of the kind so popular in Germany. Of the fences themselves there was no visible sign, and it was only when he turned his eye upward towards the forested hillside rising away into the distance that he could still make out the place where the border had once run; for although new trees

311

had been planted on what had once been the death strip, it would take many years before they had reached even roughly the same height as their companions to either side.

Robert – and inwardly he still thought of himself as Robert – pulled up a chair and sat down. Of late his back had started troubling him if he stood still for too long; a sign, he suspected, of early middle age turning gradually into late middle age. But despite his spinal problems he felt unable to feel too unhappy with his lot.

He looked again at the bridge and watched the water flowing through the central arch, swirling impatiently around the concrete pillars on either side. It must have been strange to be reincarnated as someone else at the age of two, but he had been too young to remember how it felt. Second time round, at the age of forty, he had been able to observe for himself, as if as an outsider, the pain and pleasure of a completely new start.

The pain was real enough. For Hans Peter Schmidt was allowed no contact with his previous life: no contact with Justin and Tim, no contact with his increasingly elderly English parents, no contact with old friends, not even any visits to the England he still loved so dearly. He had even trained himself to avoid the English language of his middle years, using it only in his private conversations with himself.

His thoughts turned to his father. For try as he might, he still didn't quite know how to reconstruct him in his mind's eye. On one level the man had been despicable; self-serving to the extent that he had been prepared to work for two régimes that could only be regarded as obscene. In his time, it was only reasonable to suppose that he had sent many people to their deaths and perhaps worse in the service of his chosen masters. Yet in the brief hours that Robert had spent with him, he had realised that there was another side to his father, a softness he had always repressed and that could so easily have made him a kinder and more decent man if he had only allowed it to shine through. In the closing days of his life, when they had been alone together, Robert had several times seen his father close to tears, as if he were struggling to contain the sense of overwhelming failure that was seeping through his ageing body. Perhaps his suicide had been his only way of resolving the impossible mental conflicts of his increasingly tortured mind.

Or perhaps he had simply calculated that his own death was necessary if he was to be sure of saving his children's lives. It was clear that his father had considerable insight into the way people operated, particularly the way in which people within security services operated.

His own reliability had become suspect within the senior ranks of the K.G.B., and he may have realised that the only way to remove those suspicions and throw the K.G.B. off his daughter's scent was to go down with the plane, his lifeless corpse the only evidence that would convince his political masters of his lifelong loyalty to their cause.

It was a pity that his father had not lived to see the happiness that his children had discovered behind the subterfuge of their new identities as nondescript West Germans citizens. For despite the pain of separation from the past, they had succeeded in building for themselves a life that was richer than anything they had ever experienced before. Strangely enough, it was the very repetitiveness of everyday life – the gardening, the shopping, playing with Margit and her adopted brother Johann – that they both found so exhilarating. For whereas other people cursed the humdrum of the commonplace, they had both learnt through bitter experience to recognise its profound beauty. And while others continued to strive for impossible goals, they found themselves simply glad to be alive.

It was hard to be sure that the time was right, since even an old and infirm tiger can still be dangerous and it would be foolish to taunt one unnecessarily. The signs of late had been more than promising; the crumbling Russian empire had long since seen the departure of the East German state from the fold as it had once again found common cause with its larger western neighbour. But the core of the empire had remained intact, the security services had remained intact, and with it their fear of discovery had remained intact.

But the passing of time had made the continuation of the subterfuge increasingly unnecessary. The aged tiger was rapidly turning into a tame pussy-cat, and both Ingrid and he had for several years known that the overriding need for their concealment had long since passed. For months now there had only been one lingering doubt that made them hold back.

Robert pulled a crumpled newspaper from his pocket. He had bought it two days before, but as far as he was aware, his wife had not yet read the contents. He had stumbled across the entry when he had been lying in bed alone one morning, eating a soggy biscuit that he would never have dared to dunk in his tea if Ingrid had been in the room. When he first read it, he had nearly rushed downstairs to tell her the news, but before he got as far as the door he had checked himself. Somewhere deep down inside, he knew he wanted a few hours to reflect on his own before he told her.

He turned once again to the inside page and re-read the short entry. It was written by one of the paper's regular Moscow correspondents, an affable fellow with whom Robert had often shared a drink in his diplomat days: 'General Leon Axelrod, one of the longest serving officers in the Russian security service, has died of a heart attack at the age of eighty. A surprise survivor of the sudden break-up of the Soviet Empire, General Axelrod emerged as an elder statesman of the newly-formed Russian security service and was one of the last surviving conservatives within the upper echelons of the organisation. His death is regarded by well-informed sources here as removing one of the last major obstacles in the way of reform.'

Robert carefully folded the paper and put it back in his pocket. For years now Axelrod's continuing position of power had been the main reason for their remaining hidden. For if the story had become public knowledge, Leon Axelrod would have suffered acute personal humiliation; there had always been a danger that he would have ordered their liquidation out of sheer revenge. With Axelrod dead, the last major reason for their deceit had vanished.

Yet it was still not an easy decision to take. If they came into the open with their story, the little house where they lived was bound to be filled with journalists and television cameras for several days before it all became yesterday's news; his children – both of his new family and his old – would find it hard to adjust to the new circumstances; there might even be trouble from some stupid over-officious bureaucrat arising from the fact that he was married to his natural sister.

But the lingering doubt in his mind was gradually beginning to clear. He rose to his feet, and with one last long look at the innocent little park through which the insane barrier of the Iron Curtain had once passed, he slowly made his way towards the door.

It had been a strange deception, but now the time had come to tell the truth.